His Harlot

S.M. LaViolette

CROOKED SIXPENCE BOOKS are published by

CROOKED SIXPENCE PRESS
2 State Road 230
El Prado, NM 87529

First printing May 2020

ISBN: 9781951662158

10 9 8 7 6 5 4 3 2 1

Photo stock by Period Images

Printed in the United States of America.

Chapter One

London
1868

"His Nibs Mr. Fanshawe is here for you, Nora, you've got fifteen minutes to get your arse up to the Silesia." Charles snickered and shut the door to Nora's tiny attic bedroom without waiting for an answer.

Charles Smith was her dearest friend, but Nora was glad he'd taken his handsome, smirking face and catty ways off quickly. He would tease her mercilessly if she didn't do a perfect job of concealing her body's response to the news that Mr. Fanshawe was here.

She cleaned her brush, taking care to not damage the fragile bristles as her hand shook—just the way it always did when Edward Fanshawe came to see her—especially *now* when she'd given up on ever seeing him again.

Her heart was beating a rapid tattoo as she stripped off her huge dun apron. Beneath it she was dressed for working, garbed in the same simple, modest muslin morning gowns all the female employees wore at Madame Tosca's exclusive establishment for gentlemen.

Mr. Fanshawe had not come to see her this early in the day before; he'd never come during the daylight. Nora shivered at the thought of what awaited her as she pulled the pins from her waist length pale blond hair and brushed it to a shine. Mr. Fanshawe like her to wear her hair a specific way when she came to him and her hands—long accustomed to their task—divided and braided without any instructions from her brain.

It had been six weeks since she'd seen him last. He never told her when he would return—or even *if* he would return. He'd been coming to her for eight months. Nora knew she wasn't the only woman he visited—at least not when he'd first started coming. Early on, when he'd come to Tosca's every night for six days running, he'd have a different woman each night.

Gradually, over the next five or six months, he'd come to Nora more and more. If she was taken, he might engage another woman, or he might leave.

He frequently paid for her in advance but, just as frequently, didn't return for his appointment and might show up two nights later, paying yet again.

While Madame Tosca would have liked to work Nora those nights he scheduled and never arrived—because Mr. Fanshawe *always* paid for the entire night—the greedy madam feared angering him if he either learned of her actions or, God forbid, came for Nora when she was with another.

So, Mr. Fanshawe's absences always meant more free time for Nora. She should have suspected something was wrong when she'd started to *want* him to show for an appointment rather than appreciate the unexpected liberty.

For three heady and glorious months he'd come only to her, their games intensifying with each visit.

But then—on January fifth—he'd not appeared for an appointment and she'd not seen him for almost six weeks. Six. Long. Weeks.

What kind of whore missed a client?

Her kind, apparently.

Nora secured the braid with a string and let it fall heavily down her back. She pushed her stockinged feet into her worn pink satin slippers, picked up her best shawl, and left her room.

She took the servant stairs from the attic down to the fourth floor, which is where the four largest suites were located: Silesia, Dordogne, Cantal, and Savoie. Madame Tosca was from one of the Italian States and had named her rooms after regions in the various European countries.

When she reached the door to the Silesia she paused, took several deep breaths, and tried to clear her mind. That was Nora's special trick—usually—she could go to her client with a mind as empty as a cloudless sky. She'd found that showing *nothing* to anyone not only made her more appealing to many of her clients, it also gave her a feeling of control: they only saw what she *wanted* them to see.

But walling herself off had become impossible with Mr. Fanshawe. Not because she'd had to resist his prying—in fact, he'd never asked personal questions—but because she wanted to pry into *him.*

So, her walls had begun to crumble for Mr. Fanshawe and that was regrettable because it was from *him* that Nora most needed to guard her thoughts, her desires . . . her heart.

✳✳✳

Edward paced the large suite, well aware he was behaving like a caged and restless animal. He lifted the glass of brandy to his mouth and swallowed half of it. Madame Tosca had delivered the bottle to him personally; the wily old madam knew how to keep her customers happy.

Well, *happy* might be too strong a word; Edward was not happy. Had he ever been happy? If so, he couldn't recall it. But Tosca at least knew how to soothe his irritation, whether it was with some special meal her superlative chef prepared, a fine bottle of liquor, or a girl she knew would appeal to his peculiar tastes.

This last thought made him throw back the remainder of his glass. Part of her reason for hand delivering the bottle was to ensure he'd been pleased with his last visit. Edward knew she was concerned that he'd been away so long. Six. Long. Weeks. Oh yes, he'd counted every day, to his intense mortification and disgust. And concern.

He didn't tell her *why* he'd been gone, or that one of her employees was behind his absence. No, that was not her affair. She was his abbess, procurer, bawd—not his confessor.

"Did Nora displease you the last time you were here, sir?" she'd asked after pouring them both drinks.

Edward didn't want to tell her that Nora had pleased him *too* much. So instead he gave a noncommittal grunt.

"I have a new girl since your last visit. Would you care to inspect her?"

"Is Nora not available?" The words left his mouth before he could stop them and he heard the anxiety vibrating beneath them. His faced heated. Goddammit! That was the *last* bloody time he'd expose himself—at least in that manner.

But Edward could see it was already too late; Tosca now knew that she possessed what he wanted, and she would make him pay dearly for it.

"Nora is available and waiting for you, sir."

Edward met the savvy whore's hooded brown eyes and wanted to howl at her smug, knowing look. If ever there was a woman who knew men it would be this one. She was perhaps a decade older than his own one-and-forty years, although the sin in her eyes was ancient.

"What's her name—this new girl?"

"Belinda. Shall I summon her?"

Well, why the hell not? "Yes, I'll take a look at her."

The madam rose. "I shall send her up and have Nora waiting."

Edward turned away without answering, taking his glass to the huge window that looked over the street. It was swathed in layers of heavy velvet so that it might have been midnight rather than mid-day. Mid-day: when he should have been *working* rather than here.

He shoved the drapery aside along with his dithering and surveyed the scene spread out before him. Tosca's was on a quiet street just on the fringes of fashionable Mayfair. The buildings were mostly of recent vintage. New structures constructed to offer housing and services to the growing number of clerks, bankers, and shopkeepers who served the city's most affluent, but couldn't afford to live among them.

Edward owned a goodly number of those buildings, including the one he was currently standing in. That was not common knowledge—even Madame Tosca was not aware he was her landlord.

He heard the door open and turned.

The girl who entered dropped a deep curtsy before lifting her face to him. His pulse quickened as he took in her voluptuous body.

Edward leaned against the window frame. "Come here."

She came without hesitation, stopping a few feet away.

"Closer."

A sly, teasing expression slid over her face but was quickly extinguished. Edward pointed to a spot on the floor a few inches from him.

She was very pretty; her dark brown hair braided the way he liked it. His lips twitched; Madame Tosca was up to all the tricks. Her skin was clear and creamy and slightly flushed. Big hazel eyes fringed with thick lashes held his gaze without flinching. Edward began to harden as his eyes dropped to her mouth, which was small but shapely, her pillowy lower lip just the type he liked to have wrapped around him.

He took a sip of brandy. "Turn for me."

She was tall and shapely, her unbound breasts high and full. The white muslin was so fine it did little to hide her figure, which was long-legged and narrow hipped.

Yes, she was lovely. Not so young as to make him feel like a lecher, but still dewy and sweet.

"Do you know about me, Belinda?"

"Yes, Mr. Fanshawe." Her voice was breathy and girlish but, he instinctively knew, *false.* She'd been schooled to behave the way he wanted. Or at least the way she *thought* he wanted. Belinda hoped to manipulate him. Edward smiled and, for the first time, the expression in her eyes carried a hint of anxiety.

"And what have you heard?"

She inhaled deeply, the action straining the fabric of her bodice. Large, dark nipples pressed against the fine material and his mouth watered. It was almost enough to make him forget all about her falsity. Almost.

"You like to bind and h-hurt your lovers—to *humiliate* them." Her eyelids lowered and she shifted from foot to foot. The performance was nearly perfect, but the slight tightening of her full lips—a smug little smile—told him she was a good actress but would never be a great one.

Without speaking, he left her standing there and walked to the bell pull and gave it a tug before dropping into the big black leather wing chair nearest the fire.

While he waited, he examined Belinda, whose profile was to him. Her silhouette was as beautiful as the front of her and it also showed how rapidly her chest rose and fell; she wasn't so certain any more that she'd land the big fish—*him*—Edward Fanshawe, a man whose whoring was legendary and who compensated well for his unusual tastes.

The door opened and Madame Tosca entered.

"Bring Nora to me," he said before she could start speaking and annoy him.

"Of course, sir." She nodded to somebody out in the hall and when she stepped back, Nora entered.

Chapter Two

ll the lust that had drained away when Edward identified Belinda's scheming for what it was came roaring back at the sight of Nora's rather bland features. It was true that she was no beauty, only her thick, corn silk colored hair could ever be called such.

Her pale, pale eyes—too freakishly colorless to be attractive—moved immediately to the other whore. Not a muscle twitched or tightened in her face, but something that looked like heat, and perhaps even anger, flared in those opalescent eyes. Edward's cock began to stiffen, throbbing more insistently at that tiny show of emotion than it would have done for a Dance of the Seven Veils.

The madam lifted her hand. "Belinda, if you will come with—"

"No," he said, his eyes never leaving Nora's face, worried he'd miss some emotion if he looked away, perhaps something . . . delicious. "I'll employ both for the evening." He could practically feel the older woman's greedy pleasure all the way across the room. But it was Nora's response that fed the monster inside him and brought him to full hardness.

Edward reveled in the almost imperceptible tightening of the fine, thin skin around her eyes and the slight flaring of her nostrils the same way another man would revel in having his cock sucked. Of course, he'd have that, too.

"You may go," he told the madam. Although he never took his eyes from Nora he could feel Tosca's annoyance at being dismissed like a lackey. Edward didn't care. He didn't care about anything except the woman who'd been haunting him for six bloody weeks.

He ached as he looked into her colorless eyes. Her features—nose, mouth, ears—were all small, tidy, and unremarkable. And her body was far less feminine than the girl on the other side of the room. Her breasts were smallish and topped with tiny pink nipples, the milky whiteness of her skin all but translucent, the network of blue veins clearly visible, adding to her fragile appearance: a fragility he personally knew was deceptive, having regularly taken her well beyond the point where most of his lovers had broken in the past.

Edward took a deep drink of brandy, savoring the smooth warmth of the liquid as he enjoyed the throbbing arousal that spread through his body like slow-moving honey. He marveled at the satisfaction he experienced merely looking at Nora: more satisfaction than he'd experienced in the six weeks since he'd last seen her.

But it was a satisfaction mingled with fear, not unlike opening the door to a lion's cage to test his bravery.

"How have you been these past weeks, Nora?"

Her body stiffened slightly and Edward knew the question startled her. It *should* startle her; Edward never asked whores questions. And the fact that he wanted to ask her *many* questions worried the hell out of him.

"I've been very well, sir, thank you." Her voice was always a complete surprise to him: low and husky. Their first time together he'd ordered her to call him sir, as he always did with the women he paid.

"Have you missed me?" he asked, amused by his question.

"Yes, sir," she answered without hesitation, her toneless voice inciting his lust, just as it always did. Nora had the most expressionless face he'd ever encountered. If she ever thought to enter the world of card sharping she certainly had the visage for it. Edward liked her taut, too-slender body, her heavy rope of hair, and those odd eyes very much indeed. But what he liked best about her was the slight flicker of emotion he only occasionally managed to elicit if he worked her hard enough to touch something deep inside her.

In fact, it was his unsettling '*liking*' for her and his increasingly burning need to elicit her subtle responses that had caused him to keep away from Tosca's for six weeks.

Edward recalled the day clearly. He'd been in negotiations across the table from three other men when Nora's face—gleaming with sweat, tears, and sexual agony—had intruded on his thoughts. To his recollection, that had never happened before: a woman interfering with his business.

And Edward had not liked it.

He'd vowed that day to eradicate all thoughts of her. Over the coming weeks instead of visiting Tosca's, he'd gone to another house, the Bellaire. There had been a time—before he'd discovered Nora—when he'd used the Bellaire as often as Madame Tosca's. Somewhere along the way he'd lost track of his growing ...well, there was no other word for it except *obsession.*

So, he'd returned to the Bellaire, seeking pleasure there every night for two weeks, gorging on sexual excess.

And throughout it all, he'd seen one face: Nora's.

He'd spent the four weeks after that abstaining, believing that perhaps sexual abstinence was the way to forget her.

But every time he'd woken in the middle of the night with a hard cock he'd wanted only one woman: Nora.

So, here Edward was, back at Tosca's, repeating his folly.

It simply had to stop; he had to break her—tear her apart and examine her inner workings. There had to be a point at which he grew tired of her and he would do whatever was necessary in order to find that point. He had to exorcise her from his mind and free himself to move on to other women, to move on with his life.

Edward set down his empty glass. "Come stand in front of me, Belinda. Nora, undress her."

The women moved quickly to obey him. Nora was perhaps three inches shorter than Belinda and looked more boyish than ever beside the other woman's lush figure. Edward knew such a comparison must rankle—must *pain* her—and he smiled.

She loosened Belinda's gown with nimble fingers and bent low to the floor while the other woman stepped out of the circle of fabric, wearing only a chemise so fine as to be transparent. Belinda's large nipples were tight and pebbled, two dark points that formed a triangle with the shadow of her sex.

Edward was full hard now, his body thrumming with the pent-up sexual desire of the past weeks.

"Remove her chemise—no, push it down over her shoulders," he said when Nora would have lifted it over Belinda's head.

She slid the loose straps over the gracefully sloping shoulders and the insubstantial fabric drifted to the floor without a sound, giving him a view of naked perfection.

Edward's breathing accelerated. "Very nice," he said, his voice raspy with suppressed want. "Spread your feet to shoulder width," he ordered. She kept her private hair closely trimmed, which gave him an excellent view of her puffy lips and the tip of her clitoris peeking out between them.

Edward swallowed the moisture that flooded his mouth and shifted in his chair, the fine wool of his trousers doing nothing to hide his arousal. He gave his swollen prick a languid stroke, the fabric already damp from his excitement. He forced himself to wait and wait and wait before he allowed himself a quick look at Nora.

A surge of lust almost doubled him over. Her delicate nostrils were flared and her gaze was riveted to the ridge of his erection, which jumped and strained under her attention. Her eyes rose to his and that's when he saw it—that flash of yearning that worked on his mind and body just like opium must enslave those it eventually destroyed. Just as she would eventually destroy him, if he let her.

The look came and went in a heartbeat, leaving him with an ache so punishingly deep he would do *anything* to ease it.

If only he knew how.

❋ ❋ ❋

Nora couldn't believe she was actually here. With him.

She had been about to knock on the door to the Silesia room when it opened and Madame had come out.

"Wait here but but do not enter," she'd instructed Nora. "I'll return shortly."

When Tosca had returned, she had Belinda with her. Seeing the exquisite woman had been like a knife in Nora's stomach. Once Mr. Fanshawe saw Belinda, he'd never want her. She turned to go.

"No, we will wait here," Madame instructed her, opening the door and ushering in Belinda before closing it again.

They'd stood in silence while they waited—for what, Nora didn't know. All she could think about was *him* with Belinda, his blunt, powerful, cruel, hands on Belinda's soft, feminine body. The other whore had a ripe sensuality that had quickly made her a favorite at Tosca's. Mr. Fanshawe would be finished with Nora now.

Nora told herself it wasn't agony twisting in her gut but regret at losing a very lucrative client.

But that was a lie.

It was the same pain she'd felt every day he'd stayed away, even though she'd tried to root him from her brain like weedy, pervasive vines from a garden.

It had taken him far longer than she'd expected to tire of her, not that she didn't have her small stable of admirers. Given her particular skills Nora had always managed to keep her customers for longer than average. There were not many women at Tosca's who would submit to the type of treatment Mr. Fanshawe craved, even for the money.

Nora knew exactly what her colleagues would think if they learned she would submit to him *without* payment.

She shivered at the thought of all the teasing Charles would mete out if he ever learned her true feelings for the man on the other side of the door. A man who would now be as accessible to her as the moon.

He was so vibrant, demanding, and devoid of sentimentality that she'd always assumed he would one day move on to a woman who was more beautiful and challenging. Well, today was that day.

This is your job; these are your customers and you merely engage in commercial transactions. Nobody is interested in your mind—many of them are not even particularly interested in your body. All they want is what you give to them: your pain.

That was true. Madame employed Nora for two different types of customers: young men who came to lose their virginity, whom she would not intimidate and with whom she was very patient, and those men who took sexual pleasure in causing pain to their lovers.

The first rule of whoring—or at least the first rule Nora had learned from the old woman who'd taken her under her wing at the bawd house where she'd started out—was that you should never look for love in your work. It was a bad thing to expect in many ways: mostly because it rarely came a whore's way. She'd even been cautioned to never expect pleasure, although that warning she'd ignored frequently over the years.

For the most part, Nora had done well controlling and concealing her desires. She had even managed to hide them from her first madam.

But Madam Tosca had looked right into Nora's sin-blackened heart and seen the truth. She'd seen the secret Nora had always worked so hard to hide: she *liked* being a whore—or at least certain aspects of it.

Being the excellent businesswoman she was, Madam Tosca had immediately turned Nora's weakness to her economic benefit. As a result, Nora was almost always booked even though she was the least comely of all the women who worked there—and even most of the men.

She'd learned that the shameful *thing* she'd always tried to keep hidden deep inside—the gnawing hunger to be punished and humiliated—was as visible as a bonfire to those men who needed what she had to offer.

Over the years Nora had come to terms with her sluttish desire for certain parts of her job: a desire which had once mortified her. She'd known since she was fourteen that once she took the first step, there would be no way back; she'd never regretted her decision. Life was short and brutal and if deviant sexual acts were something that gave her pleasure, she refused to castigate herself for snatching at happiness where she could find it.

Until Mr. Fanshawe.

Nora looked at him now and devoured his brutal, heartless expression, her gut bound up in that combination of arousal, terror, and all-consuming lust that overwhelmed her whenever was with him—or even when she allowed herself to *think* about him in the privacy of her bed.

Sometimes, she even thought about him while she serviced other clients. What those other men didn't know wouldn't hurt them, would it? But she suspected her obsession with him had long ago started to hurt *her*.

Mr. Fanshawe was not a handsome man. In fact, the first time she saw him she'd thought him ugly. He had a head of black wiry hair that was liberally salted with gray, even though he couldn't be much more than forty. He was a big man, perhaps an inch over six feet, certainly a head taller than Nora. His hands were massive and could span her waist and he often picked her up with no visible effort.

His body was raw-boned and heavily slabbed with muscles, his build that of a laborer, which is what he'd once been, according to whore gossip.

His hooded eyes were dark brown, opaque, and pitiless. Everything about his features spoke of excess: thick, sensual lips, a big high-bridged nose that dominated his face, and a square jaw that was as hard and heavy as an anvil.

And yet the garments he put on his too-big body were those of an aristocrat: fine soft woolens, snowy, insubstantial linens, soft, supple leathers. The gentleman's clothing should have looked incongruous on such a body, but instead it just added to his aura of wealth and power.

For months they'd done unspeakable and intimate things to one another times beyond counting and still Nora knew nothing about him beyond his surname and what he wanted in the bedchamber.

And why would you ever need to know anything more than that, Nora?

She didn't need to know—shouldn't want to know. But late at night—when her spirits were at their lowest, between three o'clock and dawn, she imagined what might be behind his cruel, iron-clad façade.

"Belinda, undress Nora."

She startled at his voice, realizing she'd been lost in her thoughts. He was watching her with lazy amusement—as if he knew she was fantasizing about him. He dominated the big black leather chair like a king did his throne. He held her eyes with his as Belinda's graceful hands worked at the tapes, ties and buttons.

The other woman was the same age as Nora, almost twenty-four, and had been in this life just as long. But while Nora only appealed to a certain subset of men, Belinda was every man's fantasy.

She was competitive but also friendly, so Nora had instinctively liked her, especially when some of the older—more jealous—whores had been unkind to her at first.

But right now, she hated her.

She hated her lush beauty, her confident sensuality, the mocking, pitying looks she gave Nora as she undressed her with painful slowness, her expression saying more clearly than words what she thought about Nora's boyish body.

But what made her hate the other woman even more was the look on Mr. Fanshawe's face as he stroked his erection.

Did he sense Nora's tightly leashed jealousy? Was that why he was looking at her with such smirking amusement, his eyes probing her in search of her pain, her humiliation, which were like nectar to him?

Her chemise slid to the floor and she stepped out of it, watching his face for a flicker of . . . anything. But there was nothing. His eyes moved over her body with the unsurprised gaze of a longtime lover: he'd seen everything she had to offer and Nora held no more secrets for him.

He sat in his chair, one hand absently stroking while the other held the glass. His eyes moved between them, as if he were comparing them; Nora knew how she would come out of such a comparison and the agonizing realization made her even wetter. What kind of woman became aroused at such humiliation?

Her kind.

His lips curled into an acquisitive smile as his eyes roamed Belinda's body, his obvious desire sending a spike of lust and yearning to Nora's already swollen sex.

He set down his glass, spread his powerful thighs, and pointed to the spot between his legs. "Belinda, kneel."

Not only was Belinda beautiful and sensual, but she moved like poetry, lowering herself to her knees in one smooth motion.

"I want you to suck me off." His vulgar words were at odds with the low, velvet of his tone and only through Herculean effort did Nora suppress a shiver of desire. He had the crassest vocabulary Nora had ever heard. She loved it.

Of course he knew that, too.

Belinda gazed up at him, her wide-eyed ingénue expression appeared incongruous with the salacious curve of her lips and Nora could not believe Mr. Fanshawe was taken in by such an act. But he gave Belinda an approving look before turning to Nora, his indulgent expression dissipating as his eyes focused on her.

"Stand right there." He pointed to a place close enough that he could see Nora's face and she could watch the other woman pleasure him. And then he turned away, dismissing her as if she were an inconvenience he'd had to deal with and could now forget.

Her body responded the way it always did when he degraded her: eager and hot and wanting, while her mind cried out like a prisoner trapped behind unbreakable bars.

Nora prayed he simply thought her behavior an act; not that God listened to prayers from a woman like her.

He cupped Belinda's rounded jaw in one hand and stroked her smooth skin with his thumb. "Proceed," he ordered.

Her hands went to work on his buttons and he shifted his hips to let her pull down his trousers and drawers. "Do you enjoy sucking cock, Belinda?"

She gave a rather dramatic shiver that conveniently caused her perfect breasts to jiggle enticingly. "Oh . . . well, I—"

"Shhhh," he murmured, his full lips curving as he rubbed his thumb on her lower lip. "Why are you so nervous, sweetheart?"

Her body jolted and her hands froze. She swallowed hard enough for Nora to hear it. "I—haven't, well, I'm new, sir."

Nora would have rolled her eyes if she hadn't been so furious.

Mr. Fanshaw's nostrils flared. "I see. Are you telling me you haven't sucked a cock before? Do you need Nora to show you how?"

Nora's sex clenched in anticipation, the contraction sending ripples of pleasure through her body.

Belinda's stiffening posture gave her away. Nora knew that she'd realized, perhaps too late, that she might have overplayed her hand. "N-no, sir. I know how. I—I just want to please you."

No, what she wanted was to *steal* him from Nora. Mr. Fanshawe was an *outrageous* client when it came to gifts of money.

Nora could tell by the way he smiled that he knew that, too. But his thumb kept stroking and probing the seam of her plump lips, which opened to accept him. She drew his thumb into her mouth, her cheeks hollowing with the force of her suction.

Although Mr. Fanshawe pointedly ignored her, Nora knew he was aware of what she was feeling right now. He would know how badly she wanted him, how she hated to see another woman supplant her and how she despised herself for feeling such things.

The right side of his mouth pulled up into a slow, cruel smile. Yes, he knew exactly what he was doing to her.

Belinda lifted the hem of his shirt, which had been covering his erection.

Nora couldn't help staring, even though she'd seen him over one hundred times—one hundred and seventeen, to be precise.

His cock was among the largest she'd ever seen, and she'd seen many. It was built along the same lines as the rest of his body: thick, heavy, and long. Already the fat bell-shaped head glistened with proof of his arousal and Nora could almost taste his salty slickness and feel the silky hardness of his shaft. Her mouth watered and her throat tightened convulsively, as if *she* were the one who'd be taking it.

Belinda's hand looked small curled around him and he grimaced as if in pain when she tightened her grip and stroked him from root to tip.

"Ah, God, yes." The last word came out in a hiss and his powerful hips lifted. "Lick me—tongue my slit and taste me."

His order sent a shock wave through Nora's body and fury battled arousal at watching this other woman touch what was hers.

No, not yours, never yours.

Belinda leaned low and kissed the weeping slit, her gentle touch causing him to shudder and groan.

"Yes," he muttered, his eyelids fluttering shut and his hips pushing up while his huge hand slid around Belinda's skull, the roped muscles of his exposed forearms flexing as he pulled her lower and filled her.

Nora felt like she was being torn apart by vicious winds. She *hated* her treacherous body and was powerless to stop its shameful, humiliating reaction. Why were her thighs wet watching a man reject her and take pleasure from another? What was *wrong* with her?

"Are you wet?"

Her head jerked up. He was looking at her and his shrewd stare reminded her of where she was and who she was with—and of *what* she was: a whore.

"Yes, sir."

"Show me."

She spread her feet, her heart thrilling as his jaw tightened and his pupils flared. It came to her, then, in a blinding flash. How stupid she was. He didn't just feed off her humiliation and pain, he *needed* it.

He *needed* her just as badly as she needed him.

The realization was almost enough to drive her to her knees, to push her over the edge and drown her in pleasure.

"Nora." The word was a sharp, harsh bark, and she met his hard, glittering eyes. "The next time I have to say something twice, you will leave."

Nora slid her feet wide, slipped her fingers between her swollen lips, and held out her hand for his inspection.

✳✳✳

Edward's control began to unspool as he stared at her glistening fingers.

He shouldn't have waited four bloody weeks.

It wasn't the girl sucking him. No. Despite her come-hither ways and blatant sexuality Belinda's technique less than impressive.

Nora—on the other hand—had the hottest, softest mouth he'd ever fucked. She had no gag reflex and worked him so hard he often straddled the border between pleasure and pain.

He hated to admit it, but Belinda, for all her beauty, was as bland as gruel.

There was no comparison between the two women.

It was Nora, always Nora, her eyes opaque and unreadable, but something about her bleeding pain and want and humiliation. Just looking at her after these last barren weeks had him teetering on the edge.

But the last thing he wanted to do was come in Belinda's mouth less than five minutes after she'd begun. While an orgasm was almost impossible to resist, this—this *whatever* it was between him and the homely, naked girl who stared at him with such ravaged wanting eyes, such exquisite suffering? Well, *that* was his opium. And he wanted it to last and last and last.

How could you make this last when the only way to take it further will end it?

Edward ignored the thought and wrenched his eyes from her; too much of her would make him spend.

He might not be able to feast on her anguish, but he could stoke her humiliation—and their mutual pleasure—higher and higher.

Edward slid a second hand around Belinda's head and picked up the heavy braid, winding it slowly around his fist, knowing how the familiar gesture would be gutting Nora, savoring the thought of her cunt and how it must be clenching with need as she was forced to watch him, powerless and wanting

"Yes," he said, rocking into Belinda. "That's right, deeper. I want your throat." He thrust and felt her gag reaction before he was anywhere close to sheathing his length. Well, so much for her intimations of expertise.

If it had been Nora kneeling between his thighs Edward would have fucked her mouth until the cords of her throat screamed beneath her white skin. If it was Nora, he'd ram his prick balls-deep and glory at the sight of her slim, taut body submitting to him and absorbing all the punishment he could inflict, her pale eyes always begging for more and more and more.

Edward closed his eyes and savored the mental image he'd just created, allowing his thrusts to grow more violent, until the sound of choking pulled him out of his fantasy.

Belinda's tears were streaming down her cheeks and her entire posture was one of grudging endurance rather than Nora's abject worship.

He risked a glance at Nora and shuddered. Lust, hate, fury, adoration, and pure misery had turned her eyes the hot white-blue at the center of a flame. His aching balls contracted and Edward rammed his cock deep, his hands like a vise on Belinda's skull as he emptied himself in violent, jerking ribbons down her convulsing throat.

✳✳✳

His head had fallen back after his orgasm, his hands limp on the arms of the chair.

Nora stood silently but inside she was screaming.

You can't let him see what this has done to you.

She looked away from him, turning to Belinda.

Belinda was sitting back on her heels, her lips fuller and redder and slick from Mr. Fanshawe's brutal use. They curved into a smug smile as Belinda rubbed the tears from her cheeks with the heel of her hand, her eyes declaring what they both knew: Mr. Fanshawe had just made his choice, and it wasn't Nora.

Nora had never been a violent person, but right then she wanted to jump on the devious whore and pummel her. Her own emotions shocked and revolted her; how had this happened to her?

Just what was it about this man?

She refused to show the agonizing pain and rejection that roiled in her belly, the constant companion of lust and arousal when she was with this man. Instead, she forced herself to smile at Belinda. After all, it

18

wasn't the girl's fault she'd become a pawn between her and the cruel, mysterious man Nora was now certain she'd fallen in love with.

Mr. Fanshawe groaned and they both turned to look at him. His head rose slowly, his eyes heavy lidded and sleepy. He looked from Nora to Belinda and then back, as if he couldn't recall where he was. And then he grunted and said, "You can go."

Nora blinked. Surely he wasn't talking to—

"Not you," he said to Belinda, who'd begun to get to her feet. He turned to Nora. "You. Get out. I don't need you."

Nora realized her jaw had dropped and closed it, her heart beating in odd, spastic jerks. She masked her reaction, but it was too late: he'd seen it. An ugly sneer distorted his face—a knowing, satisfied smirk at what she'd inadvertently exposed: humiliation, rejection, and shock.

Even worse, he saw what lay beneath it all: a gut-wrenching lust that even now—at the peak of her suffering—sent her body spiraling toward climax.

He gave an ugly laugh, stood, turned, and walked toward the bedchamber. "Come with me, Belinda," he ordered, not bothering to look back as he briefly filled the doorway between the two rooms and then disappeared inside.

Belinda trotted behind him, cutting Nora a grin that contained triumph and something else—pity? And then she shut the door and Nora was alone with the most shattering orgasm she could remember.

Chapter Three

Edward took off his spectacles and threw them hard enough that they bounced and skidded over the cluttered surface of his desk before tumbling to the floor. "Fuck!"

The explosive word caused his secretary, Simon Powell, to jump in his office chair. "Sir?" Powell's gray eyes were magnified by spectacles that were as thick as plate glass.

"It's nothing," Edward growled at his meek and mild secretary, a man whom he paid a fortune to ignore his mercurial temper and obnoxious behavior. "Take the rest of the day and go. We can pick up with this tomorrow."

Powell set about gathering his things quickly and left without a parting word, knowing how much Edward despised small talk and civilities like greetings and goodbyes.

Edward pushed himself to his feet and strode to a table loaded with decanters. He poured himself three fingers of brandy and went to stand in front of the huge fireplace, which was crackling and popping, a merry counterpoint to his bloody mood.

It had been two weeks since he'd been to Tosca's. Not since that night when he'd behaved like a bloody beast to the woman Belinda, all so he could give Nora an orgasm without even laying a finger on her.

He'd been as hard as a pike after he'd sent her away, using Belinda thrice more that night as if that would exorcise the memory of Nora's erotic suffering, which he'd only glimpsed and now *craved.*

What he'd really wanted to do that night was drink himself into a stupor but he'd kept Belinda in his bed, becoming aroused at the thought that Nora would hear the other woman boasting about how he'd fucked her all night long. As ever, imagining Nora's face at such humiliating information made him stiffen and throb.

Edward didn't fool himself that any of the whores except Nora competed for him because they liked him or the things he did to their bodies. No, they fought over him because he paid twice as much as any other customer.

He was a pig—worse, really. Because all he wanted was to go back again and do something more—something worse—to make Nora look that way again. All he wanted was to see that indescribable expression on her face. An expression he fisted himself to every bloody night, sometimes twice or thrice. Not bad for a man over forty, but it was slowly driving him insane.

Today, at the monthly meeting between the four members of the syndicate: Edward, Stephen Chatham, Gideon Banks, and their fourth member—a man they only knew by the name Mr. Smith—his three partners had threatened to take him down to the Thames and drown him.

"Good God, Edward! What the hell is wrong with you? You're always a bloody bastard but now you're like a bastard with two sore heads." This from Banks, a man who so terrified and mortified the servants at his London home that his staff turned over every six months.

"Go bugger yourself," Edward had muttered.

"Really, Fanshawe, you'd better seek medical assistance for this matter," said Mr. Smith—a man who didn't hesitate to offer his advice and observations for all that he never shared a damned thing about himself. Smith chuckled at whatever he saw on Edward's face.

Only Chatham refrained, although that was not unusual. Stephen Chatham was the quietest and most reclusive man Edward had ever met. He only spoke when necessary, and not even then. He was Edward's favorite partner of the three—not because he knew him better or liked him more, but because Chatham spoke so rarely.

Edward wasn't friends with any of them; he didn't *have* or *want* friends. They were, like him, three men driven to build their empires, to insulate themselves from poverty with walls of wealth so thick they could never be breached. He knew nothing of their individual backgrounds but their pasts were as clearly stamped on their faces as his was. Gutter trash who'd clawed their way out of the sewers and would die before they ever went back.

"Whoever she is," Banks had persisted, "You'd better do what you need to do before you make an ass of yourself."

"A bigger ass," Smith amended.

Edward ignored Smith's sarcastic comment and turned to Banks, laughing. "What? You mean I should do like you're doing and set up three bloody mistresses?"

Banks had flushed at that, but still managed a smile. "If you must." The man had the fine-boned looks of an aristocrat, his blond hair and blue eyes like the paintings of angels Edward had seen on occasion. Talk about looks being deceptive. If there was any man whose sexual excess made Edward's activities pale, it was Gideon Banks. While he'd mounted three mistresses, the man probably needed closer to five to satiate his needs. As it was, Gideon still accompanied Edward to the Bellaire and Tosca's on occasion. The whores flocked like chickens to corn to his angelic look and deep pockets.

Edward believed there was something seriously wrong with a man who required that much fucking. But, thankfully, it wasn't his problem.

"Maybe what our Edward needs is a period of quiet reflection and abstinence," Mr. Smith suggested. Even Chatham had joined in laughing at that.

Banks and Smith had continued to offer amusing suggestions, defusing the tension until they'd all gone back to the business at hand: the acquisition of an enormous parcel of buildings on the Strand.

Of course none of the men mentioned the possibility of marriage—at least not marriage to the women they all consorted with. Edward suspected the others viewed the matter of marriage much like he did: they would marry women who would advance their goals, women with connections to that strata of society they, themselves, could never hope to penetrate or join. Their marriages would be crucial business arrangements that would require more care and forethought than any other they would ever make.

Edward had even begun to consider marriage—before his obsession with Nora had seized him all those weeks ago. He'd employed a reliable man to assemble a list of ten women with the bluest blood and highest pedigree. Ten pristine virgins whose families were forced by poverty to put their daughters on the auction block for men like Edward.

He'd yet to look into the list Mr. Brock had provided him, his mind too caught up in other matters. Matters like Nora.

Although Edward had mocked Banks's suggestion, he'd lately given a great deal of thought to setting up a mistress—an action he'd always avoided as his desires could be mercurial and he never knew when he'd get bored with a woman and then have to deal with an emotional mess. Unlike Banks, however, he thought of setting up only one woman: Nora.

But then he'd recall that last time he'd seen her and how very, very close he'd been to kicking out Belinda and bringing Nora to bed and fucking her in the way that drove them both to a place that went beyond mere physical pleasure, into the realm of something almost religious.

Edward snorted at his idiocy. Religious? He threw back the rest of his brandy and went back to his desk. He deliberately opened the folder Mr. Brock had given him a few weeks earlier, selecting a carefully printed sheaf of paper with a photograph clipped to the top.

Lady Catherine Thurlow, daughter of the Marquess of Blandford. He flipped over the portrait and began to read.

✳✳✳

Nora felt as if she'd been working non-stop for weeks. It was just as well since she was less than useful when she had too much time to herself. Instead of painting or reading, she seemed to spend most of her spare moments in the only chair in her room, staring out the small square window that looked out onto sky, thinking about *him*.

It was three weeks to the day since the last time she'd seen Mr. Fanshawe and she was returning to her room after a vigorous evening with the young Duke of Glenway, a skinny, painfully shy boy of seventeen.

The duke's uncle, Lord Anthony, had been a client of Nora's since she'd first come to Tosca's when she was eighteen. Lord Anthony was a thin, nondescript, and astoundingly virile man in his sixties.

It was on Lord Anthony's last visit—after he'd sated himself for the third time that evening—that he'd brought up the subject of his nephew, the young duke.

Like Mr. Fanshawe, Lord Anthony always paid for an entire night, although he usually did not stay for the whole evening.

This last time he'd been lying on the bed, naked and slick from exertion, watching Nora as she gathered up the implements he'd used on her.

"Did I hurt you, my dear?" he asked in the lazy voice of a man who'd just enjoyed three orgasms over the course of the past eight hours.

He *had* hurt her, of course, and rather viciously, at that. But they both knew what he meant: had he caused any permanent damage.

"No, my lord, you gave me a great deal of pleasure."

He allowed himself a slight smile of satisfaction before closing his eyes.

Nora hadn't lied to him. Lord Anthony, although nearly three times her age, was one of her favorite clients. While mismatched in years, they were extremely well-matched sexually.

He'd kept her bound in various positions for the better part of six hours while he'd satisfied both himself and Nora. He went through the same ritual each time.

First he had her kneel on the settee, bend over the back. He bound her wrists and ankles with leather straps and then whipped her with a crop until he was fully aroused. He then used her mouth with unrestrained savagery, until he spent inside her.

Next they would share an extremely expensive bottle of champagne or wine and eat a light meal while conversing on topics such as music, books, and art. Lord Anthony was both interesting and interest*ed*, never failing to bring Nora tidbits of news and ask her opinion on many matters.

After that he would tie her face-down on the massive four-poster bed, her legs and arms spread wide and restrained at the four pillars. There would be more whipping and then he would penetrate her vaginally. Sometimes he came, sometimes he couldn't and just fucked her.

And finally, after he'd taken a brief nap beside her while she remained bound, he would flog her one last time, the effort required to summon a third erection usually driving him to brutality.

At that point in the evening her body had suffered not only extended, intense, physical pain but usually three times the number of orgasms as his lordship. The climax of the evening—both literally and figuratively—occurred when he entered her anally and rode them both to a satisfactory conclusion.

He scheduled her only once a month but he paid for two full days of her time—the extra day to allow for the welts to go down and for her body to recuperate. He'd left strict instructions with Nora to tell him should Madam ever try to work her the next day.

Nora had just added more coal to the already raging fire—Lord Anthony was as slender as Nora and the two of them were always cold—when his voice came from the bed chamber behind her. "Come sit with me, Nora."

He was propped up against a mountain of pillows, his thin body hidden by twice the usual amount of blankets. He flipped back the covers and patted the bed with his hand. "Take off your dressing gown and get in beside me." He smiled, which was so rare it caused a flood of apprehension; was he about to leave her, too? She didn't love Sir Anthony, but she found his habitual regularity soothing. Losing him as a client would be . . . unfortunate.

She laid her robe on the foot of the bed and did as he bade her.

"Turn onto your front, Nora so that I might admire my handiwork."

When she did so, she felt the touch of his fingers on the sensitive, raised welts. She bit her lip to keep the hiss of pain behind her teeth.

"These are lovely," he said, his voice slightly deeper as he stroked harder. "You have such beautiful skin."

"Thank you, my lord." As ever, Nora's sex began to swell with each agonizing pass of his hand. She'd long ago quit trying to understand why she found pain so arousing.

"I want to engage you for this Friday," he said, employing his closely cut fingernails on her bruised flesh to amplify his painful stroking.

"I would be honored, my lord." She barely forced the words out from between clenched jaws.

He chuckled. "You are such a naughty little thing. Quite insatiable," he added in a musing, almost wondering tone, as he caressed her harder, the action drawing a low groan from her. "You'd like me to take you again, wouldn't you, Nora?"

She grunted as he dug his fingernails into her sore flesh. "Yes, my lord."

He made a sound of regret. "I wish I could," he murmured, his voice husky as his slim fingers drifting down her back and over the curve of her arse. "I'd take you here." He slid a finger between her cheeks and probed her stretched and sore back entrance lightly. Her hips rose with no instruction from her brain, her thighs spreading to take him deeper.

He laughed and gave her bottom a sharp swat. "You are bad to tease an old man, my dear. I'm afraid three has become an increasing challenge for me of late." Before Nora could demur he leaned back against his pillows and continued, "The appointment I speak of is for my nephew."

Nora turned onto her side then, watching as he shifted his weight and grimaced at some ache or pain as he made himself comfortable. She waited silently for him to continue. It was her habit to never volunteer information or ask questions unless a client specifically asked her. After all, they were the ones paying.

"My nephew is seventeen and hasn't tupped so much as a serving wench or chambermaid yet." His lordship frowned at some distant point in the room. "He is painfully shy and requires bolstering if he is ever to grow out of this lamentable phase and take up his responsibilities." He looked at Nora. "I think you would be perfect to cure him of his virginity."

"I would be honored, my lord." Her words were not quite true. While she didn't mind breaking in young, untried boys, she always felt a sense of responsibility initiating them into physical love. Her own first time had been unsatisfactory and had made her realize just how varied sexual preferences could be.

"You're a good girl, Nora," his lordship said, the words distorted by a yawn as his eyes drifted closed. He fell into a deep sleep within mere moments and that was the last they'd spoken on the matter.

She had met Lord Anthony's nephew—the least regal duke she could imagine—and had sent him home just an hour ago with a smile that stretched ear to ear.

Now she was bone-tired and was going to do nothing more today— her one free day—than sleep. And perhaps finish her current painting if she woke up in time to catch any sun.

She reached the top floor of the house and tiptoed to her room, not wanting to wake any of the others. She opened the door to her room and then stopped in the doorway.

"Hello, darling."

Charles was flipping through her canvases, which were propped against each other along one wall.

Fury leapt inside her and she took a step inside and slammed the door—hard.

Charles flinched. "Careful, luv, people are sleeping."

"You know I don't like you poking through my things." By things she meant her paintings.

"I was waiting for you and got bored and just thought I'd take a look."

"You knew where I was—why didn't you summon me?"

"Some of these are quite striking," he said.

Nora tried to ignore the spurt of pleasure she experienced at his words, reminding herself that she was angry with him.

"What do you want, Charles?"

He grinned. "Look who's shirty this morning! What, did His Grace fail to measure up to your violent standards?"

Nora frowned and ignored his taunt.

He sighed heavily. "Herself wants to see you." When Nora turned on her heel to leave again, his voice stopped her. "No, she wants you to clean yourself up."

Nora opened her mouth to point out she'd just spent the prior eight hours being rogered six ways to Sunday by an insatiable seventeen year-old and that every part of her—inside and out—was sore.

"No, not for that, ducks. It's for something else." He came toward her, seeming to drift he moved so quietly and gracefully. The expression on his deceptively angelic features was, for once, not mocking. "She's got an offer for you, sweetheart."

Nora knew what he would say.

"From Mr. Fanshawe."

She swallowed, the gulp loud in the room.

Charles shook his head and reached out, grazing her jaw with gentle fingers before she flinched away.

"Poor Nora," he murmured, looking as if he meant it.

"Why *poor Nora*?" she demanded with more aplomb than she felt.

He just shook his head and opened the door. "Tosca says you have thirty minutes. Don't keep them waiting." He shut the door with a soft click, leaving Nora alone with the chaos of her thoughts.

❊ ❊ ❊

Edward drummed his fingers on the arm of a black leather chair that was the exact match to the one up in the Silesia room. It amused him that merely looking at this chair made him think of all the things he'd done to Nora in it—which made him begin to harden. Instead of purchasing a mistress perhaps he should get half-a-dozen chairs just like this and scatter them about his huge Mayfair house?

Of course it wasn't getting aroused that was his problem. No, it was sating the incessant lust that seemed to take over more of his mind every day, not to mention leaving him wanting in his bed with a fucking full-blown cockstand every night and morning.

"Are you sure you don't wish for something to drink, Mr. Fanshawe?"

Edward looked up at the madam's voice. He'd forgotten she was still in the room—her study he supposed—until she'd spoken.

"No, thank you," he said for the third time since arriving here almost an hour ago and pulled out his pocket watch.

"I'm sorry, I don't know what is taking her so long. I could send—"

There was a soft knock on the door.

"Enter," the madam said.

Edward had been telling himself his memories were deceptive, that she didn't have the effect on him that he'd recalled. But he'd been wrong.

One look at her pale, narrow face was enough to twist his stomach into a knot and cause his balls to ache, his cock to lengthen and harden. *Fuck. Bloody. Damn.*

"Nora, finally," Tosca said, her nervous eyes darting between Edward and the girl. "Mr. Fanshawe has come with an intriguing offer." She paused, as if expecting Nora to greet him. But she said nothing—she hadn't even looked at him yet. "What's wrong with you? Greet Mr. Fanshawe."

Edward wanted to tell the old bawd to shut the hell up, but he was too busy appreciating the flush her sharp words had caused on Nora's cheeks. It occurred to him he might employ the madam to join their games sometime. No doubt Madame Tosca was highly skilled in the areas of sexual humiliation and degradation.

He just as quickly dismissed the idea.

No amount of blushing would make him tolerate the abrasive whore's company.

"Leave us, Madam Tosca."

She blinked at his cool tone and words, her eyebrows plunging. "But I'm here on Nora's behalf."

Edward gave her a smile he knew was not pleasant. "Don't worry, I won't ask her to sign anything. I wish to speak to her, first. And then you may draw up whatever paperwork we agree upon."

She looked like a woman who wanted to argue, but finally gave a sharp nod. "Very well. Shall a quarter of an hour suffice?"

"That will be ample."

"I shall return in a quarter of an hour, Nora." She glared at the unresponsive woman as she flounced from the room, her gesture a waste since Nora hadn't taken her eyes from the carpet.

When the door shut behind her Edward said, "Look at me."

As ever, she responded immediately to his command.

His stomach lurched as if he were on the deck of a ship. No, he'd not imagined her eyes as he'd fantasized about her these past weeks—five *long* weeks since their last encounter—tormenting himself imagining all the men she was servicing in his absence and how she likely enjoyed herself with at least some of them.

"I'm here to make you an offer of exclusivity."

There wasn't even a flicker of expression on her face. "Thank you, sir, but I'm afraid I must decline."

Edward had already opened his mouth to acknowledge her grateful acceptance when his brain deciphered her response. He did a double take, his eyes widening. "What did you say?" he asked.

She flinched at his soft tone.

Finally, some response!

"Thank you, sir, but I'm afraid I must decline."

He was prepared for her answer this time, but no less stunned. Of all the responses he would have imagined, this one was not even within the realm of probability.

And then something occurred to him. "If this is your way of negotiating a higher price, you have gravely mistaken me."

Was that a glint of humor in her eyes? "No sir, I'm not negotiating."

Edward was at a loss—an utter loss. He was also bloody furious. "You don't even know how much I'm offering," he asked more heatedly than he'd have liked.

"It doesn't matter how much you offer, sir."

He gave a rude snort of disbelief. "Oh? And what if I were to tell you I'm prepared to offer you £1,000 a month?" He expected a flinch, a gasp, or at the very least a raised eyebrow at his outrageous—and certainly unplanned—offer. He got *nothing*.

"You honor me, sir. But I would still decline."

Edward wanted to-to—*hell!* He had no bloody idea what he wanted to do. He surged to his feet, pettishly pleased when she stepped back.

"So, it appears you enjoy your job too much," he sneered, refusing to make it a question—which might sound like pleading.

"I'm satisfied with my position here, sir. But I'm honored—"

Edward waved a dismissive hand. "Yes, I *know*, I heard you already. You're honored by my bloody offer."

She stood motionless, her unearthly eyes fixed on his. He could discern no smugness, no pleasure, no enjoyment of this situation in her eyes. She was, as ever, as bloody impenetrable as a castle wall.

And, as ever, it made him as hard as stone.

Edward didn't know who he hated more in that moment—himself, or her.

He picked up his cane, which he'd set against the arm of his chair. The movement drew her eyes to the ebony stick with its heavy silver ball—a stick he'd used on her more than once—and her pupils flared, her lips parting almost imperceptibly.

Edward's heart stuttered at the raw, primal desire that flashed across her face and he had to grab the high back of the chair to steady himself.

Never in his life had he experienced such a sudden, debilitating, wave of lust—not even with *her* during one of their intense sessions. He gripped the cool silver hard enough to whiten his knuckles. The gesture broke the spell and she raised her eyes to his. Only her enormous pupils gave proof to what he'd just seen on her face.

His own recovery was nowhere near as quick. His heart hammered with the violent intensity of a fist against a cell door. A shocking realization clanged in his head like a bolt securing that door: she wanted him, too, but she would not have him.

Fury—and something else, rejection?—lashed at him like the freezing wind and rain was currently rattling and shaking the building's shutters. He looked into eyes as remote as the moon, "This, my dear Nora, is not over."

✳✳✳

Nora stood in the center of the room, feeling as if all the hair had been singed off her body by the sheer heat of his rage. As ever, his presence left a dull, wanting ache deep in her womb.

His final words had been all the more terrifying—and arousing—for their chilling lack of emotion. He appeared calm, but inside—she knew—he burned to punish her, to possess her.

She allowed herself a slight, private smile at the irony of the situation: he already *did* own her. It didn't matter to her whether he put her up in a house—like a canary in a cage—or visited her once every six weeks or never again. She belonged to him.

"What happened?"

Her head jerked up at the sound of Madam Tosca's voice.

"What happened, Nora?"

"I declined his offer."

Nora had suspected the madam would be angry—no doubt she'd already negotiated a deal that would leave her with plump pockets—but what she hadn't expected was how Madam's anger would increase each day.

Even now, nine days after the interview with Mr. Fanshawe, the vindictive madam showed no signs of relenting.

Nora had just finished a grueling sixteen hour stint with insatiable identical twin brothers who'd used her mercilessly, not letting her sleep more than a few hours. It was all she could do to make her aching, sore, and bruised body climb the stairs to her small attic room.

She opened the door and closed it softly behind her.

"You know she always gets what she wants."

Nora was too tired to even startle at the voice. Instead, she collapsed against the door. "Why are you here, Charles?" she asked in a plaintive tone.

"I'm here to tell you that she'll kill you before she'll give in."

"You should have saved yourself the trip. You aren't telling me anything I don't know; I *know* she won't stop." Indeed, she would have to be an idiot not to realize Madam Tosca's plan was to break her—or to have clients break her, rather.

It was standard behavior to rest a whore in between rigorous clients. And nobody's clients were more demanding than Nora's. Usually that meant at least a day's recuperation, even when clients like Lord Anthony didn't pay for it. But since that interview with Mr. Fanshawe Nora had not gone a day without working—not even her traditional Wednesday off.

She opened her eyes and pushed off the door, going to her bed and dropping gracelessly onto it. "Now if you don't mind, I have another appointment in six hours and right now I can barely keep my eyes open." Tonight was Lord Anthony's monthly appointment and Nora actually enjoyed his visits and truly did not want to be exhausted for him.

"I brought you this."

She had to force her eyelids up at his words. He'd set a plate on her small desk and it held a thick slice of buttered bread, a leg of chicken, and a bowl of custard.

Her stomach growled.

He chuckled. "Sit up," he said, bringing her the food and nudging her over on the narrow bed. "You have to eat."

She sighed. He was right—she'd lost at least half a stone, perhaps more, in the past week and a half. And she'd had no weight to lose to begin with.

"Eat."

She picked up the bread and began to devour it, forcing herself to eat slowly.

He picked up a mug from the small night table and offered it to her. "Tea. Sorry, but it's cold. I've been waiting here a while."

Nora snatched it from his hand and washed down the bread, grimacing at the cool milky beverage.

"Why are you being kind to me? You're the most self-serving person I know."

He huffed. "I'm your best friend."

"That doesn't mean you aren't selfish," she said through a mouthful of food.

He grinned, his teeth white, even, perfect in his handsome face. "I suspect I just like to irk The Tosca however I can and she'd be pleased to see you break, so I don't *want* you to break. I don't *like* waiting on you hand and foot—I just like thwarting her."

Nora gave a bitter laugh and took a bite of chicken, unable to recall the last time she'd eaten; the enthusiastic twins hadn't stopped for sustenance.

"How long do you think you can hold out? Do you know how much he offered to—"

"Stop," Nora said. Although it sounded more like "Schtoff," through her mouthful of bread and chicken.

Charles raised his hands. "Fine, fine. Don't spew food on me. I shan't sully your virgin ears by speaking of such an obscenely *huge* sum of money." He pushed off the bed and began to prowl the small room. "I was looking at some of your paintings again." Nora snorted at his audacity, but he didn't acknowledge her. "Several of them are very good—at least to my untutored eyes."

As ever, even the tiniest scrap of praise was enough to make her heart beat faster with gratitude and her eyes prickle with grateful tears. Luckily she was too tired to weep.

"I understand there is some competition—a painting contest of sorts." He cocked an eyebrow at her.

Yes, she knew what he was talking about, the Royal Academy which happened every year. She'd considered entering two of her works, but the fee was quite high. And her debt payments to Tosca—for a period of time two years ago when she'd been too sick to work for a few months—barely left enough money to buy paint and supplies—not that she had any time left in her life to actually *use* her paintbrush these days.

Charles stopped beside the bed, looking down at her. The window was behind him and his face was in shadow. "How much do you still owe, Nora?"

Nora sighed and put the last bite of bread in her mouth, shaking her head. It was too depressing to be born.

"He would pay off the debt, you know. He'd set you up in place of your own where you'd only have his needs to serve. You'd get to keep your money and could buy more things to paint with. It is a situation we all *dream* of." She could hear the envy and anger in his voice. "And then—when Fanshawe tired of you—you would be *free*."

She shuddered at the sound of his name, which she rarely even allowed herself to *think* in the privacy of her own mind. Free? That made her laugh—which almost choked her. She grabbed the cup of cold tea and gulped down what was left in between coughs, grateful she could now blame her tears on coughing rather than her dratted, tumultuous emotions.

Yes, Mr. Fanshawe would pay off her debt and then she would be free of Madam Tosca and this place. But who, or what, would ever free her from Mr. Fanshawe once she'd given herself to him completely?

✳✳✳

"Nora?"

Her head jerked and she opened her eyes.

Lord Anthony was looking at her, his brow furrowed with concern, his glass frozen halfway to his mouth.

Nora felt her face heat under his worried look. "I am so sorry, my lord. I'm afraid my mind was wandering."

His thin lips curved very slowly into a smile. "No, my dear, you fell asleep."

Her face scalded.

To her surprise, he chuckled. "Look at you—blushing so charmingly."

"I'm terribly sorry my lord," she mumbled, suddenly too shy to look at him.

"I sensed something was amiss earlier."

Her head whipped up. "I'm so—"

He waved away her apology. "Oh, not that—you gave me as much pleasure as always." His cold gray eyes kindled at the memory of what Nora thought of as their 'greeting ritual'. "You were as obedient and responsive as ever, but I can't help noticing you've lost quite a bit of weight."

Nora glanced down at her naked chest, as if to check the truth of his words. Lord Anthony liked to eat without clothing and paid enough for coal that doing so was not uncomfortable.

"His Grace thanked me profusely for giving him a night with you," Lord Anthony said when she didn't respond.

Nora was glad to move the subject to his nephew rather than her weight or appearance. "I'm pleased to hear it, my lord. I, too, greatly enjoyed the evening." She had—and also the three times after. The duke was gentle and sweet and still learning his way with a woman's body. Although he'd taken her often during their nights, he'd been quick and undemanding.

The last time he'd come Nora had been engaged so Madame Tosca had sent him to Belinda, whom he now requested. Nora was glad. The young duke did not share her proclivities and she found it difficult to cuddle with a man. She far preferred his uncle, who needed nothing from her but the use of her body and a bit of intelligent conversation.

"I know we do not know each other—aside from our obvious enjoyment in the bedroom—but won't you tell me why you look so . . . sad?"

Nora stared at him a long moment, both surprised at his question and her sudden need to answer it—to connect with another human.

"I've received an offer."

"I'm not surprised to hear it—only that it took so long." His eyes traveled over her exposed body. "You are a singular young woman, Nora, and I speak from decades of experience." He topped up their glasses, his expression thoughtful. "I never married and I have no children," he said, looking up from the bubbling liquid, his expression wry. "As the youngest son of five my contribution in that area was not necessary. While I would not have minded marrying, I discovered my peculiar propensities when I was just a boy. My brothers and I had gotten up to some mischief—I don't recall what it was now—and were summoned to my father's study. The duke was a stern and terrifying old man." He gave Nora an amused glance. "No doubt you find it diverting to hear an old man speak so of another old man."

Nora smiled, not wishing to interrupt his interesting story. He rarely spoke of his life and she found that she wished to know more about him.

"He lined us up along the front of his big desk and had us drop our breeches. And then he whipped us with a birch rod he'd had my eldest brother—who would become duke in his time—cut from a tree. I was youngest so I was last. By the time my father reached me I wasn't only terrified, I was sporting an impressive cockstand." He chuckled. "My father was, naturally, disgusted and beat me hardest. As you can guess from what you know of me, his actions did indeed kill my lust. But that day I learned I enjoyed the infliction of pain if not the receipt of it. For the next fifty odd years I spent my leisure time seeking my other half— that woman who craved punishment as much as I wished to mete it out." He smiled. "I've had many lovers over the years—one of whom I set up in her own house and to whom I remained loyal for seventeen years, until her death. I believe what I felt for her was love—and I hope she felt at least a liking for me. But the truth is that none of my other lovers have satisfied and pleased me as much as you."

His words sent a flood of warmth through her chest. "Thank you, my lord, that means a great deal to me." It was the truth; Nora found her relations with Lord Anthony both physically fulfilling and mentally soothing.

"Of course you are lovely and skilled," he said, being kinder to Nora than she knew she deserved. "But there is just *something* about you, I don't know how to describe it—an ineffable quality, a sensuality that goes beyond anything I've ever seen or experienced." he studied her with his piercing gaze, and then shook his head and shrugged. "Whatever it is, it has made me consider offering for you many times." He smiled. "I can see I have surprised you."

"You have, my lord."

"Well, I was on the verge of doing so when I learned from my doctor I am not so well as I might appear—or feel, even."

Nora set down her glass without looking and it clipped the side of her plate and tipped over, the clear liquid spilling to the thick carpeting. She ignored it, her hand doing the unthinkable and taking Lord Anthony's slim, elegant fingers.

He smiled and gave her a gentle squeeze. "Now, now. Let's have none of that. I didn't tell you to make you sad, I told you so that you will understand when I don't show up one month. You know the only time I like to see tears."

Nora smiled at his small jest and brushed a hand against her cheek—yes, she was crying.

"In any case," he said, releasing her hand and sitting back in his chair. "I wanted to tell you to think carefully about this man and his offer. If the mere thought of it is affecting you so, you should make your decision carefully. There was pain—the wrong type," he smiled, "when my lover died, but there were also many years of joy."

Nora nodded, too emotional to speak.

"Now," he said, getting to his feet, his tone suddenly cool and brisk. "I want you to fetch the heavier of the three floggers for me. I feel like something special tonight."

Chapter Four

dward stood up from the card table.

"I say, Edward—don't leave just yet, you've almost lost enough to me tonight to buy that new pair of chestnuts I've been eyeballing."

The rest of the men at the table laughed at Mr. Smith's taunt.

"I consider it my duty to the equine species to depart now and keep you from ruining yet another soft mouth."

Everyone roared, even Mr. Smith, who was almost impossible to insult or anger.

"I think Edward has a mouth of his own to ruin."

All heads swiveled around to Chatham, whom Edward hadn't heard speak in at least two weeks.

Chatham ignored them as he scraped together the cards to mix them for another hand.

"Is that true, old chap?" Banks asked, his interest piqued—as ever—by any subject even remotely touching sex.

"A gentleman never kisses and tells," Edward said, slipping into the heavy overcoat the servant held out for him before taking his hat and gloves from another lackey. "I'll see you tomorrow?" he asked, making brief eye contact with three of the remaining five men at the table.

"With bells on," Mr. Smith muttered, his attention already on his new hand of cards.

Edward strode through the luxurious rooms of the gambling hell, acknowledging greetings as he went. It was after three in the morning but the club, known only as Number 14— for its address—was busier than ever.

The gaming club belonged to the syndicate, although even the manager did not know that. They had learned, long ago, that the best way to ensure honesty among their employees was for them never to know who might be watching.

At the front door the two liveried doormen stomped their heavily booted feet to keep warm, their breaths ghostly in the lamplight.

"Need a cab, Mr. Fanshawe?" one of the men, Ernest, asked, lifting his beefy arm in preparation of calling one of the carriages that was always hovering.

"Not tonight," he said, tossing him a coin. "I'll walk."

"G'night, sir," both men called behind him.

Edward had nowhere else to be but he simply could not stand sitting at that card table one moment longer. It hadn't been the fact that he'd lost almost every fucking hand that had driven him crazy, but the way his brain kept re-playing that brief conversation in Tosca's study two weeks ago.

Two. Bloody. Weeks. And he still couldn't put it—put *her*—behind him. Instead, every day he was worse and worse, like a man stricken with a fatal fever. But instead of the chills and a cough, his brain had simply slipped its mooring and sailed beyond his control.

He rubbed his hands together as he strode through the night, but even his fine, fur-lined leather gloves couldn't keep out the bloody cold. He should have taken a carriage but he needed to burn his restless energy somehow or he would simply go mad.

In the weeks since he'd seen Nora he'd gone to the Bellaire only twice. Neither time had been satisfactory. Oh, he'd had plenty of orgasms, but it seemed simple ejaculation was no longer enough. He needed—*craved*—something else. Something only Nora could give him. What? Just what the hell was it?

He was not a stupid man nor was he, normally, an oblivious one. He liked to consider the workings of his own mind as well as others. He'd learned to contemplate human behavior at a very young age. First, he'd done so simply to survive the orphanage. But later, as he began to gradually accumulate money and build his business, he'd observed his business opponent's behavior–rather than their words—to know their mind.

And that is what he considered Nora: his opponent. On the one hand, he knew exactly what she thought—but only about certain things. He knew what aroused her—how she looked when he'd pushed her to the very edge of her endurance, and then greedily consumed her explosive almost unbearable pain and suffering.

Further, he *knew* she fed off their encounters every bit as much as he did. But beyond that? Did she ever think of *him*? Did she care to know what was beyond the man who held the whip and doled out the pain that brought them both so much physical satisfaction? Perhaps she enjoyed such intense sexual pleasure with all her clients?

He *loathed* wondering such things. Furthermore, lately he'd begun to wonder about her with her those faceless, nameless other men, of which he suspected she had *many*. Did she worship them the way she did him—silently, utterly, and agonizingly? Did she suffer and break as beautifully for some stranger?

He'd seen, more than once, the marks on her white skin—a canvas he'd increasingly come to believe belonged to *him*, and him alone—and had always found them disturbing.

Oh, he'd been fighting this downward slide since almost their first night.

When he'd taken her the first time he'd given her the same spiel he always gave whores: If you don't enjoy pain of all kinds, leave now. Don't speak until you are spoken to—that includes both questions and opinions.

Nora, more than any other woman he'd ever had, had abided by his rules. In fact, her utter *remoteness* had increasingly intrigued him—until he'd yearned for her to ask him a question.

He'd been terrified by his reaction to her so he'd forced himself to take her only every fourth time he went to Tosca's, and then every third time, every second.

Before he'd capitulated to his raging addiction he'd begun to take her only with another woman, reveling in those brief glimpses of humiliation and—dare he hope?—jealousy she let slip while he debased her in front of another. It was his particular amusement to choose only the most beautiful whores—not too difficult as Nora was one of the least attractive women Tosca employed—and then openly admire these women in her presence.

But all too soon even that had paled for him, the presence of a third woman—no matter how willing and gorgeous had become a hindrance to his pleasure.

And then, perhaps four months into their acquaintance, he'd begun to keep her in bed with him after he'd sated himself, a behavior Edward had *never* engaged in with any other woman.

They never spoke, indeed, they lay in the huge bed without touching. Edward could never sleep with another in his bed, but she could. And when she was asleep he would study her like a hole-and-corner pervert, drinking in her plain, colorless features, which were hardly any different at rest than they were when he was flogging or fucking her. She was so very, very self-contained. And Edward wanted inside—he wanted to know what went on behind her opaque eyes.

Nora's expressionless face and blank stare would have made it too easy to assume she was stupid. And just when Edward was convinced that perhaps she was—that he'd merely imagined those glimpses of her inner self—the curtain would part and Nora would look out through the gap, but never for longer than a fraction of an instant.

Edward wanted inside; he wanted to smash down her doors, rend the heavy curtains, and invade her. Once inside he would control and dominate her mind every bit as fully as he could already dominate her body.

He'd never believed in the soul, but if it actually existed, Edward wanted to *own* hers, just as he wanted to own her body.

And once he possessed her? Once he'd made her his creature in every way? Well, then he could send her on her way as he had every other whore he'd known and move on with his bloody life. But if he did not find some release he was worried he would—

The sound of carriage wheels slowing beside him made him look up.

It was Smith's town carriage and Smith smirking out of the open window. "Get in, Edward."

Edward hesitated. Although he'd been partners with Smith for close to a decade there was still something about the older man that made him uneasy.

"Come on, get in—the horses are getting cold." He closed the window with a snap and flung open the door.

Edward sighed and climbed inside. Smith rapped on the roof with the head of his cane and they moved forward.

"You're so anxious that *I'm* getting anxious just being around you, Fanshawe."

Smith sprawled against the soft black leather interior, studying Edward with an intensity that left him feeling even more restless. Smith was a bloody mystery that none of the rest of them ever felt like probing. He was a slender man, his wiry build and shortish stature doing nothing to diminish the air of menace that hovered around him. Unlike the others, Smith wasn't native to England and every once in a while, especially if he'd been drinking, his accent would slip. He had the sort of nondescript looks that could be from anywhere: his hair was mid brown, his skin a bit olive, his eyes a dark brown, not so different from Edward's own. But for all that he looked normal and average, there was something dangerous about him.

They never talked about each other behind their backs—at least Edward never did. Their business association was so successful, he believed, in part because they didn't interfere with one another or befriend each other. They were social, but not bosom beaus.

"What of it?" Edward snapped. "You didn't need to come along and bother me if I make you so bloody nervous."

"I know of a place you might like," Smith said by way of answering, lighting up one of the foul black cigars he liked to smoke. "I think you should take a few hours and come with me—if for no reason other than I lost a wager with the others and now am entrusted with the job of seeing you don't fling yourself into the river—or commit some other act of drama, given the dramatic mood you've been in of late."

Edward laughed—but even he heard the slightly hysterical tinge. He'd not slept well in days. Even tossing one off had lost its appeal.

"Fine."

Smith's eyebrows arched at his easy capitulation and he smiled, the uncharacteristic expression showing off his sharp canine teeth. "Excellent."

"Aren't you going to tell your coachman?" Edward asked after a long moment of silence.

Smith grinned. "That's already taken care of."

"Oh, that sure of me, were you?"

Smith just looked out the window and they traveled in silence.

Perhaps fifteen minutes later the carriage stopped outside a bathhouse.

"A bathhouse?" Edward asked, his tone telling the man what he thought of that.

"Trust me."

Edward laughed heartily at that.

The next few hours were a revelation. It tuned out that this wasn't some bath house that offered perversions, but a bath house where they'd soaked in fragrant hot baths and then lain naked on soft tables while mostly naked women had pummeled and pounded and kneaded every part of their bodies except the parts he usually got handled in such a place. The women were gorgeous and young, their waist-length brown hair swinging free, their small firm breasts jiggling enticingly with every movement. Edward was wondering about how those plump nipples would taste.

"I wouldn't," Smith cautioned from the next table. He was laying on his front, his face turned toward Edward.

"What are you? A bloody mind reader?" he demanded. "And why not?"

"Their father owns this place, along with a forge and smithy a few streets away. He makes swords—*sharp* swords."

Edward pulled his eyes away from the tempting nipples. "Christ! Then why does he let his daughters parade around naked?"

"But they aren't nude." He jerked his chin toward the girl who'd just come around to his side, her back facing Edward while she pounded on Smith's back.

Like her sister her only clothing was a very slight loin cloth which nominally covered her sex while leaving her buttocks exposed, only a string running up between her full, rounded cheeks. It was an exceptionally erotic but frustrating experience.

By the end of the hour he was both erect and enervated.

Smith sat up on his table, took one look at the tented towel around his waist and snickered before handing each young woman a handful of coins and saying something in a language Edward had never heard before. The two young women cut Edward remarkably shy looks—especially for women who'd just handled naked male strangers—and giggled, leaving them alone.

"What did you say," Edward asked, not really caring he felt so lethargic.

"I thanked them for a very pleasant few hours."

Edward snorted. "Liar."

"Not at all," Smith opened his towel to display a remarkably large prick for a man of his stature—an *erect* prick. "They did give me an enjoyable time. But this was mere foreplay." He covered himself up, his knowing smirk telling Edward that Smith had intended to shock him with his unnerving display.

And it *had* unnerved him, leaving Edward with an odd snaky sensation in his belly. He'd seen plenty of men naked, but never another man's erection. His own cock, he realized, was now at full hardness. Surely he hadn't—

"Come on," Smith said, turning toward the dressing area. "Let's go somewhere we can get these taken care of properly."

Both intrigued and repelled, Edward pushed himself up and went to his, thankfully, private dressing room.

He left the building to find Smith's carriage already outside and waiting.

"Well?" Smith asked after Edward had climbed back inside. "Ready for more adventure?"

Edward gave the other man a long look. Just where was he taking him? He knew *nothing* about Smith's sexual preferences. What if the man took him to a bloody molly house? It wasn't as if Edward was as pure as the driven snow, but he'd always drawn the line at men—not even fucking in the same room back when he'd been a younger man going to cheap bawd houses with his mates, places where having the privacy of four walls had cost extra.

No, he didn't trust Smith. "I know a place," he said, rapping on the roof. "Take us to Tosca's," he told the driver when the vent slid open.

Smith grinned—the wolfish expression that left everyone in his vicinity feeling uneasy. "Ah, finally going to share your little place with one of us, are you?" Edward blinked and Smith laughed. "Oh yes, we all know about your little side investment."

Edward bristled at the insinuation in his tone. "What of it? It's not as if we agreed to engage in *every* venture together."

Smith made a soothing noise. "Of course not, Ted. It's just been amusing to watch you go to such an effort to keep your connection to Tosca's a secret."

Edward chewed on that for a moment. Had he wanted to keep it a secret? What was he afraid of? That one of his partners would discover Nora? He cut Smith a sharp look. "I take it you've already been there?"

Smith chuckled.

The bastard. But Edward refused to humiliate himself by asking him who he'd seen so they rode the short distance in silence.

The carriage dropped them off at the front door and Edward realized his palms were sweating as he led the way up the steps to the front door. He was bloody pathetic! He would ask for somebody else tonight. There was no way in hell he'd ask for her.

The man named Charles—a smarmy, handsome bastard who was an assistant of sorts to Madame Tosca—greeted them in the foyer.

"Ah, Mr. Fanshawe, what a pleasure." Humor glinted in his sky blue eyes and Edward realized all the whores probably knew of his offer and rejection by now. He clenched his jaws, refusing to exhibit his anger like a spurned lover.

"I've brought a business associate with me," he said rather foolishly, especially as Charles's attention had already turned to the other man. "This is Mr. Smith."

"My, what a coincidence," Charles splayed the fingers of one hand over the snug black waistcoat he wore without a coat and cooed in a way that raised Edward's hackles, "Smith is *my* surname, too."

"No?" Mr. Smith said with a look of faux wide-eyed wonder. "But that's *astonishing*. It's such an *unusual* name."

Both men snickered at their foolishness and Edward rolled his eyes. Just his luck: *two* clever, snide arseholes.

Charles led them into the sitting room where a handful of women— all clothed in the demure yet oddly sexual garb every woman here wore: a thin white muslin gown with only a chemise beneath it.

Mr. Smith grinned widely as he looked around the room. "Good evening, ladies."

The women giggled and called out a variety of responses. Edward knew after only a glance that Nora wasn't in the group.

Charles turned to Smith and eyed him up and down, his expression thoughtful. "I believe I have just the person for you, Mr. Smith. She's one of our favorites and you are lucky that her normal appointment cancelled and she's free for the evening."

Edward had a bad feeling in his gut—and it was amplified when Charles cut him a sly little smile. "You can recommend her services yourself, Mr. Fanshawe, having gone to her quite often. Her name is Nora," he told Smith, his taunting eyes never leaving Edward's face.

"Nora," Smith repeated musingly. "It seems I've heard that name somewhere recently."

Edward felt every bloody eye in the room on him. Each and every one of these fuckers knew he'd been rejected by a little chit of a whore and now they were waiting for him to cry and rant for their entertainment.

They could go sod themselves.

He had to reach deep inside himself to find the energy necessary to fix a bored smile on his face and shrug. "Nora's a good girl, Smith. You'll enjoy her."

Edward couldn't help enjoying the flicker of disappointment that chased across Charles's handsome features at his failure to rise to such tasty bait. Edward turned toward the assembled girls. "Now," he said, forcing himself to smile in a way that promised debauchery and pleasure. "Which of you two ladies should I take upstairs with me tonight?"

✳✳✳

Nora looked up at the knock on the door.

Maddy, one of the housemaids, stood in the opening. "You're wanted in the Silesia immediately."

Nora frowned. "But my appointment for tonight cancelled."

"This is a new one—some gent sent by Mr. Fanshawe for you." The girl gave her a saucy grin before shutting the door with a click.

Nora sighed; she would be getting such looks from everyone after this. Mr. Fanshawe, a customer many of the other girls had envied her, had finally thrown her over. She knew many of the others thought her quiet and reclusive ways were simply her way of putting on airs. They would be glad to see her brought down.

Mr. Fanshawe would have known that—he would have anticipated the humiliation she'd receive at her coworker's hands.

He would know that she would know. And he would know how his actions would cause a frisson of sexual arousal to shoot through her body and settle in her sex. It would amuse him to know he could control her body even when sending another man to use her.

Nora put down her brush. It was still fresh as she'd only a few minutes ago decided to splurge on five candles and finish the last bits of this portrait now that Mr. Lombard, her usual visitor the second Tuesday of every month, had cancelled. Nora liked Mr. Lombard, who was her oldest customer. She'd met him when she was only sixteen and had been browsing his bookstore on Bond Street. He was in his mid-forties and trim and fit. He was short of stature and not much taller than Nora, his hair a non-descript brown and his soft gray eyes magnified and distorted behind his thick lenses. Although he was excessively shy they'd gotten to know each other through the art books he occasionally ordered for her. One thing had led to another and they'd had tea. Nora had told him the truth about herself before agreeing to meet with him, assuming he'd reject her then and there. But he hadn't. Indeed, he'd seemed more eager than before so they'd gone to tea. And then gone again and again, until, one day, he'd asked her to marry him.

Nora had been heartbroken by his request. It wasn't that she didn't like him—she liked him very much—but she could never marry any man—or so she'd believed back then. He'd been deeply hurt and she'd avoided his shop for several months. And then, one day, he'd shown up at Tosca's.

He was not a rich man, so she knew he'd had to scrimp to afford to come to her. He was gentle and sweet and could usually only afford an hour. Madame had chastised Nora more than once for staying with him longer. They never had intercourse more than once, and that only lasted a few minutes, but Mr. Lombard talked and talked about himself, his past, his first wife—who'd died in childbirth—his family, who lived in Southeast London, and such things. Each time he came, he brought her a book. She'd tried to pay him—either in coin or services—but he'd never let her.

Her mind raced as she removed her painting smock and went to the mirror. She'd just gotten herself ready for Mr. Lombard an hour ago so she was still tidy but her hair was not braided. Her hands rose to take down the heavy chignon and braid it. But then she recalled it was Mr. Fanshawe's friend.

Nora's hands shook slightly and even this small sign of weakness angered her. It was just as well that he'd shown his disinterest in her so plainly. His effect on her would lessen over time. At least he'd not come to the house himself in weeks. As long as he stayed away—and took his commerce to some other house—she'd get over him eventually.

She made her way to the Silesia, a room she'd not been in since her last time with Mr. Fanshawe. Was that a coincidence? Or had he—

"Nora!"

She jumped and turned at the sound of Madam's voice.

"Yes, Madam?"

The older woman's mouth twisted with scorn. "I hope you are happy," she said, although with her accent it sounded like, 'I 'ope you are 'appy.'"

Nora had to bite her lip to keep from smiling.

"Mr. Fanshawe is finished with you."

Nora's heart stuttered. "He came to tell you that?"

"Don't be a stupid girl! Of course he didn't. But he has come with his friend and recommended you while taking Louise and Franka for himself."

Nora tried to hide her pain at this disclosure but Madam was too sharp-eyed. "Yes, you have made yourself a nest and now you will sleep in it," she said, butchering the idiom. "This new man is a wealthy businessman friend of his and could bring much money to the house. Try to please him as I should like to pull him away from Cecile Bernina."

"Yes, Madam."

The older woman shrugged away her thanks. "Now, hurry! He is waiting."

Bernina's was a house that offered *unusual* entertainments. She'd always been curious that Mr. Fanshawe didn't favor Bernina's but she knew two of the girls who worked there and they'd never heard of him.

Nora's feet seemed to become heavier as she approached the Silesia, but, inevitably she reached the heavy oak door.

She took a deep breath and raised her hand to knock.

Before her knuckles touched the wood a movement caught her eyes. She turned; it was Mr. Fanshawe, and he was just about to enter the Dordogne Room. He would have come up the main stairs rather than the servant stairs as she had.

Nora's hand froze, as did her heart. His dark eyes glittered in the low lighting of the hall and his lips were pressed into a grim line. He hesitated for an instant and she thought he might greet her, but instead he turned away and opened the door, disappearing inside.

Nora's brain performed a lock down of sorts—the type of thing the defenders of castles must have once done—her reaction to any situation which required more mental attention than she could currently spare.

Later. I can muse and mull and agonize over all of this later.

It took only seconds before she was safely locked inside herself, safe from the slings and arrows of a world that was so far beyond her control.

Her features composed into her mask of bland submission, she knocked on the door and entered the room.

Chapter Five

Mr. Smith

Smith hadn't been so diverted in ages. It was dangerous to provoke Edward Fanshawe—a man who was as pitiless as a cobra when roused—but he simply couldn't resist. Besides, he really *had* wagered with their other two partners—the loser getting the privilege of discovering what the hell was going on with Fanshawe—and lost.

The wager had only been partly in jest. The truth was, he, Chatham, and Banks had tolerated enough of Fanshawe's unbearable temper and none of them wanted to work with him for fear of inadvertently pushing him over the edge and finding themselves holding a pistol at dawn.

It hadn't taken much poking around since Smith had kept close tabs on all his partners for years—a fact that would doubtless make them all furious if they found out. Although he was fairly certain that at least Chatham—a man whose past was almost as murky as Smith's—knew all his partners' business holdings down to the last farthing. But the reclusive loner could search for the rest of his life and learn *nothing* about Smith's past—not even his name. Smith was certain of that.

In any case, it hadn't taken long to track the source of all their—and Fanshawe's—current problems to this elegant little brothel.

And it had taken *less* than any time for Smith to pinpoint the delicious young Charles as an excellent—and most pleasurable—source of information.

Of all the investigative work Smith had done over the years he believed his two evenings with Charles Smith might have been the most enjoyable.

Like most other men who engaged in sodomy Smith usually kept his personal business extremely private and didn't flit from bed to bed. Such flitting could make a wealthy sod vulnerable and the victim of blackmailers. And even though the last few people who'd attempted to bribe Smith could only be found during extremely low tides, he still didn't like to encourage such behavior.

Not only was Charles Smith a prime fuck with a throat like hot velvet, he was a clever young man who'd guessed exactly what Smith wanted after just one question about Fanshawe.

As a result of their entertaining pillow talk the visit here tonight hadn't really been Fanshawe's idea. Smith had played with the man's overflowing sexual frustration for hours so he'd not been surprised when Fanshawe had insisted on Tosca's as a destination. No doubt he'd felt a familiar place would help him regain his bearings.

Smith grinned at that thought. For all Fanshawe's acumen in the boardroom, the poor bastard hadn't stood a chance against the machinations of Smith's Machiavellian mind.

And the best part? It hadn't mattered to Smith whether they'd ended up here or Bernina's as either place would have offered up amusing distractions that would have caused Fanshawe's head to ache.

Although, he admitted to himself as he stripped off his coat, waistcoat, and cravat, until he was garbed only in black trousers, black linen, and glossy black shoes, he *had* rather hoped Fanshawe would simply choose the girl for himself and leave Smith free to spend the evening balls-deep inside Charles Smith's tight little arse.

He could—and likely would—come back for that particular entertainment another night. Tonight would be devoted to business. Besides, he was more than a little curious to finally see the woman who'd been driving poor old Fanshawe batty this past six months. Indeed, if Fanshawe had chosen Bernina's tonight Smith would have called on Nora Hudson eventually, although not necessarily in a business capacity.

But now that Fanshawe had opened this particular door . . . well, perhaps he might use this opportunity to their *mutual* advantage.

Smith's cock stirred at the possibility of sex and mental games and he grinned before taking a deep drink of the very fine brandy Fanshawe had ordered for both rooms. Right this moment the other man would likely be climbing the walls—if only inside his head—wondering what Smith was doing with his Nora.

Like the rest of his partners Fanshawe had no idea which way the wind blew for Smith. He didn't hide his proclivities from the other men because he thought they'd care—he happened to know from his investigations that all three of his partners were more than slightly bent when it came to their preferences in the bedchamber—but simply out of habit. The only men who knew what Smith liked in the bedroom were those he'd fucked, and they had their own reasons to worry about discretion. While he generally preferred male bed partners he certainly wasn't averse to bedding what he thought of as *the right kind of female* on occasion. That meant he preferred his women to occupy that amorphous zone between the masculine and the feminine. He liked women who might be men, and men who could pass for women. Young Charles, with his fine bone structure and guinea gold curls was a prime example of the type of man he craved. Painted and laced into a corset Charles represented the most erotic elements of both genders. Smith began to stiffen at the memory of their last encounter, which had—

A light knock on the door made him turn.

"Enter," he called out, a pulse of anticipation in his groin.

The door swung open and the woman who'd been tearing Fanshawe in two stepped into the room. "Good evening, Mr. Smith," the woman said in low, almost gravelly voice. "I'm Nora."

Smith swept her slender, almost boyish person with a hungry look and chuckled. "You certainly are."

Tonight, he decided, might prove to be very enjoyable after all.

Chapter Six

Edward hated the entire world: himself for being an arrogant fool and suggesting Nora, Smith for *accepting* her, and Nora for—well, for being Nora.

He'd left Tosca's not long after dawn. Rather than stride down the hall and rip the door to the Silesia Room—*his* room—off the hinges, he'd dressed, paid the whores, and left without even looking in that direction. Down in the sitting room he asked the sleepy whore if Smith had left before him. He'd been unable to hide his fury at her answer, and had stalked toward the foyer, where he'd rammed his arms so hard into the coat the footman held out for him that he'd almost knocked the poor man to the floor.

Smith was still up in that room. With. Nora.

His vision wavered and his head felt as if it might blow off his bloody shoulders. Just what the hell had happened in that room mere feet from where he'd spent an utterly miserable night? What?

He waved away the offer of a carriage. His town house was almost two miles away but Edward knew that wouldn't be far enough for him to walk off his rage; rage that was heavily adulterated by envy and jealousy and a host of other unsavory emotions as his brain staged a veritable festival of debauchery in his head: the main actors being a naked Nora and Smith, complete with whips, leather bindings, and plenty of sweat.

"You bloody fool," he grated, his words creating gouts of steam in the frigid morning air. It was all Edward's fault for insisting on going to Tosca's. And then insisting on taunting Nora at the expense of his own sanity. Besides, if you'd have asked Edward about the mysterious Smith's sexual tendencies, he would have pegged him for a sod.

He very well could be a sod—knowing Smith he would have sniffed out the situation somehow and had eagerly agreed with Edward's suggestion of Nora simply because he knew it would irk Edward.

Irk. Ha! Drive him bloody mad was more like it.

The only consolation was knowing Smith was a mere slip of a man compared to Edward and he *knew* Nora loved his size and strength because it had been the one piece of information she'd offered up without him having to beat or fuck it out of her.

So, no matter what astonishing technique Smith might have when it came to bed sport, he could never change the size of his body.

Edward's face heated at the image that flashed through his mind: Smith's huge bloody prick, which the man had insisted on sharing.

"Fucking hell!" How the devil was he supposed to scour *that* image from his brain?

It *did* occur to Edward as he strode through the frosty morning, that Nora might say such complimentary things to every customer and perhaps she'd told Smith he was precisely *her* type of build. After all, she was quiet, but not at all stupid. And Edward knew she was remarkably in demand for a woman who wasn't a beauty. It bothered him to think that other men had recognized that spark inside her—that others were even now—Smith!—plumbing her fascinating depths and trying to deconstruct her many, subtle parts to find the real Nora.

"Goddammit," he yelled, his sudden outburst scaring the hell out of a passing maidservant who scuttled across the empty street to avoid walking near him.

Edward could *not* rid his mind of the image of their two naked, flushed, slender—but wiry and strong—bodies writhing together.

His own evening had been an agony of wondering and mental suffering that had only been made worse by the need to put on a believable display for the whores he'd engaged. He'd cursed himself immediately upon speaking. Why had he needed to invite four instead of two eyes to observe him—two mouths to repeat their findings to the other whores? Yes, he'd wanted Nora to hear about the things he'd done—in great detail—but what if one of these far-too-clever whores spotted something amiss in his act? He'd end up a laughingstock.

Bloody hell. A man could go crazy playing mental games with women. Edward should have just gone to whatever bloody nest of debauchery Smith had wanted to take him to.

That thought gave him pause. He'd been too consumed with thoughts of Nora during that short carriage ride to even ask the other man where he normally went. He'd learned from questioning Louise that Smith had only come to Tosca's twice, to her knowledge. She said he'd gone with a different woman each time, neither one Nora.

Perhaps he should find out the name of the place Smith usually patronized? Lord knows he'd gotten nothing but aggravation last night. Nor had he enjoyed the last dozen trips to the Bellaire. Perhaps if he could go someplace new he would be able to *forget*. And if he could *forget*, he could get back to his life.

Edward frowned at the direction of his thoughts: all heading to Nora. Again.

Good God. All he did was try to devise ways to forget that little bitch.

By the time he reached his large townhouse he was gritting his teeth so hard his head ached.

As he tossed his hat, coat, and cane to the footman in his foyer it occurred to him—along with a gut-wrenching surge of despair—that he might very well go mad. Or, he considered as he marched up the stairs toward his chambers, he might simply lose his mental acuity. His partners would likely reject him from the syndicate—it took the vote of all three—he would whore, gamble, or drink away all his money and *still* have that gaping void inside him.

Edward flung open the door to his chambers and almost slammed into Nelson, his valet, who'd obviously been about to exit.

The other man stepped back from the door. "Good morning, Mr. Fanshawe."

"I'll undress myself—I won't need you until later." God knows he didn't need a witness to his imminent mental breakdown.

"Very good, sir."

Edward tossed both coat and waistcoat onto the floor; they reeked of whatever bloody perfume the two whores had been drenched in. Edward positively *despised* scent. Nora only ever smelled of soap when she came to him.

But after she'd spent an evening with him? Well . . . His lips curled into a smile as he pulled his shirt over his head. When she left him she smelled like sweat and fucking and Edward.

You're thinking of her <u>*again*</u>.

"Bloody hell," Edward muttered as he realized even that brief flash of memory had caused his cock to stir. How was it possible that thoughts of her could be so potent? It wasn't as if he'd not ejaculated in weeks, he'd climaxed last night—*twice*—but it hadn't been easy or even pleasurable. In fact, if he'd been at any other whorehouse he simply would have paid and then left. The only reason he'd made the effort last night was that he loathed the thought that word might get back to Nora that he'd not been able to get it up.

He dropped into a chair and roughly toed the heel of his boot, ruining the expensive leather heels with his anger and impatience. Dammit. He should have had Nelson pull them off before he'd dismissed him.

Edward grimaced with discomfort as he stood, unbuttoned his trousers, shoving them to the floor before stepping out of them, his tumescent organ springing up at him. Even when he locked all thoughts of Nora in the back of his mind she managed to keep him in a persistent state of arousal. Edward glared at his annoying cockstand and strode to the four crystal decanters he kept in his sitting room. And that was another thing—he'd begun to drink more than he liked, and he didn't even feel that it helped his foul mood most of the time. Yet he drank anyhow.

He poured himself three fingers of the best brandy money could buy and threw it back like it was cheap ale. He grit his teeth with pleasure at the burn and considered another before setting the glass down with a thump. No, he'd not become a sot for that woman.

That bloody woman.

It was pathetic, but what he wanted to do was close the drapes, crawl into bed, and fist himself raw with the memory of that two-second meeting he'd shared with her in the hallway.

His cock jumped at the memory—nothing but a quick glance and her pale eyes scored him like nails in the dim hallway of the whorehouse.

"Ah, Christ," he groaned as he rose to full hardness.

✳✳✳

Edward didn't see Smith for almost two weeks after that night at Tosca's. He'd not been avoiding the man—although that probably wouldn't have been a bad idea given the amount of enraged curiosity he battled about Smith's night with Nora—but hadn't seen him because Smith had been out of town.

They'd had a problem at one of their cloth factories up in the North and Smith—who had methods of suppressing worker disturbances the rest of them didn't want to delve into too deeply—had gone to contain the problem.

Edward had kept his nose to the grindstone since Tosca's, keeping away from drink, whores, and entertainment in general. But he'd finally had enough and accepted Chatham's invitation to cards tonight at Number 14.

It had been a good night, as far as such things went, and Smith was in an exceptionally good mood as he'd just won an obscene sum of money from some idiot with more dosh than brains.

Banks and Chatham had left much earlier, but Edward had hung about playing cards long after he wanted to be gone, just because he didn't want to go home to his empty house. Nor did he wish to go to Tosca's, the Bellaire, or the half dozen other establishments he knew about.

Part of his brain, he realized as the evening wore on—wore being the operative word—wondered about asking Smith—in the most casual way possible, of course—the name of the place he frequented.

He should have known that subterfuge never worked with the bloody man, who seemed to have some kind of mind-reading powers.

"I sense you are waiting for me," he said, grinning at Edward as he gathered all his markers into a huge pile. "You look like a man who desperately needs to get his knob polished." Before Edward could answer he pushed up from the table and summoned a nearby waiter. "Take this to Malcolm and tell him I want it in small denominations." Malcolm was the manager of Number 14 and saw to the house's bank.

"Of course, Mr. Smith."

"Well, it just so happens I'm in the mood for some. . . diversion myself, Fanshawe. Want to try something new?"

Edward shrugged, determined to appear casual. "Why not?" he said as they descended the sweeping staircase and made their way to the cloakroom, where Malcolm himself awaited them.

"Good evening, Mr. Smith, Mr. Fanshawe." The youngish, rotund manager turned to Smith. "Here you are, sir." He handed Smith a roll of banknotes, bowed, and left them.

"How much?" Edward asked as the Smith slipped into the very plain and very expensive black cashmere wool coat a servant held out for him.

"A little over two."

Edward gave a low whistle; two thousand pounds was a pretty haul for an evening's work. He knew the toffs never asked each other how much they won or lost, but his business associates were men from the gutter who enjoyed sharing their successes.

Smith's carriage was waiting for him when they stepped out into the frigid night. Edward tipped the doormen while Smith climbed inside his luxurious town coach. Like everything Smith owned the coach was black on black. He knew Smith owned a house somewhere in London, but he'd never seen it. He imagined it as a dreary cavern of a place with black floors, black walls, black—

"I have to thank you for your referral at Tosca's," Smith said, his voice smooth and uninflected in the darkness of the carriage.

"Oh?" It was all Edward could manage to squeeze out when what he really wanted to do was grab the man by the throat and shake the truth of that bloody night out of him.

Smith chuckled, the sound evil. "Oh, indeed. Nora turned out to be just exactly what I like."

The inside of the coach seemed to become suffocating. Edward had to clench his jaws to keep the words back, reminding himself he didn't *want* to know. That he would pay good money *not* to know. That—

"I had such a lovely time I stopped by again the very night I got back from Manchester. And then again last night." Edward felt his self-control fraying like the strands of a poorly braided rope. Smith gave a low, primitive grunt and said, "I just can't get enough of that—"

"So why aren't you going there tonight?" Edward demanded, his pulse pounding in his temples.

"Ah, well, variety is the spice of life. Besides, when a friend waits all night for you to take him out whoring—"

"I wasn't waiting for you," Edward gritted out.

Smith laughed in a way that made Edward's hands clench. "What is the name of this place?" he asked before Smith said something that made Edward kill him.

"Bernina's."

Edward frowned in the darkness. "I thought that closed some time ago?"

"It did, but it moved to a new home and re-opened late last year." He paused and then added, "You might have noticed if you'd not been so . . . busy with other matters."

Edward bit down on his retort, refusing to feed the man's curiosity any more than he'd already done.

After a moment, Smith continued. "It's a very small establishment that caters to unusual tastes."

Edward's cock, which had only responded to thoughts of Nora for days and days, began to stir.

He cleared his throat. "Unusual, how?"

"Oh, a variety of ways—I wouldn't want to spoil it for you."

Before Edward could tell him to quit being a tosser and just tell him, the carriage rolled to a stop.

The building looked remarkably like Tosca's, which was to say the type of place you'd never notice unless you knew where to look.

They mounted a half dozen steps and the door opened before they knocked. An exceptionally tall, thin woman stood just inside, in a very elegant foyer.

"Welcome back, Mr. Smith," she said in a low voice.

"Ah, Cecile, how lovely to see you—it's been a while. I understand you had family come to visit. I hope that was enjoyable."

The woman gave a low chuckle as she and another servant—a very young boy dressed in livery—helped them with their coats, hats, and gloves.

"Ah, family. So good to see them, but even better to see the back of them."

Smith laughed. But Edward, who'd grown up in a workhouse, failed to see the humor.

"Did you wish for your usual tonight, Mr. Smith?" Cecile asked as she escorted them up a broad flight of stairs.

"No, I think I shall try the Rose Salon."

Cecile paused before saying. "Of course. I think you'll be very pleased with the selection tonight."

"What's the usual?" Edward asked Smith as the two of them followed the madam to a set of double doors.

Smith just chuckled.

Cecile opened the right-hand door and ushered them into a large sitting room where a handful of women, all garbed in rich silk dressing gowns, were scattered about. A couple were reading, several were chatting, and one appeared to be bent over needlework close to a brace of candles.

They all stopped what they were doing when the door opened.

Edward paused, standing back as Smith smiled and greeted several of the women by name.He bestowed kisses all around and then turned to Edward. "This is my good friend Edward. He's never been here before."

Edward nodded at the women, pleased to see they wore very little face paint and all appeared clean and well-groomed.

Smith cocked his head and grinned. "I tell you what, Edward, why don't I choose for you? After all, you were so kind as to choose for me that last time." Without waiting for an answer Smith said, "Victoria, I think."

A smallish woman with dark straight hair and exotic eyes stepped forward and offered her hand to Edward. He took it but looked at Smith who was grinning more than usual. Edward couldn't help feeling there was something . . . off with the other man.

"Now, who shall I pick for me? Hmmmm." He tapped his chin with one finger, as if deep in thought. "Ah, is that Emma I see hiding in the back?" The women parted to reveal a woman Edward had somehow missed seeing.

The room seemed to tilt slightly when she fixed her pale blue eyes on him.

The resemblance was astonishing: it could have been Nora's sister. Same slight build, same pale, narrow face, same straw-colored hair. Same impenetrable expression.

"Yes, Emma," Smith's voice brought Edward back to himself. "I think Emma will do very well for me tonight." The sly note in his voice pulled Edward's eyes from the girl.

Why the devious little bastard.

Smith took the girl's outstretched hand and kissed the back of it. Only then glancing up at Edward. "Are you quite satisfied with my selection, old man?"

Edward seethed inside, but managed a pleasant, "Excellent choice, Smith."

Smith chuckled and led Emma toward the door. Victoria took Edward's hand and guided him after them.

Edward had assumed Cecile would take Smith and his disturbing companion to their room and then show him to another, where he'd likely spend the night imagining the swine with Nora's bloody look-alike.

Cecile led them to a set of doors on the third floor. She flung both open, exposing a room that resembled some eastern potentate's harem. "Will this do?"

"This is exactly what we wanted, Cecile," Smith said, having to stand on his toes to kiss the tall woman's cheek. Edward saw an odd look pass between the two, but he was too distracted at the notion of sharing a room with Smith and his Nora-whore.

"Come in, come in," Smith said, waving to the room behind him, which was filled with padded divans, chaises, and piles of cushion in lush silks and decadent colors.

When Edward hesitated Smith cocked his head. "Oh, I'm sorry— you don't mind sharing, do you Edward? I thought we might make a party of it."

Edward stared into Smith's black-as-hell eyes, warning bells going off in his head at the other man's hard, challenging smile.

He should have turned and ran.

But, idiot that he was, Edward heard himself say, "It would be a pleasure." And then he entered the room.

Chapter Seven

Smith's thin lips curved into a carnivorous smile. "Excellent," he said, turning to Victoria. "I see some champagne on ice near the bed, darling. Why don't you strip off that gown and go fetch us a glass." Smith's hands were already at his cravat.

Victoria tugged on her sash and shrugged out of her robe exposing a curvaceous body with full hips and a tiny waist. When she turned to lay her robe across the back of the chair Edward stared first at her luscious breasts and then at her sex. A noise of surprise escaped him at what he saw. She'd been shaved of all hair and a small silver ring glistened between her plump, smooth lips. He cut a quick look at Smith, who smiled at him.

"Lovely, isn't she? Why don't you show Edward your pretty little jewel, my dear."

Victoria used her delicate fingers to spread her lips.

"Christ," Edward muttered, as hard as a bloody pike.

Smith laughed and swatted her ass. "Drinks, my dear." When she went trotting off, her bottom bouncing fetchingly, Smith tossed his waistcoat on top of Victoria's robe, his eyes moving to Edward's side. "Emma, has the same—show him, Emma."

Edward had avoided looking at the quiet whore but now she stepped between him and Smith. She pulled the sash on her sapphire blue robe, letting it puddle on the ground. Edward sucked in a breath: her breasts were just slightly larger and her hips more rounded than Nora's but the resemblance was uncanny. The only real difference was her sex, which was smooth and hairless with a silver ring protruding from between her lips. Like Victoria she spread herself for his viewing. Edward dropped to his haunches, mesmerized. The ring pierced the thin bit of flesh that protected her clitoris. He reached out a finger, which looked obscenely big and dark against the delicate pink of her skin, and lightly stroked the ring.

A shudder went through her body and he looked up to find her lids heavy over her light blue eyes.

"It feels good, doesn't it, Emma?" Smith asked. Edward saw that he was naked as he came to stand behind Emma. He laid his hands on her shoulders and looked down at Edward. "The ring brings her pleasure when she becomes aroused." His hands slid down Emma's back and reemerged beneath her arms, snaking beneath them and lightly cupping her small breasts.

Edward swallowed, unable to take his eyes from Smith's hands. His olive skin tone was more noticeable against Emma's milky white skin, and his hands—long fingered and elegant—caressed the undersides of her slight breasts, bringing her tiny nipples to tight points.

"Go on," he urged Edward, the nostrils of his narrow, blade-like nose flaring as he stroked. "Taste her—I don't mind sharing."

Edward's mouth flooded and his eyes dropped to her pierced sex, only inches from his face.

"Open yourself to him, Emma," Smith urged.

Edward's heart was pounding so loudly in his ears he wondered if it would do his hearing permanent damage.

Slender white fingers pulled apart her plump lips and he sucked in a breath at the slick pinkness she exposed.

"She needs release, Edward."

Smith's voice was mesmerizing and compelling and Edward leaned forward and flicked the silver ring with his tongue.

The groan that issued from her small body made his head spin.

"Again," a soft, hissing voice commanded.

Edward dropped from his haunches to his knees taking her slim hips in his hands and lowering his mouth over her engorged peak.

She shivered beneath his mouth and hands, her fingers pulling her lips wider.

It was unfortunate that she tasted, felt, and sounded different enough from Nora to keep him from slipping entirely into his fantasy, but she was responsive and her needy whimpers spurred him on. There was also the knowledge, lurking at the back of his mind, hiding in the shadows, that Smith was watching him. The disturbing thought sent a sharp arrow of arousal to his already hard cock, he seized her narrow hips hard enough to leave bruises and lost himself in her.

Edward felt as though he'd barely begun when she shuddered, her sex contracting beneath his tongue.

"Shh, there now, my little darling. Was that good?"

Smiths' voice shook Edward from his torpor and he released her sensitive nub with reluctance. Two hands landed on his shoulders and he realized, quite suddenly, that he'd forgotten all about Victoria.

"Undress him, Victoria," Smith ordered, smirking down at him as Victoria helped him up. "Don't worry, Edward," Smith said, "I'll keep Emma busy until you're ready to play with her again."

Smith lowered himself onto the low-slung chaise just behind where he'd stood with Emma. When Emma made to turn toward him he shook his head. "No, darling, you face away from me—toward Edward, so he can watch you."

Edward was only vaguely aware of Victoria's hands moving over his body. All his attention was on the show in front of him. And there was no doubt in his sex-addled mind that Smith was putting on a show.

The other man's cock was every bit as big—and erect—as Edward remembered from that night at the baths.

It was ruddy and jutting up proudly from his lap. "Sit down, darling," he said to Emma, his eyes on Edward, his smile lazy and amused and aroused. "I want you to keep your eyes on Edward. He likes to watch. He's been wondering what type of things I do to girls who look like you."

Edward breathing quickened at what he knew Smith was saying: he would show him exactly what he'd done to Nora.

The fucking, vile, weaseling—

Victoria tugged on his shirt and Edward ducked to help her remove it, grateful for the brief moment away from Smith's knowing gaze. But the moment was over too quickly and when he opened his eyes it was to see Emma on Smith's lap, her legs spread wide and draped over Smith's, her sex open and exposed with Smith's enormous erection jutting up and pressing against her slit.

"God, that feels wonderful," Smith groaned, the flared head of his cock rubbing the silver ring. "But I want you to put me inside, darling, Edward wants to see me fuck you."

Edward shuddered at his words, his jaw sagging to deny it— But nothing came out. *Because it's the bloody truth, Edward!*

Lust and sickness roiled in his tight belly. Why would he enjoy looking at another man's prick in a woman? Why? Especially a woman who so closely resembled Nora? He'd always known he was depraved— but this?

Emma's small hand slid around Smith's shaft, barely able to encompass its girth. Edward's entire body clenched and he could not look away.

Deep down he knew what he was feeling would come back to haunt him. But he just didn't give a damn.

Emma didn't hesitate to bring Smith's swollen head to the entrance to her body. Edward was close enough that he could see the effects of her arousal. The little triangle was engorged and had pushed back the hood, which pulled the silver ring with it, drawing it tight against her slick nub. He imagined the friction would be pleasurable at first but might very well become excruciating after too much stimulation.

A sudden image of Nora the same way slammed into him and his cock almost exploded. Nora, shaved and pierced, her pink skin darkly flushed, her clitoris hard and slick and painfully sensitive after multiple climaxes. *God!* How he would use that little silver ring. It would bring them so much—

He blinked away the erotically charged image: *they* wouldn't do anything. Nora had rejected the chance to be his—to belong to him.

Agony and fury followed on the heels of the memory of her rejection.

Forget about her, a greedy, lustful voice cut in. *The woman across from you could be Nora.*

Edward gritted his teeth against the voice, but the damage was done and the image of his pierced fantasy-Nora disappeared. Instead there was Emma.

She was wiggling her hips and making soft little noises, clutching her lower lip beneath her teeth, obviously putting on a show for Edward.

Instead of reminding him of Nora—who would *never* be so obvious—and arousing him further, it gave him some distance— although far too little. He still couldn't tear his gaze away as she positioned Smith's big crown at her entrance, her eyes creasing in discomfort as he breached her.

Smith grunted and held her there, not allowing her to lower any further. Edward didn't need to look at the other man to know he was watching *him*. Once again, he didn't care how he was exposing himself—his yearning. He simply could not look away.

And then she began to lower herself and it was—quite honestly—a bloody mesmerizing sight. It didn't seem possible that she could stretch to accommodate Smith's huge cock without ripping in two. But she did—inch by inch by inch by inch—not stopping until only the underside of his thick root was still exposed.

Smith grunted and flexed his hips pulling his glistening shaft almost all the way out, until just the bell end remained inside her. He pulsed his hips lightly, the crown massaging her opening. And then, suddenly, he drove into her, hard and deep, drawing a startled gasp from both Emma and Edward.

Smith propped up his body with his elbows while Emma straddled his hips, the muscles in her legs quivering as she held herself in a low squat, meeting him thrust for thrust. Smith's body was almost hairless and his olive skin had begun to sheen from his exertions, his abdomen and chest tightening with each precise, vicious thrust of his hips.

Edward's mouth watered as he stared at the spot where they were joined. He wanted to tug on her ring with his teeth—suck her taut nub—and lick the pink skin that stretched around Smith's hard—

He jolted at the horrifying thought and his erect cock bumped into something soft. He looked down to find Victoria kneeling and looking up at him, her lips parted. She'd managed to strip him without Edward even realizing it and she was staring at his hard, weeping prick.

God Yes. He nodded and her cool hand slid around him and he groaned, letting his eyes close and his head fall back as she lapped at his swollen head. This was better—more normal, a woman sucking him off, not some bizarre sex show put on for Smith's perverted entertainment.

She didn't take him inside her mouth her right away, but cradled the end with her curled tongue, massaging the sensitive flesh just beneath his crown. He sucked a noisy breath through flared nostrils at the exquisite pleasure of her mouth and looked down while she worked him.

He'd not ejaculated in days and his balls were primed to come, tight to his body and eager to shoot their heavy load.

It was a struggle to hold himself in check as her skillful tongue danced and probed and caressed, but he gritted his teeth and began to pulse his hips, an action that was Nora's signal to take him deep in her throat—that he was ready to fill her, spend in her, mark her.

God. Nora again. Even when he had a beautiful woman's mouth on him. But maybe he could just imagine . . .

He closed his eyes and sighed. "Yes, Nora."

A low, rough chuckle jerked him from his reverie and he opened his eyes to find Smith watching him, his smile telling Edward he'd seen his lips move, if not heard his voice.

The thought was thrust away by the sight of Smith's slick body and the way the muscles of his abdomen and chest—more distinct and defined after only a few minutes' labor—bunched and flexed with each brutal thrust. Smith was not a big man but Edward realized, for the first time, just how fit and muscular he was.

Some part of Edward's recoiled against the observation. *You're staring at another man's body while a woman is sucking your cock. What the hell is wrong with you?*

Edward would have liked to attribute his arousal to Victoria's very skilled mouth, but that was a lie. He was aroused by watching Smith fuck a woman who looked enough like Nora to be eerie.

And, yes, *yes!* Maybe his cock *had* hardened at the sight of Smith's taut, corded body thrusting, pumping, and sweating.

What of it? some part of his brain demanded in defiance. *There is nothing wrong in watching others copulate and enjoying it. How many times have you watched Nora pleasure another woman? Or made her watch you?*

But those were women and this is a man, my bloody business partner for fuck's sake! And I'm getting hard watching his cock slide in and out.

Edward waited for horror to rush in and kill his arousal, but it didn't arrive. Instead, he just ached all the harder.

He wrenched his eyes away from Smith's pumping cock and looked into the other man's eyes, which were dark and unreadable.

Smith's teeth were exposed in a feral grin, the sharp points glinting in the low light as he grimaced in anticipation of his impending orgasm.

Edward's own balls clenched in sympathy and his hands dropped to Nora's soft hair—no *Victoria's*. He wove his fingers deep and grasped her skull, his hips jerking in time with Smith's thrusts, which were becoming harsher, his pumping harder and less controlled, until—finally—Smith rammed himself inside Emma and froze, the muscles in his arms standing out like thick ropes as he held her hips immobile, the base of his thick cock pulsing as he emptied his balls into her.

Edward's last thought before he thrust deep into Victoria's throat and spent was that Smith had looked fucking glorious.

Chapter Eight

Mr. Smith

mith rarely slept, and when he *did* sleep, he did it in a locked, dark room by himself.

Edward, on the other hand, had gone down like a man who'd been punched in the head.

Smith had sent the two women away while Fanshawe slept the sleep of the dead in the big, four poster bed where he'd collapsed after their brief bout of sex.

He poured himself a glass of whiskey Cecile kept just for him and lit one of his specially made cigars before collapsing into a chair in front of the fire, which Emma had stoked to an inferno before leaving. He couldn't help grinning at the thought of Emma.

When he'd seen Nora that night two weeks ago he'd been bloody stunned: the women might have been twins. He'd learned, after an evening with Nora, that even their temperaments were similar. But their personalities and tastes could not have been more different.

Emma was rather lazy and silly beneath her quiet façade. She was satisfied with the life of a whore and found sexual encounters a minor inconvenience compared to the money.

Nora, Smith had discovered from a little bird named Charles, had a passion other than tormenting poor Fanshawe: she was a painter. And a bloody good one. Smith knew that not from her—she had no idea that Charles had actually brought him several of the girl's paintings—but because he happened to possess a rather fine collection of paintings, himself.

Charles had told him a big reason she still worked as much as she did was the debt she owed to Tosca. He smiled and shook his head: there was nothing worse than falling into the clutches of a greedy whore.

Well, except falling into *his* clutches, of course.

Nora's paintings were exceedingly potent and Smith knew she would one day achieve fame; the woman had plans and desires that extended outside the brothel. He couldn't help wondering if there were nudes in her collection.

Emma, with her Sapphic tastes, would probably work at Bernina's quite happily for the rest of her life. Bernina's catered to clients who preferred their own gender but it was never wise to advertise such a specialty, which is why Cecile had needed to rapidly close her last establishment and wait two years before reopening in a different location. This time, at Smith's recommendation, Cecile serviced heterosexuals along with the clients who provided the bulk of her business.

Smith inhaled deeply, held it until his lungs began to burn, and then exhaled a narrow stream of brow smoke. He'd come up with the idea for tonight while he'd been trapped in bloody Manchester dealing with discontented weavers.

Sometimes Smith had to marvel at his own thought processes—at just how bloody devious he was. A normal man—and even most normally abnormal men—wouldn't have come up with tonight as a solution to Edward's problem. And, even now, he couldn't be positive it had worked. Even so, he'd bet all the money he'd earned tonight that Edward would wake up in the morning, pillory himself for getting aroused watching another man fuck, suffer night- and day-terrors for a week worrying that he was turning into a sod, and then get busy drawing up a plan to acquire the only woman in Christendom who could keep him from straying down the path of sodomy.

Smith chuckled. Lord it had been fun watching Edward's face tonight. Not to mention that he'd enjoyed seeing the man naked. Edward Fanshawe was a bloody bull—in every sense of the word—and Smith had enjoyed watching Victoria throat Edward's enormous cock.

He experienced a slight twinge in his groin recalling it—leching on a man who had no idea he was being leched on was beneath him, although very amusing.

While Smith had always prided himself on his physique, he knew that at just a hair over five foot nine he was on the smallish side. He'd always made up for that shortcoming by ensuring that his body was fit and hard and muscular. He'd discovered that physical exertion also kept his more violent, baser impulses in check. Those urges had lessened as he'd become older, but he still had to remain vigilant against the murderous rages that occasionally overcame him.

He took a final draw on his cigar and flicked it, sending it arrowing over the table and hearth and directly into the heart of the fire.

Smith ran his hand over his hairless chest, enjoying the feel of his body and imagining another set of hands on him, his prick thickening.

Hopefully tonight would be the last evening he'd have to spend with miserable, obsessed Fanshawe for a while. While he liked the man's company well enough, he was eager to go back to Tosca's on his own business.

Chapter Nine

*B*ang, bang, bang!

"Nora? *Nora!* I know you're in there! Wake up, ducks."

Nora blinked, her eyes dry and sore from remaining open so long. It took a moment for her vision to focus on the canvas. What she saw sent ripples of joy throughout her body. She'd caught it and captured it. It was *there*.

Bang! Bang! Bang! "I've not got all day, Nora!"

No matter what happened now—even if the building were suddenly to be consumed by fire—the image on the canvas would live forever in her mind's eye. She vaguely registered the sound of Charles pounding the door, trying to dislodge the chair she'd set under the handle.

"That's it! I'm coming in so you'd better cover all your naughty bits." Raucous laughter and then the sound of her door flying open, the chair skittering against the wall. "Oh. You're not sleeping."

"What do you want Charles?" She asked without turning, not yet willing to look away.

"You've got a visitor, sweetheart."

She sighed and laid down her brush, reluctantly turning just as Charles came up behind her.

"Oh, I say. That's rather good, isn't it?"

Nora pushed past him, leaving him standing in front of something that should have been hers for a while longer before she had to share it. But she had years of practice when it came to tucking away her expectations.

She reached behind her neck to untie the smock. "Who is it?"

"Hmmm?" he said, not turning from the canvas, a small, unconscious act that was more flattering that a thousand words of praise. Yes, what she'd done deserved his absorption. This year, she would enter a goddamned painting even if it broke her to do it; even if she had no money left to buy more paint or canvas.

Nora hung the stained smock on a hook and turned to examine her reflection, grimacing at what she saw: a sad little waif with pale unexpectedly curly corn-silk colored hair that hung just to her jaw.

She'd cut it one night in a fit—after Madam Tosca had sent her to a customer she knew Nora hated. Madam was usually very good at making sure her employees didn't have to service customers who repelled them—as long as that number didn't include too many. Nora was one of the easiest workers in that regard, but she absolutely could not tolerate Viscount Rowland. Oh, he was handsome enough—*very* handsome, in fact—but he had an ugly, ugly soul.

Madam had originally given him to Nora because of his proclivities: lots of leather with heavy whipping.

It astonished her how two men—take the viscount and . . . well, Mr. Fanshawe, for instance—

Nora couldn't help the slight shiver that went through her at his name. A name she allowed herself to think only one time each day. So that was twenty three times she'd thought of him since last seeing him in the hall that night. The night she'd gone to his friend, Mr. Smith.

She told herself her yearning was diminishing—but that was a lie that had ceased being convincing long ago.

Charles's handsome face appeared in the mirror beside her. "You'd better change your gown," he said, his fingers already going to the buttons that ran down her side—designed to allow either a whore or her lovers to easily remove her garments.

Nora ignored his prying eyes, allowing him to undress and dress her as her mind went back to the thought he'd interrupted. How could two men do the exact same thing to her: bind her immobile and then whip her, for example, and one man could bring her multiple orgasms while the other left her wrecked and in a state of self-loathing? Enough hatred for her own person that she would chop off all her hair.

There had been one positive result: Madam Tosca had stopped punishing her that day. Life had gone back to normal, with the exception of one of her clients—a man she didn't particularly care for and only saw infrequently—who saw her short hair and requested some other woman, claiming that, "he didn't want to feel like he was fucking a bloke."

Nora had found his flustered anger amusing rather than insulting and had been glad to pass him to another woman.

"Lift your arms, ducks."

Nora complied and the soft white muslin slipped down over her head.

Tonight she would see Lord Anthony for the first time since she'd cut it. Her lips twitched at the thought of what he'd say; she thought he would like it.

"What are you smiling about?"

Her eyes met Charles's in the mirror and she frowned, in no mood to engage in banter with the snake—who'd told her not long after she was with Mr. Smith that he'd cooked up that evening with Mr. Fanshawe's strange business partner to play some sort of trick on him—using *her*. Nora almost never lost her temper, but she'd been furious. Charles had been groveling ever since, bringing her food, taking her laundry down with his, and other small acts designed to weasel his way into her confidences. Probably so he could sell the information to Mr. Smith.

"Who is it, Charles." It was not a question, it was a demand.

Charles was only a few inches taller than her and with their faces side by side in the mirror she realized they looked enough alike to be siblings, although his lips were fuller, his face slightly broader, and his features prettier than hers. But the biggest difference was his eyes, which were a startling sky blue rather than her strange pale, pale gray.

"It's Mr. Fanshawe," he admitted, not smirking for once. "Are you going to—"

Nora whipped around, sending a button he'd been working on flying. "You have no right to ask me anything when it comes to him. You're a snake and a traitor." His haughty, handsome face crumpled. "I said I was sorry, Nora, and I meant it. Christ," he said, flinging up his hands in one of the dramatic gestures he was so fond of. "Do you never forgive people for making a mistake?"

"A mistake is borrowing my hairbrush and breaking off the handle."

Charles gave a guilty shrug. "I apologized for that."

"And I forgave you. But this? Telling some stranger about me—my life? Sharing the little bit of privacy I get in this room?"

He groaned, his expression genuinely remorseful—although she suspected more from being denied something he wanted, rather than from wanting her friendship very much, or regretting being a tittle-tale.

She lifted up her left arm. "If you want to be helpful you can finish buttoning me and keep your questions to yourself." That was the most forgiveness she could muster with her mind down in Madam's study and the man who waited there for her. She was almost relieved that he was here—finally, she could put an end to the misery of the past weeks and embrace a new kind of suffering. One that would likely destroy her.

✳✳✳

Edward had worked as if he were hooked to a plow these past weeks. True, he'd done all that work for himself rather than his partners or his other business interests.

That night with Smith at Bernina's had been . . . well, it had been the last bloody straw. He couldn't even blame his arousal on being cup-shot as he'd only had two glasses all night.

What the evening had done—after he'd stowed away his mortification at how much enjoyment he'd derived watching another man fuck—was motivate him to act. If he didn't do something about this obsession with Nora he was likely to end up doing the hangman's waltz for buggery.

So, he'd put his mind to work, locked his study door, given poor Powell a much needed two-month holiday and formulated his plan. A plan that had required the assistance of a great number of workers: carpenters, builders, and the like.

The final work he'd done himself. It had been a pleasure to work with his hands after so many years sitting behind a desk. By the time he'd finished everything, he'd gone for over three weeks without drinking, a woman, or even frigging his own bloody hand. He felt like a racehorse that had been training for Newmarket: fit, focused, and eager to test his mettle.

So, here he was, waiting in this bloody study again.

His mortification at showing up if not exactly *hat* in hand, then at least contract in hand, was only partially ameliorated by Madam's joyous reception of him.

Her joy had gradually dissipated the longer they'd waited, the only sound in the well insulated room the sound of a ticking clock—and likely the sound of Edward's blood pounding the longer he sat there.

"I don't know what Charles could be up to." She stood, her expression nervous. "I shall go and check."

"Tell her if she's not down here in five minutes I'm leaving." Which meant he'd then need to resort to Plan B, because—this time—he wasn't taking *no* for an answer.

Tosca moved from the room with more haste than grace. Relieved to be alone, he tossed his contract onto the smooth mahogany desk and stood, examining the contents of the madam's bookshelves.

Rather than the Gothic novels he'd expected there were books on a wide variety of subjects: philosophy, science, religion, and even several books on gardening.

But none of them were interesting enough to distract him from the task at hand. He pulled out his pocket watch, gritting his teeth and praying the minutes hadn't slipped past—and then hating himself for praying—when there was a soft knock and the door opened.

He'd anticipated feeling some shock—or other emotion—at seeing her, but he hadn't expected *this*.

"What the hell happened to your hair?"

She dropped a quick curtsy. "Hello, Mr. Fanshawe."

Edward frowned. *Already* she was disobeying him. "I asked you a question," he snapped, realizing that perhaps this wasn't the best way to start their negotiations but unable to stop himself.

"I cut it."

Edward blinked. What the hell could he say to that? Besides, he realized as he looked at her small face fringed by surprising curls, she looked rather . . . well, *good*, goddammit. She looked good. Who gave a damned about hair? He'd always had his women bind theirs back so it wouldn't interfere with what he liked to do. Now she wouldn't need to waste time braiding it.

That's if *she'll come.*

He gritted his teeth against his traitorous, mocking inner voice and marched back toward Madam's desk, snatching up the contract and striding back to where she was still standing. "Here, this is my offer to you."

She took it without looking at it and then walked toward the desk.

Edward gaped at her back, dizzy with—well, with *relief* and gratitude. More than three-quarters of his brain had expected her to reject it out of hand. His puppy-like joy sickened him.

"I shan't change any of the terms," he said to her back. "So don't even think of requesting anything more. Indeed, my man of business almost had an apoplexy drawing up this dratted—"

Edward saw her arm—her left hand—move in a way that indicated writing.

He steadied himself on the black leather wingchair, the action giving him an odd sense of *deja-vu*.

"You'll need to initial both near the—"

She flicked a page and wrote, and then flicked another page and another and another. She then put the pen in the holder, turned, and held the papers out to him. "Sir."

Edward looked into her impenetrable eyes, searching for *something*. Some sign of triumph, smugness, amusement—*anything*. There was nothing.

"May I have tonight to pack my possessions and finish one last piece of business?"

"What—" Edward began, wanting to know what *business* she had to finish. Wanting to know, quite bloody honestly, every tiny, infinitesimal, insignificant thing about her. But he'd already exposed himself quite enough for one day, hadn't he? So, he nodded sharply and strode toward the door, where he paused with his hand on the handle. "I shall send a carriage for you tomorrow at three o'clock sharp." And then he opened the door, not bothering to shut it behind him.

Chapter Ten

Edward pulled out his watch: it was 3:01. One minute later than the last time.

"Great bloody bollocking hell." He yanked at the watch, tearing the chain from his vest with a loud rip. And then he strode to his desk, pulled opened a drawer and threw the watch inside, slamming it shut with a satisfying crash.

There. That was better. What did it matter what time it was?

His lips began to curl up at the corners and he felt like rubbing his hands together with anticipation and glee: Nora had signed his contract. Signed and sealed. And if it bothered him a bit that she'd not even wished to read it, well, that was not his affair, was it? She was a woman of three or four-and-twenty—he should probably ask her age—not a girl, no matter how much she might resemble one.

He resumed his pacing, cutting frequent glances out the window, which overlooked the square below. He'd paid a bloody fortune for this spot on Grosvenor Square. And then he'd torn down the outdated old shack that had occupied the spot and put up his own house, an action he knew affronted his toffy-nosed neighbors. Well, they could lump it, he was here to stay.

He glanced around the study and grimaced; it was probably time he put some effort into filling the house with furniture, books, knick knacks, art or whatever frippery people crammed into their houses. He shrugged off that thought. There would be plenty of time for that after he got a wife, a project he could focus on now that he'd gotten Nora sorted. Yes, now that he would have her *here*, under his own roof where he could have access to her whenever he wished—and where nobody *else* could have her—he would be able to concentrate on other, more important matters: like getting a wife.

In fact, he'd celebrated yesterday's triumph by writing a brief note to the parents of one of the ten prospects—now eight prospects as two had married while Edward was carrying out his current plan—on his marriage list. It didn't matter that the list had shortened, he was sure there would be others if none of these eight suited his needs. Needs that were quite simple: be decorative on his arm, manage his gradual entry into society, and bear him children. He stopped in front a blank wall and frowned: *and perhaps buy some bloody artwork to fill all these blank walls.*

He spun on his boot heel and marched to the other end of the vast room—his study, but initially meant to be a library, which accounted for the hundreds of empty bookshelves.

Yes, his wife could live a life of luxury that many aristocratic women could no longer enjoy thanks to the plummeting fortunes most of the great houses had suffered over the past fifty years. While he wasn't unrealistic enough to imagine himself chumming around with his father-in-law—at Whites or Boodles or whatever bastion of upper class superiority such a man was likely to inhabit in his free time—the mere fact of being related to one of these families, no matter how impoverished, would increase his standing in the world.

Edward realized he'd stopped in front of the window as he'd imagined the pleasant future now open before him. Yes, everything would fall into place now that Nora belonged to him.

✳✳✳

Nora felt deep, almost hypnotic, serenity—and had done—since the moment she'd signed his contract.

There! The voice inside her had declared. *Now it is out of your hands.*

And what a relief it was. She didn't care what was in the pages she'd signed; she would do whatever he wanted and enjoy it for as long as she could. Why not? So what if she ended up crushed and broken when he tossed her aside? She was already crushed and broken from months without him. Besides, pain was part of life, and she liked pain, didn't she?

Nora had never ridden in a coach as luxurious as the one Mr. Fanshawe sent for her. Indeed, when she had time away from Tosca's she usually preferred to walk, to explore the city. Although she'd lived in London for ten years there were still many parts of it she had yet to see.

She tried to take at least one out of every four days off and see something new. But most often she gave in to the urge to paint. After all, the luxury of painting for most of an afternoon was a rarity.

The scene outside the window subtly changed. Although Tosca's was located in a part of town that was considered respectable, the houses they were passing now were bigger, more space between the buildings, until some houses seemed to take up entire blocks just by themselves.

She knew Mr. Fanshawe must be well-off to afford Tosca's as often as he did, and at such a level. He'd never had anything but the best Madam had to offer. Nora smiled. Well, except her. Although he'd taken high-flyers like Monique, Louise, and Bettina—Madam's most beautiful, skilled, and expensive women—he'd ended up with Nora.

The carriage slowed and then took a right, and Nora sat closer to the window to enjoy the sight: it was a pretty little square, complete with benches, a tiny gazebo, and a path that would be surrounded by flowers when spring finally came. It was magical.

The carriage slowed before a massive gray stone house that appeared bigger and newer than the two beside it. She felt the carriage shift as the footman jumped off the back. Surely there must be some mistake? Mr. Fanshawe would not engage a house such as this for a mere mistress?

The door opened and the footman pulled down the steps before holding out a gloved hand, "Miss Hudson?"

She frowned. "I think there must be some mistake?" She paused, uncertain—should she tell the man she was Mr. Fanshawe's mistress?

The huge black door at the top of the steps opened and Mr. Fanshawe stepped out. His frown told her that he anticipated a problem. Nora rapidly took the footman's hand and stepped out of the carriage, turning around for her bag.

"Leave that," Mr. Fanshawe ordered.

Nora turned at the sound of his voice.

"Thomas will bring in all your belongings and take them to your room." He held a beckoning hand toward her. "Come, Nora."

Nora mounted the steps without hesitation. Mr. Fanshawe hated to repeat himself and she'd just sold herself to him for the conceivable future.

When she reached the top he didn't touch her, but ushered her inside.

"You don't have a heavier cloak than that?" he asked as she unclasped her *only* cloak, a serviceable gray she'd had for as long as she could remember.

"No, sir."

A distinguished looking man who could only be a butler took her cloak. Nora smiled at him and he nodded but did not speak.

"This way," Mr. Fanshawe gestured toward a grand staircase, all but pushing her up the stairs, their footsteps muffled by the plush carpeting. "When you reach the landing you will continue to the next floor and then take a right."

The house felt half-finished—as if nobody inhabited it. The walls, she noticed, were bare. The lamps, woodwork, and carpeting were all of the finest quality, but there was no sign of human habitation.

When they reached the next floor, she took a right.

"The third door down," he said behind her, his voice sounding odd, as if he had a sore throat.

As they approached the door he stepped around her and reached for the handle. Not expecting the courtesy, Nora reached for it at the same moment and her hand landed on his. She felt his entire body stiffen and her own fairly hummed in answer. He wanted her—quite badly. She took her hand off his and he opened the door.

✳✳✳

Edward wanted to fuck her against the bloody door. It was only through a monumental force of will that he restrained himself.

He couldn't take his eyes off her—and there something about having her *here*, in his own environment, that was beyond erotic. His prick was so bloody hard he could quarry stone with it.

He stood back and watched her as she took in the room, turning in a circle and stopping when she faced him, a quizzical expression on her face. Was that the first time he'd ever seen her exhibit curiosity? His chest tightened with excitement—as if he'd just discovered something precious and rare that he wanted to snatch up and hide. Like a squirrel with a nut that he could take out later and gloat over, alone.

She looked up at him. "I don't understand? This is your house?"

He forced himself to use a dismissive and slightly admonitory tone. "If you'd read the contract—as you should have done—you would have known I was bringing you here." If he'd hoped to chastise her into

81

blushing or an expression of regret, he was destined to be disappointed: she merely looked at him with her strange colorless eyes. He sighed. "Yes, this is my house. This is your suite of rooms. You are Miss Nora Hudson, my ward. The daughter of my sister who died some time ago."

Her eyes widened and her bow-shaped mouth opened.

Edward felt like leaping up and down. *Finally! Finally a bloody reaction!*

"But—the servants who picked me up at Tosca's? Surely they know?"

Edward shrugged. "If they do, they'd better keep their mouths shut or go look for another employer."

She absorbed that, and then asked, "Did you have a sister?"

Edward almost laughed. His Nora—always one to do or say the unexpected. Most people would openly scoff at the notion of such a ridiculous charade—a twenty-four year old niece living with a bachelor uncle—but she was more interested in some fictitious sibling.

"Not that I am aware of." He strode to the door on the right, eager to show off the fruits of his labors. "This is your study and that door on the other side leads to a small sunroom—you may explore that at your leisure." He opened the door in front of him. "This is your bedchamber," he stepped back to let her precede him. The room had a huge bed, complete with four heavy posts. A massive fireplace raged across from it as he had noticed Nora was so slender she became cold easily. He kept walking. "Here is your dressing room," he opened the door to an exceptionally large dressing room, which all the suites in the house contained. Edward despised paltry little rooms and had opted for fewer rooms—he had no friends to fill even one guest room—in exchange for more luxurious spaces.

He stopped and waited while she looked around at the vast number of shelves and armoires that were full of articles of clothing, shoes, hats, and other bits of feminine frippery.

Her eyes grew satisfyingly round. "But—what is all this?"

"It looks like female clothing to me."

She appeared not to notice his sarcasm. "Is it . . . somebody else's?"

Edward snorted.

She shook her head in obvious disbelief and he couldn't help being pleased that he'd elicited such an unprecedented reaction from her. "But—who chose all of this?"

"I did."

She considered that for a long moment, wearing her usual non-expression, and then opened a wardrobe that was filled with gowns. Edward squirmed a bit as she thoughtfully rubbed a piece of sapphire blue silk between her fingers. He recalled that gown and how he'd thought it would look on her. Perhaps he'd gone a bit mad when it came to clothing, but he'd not been sure what would suit her, so he'd bought one of whatever seized his fancy. The other—less traditional garments—were locked away elsewhere.

"Thank you," she said when her eyes settled on him.

Edward turned away from her gratitude—one of the few things he did not want from her. "Through here," he opened the door beside him, "is the bathing chamber."

She stepped into the pink marble room and stared at the huge copper tub that sat in front of a crackling fire—which he'd had lighted just in case she wished to bathe.

There was a painted panel above the fireplace that the carpenter had installed to cover some of the machinery required to plumb the tub, sink, and commode.

She stared at the painting on the panel, her hand absently caressing the rolled copper.

Edward shifted his cock, which had just begun to subside but reawakened with a vengeance. He was rather unnerved by her silence. He'd not realized she was so quiet *all* the time. He'd believed it to be part of her act or routine. Did she never chatter or rabbit-on like most other females?

He finally cleared his throat. "If you don't care for the painting I can engage another artist," he said.

"No," she said, the word more thoughtful than definitive. "You needn't do that." She turned to him. "This is lovely. Thank you, sir."

His neck and face flamed and he was bloody grateful his complexion was not of a type that showed blushes. "You had better call me Edward from now on."

She stilled, like a startled forest creature, but then nodded. "Thank you . . . Edward."

Hearing his mundane name on her lips should not have caused the thrill in his body it did. He turned on his heel, needing, quite suddenly, to get away from her. He strode to the last door, which was fitted with a lock. He produced the small key—one of only two, both of which he kept in his possession—from his pocket and unlocked the door. He'd been up here earlier—pacing and, he was embarrassed to admit, fisting himself for the first time in weeks. It wouldn't do to ejaculate as soon as he touched her, after all.

Although the heavy drapes were closed he'd left two of the wall sconces lighted. He stepped back and waited for her to enter.

✳✳✳

Nora's head was pounding and she knew it was from the effort of containing her emotions and reactions.

She would *live* with him? He'd purchased clothing—and not a small amount, but a *vast* array—for her.

Good God, what a fool she'd been to sign that contract the way she had—and all to make a grand gesture. She'd let her emotions out from under lock and key for just a few moments and had done something unspeakably foolish.

How could she maintain her defenses in the same house with him? Especially *his* house, not even the neutral ground of Tosca's. She'd only been around him for a few minutes and already she could sense how different he was outside the brothel, more confident, assured—in his element. His *lair*. And that was saying something because he'd been overwhelmingly confident—to the point of arrogance—before.

He would learn the truth and he would destroy her.

He reached into the breast pocket of his coat and extracted a small bronze key, turning toward a door that she'd believed to be just another section of wooden wall paneling. There was, she saw, a small keyhole. He inserted the key and turned it, opening the door and stepping back. His expression was the same aggressive, proud, arrogant look that he always wore, but something in his posture told her he was . . . excited, and perhaps even a bit anxious.

Nora forced herself to walk toward the door, pausing on the threshold.

Well.

She felt like her eyes were not big enough to take it all in.

There was a slight pressure at the small of her back and she turned to find him beside her. It was a long way up to meet his eyes. She recognized the hunger that flared in the dark depths and her body began priming itself at his slightly flaring nostrils. She had missed him and he must *never* know how much.

"I had it built specially. For us." His hoarse tone told her all she needed to know about his condition: he was long, hard, and thick for her. She stepped inside.

It was beautiful and stark and utterly unique in her experience. The floors were a milky white that seemed to glow beneath the heavy, exotic hides scattered about the room. There were mirrors in several places, their positions obviously chosen with great care.

On one wall was the largest armoire she'd ever seen. She knew without looking what would be inside it—the tools and implements he delighted in using on her—and which she'd missed with every fiber of her being.

A fire burned in a corner fireplace and before it—in a position of honor—was a low-slung black leather chaise resting on the thickest, fluffiest sheepskin she'd ever seen. Nora could visualize them using it and a fresh onslaught of sensation swelled her sex.

Other, less easily identifiable pieces of furniture lurked in the darkened recesses of the room.

But the centerpiece of the giant room was undeniably the magnificent bed; a bed equipped for something other than sleeping.

It had obviously been made by the same craftsman who fashioned the armoire. It was carved from the same heavy black wood pitted here and there with wrought iron rings. The posts were massive and also set with rings.

The bed was an erotic work of art but it was the bedding that was the biggest surprise.

Nora was accustomed to dark, sensual shades—blood red, majestic purples and blues—and touches of gold which Madam Tosca used elegantly, but, Nora had always felt, rather predictably.

This entire room was without color. It was, she realized, rather like her.

She walked toward the bed, needing to feel it—to confirm it was what she thought it was.

Her hand sank into it—a feather-stuffed blanket that was beyond soft—the cover made of the finest lamb or kidskin that had been bleached as white as the exquisite linen Mr. Fanshawe—*Edward*—always wore on his person.

She felt him approach her from behind and her breath hitched. Without any commands from her brain Nora's feet spread slightly and her pelvis tilted in a way that pushed her bottom toward him. If she were to paint herself in this position she would title it: *Female Eager for Mounting.* Not that Edward would need any help to read her posture. He would have noted the subtle shifts in her body and would recognize her wordless supplication.

He was close so that she could feel his heat—smell the familiar scent of his cologne. But he did not touch her.

"Do you like it?" He asked and then reached around her and laid his brawny, sun-browned hand on the fine white leather, his body finally pressing into hers, the hard length of him thrusting against her lower back, "I imagined you on it, Nora—your skin as white, but infinitely softer and finer. I imagined your body marked with lovely red welts of my making."

She shivered at his words and he dragged his mouth down her throat, inhaling her. "You know I'm going to whip you hard for the way you treated me—rejected me, Nora."

It wasn't a question—nor did he have to explain what he meant, she knew.

He chuckled against her hot, damp skin. "My bad, bad girl." He gently rocked his hips against her, his stiff rod abrading her through her clothing.

Nora stood ready and waiting to obey his command and lift her skirts for him.

"I'll bet your cunt is tight and swollen. I'll bet your juices are already running down your sweet thighs, making them sticky. Is that so?"

It was work to grind the words out, "Yes, Edward."

He groaned. "Oh, I *do* like hearing you say my name. And I'm really going to enjoy hearing you say it when I make you beg."

"Please," Nora begged as his hot breath brushed against her neck. "Please, Edward." Her breathing was so loud and ragged she sounded like a lathered horse. "Please."

"Shhhh," he murmured, his mouth moving to where her neck joined her shoulder. "I'm not finished speaking yet—there will be ample time for you to beg . . . later. I have to be honest, Nora, I'm a bit . . . peeved with you." He kissed and bit her, his touches maddeningly light. "Did you know that I've been alone here for weeks while you've been lying with any man who will pay you?" Nora stiffened, and this time his chuckle sounded more like a predatory rumble than an actual laugh. "Every night I lay in my bed, hard and wanting—oh *God*, so bloody hard—but I never touched myself. I would think of you even though I didn't wish to and even though such thoughts only tortured me further." He caught a bit of skin between his teeth and pulled hard enough to bring tears to her eyes and send a savage rush of pleasure to her thumping sex.

"Tell me, Nora, how long has it been since you've had a stiff cock in your mouth."

She hesitated and one of his arms slid around her more quickly than a snake, pulling her tight against his rock-hard body. "Don't lie to me, because I'll know it, and then things will go even worse for you."

"Last night, Edward."

His arm tightened until it was painful but Nora knew better than to make a sound.

"And the last time you had a cock in your cunt?"

"Last night, Edward."

She felt, rather than heard, the growl that emanated deep in his chest. But instead of asking her another question he trailed kisses back up her neck, lingering sweetly until she began to believe—

He shoved himself against her, his erection ramming between her cheeks hard enough to give her a friction burn. "And here, Nora—when have you last had a stiff cock *here?*" He punctuated the question with another vicious thrust.

Nora bit her lip, unable to utter a sound as the pleasure that had been building like a tight knot inside her began to loosen and unfurl.

His hand slid to the front of her body and grabbed her mound in a painful grip that startled a gasp out of her. "If you have *any* notion of coming right now, I caution you to rethink it. Now, answer my question. I'll repeat it just in case you might have forgotten: when is the last time you had a cock in your arse?"

Nora gritted her teeth, willing her body not to squirm in his painful grasp. "Last night, Edward."

He swore and pushed away from her, leaving her hunched over the bed, her chest heaving, her hands bunched in the soft leather.

"You. Fucking. Whore." The words were so low it was difficult to hear them. "You *knew* you were coming to me today—Tosca received her bloody money for you yesterday so I know she didn't make you work last night. Did she?"

Lust, shame, pride, and other, even less savory emotions whirled in her belly and she teetered on an orgasm even as her sex ached from his rough handling.

"No, Edward."

He swore. "You *wanted* to work—" he sounded as if he had to force the words through clenched teeth. "You bloody well *liked* it."

She heard the strain in his voice; he was near his breaking point, a place she was more than familiar with herself, thanks to this man.

Nora considered her next answer—wondering what she would say—whether she would give him that one last push to send him over or spare him. After all, pushing him might also push her towards her climax, and she *knew* he'd not hesitate to punish disobedience. As much as she swelled and thrilled at such a thought, he would be dangerous with a whip after he heard the truth.

But of course that didn't stop her.

Her mouth curved into a smile as she stared at the white leather beneath her hands and said, "I didn't like working last night, Edward." She paused only long enough to hear his slight sigh of relief, and then added, "I loved it."

Chapter Eleven

he words were stuck in his head like a chant—a mantra: *"I didn't like it, Edward. I loved it."*

His cock, instead of wilting at her admission, wept copiously, soaking the front of his trousers.

Edward stared down at her bowed figure, at her white hands almost indistinguishable from the leather. He should strip her—tear the clothing right off her back and then tie her between the posts, her arms and legs stretched so tight she'd feel in danger of ripping in half. And then he would raise the welts on her body he'd been dreaming about for *months*.

He savored that vision, his swollen prick needing only a touch to embarrass himself.

But instead of acting on his fantasy, he stepped away. His rage was consuming him. If he started on her—he'd not be able to stop.

Rage? Ha! That's a lie and you know it. It's not rage but nasty, vile, poisonous green jealousy that runs through your veins, my boy.

Edward ground his teeth, wishing he could deny it. But the shame of it—even if it was only partly true—seared him like a white-hot flame.

Not partly true, old son, but painfully, utterly, completely true: the green-eyed monster is feasting on you.

Yes, it was. It was jealousy that twisted and clawed inside him, leaving his chest raw and sore as if something had been gnawing on his heart, while at the same time—impossibly—making him harder than he'd ever been in his life.

He was a sick bastard and always had been—he'd accepted that years ago. But this stunned him—how could he become aroused at the thought of her taking another man's cock? *How?*

And yet he was aroused—insanely so. But even his arousal could do *nothing* to subdue his jealousy. He wanted to find out who had fucked her—whose body she might be sore from—and beat him to a bloody pulp. He opened his mouth to demand a name but caught the words just in time.

Instead, an image shot through his mind—a brief, priceless flash of their last time together.

He knew the grin that twisted his lips would be ugly, but he truly didn't give a damn. He would begin holding her to the terms of the contract this very night.

"We're going out tonight. I want you to clean yourself—both *inside* and out." Her shoulders flinched. *Good. Behave like a whore and I'll treat you like a whore.*

Because that's what she was: a whore, and he'd been running after her like a lovelorn swain. Well, those days were long gone.

His body hummed with pleasure and power: pleasure at coming back to himself and power at having her in his control. Gone was the puling idiot who'd sniffed after her for months and then been crushed and lost when she'd rejected him.

She'd been so secure in his *obsession* for her that she'd signed off on a contract she'd been too bloody arrogant to even read. And she would pay the price for it.

He strode toward the door. "I want you out of here. You're only allowed in this room when I tell you."

She straightened slowly and turned to him.

Edward hadn't known what to expect when she faced him, but it sure as hell wasn't what he got.

She was smiling.

He gave a mirthless laugh and shook his head. "You *bitch*."

Her smile grew even bigger and then, for the first time since he'd met her, she laughed.

That was when Edward suspected he might have gotten more than he bargained for.

Chapter Twelve

ora's father had always told her that pride was her besetting sin. If he'd seen what she'd done in that decadent bedroom he would have changed his opinion to arrogance—or perhaps stupidity.

Nora's body was limp and she felt utterly drained by their encounter—not to mention horrified by her continued stupidity. But his accusations had simply been too much. Could he really believe that giving her body to another man changed the way she felt about him? If he did, then she was bloody lucky. Perhaps he'd *never* look past his own jealousy to see what she really felt about him.

She kicked off her shoes and crawled into the soft cocoon of her bed, this one covered in silk and finely combed wool, but just as pristinely white.

It felt like only a few minutes later when some slight sound made her open her eyes. It was night outside the tall windows; she must have slept for at least several hours.

She yawned, grimaced at the stale taste in her mouth—she'd not eaten breakfast and only tea and toast at noonday. She was famished.

Something clinked in the next room and she followed the soft sounds, which were coming from the dressing room; a girl inside hanging up Nora's few bits of pitiful clothing among all the sumptuous silks and satins.

"Oh, you needn't do that," she said.

The poor thing jumped and squeaked before whirling around. "Oh, Miss, you gave me a fright you did."

"I'm sorry, I didn't mean to frighten you. This carpet is so very— luxurious, it quite muffles one's steps. I said you didn't have to unpack my clothing—I will do it."

The girl—for that was what she was, Nora saw now that she was closer—shook her head, her plump freckled cheeks flushing. "But that's my job, Miss Nora—I'm your maid." Whatever she saw on Nora's face made her own face crumple. "Oh, Miss—please don't send me away. I promise you, I mightn't look like much, but I know my way around hair and clothing. If you send me away, Mr. Fanshawe," she shivered, an expression of abject terror on her face, "Well, he'll give me the sack."

Nora frowned. "Has he hurt you? Been cruel to you?"

"Oh, no, no, no," The girl exclaimed before the last word was out of Nora's mouth. "Nothing like that at all."

Nora sagged; thank God. Beating, degrading, or humiliating her in the bedroom—all actions she craved and schemed for—was one thing. Doing so to one's servants, especially a mere girl, was another matter altogether.

"Well, I'm relieved to hear that, er—I'm sorry, I don't know your name?"

"It's Mary, Miss." She dropped a curtsey, forgetting she was holding a handful of Nora's ragged clothing, her painting smock among them. She wrinkled her stubby nose and held it away from her. "I think perhaps some servant's clothing got mixed in with yours?"

Nora smiled and took the paint splattered smock. "No, this is mine." She glanced around, her heart in her mouth as she realized the chest that contained her painting materials was nowhere to be seen, nor were her paintings, which she'd taken from their stretchers and wrapped up in old bedding. "Have you seen a trunk?"

"I dunno, Miss. The Thomases put several things in that small sunroom."

Nora turned and went to see, her palms sweating. The painting she was planning to enter into the competition wasn't in there—it was too wet to be rolled and she'd left that one and three others with Charles after he'd sworn on his life to keep them safe in his room and not let anyone else see or touch them. Still, the roll of paintings held many that were precious, like paintings of her parents and sister.

She opened the door to the sunroom and heaved a sigh of relief when she saw her trunk and paints looking forlorn in the rather large room. It was on the southwest corner of the house and her heart leapt: perhaps this would be a nice place to paint?

Her heart plummeted again when she recalled what she'd said to Mr. Fanshawe—*Edward*—only a few hours ago. Nora groaned. She was such a fool. She'd likely find herself out on the street in the morning.

There was a light knock on the door that led out to the hallway. Before Nora could answer it, Mary was there, speaking to whomever had called in a low voice out in the hall. When she came back she was bearing a heavy tray.

"It's a light supper from Mr. Fanshawe, Miss Nora. Where would you like to eat?"

"Oh. Well, you could put it here, I suppose." *Here* was a low table in front of the study fire.

Mary proceeded to fuss with the tray's contents, setting things out. She was enjoying herself so much Nora didn't have the heart to tell her she was accustomed to serving herself. Instead, she pulled a few cushions onto the floor and sat down beside the table.

"Oh." Mary frowned. "Are you sure you wouldn't like the proper table?"

"No." Nora smiled. "I like sitting on the floor."

Mary made a skeptical sound but forbore commenting. She reminded Nora of a plump little bird organizing her nest.

"I don't know what this is, Miss Nora." She handed Nora a leather document folder that had been rolled and tied up. She knew before she opened it what it was.

There was a brief note on piece of paper affixed to the front of the contract.

"Nora, I've taken the liberty of having a copy made of the contract you signed. *Given our conversation earlier in the day, I would like you to familiarize yourself with the document. Section 2, 7, 8, and 14 are of particular importance. You will recognize them as being areas you were required to initial. I shall expect you in my study at nine o'clock sharp. Mary has been instructed which clothing to lay out for you."*

He'd not signed it, but his handwriting was just like him: bold and aggressive and commanding.

"There you go, Miss. I've got your outfit for this evening picked out and will just press a bit of a wrinkle I found." She chewed her lip, uncertain. "Mr. Fanshawe instructed me, Miss. I hope that's all right."

"Oh, yes. Perfectly. He is more familiar with our destination and knows what clothes will be best. Please don't hesitate to follow his instructions to the letter. It is a relief to me not to have to concern myself with such matters." And that was the truth. One of the things she'd like most about Tosca's was the fact they had a uniform of sorts: the same muslin dresses for both day or night. Just thinking about the variety of outfits in that massive closet made her head ache.

Nora spooned some delicious seafood stew into her mouth and began reading the contract.

✳✳✳

By the time nine o'clock rolled around Edward had cooled down considerably. That didn't mean he wasn't going to carry out what he'd planned. His mouth curved into a smile at the thought of the evening ahead.

Going to Bernina's with Nora had been a part of his plans—one of the most obsessive parts, really—but he'd not necessarily thought to go soon. Still, going tonight would actually suit him better and he could kill two birds with one stone, so to speak.

The door opened and he looked up from the messy pile of paperwork he'd been staring at and not seeing. His jaw dropped. Good. God.

He shot to his feet as she entered the room. He'd known what she would be wearing—hell, he'd bought every stitch of it—but he'd had no idea of how it would look.

"Good evening, Edward."

His eyes settled on her mouth. Was that rouge? He frowned, not sure he liked it. Still, the glossy red color did make her mouth . . . inviting.

"Turn around," he ordered. His groin—as ever—becoming heavy when she obeyed without hesitation, making him wonder if there was any order she *wouldn't* obey. He shoved away the distracting, arousing, speculation and looked at the result of some of his labor.

The gown was a silvery white silk and the crinoline beneath it smaller and less egregious than was currently fashionable—he despised crinolines, truth be told. He knew she wore stays and stockings, also virginal white. It was more concealing than the gowns she wore at Tosca's—which he'd like very much—but he didn't want anyone else looking at her in such clothing. That type of garment was for him alone and up in *their* room.

He opened the top drawer of his desk and pulled out a large velvet box, which he handed to her. Her hesitation was almost imperceptible.

His heart beat in his ears as her slender white fingers opened the box. She stared at the contents without speaking, her face the wall it usually was. Only the fluttering of her pulse at the base of her throat gave away any emotion.

She swallowed and he drank in the fragile musculature of her throat. She was so very *different* than him. Oh, not just the obvious differences—her a woman and him a man—but her delicacy, her cool, concerted way of moving.

She raised her pale eyes to his. "Opals. They are my favorite."

"Are they?" the surprised words left his mouth before he could stop them.

Her lips curved into a slight smile. "Do you wish for me to wear it tonight?"

"Come here and I'll put on the necklet and bracelet."

The necklet he'd chosen was four rows of opals set in silver. He'd wanted gold as it symbolized the finest money could buy, but the jeweler had suggested silver with these particular stones, and once he'd seen them near silver he'd had to agree.

He took the necklet from the box and draped it around her throat, inhaling her hair, which smelled different. He paused. "What is that scent you are wearing?"

"It must be the soap Mary used to wash my hair."

He took another sniff and frowned. "I don't care for it—I like the way it has always smelled. What was that you used?"

"Whatever Madam provided for us—something very inexpensive, I would guess."

Edward grunted. Whatever it was, he'd get some and have the rest of the bottles and jars he'd stocked her bathing room with thrown away.

He returned to his task, savoring the way the delicate hairs at the back of her neck stood up at his touch. There were ten rings on the clasp, depending on the wearer's neck size and level of comfort. Edward brought the hook to the ring that was roughly in the middle. The necklet sagged so he unhooked it and tried one smaller. This fit well enough but was not snug as it was designed to be so he unhooked it. He had to pull the ends tight, the cool metal biting into the tender flesh, in order to hook the clasp into the next ring.

Edward stroked her throat, his fingers grazing the cool metal. "Shall I loosen it? Is it too tight?" he asked, already knowing her answer.

"No, I like it tight."

Her answer had the predictable effect on his cock. Yes, he knew she liked it tight. He also knew they'd both be thinking of the times when he'd fastened a different collar around her elegant throat.

Upstairs, in the armoire there were half a dozen collars he'd had made especially for her.

But not for tonight.

Edward screwed in her earrings and then clasped the bracelet around her delicate wrist, leaving that much looser.

He reached for the box and she said, "There is one more piece—a tiny ring of some sort."

He slipped the small ring into his trouser pocket before closing the box and laying it on the desk.

"Turn around."

Edward tried not to gawk. How had he ever thought her plain? Her hair style suited her to perfection. Her maid had swept her curls to the side and held them in place with a hairpin of some sort. Edward squinted and saw it was shaped like a tiny silver bee. It looked cheap but was effective. He would buy her something similar but more suitable the next time he went to the jewelers.

The necklet bit hard into her flesh and he could see that swallowing must be uncomfortable. He liked that, too—a great deal. In fact, it was difficult not to put his hands around her throat, bend her over his desk, and ride them both raw. But the entertainments he'd planned for tonight beckoned.

"You look beautiful," he said, not lying. "White suits you."

Her lips twisted slightly at that—a sardonic smile he'd not seen before. Edward realized, quite stupidly, that he knew almost nothing about this woman aside from what she liked in the bedroom. Where was she from? What had led her to whoring? Did she have family?

He shrugged those thoughts aside. There was plenty of time for that.

"Come, John Coachman will have the carriage waiting."

They were almost to the door when he remembered something. "Hold a moment, I almost forgot." He strode back to the low table in front of the fire and picked up a huge garment box in one hand and a hat box in the other and carried both toward her. "This one first," he said, holding the big box toward her.

She removed of the lid and he heard a soft intake of breath.

"Just toss that onto the floor," he ordered when she continued holding the lid.

She complied and then slowly sunk her hands into the snowy white garment, her pale fingers only a few shades darker than the white fur. His body coiled even tighter and he knew he'd likely ruin yet another pair of trousers if he didn't take control of himself.

She pulled the garment from the box without further encouragement. The look on her face well worth the thousands of pounds the cloak had cost him.

Edward set the hatbox on the nearby console table. "Here, let me."

He shook out the cloak, pleased by the way it had turned out. "I understand the fur goes on the inside," he told her, draping it fur-side down on her shoulders and exposing the thick crème-colored velvet that was quite beautiful, but nowhere near as luxurious. The clasp was hammered silver and necessarily heavy to hold the substantial garment closed.

He opened the hatbox and offered it to her. "You'll have to manage this as hats are quite beyond me."

It was a tiny confection of matching fur and velvet with a veil that looked to be made from mist. He'd bought it with the knowledge he wouldn't want others gawking at her when he took her to places like Bernina's. She was *his*, now. Bought and paid for.

Once she'd adjusted it Edward took her hand—gloved in the finest icy white kid, which extended several inches above her elbow—and turned her toward him. Again, he could have stood and gawked for hours. Instead he said, "It suits you. Is it warm?"

She nodded and he saw her throat work with the difficulty of swallowing. "It's lovely. Thank you, Edward."

He turned away from her eyes, which had darkened and gave her an oddly knowing aspect. "Come, let's not keep the horses waiting."

✳✳✳

97

Nora couldn't help feeling a bit like a princess. She'd never worn such beautiful clothes. She'd never even *seen* such beautiful clothing. Some of the women at Tosca's spent every penny they made on clothes. Nora had only paid for the dresses she was required to wear and one serviceable day dress for her afternoons off.

The carriage was a different one than she'd ridden in earlier. Edward was, she realized, a very, very wealthy man. Why, the cloak alone—some type of fur that was softer than feathers—must have cost hundreds of pounds.

His own person, she had always noticed, was garbed in plain clothing but of the finest material and cut. The severe style suited his large, bulky body and enhanced the aura of power that surrounded him. Nora had often thought that it was exactly that aura—a man who was used to getting what he wanted and being obeyed without question—that had first begun to chip away at her professional wall of reserve.

"Are you London born and bred?"

The question was both abrupt and unexpected. Since when did Edward favor small talk? Not that she minded. Just because she never spoke unless spoken to with her clients did not mean she was so taciturn with her friends. But she must never, ever forget Edward was not her friend. Answer his questions; volunteer nothing.

"No, I'm from a small village about fifty miles outside of London."

"Oh." She heard his fingers drumming on the wooden panel, a nervous gesture she did not recall seeing before. Just what was making him nervous—where were they going?

"I suppose that explains the lack of accent—not growing up in London." Edward's own accent had been softened somewhat by proper speech, but she'd heard plenty of men and women who sounded like him and knew he would have come from one of the worst parts of the city.

"No, my father was the reason for the lack of accent." The vicar had been a stickler for grammar and correct pronunciation.

They rode in silence.

"Did your parents die when you were quite young?"

Nora looked away from the window. "What makes you think they died?"

"Well, you are here—in London—working at Tosca's. I just thought—" he trailed off.

She knew exactly what he thought: he believed she must have suffered some setback that had forced her into this life. She wondered what he'd look like if she told him the truth?

"My parents are both alive and well—flourishing, in fact." Nora allowed herself a small smile; she knew she was bad to enjoy his stunned silence, but he held so much power that she had to take her small pleasures where she could find them.

"Do they know what you do?"

"Oh, yes."

She heard an amazed huff of breath in the darkness. Before he could pursue the story of her downfall, the carriage rolled smoothly to a stop.

"Oh," she said, recognizing the building immediately. "We are at Bernina's."

"You *know* of his place?"

She had to bite her lip to keep from laughing at his scandalized tone. For being such a sophisticated man of business and so unconventionally skilled in the bedroom, Edward was, she realized a rather innocent man.

"Whores talk among themselves," she said, only partly successful at keeping the amusement from her tone.

The door opened and one of the footmen—they were all called Thomas—flipped down the steps. Edward hopped out first and then turned to hand her out.

"Pull down your veil," he instructed, and then snorted while she complied. "Although it sounds as if I'm protecting your identity for no reason."

"Oh, is this for my protection? I thought it was for yours."

Rather than become offended his harsh features twisted into a rare smile as he guided her up the steps. "Perhaps you are right."

The door opened and the whore who went by the name of Cecile ushered them in.

"Good evening, Mr. Fanshawe. It's such a pleasure to see you again." Cecile studiedly avoided looking at Nora. "Everything is waiting for you, just as you instructed. Right this way."

Nora had never been to Bernina's before, but she'd worked with several women and at least one man who'd come here. While it was true whores talked among themselves, they rarely visited other whorehouses on their brief days of freedom.

She wondered, as they followed the tall, slender madam up a staircase if Edward had realized yet that Cecile was a man who preferred to dress as a woman. In the scheme of human sexuality, Nora did not find such behavior unusual. But she knew others—non-whores, for example— were far from sanguine about such matters.

The room Cecile led them to was large and spacious, filled with chaises, silken pillows, plush rugs, and—thankfully—a raging fire. The bed loomed in the adjoining room, the ceiling above it coved and, she suspected, mirrored. Again, it all felt familiar. After today—and seeing the stark beauty of the room Edward had designed—she found the overstated luxury almost tawdry.

Edward turned to face the madam. "Thank you, this will serve."

Cecilia curtsied with admirable grace. "I've taken the liberty of having Amaya set up in the bathing chamber. Shall I send Emma up?'

Edward's mouth curled into something that resembled a smile. Nora shivered with anticipation at the cruel glitter in his eyes and the quick glimpse of his crooked teeth. Her heart sped; oh, this man.

"Yes, do so." He turned away from Cecile with a clear dismissal, his hands going to Nora's throat—to the clasp. When the door shut he lifted the remarkably heavy cloak from her shoulders, his blunt fingers and broad, ugly hands clutching the white fur briefly before he tossed it carelessly over the back of a nearby chair. "One day I'm going to fuck you wearing only that," he told her in a conversational, utterly uninflected voice that worked like an invisible tongue on her already swollen sex.

He turned on his heel and strode off toward the bedchamber. Nora took the pin from her hat with trembling fingers and set it on a nearby console beside his.

The slippers he'd purchased for her—every pair—were heeled and higher than what she was accustomed to wearing. But she wasn't completely inexperienced with them as some of her clients had been inordinately fond of shoes and had often taken her only wearing shoes they'd brought with them. She wondered idly if Edward had such a fondness as she followed him into the next room.

The bedroom held no surprises except the bathing chamber, which was adjacent, both doors wide open. Nora had to smile as she realized why she was here tonight: here was paragraph 8.

Edward was speaking to somebody he could not see but turned when he heard the rustle of her gown. His expression was the same harsh glare as ever, but she knew him well enough by now to recognize it masked a great deal of sexual excitement.

"This is Amaya," he said, gesturing to a very old, tiny woman who stood near a shaving tray and large hip bath that was full of steaming water. "I think we have reached the limit of her knowledge of English."

The old woman smiled and Nora saw she was missing several teeth.

Edward looked over her shoulder and the evil smile she loved so much appeared. "Ah, welcome, Emma."

✳✳✳

Edward shifted his stance slightly so that he could see Nora's face when she saw the other woman.

Once again, his Nora surprised him. "Hello, Emma."

If anyone was surprised it was Emma. "Nora!" Her face broke into a huge grin that exposed a missing tooth and almost demolished her resemblance to Nora. "It's been a long time." She embraced Nora who, he noticed with interest, responded warmly.

"You *know* each other?" he asked stupidly. Obviously they bloody did.

"We worked together for a while." Emma said, still grinning. Now that they were so close together Edward realized their resemblance was rather superficial. While they shared the same hair coloring, skin tone, and general build he could see that Emma looked rather like a poor reproduction—a picture in a magazine that had been printed without enough ink.

Not only that, but she looked rather—well, there was no other word for it—*thick*. Instead of Nora's intoxicating reserve, she seemed to be a rather happy, simple sort.

Edward looked at Nora to find her studying him in that way that made him mad to know what she was thinking. If only he could open her head and lay her thoughts bare the way he laid her body bare. Which reminded him.

101

"This woman—Amaya—doesn't speak English," he told Emma. "Go fetch somebody who can talk to her."

"I speak Basque," Emma said, smiling at the old crone and saying a few incomprehensible words.

"*Basque?*" he repeated; he'd never even *heard* of such a language.

"It is in Northern Spain—not far from the French border," Nora volunteered.

Edward's eyes narrowed, both at the information itself—how did she know such a thing? And also the very act of volunteering it. Had she ever told him anything he'd not *dragged* from her? If she had he could not recall it.

"Amaya says Nora should remove her gown and get into the tub, that the hot water makes the hairs easier to shave." She turned from Edward to Nora and grinned. "I can attest to that. You'll *love* the way it feels rubbing on your nub, Nora—and wait 'til you feel somebody's mouth—"

"You," Edward said, pointing a finger at the talkative whore, "will only speak when spoken to, and will answer my questions without volunteering information. Is that understood? And you will address me as *sir.*"

The girl's face immediately shifted, the amused light draining from her blue eyes and her features shifting into a blank, bland expression. "Yes, sir. Of course." Her tone was low, modulated, with just the amount of supplication he liked.

"Ask her how this will proceed. And then ask her how long the healing will take and any limitations on Nora's behavior."

Emma turned to the old woman and fired off a volley of words, waiting while the woman responded.

Edward knew he could have just asked the whore to recount her own experience with the piercing, but he didn't care to hear it. He wasn't here to *get to know* her. She was a vessel for his pleasure and a prop for his performance and nothing more. Well, except now a translator.

She turned to him. "She will soak in the tub for a short time and then Amaya will remove her hair with that razor." She gestured to a wicked looking razor that was stropped and ready on the tray beside a boar bristle brush and cake of soap. "After that, she'll lie on the chaise." Everyone glanced at said chaise. "She will numb the area with ice and then make a quick puncture with her needle." Again they all turned, this time to the tray where he saw a needle in a glass of water.

The old lady spoke again.

"Nora should abstain from intercourse—" Amaya said something and then chuckled, her dark eyes glinting. "But only in her cunny."

Edward didn't care for the sound of that restriction. "How long?"

"Three weeks, at the least."

The room was silent as he considered this unwelcome news.

Amaya was the one who broke it.

"Two at the minimum, if it heals quickly. She says you may touch her with your mouth and fingers but avoid chaffing the ring."

Although Nora had not moved or changed expression, he *knew* she was enjoying this. Well, three weeks—two at the minimum? What of it? He could enjoy himself—and her—in plenty of other ways.

"Go on," he said.

"She asked if you brought a ring or would like to use one of these." There was a selection of silver rings, all similar to the ones Victoria and Emma wore.

Edward brought the small diamond-encrusted ring from his pocket and handed it to the old woman. She examined it and said a few words.

"Amaya says it is very beautiful and will look well."

Edward didn't need the old woman's opinion to know that. He turned to Nora, who was merely watching and listening as if the procedure was about to happen to somebody else.

"You read the contract."

"Yes, Edward. Shall I disrobe?"

His balls clenched so hard at her quiet obedience it was difficult to remain upright. "Emma will undress you." He went to the chair that had been set up opposite the hip bath and placed to give him a clear view of the proceedings. Before sitting he shrugged out of his coat and pulled off his cravat. Amaya came scurrying over when he tossed them onto the cool marble floor, muttering something under her breath.

"She says it's a shame to treat such lovely clothes in that manner," Emma translated.

Edward snorted and dropped into the wingback chair which was large enough to support his big frame. Madam Cecile knew her business.

Emma had already unfastened the many small buttons that ran down the back of Nora's gown. He knew the simple dresses she wore at Tosca's had been devised for women who had no servants and needed to dress and undress themselves. Every garment he'd bought for her—including the perfectly fitting leather gloves that sheathed her arms—required assistance. He liked the thought of her being waited on hand and foot. He liked it even more because he suspected she wouldn't like it—not that she would ever tell him.

Emma—who was even shorter than Nora—had to stand on her toes to lift off the gown, leaving Nora standing in a narrow cage crinoline and her corset, chemise, and stockings. He'd had no drawers made for her. What intelligent man wanted such a thing to get in his way?

He'd never seen her in a corset before. Madam Tosca had provided some in her arsenal of toys, but Edward disliked the thought of putting her into something made for some other woman. So he'd done without. Until now.

She was very slender but the corset, designed to fit an inch or two down the hips, had pulled her into an unexpectedly curvaceous shape. His hands itched to span her—to feel her confined, bound body.

He laid his palm over his straining cock but did not stroke himself. Nora's eyes followed his movement, the pulse at the base of her throat, as always, giving her away.

Chapter Thirteen

ora was amused that Edward had found Emma. She'd worked with the other woman for over a year when she first began. They'd both worked for a madam who promoted them as twins and they'd been very successful with men who found the idea of fucking sisters arousing.

Emma had found the arrangement arousing, as well. The other woman—actually two years older than Nora—preferred women and had, over time, developed a liking for Nora she could not reciprocate. Although Emma had been disappointed, she'd not been upset. She was exceptionally easy tempered and not particularly clever. She appeared to be blooming and Nora knew the clientele at Bernina's—with the exception of a few like Edward—would be far more to her liking.

She heaved a sigh of relief as Emma loosened her corset, aware of Edward's increased interest at the action. Corsets, she suspected, would become a permanent part of her life while she was with him. While she didn't mind them, it had been several years since she'd worn them regularly. Several of her clients enjoyed having her wear those provided at Tosca's but she'd not worn one all day for a long time.

The corset slid to the floor and Emma bent to retrieve it. Edward, she could see, was tightly coiled with anticipation. She'd seen the piercing she was about to receive several times before. It was not as prevalent as nipple and apadravya piercings, but she knew both piercings were increasingly popular with members of the aristocracy. She'd once serviced an earl and his countess, who'd each had several piercings.

Nora had never considered getting one but, predictably, could not deny Edward and was aroused at his obvious excitement. If he liked it, she was bound to enjoy it.

As Emma removed her chemise and left her standing naked but for her shoes and stockings, Nora looked at the man for whom she would do anything. His eyes were flickering up and down her body, consuming her, leaving her wet and throbbing for him.

He constantly returned to her face, searching, she knew, for something—anything—in her eyes. That was the hold she had on him: her inaccessibility. If she ever showed her true feelings—that she bled for him? He would discard her, his goal finally achieved.

It was good to remind herself of that—and she vowed to do so every day, perhaps multiple times on days like today, when it would be so easy to sink to her knees and declare her love for him.

✳✳✳

Edward wished to God he had another set of eyes to drink her in. Nora, his untouchable, forever-out-of-reach, ice queen.

She'd remained motionless and distant as Emma stripped her. Even now—seated in the hip bath, her slender legs over the sides of the copper tub, her sex spread and open to his view—she was as ripple-less as the surface of a frozen winter lake.

He'd been a fool to ever imagine Emma was anything like her. Still, the girl would be useful to him this evening.

"Remove your robe," he said without looking at her, unable to wrench his eyes away from the old woman's hand sluicing water over Nora's elevated pelvis. "And then come kneel between my thighs."

He heard the rustle of silk, his eyes locked with Nora's, the pulse at the base of her throat beating wildly. Edward loved that *she* loved watching him use other women—that she would suffer for his pleasure.

As Emma knelt between his wide-spread legs, her head bowed, he couldn't help wondering how Nora's aroused state would affect the piercing procedure. But Amaya didn't seem to find anything out of the ordinary and was perfunctorily washing Nora's swelling sex, her gnarled fingers spreading her lips to inspect her more closely. She grunted at whatever she saw and then turned to her tray, leaving her patient spread and waiting.

Edward would give Nora something to watch—it was only fair. "Unbutton my trousers."

Emma's deft fingers responded without delay and Edward lifted his hips when she'd unbuttoned him all the way. His cock sprang free as she removed his drawers along with his trousers.

He bit his lower lip to hold back a groan as Nora's pale eyes flared, her throat working beneath the cruel embrace of the necklet.

"Stroke me," he ordered softly, his breath quickening as the old woman turned back to the tub holding the long silver blade. He saw the muscles in Nora's taut stomach clench and flutter. Ah, so she wasn't as untouched as she appeared. He smiled, relaxing into the pleasure of Emma's hand.

Amaya was more skilled with the blade than Edward's valet and cleared her mons of hair in a few deft passes. And that was when it became fascinating.

Edward laid a hand over Emma's to still her stroking, not wanting any distraction, no matter how pleasurable, to interfere.

Amaya spread her fingers to make a V and used them to open Nora wide, exposing her delicate pink flesh. She moved more carefully, taking only one swipe for each area, clearing the hair from the tender skin around her opening in far too few strokes: Edward could sit and watch this sight for hours.

She matter-of-factly rinsed her, inspecting her work closely and manipulating Nora's sex in a no-sense fashion before she was satisfied. She tapped Nora's thigh and made a motion that indicated she wanted her to get up and turn to face the opposite wall. She positioned her over the hip bath, her legs spread wide by the tub, her hands gripping the high back. And then pushed her shoulders low, canting her bottom high.

She took the pitcher of warm water and poured it over Nora's ass, spreading her cheeks and washing her thoroughly.

Edward's twisted brain flooded with images of some other—younger, more nubile and naked—woman doing this very same thing Nora and he felt a bit dizzy.

Amaya pulled back a cheek, exposing Nora's tight pink rose, and then soaped her, once again performing her work far too quickly before rinsing. Again she inspected closely and touched up a few spots with a flick of her razor. When she was done, she set a hand on Nora's shoulder and muttered something. Nora stood and the old woman took a fluffy towel from the heated bricks by the hearth and proceeded to dry her using vigorous and non-erotic motions.

When she was dry, she motioned her to the chaise beside the tub, which had been strategically placed for his pleasure.

She positioned Nora like a doll. Laying her all the way back and then sliding a pillow beneath her hips. She then placed the bottoms of her feet together and opened her like a butterfly.

Edward couldn't bear it any longer. "Suck me."

Emma's mouth slipped over his cock, her lips stretching wide to accommodate him. She knew her business well and didn't stop taking him until his sensitive head bumped the back of her throat. And then she swallowed and he groaned and jerked his hips into her, grinding his balls against her chin and holding her head immobile while he ejaculated down her throat in an embarrassingly quick amount of time. But he didn't care.

He pushed her head off him and blinked his eyes to clear the haze of lust, reaching down to pull up his bunched drawers and trousers, buttoning them as he strode toward the chaise, worried he'd missed the most important part of tonight's show: his permanent branding of her as *his* possession.

But the old lady was just removing the ice when he came to the chaise. Nora's breathing was slightly elevated but otherwise she appeared normal—if you didn't notice her white knuckles grabbing the side of the chaise. Without thinking, he took one of her hands in his. Her eyes widened with surprise, and that was when Amaya used the needle.

Chapter Fourteen

Nora laid down her brush and stepped back from the canvas, squinting. There was still something not right. She sighed, her eyes flickering to the fading light outside the windows. She'd been in here for hours every day this past week.

Tonight Edward was to return from his business trip up north. Her stomach fluttered with excitement and need and longing.

She wiped her hands on the turpsy rag and then reached up to untie her smock. Beneath it she wore one of the loose gowns from Tosca's, which she'd worn all week. Tonight she would have to wear one of the many gowns Edward had chosen for her. He'd not written her all week, but he'd left a terse note for her the morning after their night at Bernina's. It had just told her he'd be gone and would return in a week. And that he was taking her to the theater and dinner with several of his business acquaintances when he returned and she should dress accordingly.

She closed the drapes in the room and shut the door behind her. Now that he'd returned, she supposed he would have a schedule and her days spent painting and reading would be over.

She went to her dressing room without ringing for Mary, passing through it to her bathing chamber, which she loved.

While the huge tub filled with water she unbuttoned her gown, chemise, and old woolen stockings, standing in front of the massive gold-framed mirror that leaned against one wall.

The hairs had begun to grow back and were only now stopping their incessant itching, but she supposed she'd better get accustomed to shaving herself so she had purchased a razor and planned to use it for the first time this evening.

She'd not become accustomed to the look of her exposed lips, which appeared rather petulant with the silver ring protruding between them. She'd not touched herself other than to wash since Edward left. He'd told her that night, after bringing her back from Bernina's far earlier than she'd expected, that he would abide by the instructions and that he expected the same from her—forbidding her release until he told her otherwise.

The last week had been the longest she'd gone without sexual satisfaction since—well, since she could recall. While her life as a whore had been far from perfect, she'd managed to accumulate enough clients she enjoyed—in one capacity or another—over the years and was not accustomed to such solitary days.

At first all this time had been glorious, but she could only paint so many hours in the day. His library, while huge, had been almost utterly devoid of fiction. That had been fine as she'd enjoyed spending a couple afternoons at Hatchards. She'd even gone to visit Mr. Lombard, who'd been so happy to see her, but so devastated to hear she'd left Tosca's that it had been uncomfortable to stay too long.

"Come back again," he'd pleaded as she left. "I will be…better the next time."

Nora had smiled and kissed his cheek. "Of course I'll come back." And she would, even though taking excursions was not as simple as she'd hoped. First, she had to dress appropriately (paragraph 16 in the contract) and then, after she was trussed and buttoned and shod and bundled, she had to take one of Edward's carriages for all except the shortest journeys—that was the same paragraph that included the stipulation about a footman. Each and every time she stepped out of the house, she had to be accompanied by one of the footmen.

Nora had known many men in her life, but never had she met such colorless, witless dolts as Edward's footmen.

First off, they'd been selected for their resemblance to a common type: tall, hulking, brown hair, brown eyes, and dull, incurious expressions. She thought there were as many as five of them, but it was impossible to be sure as they all looked alike and answered to the name Thomas.

That affectation, she'd learned, came from the aristocracy. Apparently, giving all the footmen the same name was meant to display one's complete disregard for one's menials—to the degree that one couldn't be bothered learning their names. The same went for John Coachman.

Nora snorted as she stared at her reflection, taking a few steps closer and pulling back her lower lips to examine the piercing. It was clean and the swelling had disappeared quickly. Sometimes the jeweled ring caught on clothing and that could be uncomfortable, but, by and large, she felt the tiny puncture was healed.

Just pulling aside the sensitive skin to examine it caused a wonderful friction on her clitoris. Indeed, just walking jostled the ring and kept her in a heightened state. She dropped her hands and turned away, frustrated by her body's insistent attempts to lead her toward temptation. Late at night, when the soft muslin of her nightgown would chafe against the ring, she'd have to put her hands beneath her body to stop from rubbing or touching herself. The voice in her head, most insidious at night, would tell her there was no way he would ever know.

And he wouldn't—at least not until he asked her. And Nora would tell him the truth—she always did. In fact, lying was the one characteristic she could not abide in herself and others. She'd lied for the last time when she left her parents' house at the age of fifteen, when she'd told them she'd been going to stay with her friend in Winchester but had, in truth, gone to London.

Only when she could no longer go back had she written to tell them the truth.

She submerged herself in the too hot water, enjoying the painful burn and shivering in anticipation with thoughts of tonight. Although she kept no journal, she recalled the last time he'd been inside her body. The last two times they'd been together he'd taken another woman instead of her. The memory of Emma's blond head bobbing up and down in his lap and his feral grimace of passion when he'd climaxed came back to tease and taunt her nightly.

It was part of what made her feelings for him different from any other man she'd met. The mix of jealousy and lust and humiliation was an aphrodisiac unlike any other. The emotions were so intermingled and entangled it was impossible to sort everything out. All she knew was that the more he degraded her, the more she wanted him, the harder she climaxed when he finally touched her or—like that last time at

Tosca's—even *looked* at her. She hated but loved to see him with another woman, using her the way *she* wanted to be used. It was a humiliating rejection that made her crave greater and greater debasements.

Their association would not end well for her. But oh, how she would cherish the journey.

✳✳✳

Edward cursed himself for an idiot. Why had he accepted Banks's offer and gone to the bloody theater his first night back when all he'd wanted to do was unlock the door to his fantasies and use Nora's body the way he'd dreamt every damned night since he'd been away?

Instead he was here in a bloody restaurant with Banks and his mistress, Chatham and one of the actresses from the play, and Smith, who was currently monopolizing *Edward's* mistress.

Edward wanted to jump across the table and jerk Nora away from the smooth, clever, and oddly magnetic man. And then he wanted to punch Smith in the face. But he simply couldn't bring himself to do it. Why? Because he was too mesmerized watching her—just as he'd done during the play—a play he couldn't have named if his life had depended on it.

She was laughing—*laughing!*—smiling, flirting, and *talking* more than she'd spoken to him the entire time they'd known each other. Just who the hell was this woman?

"I think you might have burnt a hole in Smith's evening coat, Edward."

Edward turned to Chatham, his lips already twisted into a snarl. He looked from the usually quiet, giant of a man—easily five inches taller than either Edward or Banks, both of whom topped six feet—to the actress he'd brought along, who was currently sitting captivated by Banks and almost in his lap.

"Instead of giving me grief you should be looking to your own business."

Chatham cut a languid look in the direction Edward indicated and gave his version of a smile—a shift of the lips so slight you had to know the man to even notice. "Our Gideon is quite the charmer," he said with obvious unconcern.

Edward snorted. Banks was a whoremaster and had the most insatiable sexual appetite of anyone he'd ever met. Even three mistresses didn't seem adequate to suit his needs. He wouldn't be surprised if he added Chatham's bit of muslin to his rapidly growing collection.

"She's very pretty."

Edward followed Chatham's line of sight to Nora, who was laughing hard enough to bring tears to her eyes. Bile and envy rose inside him.

"She lives with you?" Chatham asked.

Edward knew the other men had been floored by that news.

"Yes, she lives with me because it is convenient, Chatham."

"Nothing more?"

"When did you become so bloody chatty?" Edward demanded. "She's a whore, Chatham, not my betrothed."

The other man's brows rose, but he remained silent.

"I've got a list drawn up and will commence courtship this very week."

"List?"

"Yes, all young women as pedigreed as race-horses but without a guinea between them."

Chatham made a noncommittal humming sound.

"I'll be dining at the Earl Sutcliffe's one night and a baron and viscount's houses the next nights. And after that, I've got my eye on a marquess's daughter. I'll keep looking until I find what I want."

"And what is that?"

Edward gave Chatham a look of surprise. "Why, a wife who will forge a connection to those men who are forever beyond our reach. A woman with the blood of kings in her veins who will breed my children. With my money and the right bloodline a son of mine would be unstoppable." He frowned. "Isn't that what you want?"

"Hmm." Chatham took a drink of wine—a wine Edward knew cost a hundred pounds a bottle—and studied Nora and Smith. Smith was currently whispering something into Nora's ear to make her smile. And making Edward vow to have words with him at the first available moment.

Chatham shook his head and turned toward Edward. "No."

Edward blinked. "What?"

"No, that's not what I want."

"Oh, that." Edward threw back the contents of his glass—at least five pounds-worth—and waived to their waiter. He would need another bottle to float him through the rest of this bloody evening.

✳✳✳

Edward was very quiet on their way home. For her part, Nora couldn't recall an evening she'd enjoyed so well. Mr. Smith was wicked and funny and irreverent, Mr. Banks the most beautiful man she'd ever seen, and Mr. Chatham reserved but courtly and polite. Only Edward had not appeared to have a good time. Of course she knew why, but his moods and jealousies were hardly her concern. Well, not unless she could get pleasure from them which, admittedly, she'd done tonight.

Smith, also, had found his grim partner amusing.

"You know he will take this behavior out of your sweet bottom later tonight," he whispered in her ear at one point.

Nora whispered back, "I certainly hope so." And they'd laughed like children.

All night they'd discussed Edward without his knowledge. Oh, they'd not said anything disparaging, Nora would not have tolerated that, but Smith had told her how he'd taken Edward to Bernina's and then mounted Emma right in front of him. He'd shared the details of Edward's conflicted expression that night.

Nora realized tonight, as she gossiped and played with Smith, how much she missed Charles. He could be a nosy pest, but he reminded her of Smith, only far younger. She wondered what the two men would make of each other.

But that was not something she had time to ponder now. Right now she needed to give all her attention to Edward, who was pouting.

He remained silent until they reached the house, waiting until he'd handed her out of the carriage and then barked, "I shall come to you in a half hour." He said it right in front of the footman.

Well, so much for his ridiculous façade that she was his niece.

Mary was waiting for her and chattered while helping her to disrobe. Nora never let the girl remove her chemise for fear she'd faint with shock at her shaved, pierced genitals. If the girl thought her behavior odd she made no mention of it while she hung up the various garments and gathered a small pile for washing and pressing.

"Thank you, Mary. That will be all for tonight," she said when the girl seemed predisposed to linger, an activity she'd encouraged, but not tonight—not now that Edward was back.

Once the door closed behind her she pulled off her chemise and went to the nightgowns in her dressing room. There were only a handful and they were rather prosaic. She suspected Edward kept far more intriguing garments in the room she thought of as his special play area.

As if on cue, the panel door swung inward. Nora dropped the nightgown over her head and fastened the small row of buttons before padding toward the open door.

Edward was inside, sitting on a large black leather chair that faced the fire, reading something on a sheet of paper. She watched him, enjoying this opportunity to observe him without his knowledge. He'd taken off his cravat, coat, and waistcoat and wore only his trousers and white shirt, his feet still in dark stockings. His hair, wiry and thick, was overlong and hung down over his forehead, brushing his collar.

She allowed her heart a brief moment to appreciate his massive shoulders and how vulnerable they appeared as he hunched closer to the light to read, his posture tense.

And then she took her love for him and bound it up with a leather cord like the type he was so fond of. Once it was nothing but a small square, she tucked it into a trunk at the back of her mind. And none too soon because he looked up.

He wore a scowl, his skin flushed dark. "Do you know what this is?" he held up the single sheet of paper in his clenched fist.

She went to him. "No, Edward. What is it?"

He thrust it at her. "Read it—it's about you, after all."

Nora took the page, which was filled with cramped, inelegant writing. There were dates and she realized they began the day he'd left. Each day there was a description of somebody's activities—*her* activities.

"Monday February 19: Miss N. left house at ten minutes past noon and stopped at an apothecary's (purchased one razor, a cake of shaving soap, and various feminine items) and next went to Hatchards. Read for two hours but did not purchase anything. Next went to an address at—"

Nora looked up when she saw it was the address for Tosca's.

"I want you to tell me what you did at Tosca's," he demanded. "And if you lie, I will find out."

She bristled slightly at his imputation that she was a liar when she'd never told him even the smallest fib. Of course she kept that to herself.

"I went to visit a friend of mine there, Charles Smith."

She could see her answer surprised him.

"That was all—you wished to talk to him?"

"That and I wished to check on a couple of paintings he is keeping for me."

"Paintings?" he repeated, arrested.

"Yes, I like to paint and several of the pictures were too wet to transport. He is keeping them for me until they have dried."

He gave a dismissive grunt, clearly not interested in the news she painted, looking oddly deflated by her answer, as if he'd expected—or hoped for—something more illicit or prurient. Nora felt almost bad to disappoint him.

But then he sat up again, his anger returning. "And what about Thursday? Hmm? How do you explain *that*?"

She glanced down and immediately saw what he meant.

"I went to visit an acquaintance of mine who owns a bookshop— Mr. Felix Lombard."

"An acquaintance," he sneered.

"A former client."

He shot to his feet. "Do you not recall what you signed your name to? I'll remind you. It is in paragraph—"

"Seventeen," she completed for him. "The paragraph that says I will not engage in any sexual congress other than at your direction." It was actually far more explicit than that, and enumerated what, specifically, was prohibited. She'd considered telling him about the loophole his language left out, but decided it was not her business to be his solicitor.

He strode toward her and grabbed the front of her nightgown with both hands and tore it in half with a deafening *riiiip*.

He was breathing hard as his eyes swept up and down her body, his lips parted, his nostrils flaring. "Where the hell did you get that vile garment?" he demanded.

When she opened her mouth to tell him that he'd bought it, he raised a hand to silence her. "Never mind. You will never wear anything to this room again. Come to me naked. If I want you to wear clothing I'll tell you. Is that understood?" he said, his eyes at the level of her pelvis.

"You shaved." It wasn't a question. But he looked up when she didn't answer.

"Yes, Edward."

"Well don't—I'll do it for you." He gave her one of his non-smiles. "Unless you don't trust me down there with a razor."

"Of course I trust you."

He snorted. "Go lie on the bed, face up, on top of the comforter," he said when she moved to pull back the undoubtedly expensive white leather cover.

She complied and watched as his hand went to the neck of his shirt and he began to flick open buttons.

"It's only been eight days," he said.

She knew what he meant. "Yes, but I believe it has healed enough."

He gave another of his noncommittal grunts, tossing the shirt to the floor and exposing his powerful chest. He had a great deal of chest hair and it thinned to a line that ran down his belly to his groin. She loved his body hair—so unapologetically male—almost as much as she loved the muscular body it covered.

He was out of his trousers and drawers in the blink of an eye and then crawled on to the bed, taking her ankles and spreading her legs until her hips ached. He released her, but she knew well enough to keep them spread.

He lowered himself onto his elbows and brought his face close to her sex, his warm breath delicious on her already swollen clitoris.

He pressed a big finger at the base of her erect peak and she sucked in a breath, her body tensing against the acute pleasure.

"Mmm," he hummed, stroking from the base to the entrance to her body. "You're wet, swollen."

"Yes, Edward." Her voice tremored and he looked up over her bare mound, flat belly and slight breasts.

"Have you had an orgasm?"

"No, Edward."

His lips curled and his eyelids lowered. "Good. Do you ache from denying yourself?"

"Yes, Edward."

He shoved a finger into her without warning and her entire body tensed, her buttocks lifting off the bed. He moved his digit in a beckoning motion that rubbed an exquisite spot inside her and she moaned. "Oh, yes."

Just as suddenly, he was gone. She opened her eyes to find him on his knees, his enormous erection jutting straight up, his smile derisive and cruel. "You like that, do you?" He gave a bark of mean laughter. "That's too bad, because you'll not get any relief tonight. Now get on your hands and knees."

✳✳✳

Edward loved her on her hands and knees the most. When he brought himself off, it was usually thinking of her in that position. It was such a primal, base position and fed the animal need he had for her.

And now, with her shaved bare, he could see her more clearly—the way her lips spread as she became aroused and exposed the most delicate parts of her to his prying eyes.

He enjoyed the sight of her submissive pose for a moment, walking around the bed to see her from all angles. Her body was flushed with arousal, her nipples sharp little points, and her thighs slick with moisture. He was more than a little aroused himself. And because he knew that he was supposed to avoid agitating the silver ring with intercourse, that was *exactly* what his contrarian cock wanted: her tight sheath wrapped around him, milking him.

He leaned close behind her and thrust his tongue deep into her cunt, fucking her with it while she shivered. She tasted delicious and he wanted to let her come—*make* her come—but then he recalled the list he'd just read from the men he paid to spy on her every move and he stopped, pulling back abruptly.

"I don't want to hear you've been kissing another man, even on the cheek." He swatted her arse hard enough to leave a handprint, thrilling at the sight of her skin bruising for him. He slapped her other cheek, harder. "I didn't hear you?"

"The contract doesn't say anything abo—"

He swatted her again, so hard his hand hurt. "I cannot believe what I am hearing." It was true—he couldn't. But he was enjoying the hell out of her rare act of rebellion all the same. "Are you saying you will disobey me?"

His hand hovered over her arse, which was scarlet with the force of his punishing blows. His hand stung so he knew she must be suffering.

"No, Edward."

"Good." But he gave her a hard swat just for taking so long to answer. When he stepped back, he saw there were tears sliding down her cheeks. He kissed them away, savoring their salty, familiar flavor. "You know it's for your own good, don't you?" he whispered in her ear.

"Yes, Edward."

He crawled up onto the bed on his hands and knees. "Are you going to behave in the future?"

She gave a barely audible sniff that made his cock as hard as steel. "Yes, Edward."

He smiled and tapped on her jaw. "Good girl, now head up for me, mouth open."

He positioned himself in front of her as she raised up higher. He took his shaft in his hand and rubbed the fat bell end over her lips, smearing them with slick fluid. When she opened her mouth to take him, he gave a slight shake of his head. "No, not yet. I'm not sure you deserve it." He swatted her wet cheeks with his cock, hard enough to hurt both of them. "You were teasing me tonight—you and Smith. Weren't you?"

She swallowed hard and he reminded himself to try out one of his new collars on her before he finished with her tonight.

"Yes, Edward."

He chuckled, an evil sound that broadcast all the jealousy and bile inside him. "I think you may not remember who you belong to—who owns you. You need a reminder and I've got just the thing. But right now I want you to throat me—I want to see if you compare to Emma or if I need to send you to Cecile for some training. Open up wide, that's my good girl."

✳✳✳

Nora would never make it through this night without disobeying him and coming. It was as if he'd spent the last week thinking of all the things she liked best and was now going to torment her beyond sanity.

Her buttocks burned and she knew there would be hand-shaped bruises for a week. He'd never struck her so hard before and she'd almost come after the last one.

And now this . . .

She opened her body to him and he slid all the way in, not stopping until his thick shaft blocked her throat. She experienced that second of panic just before she reminded herself not to gasp—not to struggle for breath.

"Ah, yes," he said, his voice pulsing with pleasure over his mastery of her. He held her full, his balls against her chin. He groaned. "I could stay tucked inside here all day."

Knowing Edward, he would try.

"Swallow," he ordered

She did and he shivered and laughed—a genuine boyish laugh of pleasure that tickled her so much she did it again and again until he pulled all the way out.

She gasped for air, filling her burning lungs to bursting.

Edward chuckled. "That was very bad of you," he slapped her cheek with the head of his cock and then backed away. "But I enjoyed it—too much." He leaned close and whispered, "Oh, Nora! I wish I had three cocks so I could fuck all your holes at once." He turned and hopped off the bed, leaving her reeling from his hot, vulgar words.

Nora watched him stride toward his massive armoire, his tight cheeks flexing enticingly, the corded muscles of his narrow waist flaring into his massive back. She had to swallow several times to keep from drooling.

He opened both doors of the big cupboard wide and she sucked in a breath at the profusion of implements. And then he dropped into a squat. The sight of his balls—hanging tautly between his spread thighs—caused her to clench, which sent a dangerous cascade of sensation rippling outward from her sex. It wasn't the thought of displeasing him that made her grit her teeth and stop the orgasm that threatened to explode—but a competitive dislike of losing. And the tug of war between them could have only one winner. If Nora had any say, it would be her.

He came back to her with full hands. Thankfully, neither of them held any of the floggers or crops she saw hanging. But when she caught a glimpse of what he had in his right hand her entire body tightened.

"Ah," he said, his sharp eyes catching her body's reaction. "Are you looking at these?" He held out a black leather case that held seven implements, all made from black marble. They ranged in size from the diameter of perhaps a hazelnut to slightly larger than a walnut.

He tossed the plugs onto the bed along with a small bottle of oil. "I might not have three cocks, but I've got the next best thing—don't I?" He smirked at whatever he saw on her face.

In his other hand was a wide leather collar with a silver ring attached.

"It is a posture corrective," he said in a conversational tone as he slipped it over her throat and pulled it tight to fasten the buckles.

Nora resented the implication that her posture was in need of correction.

"Not that you need it, as you have such lovely posture."

She couldn't help preening a bit at his praise.

"But I knew I'd like the look of it around your slender neck." He pulled the last buckle closed and then took her throat in his hand, roughly caressing her. "There, nice and snug. Can you breathe?"

She was surprised he'd bothered to ask. "Yes, Edward." But just barely.

"Ah, well, next time I'll tighten it up a notch."

He disappeared behind her and she felt his hands, one on each cheek as he spread her. "I must say I like this smoothness," he said almost to himself, his thumbs stroking the shaved skin that surrounded her back hole. "It seems like you might have missed a bit, right here." He flicked an area that had been particularly difficult to reach. "I shall do better," he promised. His hands disappeared and when he touched her again it was with fingers slicked with oil. He poured more at the top of her crack and she felt it slither down toward her anus. His thick finger spread the oil up and down, stopping short of her other opening.

"Mmm, I've been dreaming about this—but I think I already said that." He probed at her tight hole and she bore down, pushing against him as he breached her with just the tip, twisting his finger from side to side, lightly stretching before invading a tiny bit more.

Edward was cruel when it came to her feelings, but he was always meticulous about preparing her body. Many men did not want to get too close to either opening, not even wishing to touch her with their hands, instead preferring to simply bull into her, often tearing skin and causing the wrong type of pain.

Edward, on the other hand, seemed to relish exploring her body, no part too distasteful or beyond his interest.

"God, yes, Nora," he groaned as he pushed ever deeper, drizzling more oil on his invading finger. His breeding organ was so huge that even considerable preparation would not make taking him easy. Still, she enjoyed his efforts as much as the actual penetration.

Soon he was pumping in and out of her, burying his finger with each thrust. He paused and lightly kissed one of her still aching cheeks. "Are you ready for two?"

She was never ready for two, but she said, "Yes, Edward."

He made a sound of pleasure and soaked them in more oil as he carefully worked another huge digit into her, stretching her slowly before pumping her with hard, deep strokes.

"You look so beautiful," he breathed against her bottom, his voice raw with want. His cock, she knew would be hard and weeping.

"Please, Edward. I want you."

He gave her a stinging slap with his free hand and rammed his two fingers into her hard. "I wish I cared what you wanted, Nora. But I'm afraid I don't. You'll have to earn my care."

She bit her lower lip to keep from crying out, the tears streaming down her cheek, her pelvic muscles convulsing.

"And if you come, I'll whip you bloody."

And he would. And she would love it.

✳︎✳︎✳︎

Edward loved fucking her back hole—it felt like such a filthy, taboo activity. He especially loved to watch her take him. He was big, he knew that. Some women couldn't bear it and didn't find such impalement pleasurable. But Nora reveled in it, her slender body accepting anything he offered. Sometimes he filled her anus with a plug while fucking her cunt, the sensation of another hard object inside her more curious than pleasurable. He'd considered what it would be like to have another man inside her when he took her, but the idea of getting so close to another male repelled him.

An image of Smith's big cock sliding in and out of Emma assaulted him.

Liar.

He shoved the thought away as fast as possible, but his cock had already noticed it and pulsed with a demand he could no longer deny.

He considered tonguing her again—her anus this time—the thought making his mouth water. He loved tasting her—every part of her. He knew it was just another sign of how deviant, animal, and low he was— wanting to lick her arse out. But he'd accepted it. He'd always liked exploring his women, but never as much as her. And now that she was his and he no longer had to worry about the last man who'd been inside her, well, he could taste her whenever he wanted. Feast on her.

But not right now. Now he needed to fill her and mark her. He took out his fingers and drizzled oil on his already slick cock, giving it a few strokes and appreciating its rock hardness. Not every man his age could claim such stamina and he felt sure it was the result of vigorous bed sport since the time he'd discovered his prick and what it was good for. Nights in the workhouse dormitory had been a veritable symphony of boys groaning as they tossed one off. And other things.

He positioned his head at her tight pucker, enjoying the sight and tucking it away for later. He breached her slowly, not wishing to tear her. Edward wasn't an utter deviant, he never enjoyed hurting a woman with unpleasant intercourse.

He gritted his teeth until his jaw ached as he eased into her, past the outer ring that squeezed almost painfully tight, deeper and deeper up her impossibly tight canal until his balls rested against her.

"All right?" he asked gruffly, holding her full and stretching her.

"Oh, yes." She made a purring noise and he smiled. He'd never in his life met a woman who liked to fuck as much as Nora—and in so many ways.

Images of her fucking Smith and nameless, faceless others, assaulted him and his smile evaporated. He pulled out and slammed into her, as if such brutality could drive those phantoms away. The savage action jarred a guttural grunt from her and he gripped her narrow hips with white knuckled hands, his hips shaking as he struggled to control his unreasonable rage.

Jealousy.

"Yes, goddammit!" he ground out.

"Edward, please."

He thrilled at the raw need in her voice. She would come tonight— he would make sure of it. And tomorrow night he would punish her for it. He pulled out slowly and slammed in, making both of them grunt with the violence of his thrust.

"I have a surprise for you, Nora."

Thrust, grunt.

"Next week I shall embark upon a new project and you'll join me."

Thrust, grunt.

"It's paragraph 9 in the contract—the part where you will act as my hostess, my ward, the shy and reclusive Miss Hudson, my poor sister's only daughter." He gave an ugly laugh.

Thrust, grunt.

"We shall be entertaining at least twice a week. Just small dinners."

Thrust, grunt.

He wanted to draw this out—to make her suffer with doubt and anticipation, but he simply couldn't hold back. "They will all be young ladies with their parents." She clenched around him and he yelled. "Fuck! You just about broke me in two, Nora. I think that news excited you."

Thrust, grunt.

"Or does it make you feel something else? Some other emotion." He paused, breathing hard, grinning as he made her wait, knowing she would *never* tell him what she was thinking.

He resumed his thrusting, even harder this time, until it was difficult to fuck and speak. "I think you know I'm going courting, and these are my prospective brides you and I will be entertaining."

Her body was so rigid beneath him he was surprised she didn't fracture into a thousand pieces like glass, shredding him in the process.

He dropped onto his hands, covering her back with his chest, enveloping her smaller body with his, dominating her. He turned to look at the mirror across from the bed. "Look at us," he ordered, their eyes meeting in the glass. He pumped his hips, relishing the sight of his powerful body covering hers. "We look like two animals in rut," he said, demonstrating again but harder, devouring the pain and lust and—yes, if he wasn't mistaken—jealousy on her face. "We're two of a kind," he whispered in her ear. "Two mutts who like to fuck like the animals we are." He thrust again, very close to his climax now. "But my wife, Nora, she will be a purebred." His dark eyes held her pale ones in thrall: black and white just like this room—*their* room.

"And I'll pump my seed into her purebred cunt and breed my mutts inside her gold-plated womb." He leaned close enough to kiss her ear. "And you'll have to watch and suffer and want."

He gave one last vicious thrust and they came at the same moment, Nora climaxing as he spent deep inside her, tears streaming from her eyes.

Part 2

Chapter Fifteen

Catherine

All her life Catherine had been groomed for this—to become the broodmare of a wealthy man and bear him two sons—one after the other, no daughters to get in the way, if she was fortunate. She'd accepted her lot in life long ago.

But this? No, she'd never expected *this*.

The man across from her, Mr. Edward Fanshaw, a cloth and coal and tin and whatever merchant, strained the seams of his well-made suit as he leaned toward her.

"How are you enjoying London, Lady Catherine? Your father tells me you've just come from the country?"

Cat was amazed when her voice—as normal as ever—came out of her mouth. "Very well, thank you, sir. Although it is dreadfully thin this time of year."

"Thin?" He frowned, his great bushy black eyebrows descending over eyes that were almost black and far too penetrating. She tried to avoid looking at his mouth, whose fullness and sensuality made her tummy flutter with emotions she did not like.

"There is very little company, as yet," she explained patiently. *Could the man really be that thick? He was undoubtedly a barbarian, but surely even* shopkeepers *knew when the Season began?*

"Ah."

Cat couldn't resist a little dig. "We normally don't come this early, but Papa had some manner of business." She knew exactly what that business was: the auctioning of her person to the highest bidder.

His disturbing lips curved into a slight smile and his heavy lids lowered. Everything about him was dark and thick and heavy—his too wiry black hair, his huge nose, his massive laborer hands with disgusting black hair on his knuckles.

Cat shivered at the thought of them coming anywhere near her.

"Are you cold, my lady?"

She wasn't, but it was as good an excuse to go back inside as any. "A little."

He stood immediately, his huge person all but blocking out the weak winter sunshine. Cat took the arm he offered and they walked through Blandford House's pitiful gardens. Everything about her entire life was pitiful. But the most pitiful thing yet was having to submit to being drooled on, gawked at, and pawed by this pushing cit.

"I'm looking forward to showing you Fanshawe House tomorrow evening, my lady."

Cat was looking forward to the wretched dinner party the way a martyr looked forward to their burning pyre. But she smiled demurely up at him and fluttered her eyelashes—luxuriant and beautiful, just as everything about her. "As am I, Mr. Fanshawe." She could already imagine it—scarlet, black, and lots of gold—the way her brother had described a brothel he favored.

"It is a well-built and spacious house," he boasted, "but in need of a woman's touch."

Cat wanted to retch, but instead murmured appreciatively. As if *she'd love* to provide that touch or any other kind of touch for a man who likely was born above a stable, if not actually inside a stall.

"My ward, Miss Nora Hudson lives with me, and you will meet her, as well."

Yes, another thing she could imagine, some great cow of a girl with the wit of a bale of hay. "I'm looking forward to making her acquaintance. Is she my age, sir?'

"Er," he hesitated, clearly unsure of whether to ask how old she was. Cat considered letting him dangle but decided not even that was worth prolonging his presence in her father's house.

"I am seven-and-ten, sir."

"Ah." He sounded rather nonplussed, as he did quite often, in fact. She was beginning to wonder how such a man had ever managed to accumulate a great fortune.

"Nora is, I believe six years your senior."

So, an old crone.

"Will she be joining the festivities this Season?" *Or has she given up after so many years?*

He coughed on something, seemingly unable to walk and speak at the same time.

"Er, no. She is very . . . well, shy. She's never been, er, out."

Cat stopped and turned to him, having to look up an obscene distance for very little reward. "Truly? Not even when she was young?"

His lips twitched as if she'd said something amusing. "No, not even then."

"But, what does she do all day?"

He blinked and then gave a helpless sounding chuckle. "I have no idea. But you can ask that and more tomorrow evening."

Cat watched with widening eyes as he pulled out his watch, popped open the gaudy cover, and looked at the time. Why the rude, despicable—

"Dammit," he muttered beneath his breath just before his head jerked up. "I apologize for my vulgar language, my lady. It's just that I'm late for a rather important appointment."

She frowned.

He grimaced as he realized the implication of his words. "Not that *you* aren't important, of course. It's just that—well, I'm afraid I must go. Would you like me to walk you back inside?"

"I shall be quite safe out here on my own, Mr. Fanshawe."

Something like suspicion flickered across his face but disappeared when she smiled vapidly up at him and dropped a curtsey. "It has been a pleasure, sir. Until tomorrow."

He took the hand she offered and actually laid his foul mouth on it. Thankfully she was wearing thick gloves for the chilly weather.

She waited until his broad shoulders disappeared into the house before flinging herself onto the nearest bench.

This was it, then. She was not even to have one Season before she was auctioned off like cattle.

"We simply cannot afford it, Catherine, and getting into a pelter about it won't change anything," her father said the night before they left for London. He'd taken a drink of the dreadful wine the steward had found in some dark recess in the cellar and grimaced. "Good God. Fish!" he yelled, even though their aged butler was right beside the table, helping clear the last course because they couldn't afford another footman.

"Yes, my lord?" Fish asked coolly.

Her father waved the glass of wine rudely. "Don't we have something else? *Anything* else?"

Fish's expression changed so minutely only an expert in Fish-watching would have caught it. "I'm afraid not, my lord."

"Bloody hell," the marquess muttered.

"Blandford," Cat's mother chastised, but without any real heat.

They'd been dining in the gloomy cavernous dining room, just the three of them, her vile brother Ceddy having skived off somewhere, no doubt to whore and gamble and do other things that cost great gobs of money. And which *she* would have to pay for, with the sacrifice of her person.

When Fish and the footman departed to fetch dessert her father turned to her, his expression hard. "This will be the last time we discuss this, Kitty. I spoke with Fanshawe when he came to meet you two weeks ago and the terms he is offering are—" he sputtered, "Well, suffice it to say none of us will suffer."

Except her.

Her mother turned to her, clearly reading her mind—and why not? She'd not wanted to marry her father, either—they loathed one another and always had. No doubt they'd move to separate dwellings the moment they received the money from *selling* her.

"His sort of man will expect very little, my dear," her mother said.

"His sort?" Cat laughed without any humor. "And what sort is that, Mama."

"The well-larded sort," her father snapped. "You'd best mend your ways, Catherine—nobody likes a spiteful little cat—not even social climbing mushrooms."

"Blandford," her mother murmured.

Cat rolled her eyes. Quite truthfully, she would be grateful to get away from both her parents—and Ceddy, who'd done his part to land them all in this mess.

"He works all the time," her father said, his level tone saying he'd relented toward her slightly. "I doubt you shall even see him most days."

But what about at night, Papa? What about then?

Cat knew they were all thinking it—about what she would have to do to uphold her family's part of the bargain. Cat had once seen a stable boy's bare bottom pumping away into the body of one of their chambermaids. She'd hidden and watched the whole thing—it had been *revolting*. It had also left her with an annoying itch between her legs that still bothered her from time to time. Was *that* what she had to expect with Mr. Fanshawe? Him with his trousers around his knees, his bottom thrusting and—a small whimper escaped her mouth and drew her mother's attention.

The marchioness smiled at Cat and patted her hand lightly, "There, there, my dear. Don't worry. Fish says there is to be a custard for dessert."

Chapter Sixteen

Edward rolled off Nora's body with a deep groan of satisfaction. "God, that was good."

It had been better than good—it had been … transcendent.

Nora felt him shift and move on the bed and knew what was coming. He spread her cheeks and pushed a well-oiled cold, stone plug into her anus. "There we are," he said with a tone that pulsed with possession and smugness. "Shall we aim for a new record today, my Nora?" He chuckled as if he'd made a jest and then bit her sore buttock.

By record he meant the number of times in any given evening when he spent in her back entrance.

He pushed himself off the bed and made his way to the small water closet off the other side of the play room. She knew now that his chambers were on the other side: a study, dressing room, and then bedroom—and idly wondered if he would change the situation once he brought his bride home.

Nora rolled onto her back and sighed, wiggling her hips to adjust the large plug of marble. Edward had recently become obsessed with her bottom. Specifically, he'd decided he liked fucking her and then plugging her. And then fucking her again and plugging her. And so on.

"I like thinking of you filled with my spunk," he'd told her the first time, his tone proud—as if he were the first man to think of such a thing. "I wish I could keep you filled all the time, but I know that's not possible." Yet he'd done a bloody fine job of trying. So far his record in one day was six times. He seemed concerned he'd not be able to top that.

Nora adored his obsessive and creative approach to sex, but his behavior had taken on a frenetic edge lately. And it concerned her. She knew the cause, of course, although she'd never said a word on the matter of his courtship: but he'd said plenty on the subject for both of them.

He came padding back into the room and crawled onto the bed, forcing apart her thighs. "Open wide for me, Nora, I want to play with my favorite toy."

That was another of his obsessions: her piercing. Some nights he licked and fingered her almost raw.

Some nights he fucked her for an hour or more, transfixed at the sight of his body penetrating and stretching hers. "You're so small and tight," he'd marvel, as if he'd only then seen her for the first time. "I can't get enough of watching you take me."

Yes, she knew that.

And then there was his fascination with the diamond encrusted ring and the way it chafed at her exposed clitoris. "I wonder if we should get you a bigger ring," he'd mused a few nights ago—the same night he'd decided he would see how many orgasms he could give her in a single evening. The answer to that, by the way, was a *lot.*

She felt his hot breath first and then his warm, hot tongue on her sensitive flesh. He licked her from cunt to piercing.

"I love the taste of my come on you," he murmured. "Do you think that makes me odd?" he asked, pausing his licking to look up at her with a serious expression.

Nora could only laugh.

"I'll take that as a no," he said, returning to his nuzzling and licking, thrusting his remarkably hard tongue up her entrance and fucking her with it.

She looked down at his big head, his hair wild and mussed, his powerful body propped up on thick, muscular biceps. She rarely had a chance to see him so clearly, but he'd come back in the middle of the day so they'd opened the drapes on the windows, risking exposure if anyone happened to be looking in from the third floor across the street. He'd been so hard and desperate for her that he'd actually ripped part of her gown to get to her.

Something was bothering him. If they were normal lovers, she would ask. Of course if they were normal lovers, he wouldn't share the inner details of his recent wife-hunting with her every night in this bed, before, during, and after he'd taken her.

He tugged on her sensitive piercing with his teeth and she stiffened. He laughed and then sucked her still aroused, hard nub into his mouth, his finger nudging at her opening—the one not plugged with marble.

She relaxed her body, spreading wider for him. The truth was that she couldn't get enough of him, either. Their contract ran for a year, at which time she would leave. And she *would* leave, because to stay under such conditions—Edward bringing in a wife, having children—would eventually kill her. Part of her wished he'd put five years in the contract so she would have to stay with him, dying a slow death until he eventually paid the stiff forfeiture and ended their agreement early— which she knew he would.

But, unfortunately, she only had this one year, less now.

She knew most people would consider her willingness to whore for a man in his house, with his new wife, unforgiveable. She would have despised herself, too if it was a normal marriage. But she'd met all but one of the women on his bloody list. He'd brought them one by one, to the dinner table and forced her to socialize, smile, and be looked down upon. Every single one of them had looked at Edward with barely veiled hatred. Nora had read their expressions as clearly as a book: none of them would care if Edward stocked his house with ten mistresses if that meant they never needed to submit to his loathsome, plebian embraces.

"Mmm," his groan shook her from her unpleasant thoughts and she tilted her pelvis for him, focusing all her attention on his clever tongue working her aching flesh while a second and then third finger pumped her. As ever, he brought her to a shattering climax with very little effort. She didn't always come so quickly; only with Edward.

He chuckled while holding her spasming clitoris clamped between his lips, stilling his hands and tongue to allow her to enjoy the sensation.

He released the small triangle of flesh with a vulgar *pop*. "Oh, Nora, I so love your cunt."

She knew that. But why couldn't he love *her?*

He pushed himself up even with her and propped his head up with his hand, looking at her while his fingers circled her nipples—also painfully sensitive. He said the same thing he always did. "I can't decide if I'd like these pierced. Perhaps just one. But which one?" He leaned down and sucked the right one into his mouth. Sometimes Nora thought she would die from an overabundance of physical pleasure. She wondered if that was possible.

He was pressed against her hip, his thick organ already beginning to harden again. He moaned against her breast and released her, rolling onto his back.

"I just want to fuck you all day long but I have to go and check with Mrs. Loring—about the dinner."

Yes, she knew. She also knew his plaintive tone. They'd had their first ever argument her third week with him, when he'd told her about the first dinner. Nora knew her refusal to do his bidding—for only the second time, the first when she rejected his initial offer—confounded him. And infuriated him. That was her fault for always submitting to him—he was like a spoiled child accustomed to getting what he wanted. A spoiled six-foot, fifteen-stone child.

She refused to act as the mistress of his house. He could pay somebody to decorate or arrange his bloody dinner parties. She'd signed a contract to accept dominion over her body, not to act as his wife.

"I think Lady Catherine is the one, Nora," he mused beside her, staring up at the mirrored ceiling, at images of themselves, naked and sated. He shoved a hand through his hair, his muscular bicep bulging—the sight stirring her even though she'd climaxed not five minutes earlier. Oh, how she adored his body.

"I paid a call on the marquess's house on Berkeley Square," he continued, no response from her necessary. He snorted derisively, just as he always did after visiting one of these down-at-heel old houses. "What a disaster. Instead of franking that lout of son they could have fixed at least the roof. It's even worse than their country home." He absently rubbed his chest, the action making his muscles move in fascinating ways and making her mouth water.

Truly she was born to be a whore. But then she'd known that.

He turned to her suddenly. "What do you suppose these blokes *do* all day?" He appeared genuinely serious.

She shrugged. "Wake up at noon, have a leisurely meal and read the paper, spend several hour at their toilet, go eat at their club, go to some society function, pay a visit to a gambling hell or brothel or both, tumble into bed at dawn and do it all over again."

His eyes had widened. "Did you just make all that up?"

"Yes," she admitted.

He frowned. "But it sounds bloody plausible, doesn't it? What a dreadful way to go on with one's life."

Nora thought back to the vicious young viscount who'd hurt her so badly and had to agree. Boredom was a deadly emotion.

On an impulse, she asked him, "What do *you* do all day, Edward?"

He couldn't have looked more surprised if she'd pulled out a croquet mallet and hit him in the forehead. Well, she supposed she'd not asked very many questions. She'd learned, since moving into his house, that he'd begun to open up and usually gave a good deal of himself away if one just waited and watched.

His face and neck flushed, and she knew her interest pleased him. She couldn't decide if that made her happy, or not.

"Hmm, well. I usually spend a few hours with Simon Powell going through paperwork."

Nora had met the quiet young secretary only once. She tended to avoid the second floor when she knew there might be others around—Edward's associates or other businessmen. She especially avoided Mr. Powell because she suspected Edward had used him to copy the contract. The way the younger man—perhaps her age—had flushed when he'd met her had confirmed that suspicion. She could only imagine what he thought of her.

"Then I might meet with one of the others to discuss our various investments." By others he meant his small syndicate. "Sometimes I go to check on things in person." He paused and scratched his jaw, which was already dark with hair although it was only midday. "Like that damned brewery Smith convinced us to buy down by the London Docks." He turned to her. "Do you know the one I mean?" he asked, clearly forgetting to whom he was speaking.

"I'm afraid I don't possess an extensive knowledge of breweries."

"It's the Gateshead," he said, not noticing the mockery in her voice. He shrugged. "In any case, I might do that and then come back here to get in a few more hours once Powell has gone home." He cut her a quick look. "I know you haven't met him but—"

"I have."

He frowned, his dark eyes suddenly focusing on her in that way that exhibited total focus, like a marksman taking aim. "When was this?"

"One morning downstairs."

Storm clouds gathered so fast in his eyes she wanted to laugh. Here he was jealous that she might *speak* to another man when he talked of nothing but marrying another woman—and *breeding children on her!*

"What were you doing on the second floor?" he asked, leaking suspicion like a cracked jar leaked water.

"Likely walking through it to get to the first."

He blinked at her tart answer, and then, to her surprise, laughed. "Ah, Nora shows her claws."

Oh, you've not even seen the tip of what I keep sheathed, Mr. Edward Fanshawe, she wanted to tell him, but of course did not.

Besides, he'd already lost interest in her, or her claws, and he turned back to the mirror. "I have to admit they aren't the mother-and father-in-law I'd have chosen, but I think Lady Catherine is the best of the lot—and certainly the most beautiful," he said in an admiring, covetous tone.

The "lot" being the parade of young, impoverished women and their eager but arrogant parents who'd come through the house in the past weeks. She'd known for some time he was becoming bored with the process and wanted to get things finished—just like he'd gotten Nora installed in his house—so that he could marry, impregnate his wife, and then move on to the next item on his list.

At first the thought of him marrying another—bedding another—had driven her nearly mad. She'd wanted to tear off her own head to get away from the horrific thought. But, of course, some base part of her brain had thrilled at the notion he would humiliate and debase her so *thoroughly*—and *she* would not only accept it, she would revel in it.

So, for these past few weeks they'd engaged in the most torrid, violent sex she'd ever had; it had also been the very best in her life. Neither of them could get enough—which was saying something considering they never seemed to get enough.

He'd developed his obsession for anal plugs then. For at least five or six days he'd fitted her with *two* plugs, which he'd kept inside her with a special pair of drawers made of straps of leather.

He would ride her for most of every night. his whippings the most severe he'd ever given her because she would purposely disobey him, usually by stimulating herself to orgasm without him, and then boasting of it when he came to her, just to make him beat him harder.

Every night when he was finished with her, he'd disappear until late the next evening when he'd summon her to their room and they'd do it all over again.

That was another thing—he worked a great deal. More than anyone she'd ever known. Some nights he didn't come for her until just before dawn. He'd use her with a franticness that both terrified and incited her, sleep for half an hour, and then head for his chambers to bathe, shave and dress and go to work.

He seemed to have no friends. Even his business partners were just that: business. He had no hobbies or pastimes, didn't appear to enjoy gambling, drinking, buying expensive cattle—nothing except working, fucking her, and planning his upcoming nuptials.

The days leading up to the first "dinner party" with his prospective bride had led to an almost unbearable tension inside her chest, until finally, one night after he'd left her, she pulled down her small cloth bag and threw in her old clothing. She would leave—go back to work in some other whorehouse—not in London because he'd find her if she stayed. But someplace far away.

Even as she'd been packing, she'd known she could never leave him—not until he kicked her out.

And then the night had come when she'd met his first "prospect" and all her envy and jealousy had dissipated quicker than a wisp of smoke. That's when she'd seen what a horrible, horrible mistake he was making.

The aristocrats who brought their daughters to his house, and allowed him into theirs, would never accept him. Even if he were a modest and self-effacing man, and he most definitely was not, they would hate him for recognizing their need—money—and knowing the depth of their poverty.

If any of them thought it was odd that he had his twenty-four year-old ward living with him—she'd passed her last birthday the way she wanted it, with Edward unknowingly gifting her with several magnificent birthday orgasms—nobody said anything. She believed that was largely because all the players in the little farce were consumed by their own concerns. Only Nora watched them all and learned.

Without exception, every single one of the young women stared at Edward with thinly concealed abhorrence. The same barely leashed sexuality that she adored in him they instinctively recoiled from. Oh, she'd met plenty of aristocratic women over the years who'd reveled in sex—they filled the brothels of London in numbers that would have shocked decent society—but these women—girls really, as most were below twenty—were not among that number.

So, Edward would get the pedigree he wanted and then spend the rest of his life with a family that hated him. Likely his wife would make sure their children despised their rough, rude, upstart of a father.

And he simply couldn't see it. Indeed, after that first dinner he'd come to her afterward like a conquering general—he'd had an earl at his table, *begging* for Edward to marry his daughter—and he'd then fucked Nora silly. Afterward he'd spoken of all the opportunities and doors that would open up for him with such a wife.

When he'd taken her every way he could and was physically sated he went off to his bed—they never slept together—and Nora went to her own cold bed and wept for him. How could he not see the life he was making for himself?

But it was not, and never had been, her place to tell him such things. Whether he married the daughter of a duke or an earl, didn't matter— he'd *never* deceived Nora that he would consider marrying a whore. And Nora would not take him if he asked her. She could not bear to think of the years ahead when he'd tire of her and go back to the brothels for his pleasure. As a wife, she would be forced to tolerate his treatment. As a whore, she could go away and lick her wounds.

No matter which way this story went, it always ended the same for her: he would tire of her and move on.

But life was not all grim. She spent every night with Edward and most days she had to herself. As long as she took a footman with her and avoided old clients, he didn't seem to care what she did.

He'd never once asked to look at her paintings, which was just as well because her current one was of him. It was, she suspected, one of the best things she'd ever done—perhaps it would be the best thing she'd ever do.

It was her first nude, which seemed astonishing given her background.

The canvas, like the man, was huge—another first.

She would submit this one and two others to the Royal Academy which opened for submissions in a few weeks.

The thought of Edward's powerful, naked body being viewed by thousands made her smile. And the painting was hers, all hers, the only part of him she could ever call her own.

Chapter Seventeen

Catherine

The Tin King's dinner party was going along as abhorrently as she'd expected. Her parents were fluctuating between toad-eating and openly despising her betrothed, exactly as she'd known they would; Ceddy had failed to show up—risking insulting the only man in England with enough money to save them all; and her husband-to-be—because that is what Edward Fanshawe was, she'd finally accepted it—had cemented her impression of him as a gross sensualist who imagined her bulging with his child every time he looked at her.

But there was one bright spot in the wretched evening. Cat cut a quick glance at Mr. Fanshawe's rather surprising niece, Miss Nora Hudson.

Cat had arrived prepared to despise her as much as her uncle, but other than have Fanshawe as an uncle, there was nothing despicable about her.

On the contrary, she was utterly fascinating looking and *completely* different than her relative. How could such a dark, vulgar, hulking oaf be related to such a slender, delicate, and almost celestial-looking being?

While Nora Hudson would never be called beautiful, Cat had needed to force herself to quit gawking at her almost ghostly eyes and serene, ethereal expression.

She was well-spoken, but reserved, graceful, and oddly still—as if she didn't wish to attract attention to her person.

For her part, Cat thirsted for adulation and attention; she'd yearned for a Season as long as she could remember. She'd been the most beautiful girl in her village, but country swains meant nothing to her. She'd wanted to captivate the hearts of dukes and maybe even a foreign prince.

Ceddy had laughed unpleasantly at her yesterday upon hearing about the dinner with Fanshawe—calling him her Tin Prince.

He'd not met Fanshawe yet or he'd know the man was no prince. A king, perhaps—a barbarian king from Biblical days who had a thousand wives and cut off peoples' heads who displeased him. But a storybook prince? She snorted.

"My lady?"

She looked up from her thoughts to find Mr. Fanshawe looking at her with an expression she guessed was meant to appear solicitous— rather than salacious.

Fanshawe glanced at her untouched plate. "Is aught amiss with your meal, my lady? Could I have anything else brought out for you?"

As far as Cat could tell the only thing that *wasn't* on this table was his head on a platter. She'd never seen so much food in her life.

"Oh, thank you Mr. Fanshawe, really." She fluttered her eyelashes at him, which always made color rush into his ugly face.

"Our Kitty is quite a sparing eater," her father said, using a pet name he *knew* she loathed while looking pointedly at her and giving a false-sounding chortle.

Mr. Fanshawe's beastly eyebrows arched with interest. "Kitty?"

"That is what her family calls her," the marquess said. "Our sweet little kitten."

Cat's face scalded at her father's vomitous words. She jerked her eyes away from his hateful face, afraid she might throw her floating island across the table at him. Instead, she looked at Miss Nora, prepared to see mocking superiority.

Once again, the woman surprised her. Her expression of sympathy was so subtle, Cat almost missed it. But, for the first time that evening, Miss Hudson opened her mouth without prompting, changing the agonizing topic, Cat knew, for *her*.

"I understand your seat is in Hampshire, my lord?"

Cat felt Mr. Fanshawe startle beside her, as if he'd never heard his own niece's voice before. Being the arrogant hog of a man that he was, he probably never listened to her.

"Yes, it is—not far from Sherbourne St. John. Are you familiar with Hampshire, Miss Hudson?"

"I spent some time in Basingstoke," she admitted, again drawing a look of surprise from her clod of an uncle—almost as if he didn't even know where his niece had lived.

"Ah yes, Basingstoke. I know the vicar there—he's had the living for a very long time. A Reverend Hartwicke—perhaps you've heard of him?"

Miss Hudson was so pale it was hard to tell if she'd just become paler, but Cat would have wagered a pony—not that she knew what that meant, it was just a vulgar phrase she'd picked up from Ceddy—that Miss Hudson had been surprised.

"Yes," Miss Hudson said in her soft voice, which was so well-modulated Cat must have imagined her change in color. "I do recall Mr. Hartwicke and his two daughters."

"Mmph," the marquess, said, his mouth full of superlative wine, which Cat thought he was consuming with revolting enjoyment. When she married Mr. Fanshawe Cat would see to it that her parents were served only the most repulsive vintages whenever they visited—which would be *rarely*.

"Only one daughter now," her father corrected. "I believe the younger one died quite tragically. Isn't that right, my lady?"

But the marchioness had obviously not been listening to her husband—as usual—and turned to their host instead. "I see you've chosen to situate your dining room on the northeast corner, Mr. Fanshawe," she began, initiating the type of jaw-droppingly tedious conversation about rooms and aspects and such that she seemed to live for and which made her listeners want to take pistol and blow their own brains out.

Unfortunately, her ladyship's boring conversation continued throughout the rest of dinner, making Cat eager for the moment they could leave the tiresome men to their port and she could get Miss Hudson to herself.

Three weeks later . . .

Nora was staring at the canopy over her bed into the darkness when she heard the panel door open. She glanced toward the playroom and saw he'd left the door open, a few candles burning inside the room. She sighed. If she didn't go to him, he'd come get her.

She pushed back the covers, astounded that even Edward would have the gall to come to his mistress on his wedding day.

And what a day it had been: long and grueling. Life had been at a fever pitch for three solid weeks leading up to the rather hasty marriage—which Edward had demanded—and she'd hoped to sleep for the next two days and then wake up in her old bed at Tosca's not worrying about anything but snatching enough time for painting.

Nora sighed. No, that was not true. Life was hellish, but she would not give Edward up—no matter how bull-headed, ignorant, maddening, and selfish he was.

She removed her nightgown so he would not tear it off her person— it was the last one she owned, having forgotten a few times and sacrificed the poor garments.

She hesitated in the open doorway: he was sitting in the big black leather chair facing the fireplace and she could only see the back of his head and bare knees on both sides of the chair. He only sat in this chair for one purpose.

Nora's cunt—which didn't care how shameful this was—or, rather *did* care, and loved the filthy idea of submitting to Edward on his wedding night—tightened, sending shivers of pleasure to the rest of her body.

"I can feel your eyes on me, Nora," he said, his baritone voice startling her. "Come here."

She went to him, not surprised to find him naked and erect. His eyes kindled as he looked at her, his face flushed with triumph.

"Kneel," he ordered.

She could hardly drop quickly enough. He took his thick shaft in his hand and tilted it toward the light and she saw the faint dark smear and then sagged back on her heels as every drop of blood in her body rushed to her sex.

"Such a dirty, filthy thing you are," Edward praised, reading her correctly and grinning down at her, well pleased by her reaction. "That makes you hot—hot enough to come." He frowned. "But don't even consider it." His harsh features flickered red from the reflection of the flames and he looked so savage and cruel that the first ripples of her orgasm licked at her.

He gave a vile, low chuckle. "Ah, my poor, lusting, little whore," he whispered stroking his cock, which was leaking freely, the fluid glittering in the candlelight. "But I brought a treat for you—a wedding present of sorts—I didn't wash myself after I took her because I knew you'd want to taste her on me. I was right, wasn't I?"

Nora swallowed convulsively to clear away the lust and loathing that almost choked her. Her voice when it came, was a husk. "Yes, Edward. Please."

His eyes fluttered closed and he groaned and pulled hard on his cock, his jaw so tight it looked ready to crack.

Nora waited for what was coming.

His eyes opened to mere black crescents, his smile that of a lazy, sated predator. He tilted his glistening crown toward her. "Just a taste, my Nora."

She lowered her mouth without hesitation and flicked his slit with the pointed tip of her tongue, glorying at the way his body shook and tensed.

"God, yes. You're in heat, aren't you?" he gasped as she pursed her lips and sucked the tiny slit—his *meatus* she knew it was called, the word vulgar and erotic—hard, as if she could suck an orgasm from him. "That's right, suck me clean and make me weep for you,"

She shuddered at his words and a strand of drool dropped to this thigh and made him chuckle.

"My little bitch is in heat," he soothed, petting her head like animal she was as she sucked him as if he offered sustenance rather than humiliation and pain. She couldn't stop sucking, her lips milking, wanting more, wanting—

"That's enough."

God, he tasted—

"Nora," He warned, pushing her back when she didn't release him.

She trembled from the struggle inside her—sitting back on her heels. So ashamed. So very, very ashamed.

"Look at me."

She did, raising her eyes slowly. He gasped at what he saw on her face—as if struck by something wondrous. He shook his head back and forth.

"You wished you'd been there tonight—watching—don't you? You'd liked to have prepared me for her—or perhaps even readied Catherine."

She shuddered and his pupils flared and she knew he was envisioning it.

"You would have liked that."

It wasn't a question, but she told him the first lie she'd ever spoken. "No."

He threw back his head and laughed and she winced. When he stopped, he said. "Oh, you're worried my *wife* might hear me?" He chuckled, not waiting for an answer. "Don't worry, my greedy little whore—the doors and walls have cork an inch thick. My little kitten won't hear a thing. Besides, tonight was rather exhausting for her—I left her sound asleep." He grinned proudly and beckoned her with his cock. "Come here—I'm going to come in your mouth so you can enjoy us mingled. And then I'm going to spend the rest of my wedding night fucking you."

He tilted his cock toward her and—God have mercy on her blackened, rotted soul—she opened her mouth wide and took it.

"That's right," he said in a low, soothing voice. "No," he chastised when she would have throated him. "I want you to lick me first. Yes, like that—like you are licking something delicious." He made a humming sound, shifting his hips to widen his thighs. "And I want you to do my balls, too. Do that thing I love—when you take them in your mouth and massage them with your tongue."

She obeyed him, not making a sound, but he knew—he always knew—and his hand slid around her jaw as his thumb wiped away her tears. "Oh, poor Nora," he teased in a voice rich with amusement and lazy with lust. "I'll bet you're weeping just as much between your sweet thighs, aren't you?" He didn't wait for an answer, he knew it already. "You want to hear about my wedding night, don't you?"

No!

But her body clenched so hard she almost came.

He laughed. "You'd better not come," he warned, and then heaved a contented sigh. "I've never fucked a virgin before Nora," he said, his tone musing while his hips pulsed gently. "She was *so* tight and small—even tighter than you, my Nora—that I worried I might rip her. I would have liked to have the lights on to spread her open and see her—or at least remove her huge bloody nightgown—but there was none of that." He grunted. "It was lucky I'd thought to bring oil with me because she was as dry as a desert. But even oil did not ease penetration very much." He paused, and then said in a less amused tone. "I thought to touch her—you know, stretch and ready her a bit, maybe even give her some pleasure—and she all but scratched my eyes out. I suppose that is virgin behavior."

Nora had a quick flash of her first time—when she'd begged for Brandon Sealy to touch her, to pinch, pull, and *hurt* her. No, virgins behaved as differently as anyone else.

"I suppose I shouldn't go to her tomorrow as I daresay she might be a little sore. I'll wait until the following day. But the doctor I consulted said I should breed her most of the month if I'm to have any success."

That, in a nutshell, was classic Edward: not if *we're* to have any success, but if *I'm* to have any success, as if Catherine's contribution to the process was negligible.

"It will become easier for her. Perhaps she might even come to enjoy it—although I am given to understand that women of her class rarely care for such things."

Nora would have fallen to the floor laughing if she'd not had his balls in her mouth.

Putting aside his incorrect assumption about the frigidity of an entire class of women, Nora suspected his wife would never care for sex with him.

Whether because of Edward's too-huge cock, her too-tight cunt, or the amount of loathing Catherine bore him, Nora simply couldn't envision a day when the other woman would want him. She tried not to gloat too hard about that but was largely unsuccessful.

He suddenly chuckled. "My kitten is a cat. I *know* she wanted to spit and claw and scratch and keep me out, but she's made a bargain and is an honorable little thing."

Nora spared a moment's pity for the poor woman in the other room—in between sucking the same woman's husband and trying to hide her first orgasm. Poor Catherine was honoring a bargain she'd never made, but one her father had.

"Nora?" Edward's voice was sharp. "You'd better not have done what I think you did. Do I need to get out the crop?"

She smiled, shivered, and released his testicle with a soft pop. All the while, tears ran down her cheeks. "Yes, Edward. I need to be punished."

Chapter Eighteen

"*I hate you!*"

Edward barely ducked in time to dodge a heavy marble statue that Smith had given him as a wedding present. The marble knocked a stack of papers off his desk and skittered over the smooth surface, barely missing the window behind him before thudding to the floor. Edward glanced at it and saw it appeared unharmed. He didn't care for it, but he believed it might be worth a good deal of money. Smith had smirked that it was a fertility totem—whatever the hell that was.

He stood. "Kitten—"

"You bastard!" She yelled, blindly reaching for something else to throw but finding nothing. So, that was one good thing about having an artless, empty house. "Don't you ever call me Kitten again," she shrieked through her tears.

Edward was impressed by both her throwing arm and lung capacity. Powell, on the other hand, appeared terrified. He'd been taking dictation when Kitten, er, Catherine—flung open the door to his office and began hurling insults and objects at him.

Edward turned to the poor man, who was crouched behind his small writing desk. "Will you give me and my wife a moment, Powell." It wasn't a request.

As soon as Powell scuttled from the room Edward strode toward the door and closed it before turning to the woman who hated him more than anyone she'd ever met—or so she told him daily.

He took her arm. "Please, Catherine, will you sit."

She shook his hand away violently enough to cause herself to stagger back. He considered letting her fall on her cute little arse, but relented, catching her, steadying her, and just as quickly releasing her. "Sit," he ordered, using a tone he'd never thought to employ on an aristocrat, but now used daily.

She dropped into a chair hard enough to make him wince.

He considered sitting on the chair beside her but then decided he wanted a desk between them if she started hurling things again.

"Now," he said, adjusting his waistcoat and cravat before sitting back. "What is the problem?"

She glared at him through eyes that were red-rimmed from crying. She was one of those women who looked beautiful even when she cried. She was the most exquisite woman he'd ever seen. She was also a hellcat of exactly the wrong type—not a spitfire in bed, like Nora, but a willful, demanding, ungrateful, frigid little bitch who hated him and took no pains to hide it.

"I'm p-p-pregnant!" she wailed and then collapsed her head onto the arm of the chair and cried noisily.

Edward had a devil of a time not leaping up and yelling *Huzzah!* But he decided that reaction would only upset her more, and he'd read somewhere that pregnant women needed peace and quiet and calm.

"Why are you so furious?" he asked, hoping to make her see reason and get her the hell out of his office as quickly as possible. "That means you won't have to allow me into your bedchamber for nine," he amended, "ten months."

Her sobbing briefly paused and then she wailed, "But I shan't be able to go to parties or balls and I'll have to sequester myself in the country and get big and fat and—"

Edward's brain latched on to one thing she said and started whirring: yes, she needed to be in the country. There was too much excitement in the city—especially with the bloody Season still in roar. He'd pack her off to the country immediately. He'd have to lease something first—but only until he built a new house. He didn't like the notion of living in a used house.

His mind leapt ahead as she complained.

Once he'd established her in the country, he and Nora could go back to the way things were. Oh, it wasn't that things had been *bad* since his marriage, but Catherine's incessant demands for balls and parties and routs had turned everyone's life upside down. Although he wasn't expected to attend her at these functions—indeed, she'd made it quite plain she did *not* want his presence—she'd somehow managed to do the impossible and convince *Nora* to be her companion on some of these miserable romps. The two women had become as close as sisters in the two months since he'd been married. Who knew what they'd be like after six months?

And if Nora went to a bloody ball with her, that meant Edward *had* to go. Because God only knew what Nora might get up to without him watching her. And he could hardly employ a footman to spy on her at balls.

He'd been almost too furious to yell at her when he'd learned she'd agreed to accompany Catherine to some fool function.

"But you always refuse to accompany *me* to such *ton* functions when I asked during the courtship process," he'd whined in a most mortifying manner.

Nora, as impervious and unreadable as ever, had merely said, "Yes, well Catherine asked me as a favor."

That had made him howl. "What about *me*? When are you going to do *me* any favors?"

Her lips had twitched in that slight way that gave him an almost instant erection. "I believe I have at least three favors plugged up inside me as we speak."

He'd blinked at her unexpectedly vulgar response—which also made him hard as it reminded him of his virility, and his responsibility to break the current record for ejaculations—which had been, rather disturbingly, eluding him.

So, that had been the end of *that* discussion. The woman was a wizard at distracting him and they'd not had a moment since that night to re-negotiate this foolishness.

"Edward!"

"Hmm?" He looked up and saw his furious wife glaring at him. *Ah, that was right—she was pregnant.*

"It's no use trying to hide your disgusting smile," she said. "I *know* you're over the moon."

Edward grinned. "Of course I am." He cut a glance at her midriff. "I want to see your belly." She shrieked so loud he had to cover his ears.

"You-you-you—"

"Degenerate pig?" he suggested, when he thought she might be stuck.

"I *hate* you. And I hate the thought of having your child inside me."

Edward loved it—but he suspected she already knew that. He shrugged and stood up, tired of her dramatics. "That child is costing me hundreds of thousands of pounds, Catherine," he pointed out as he strode toward the door. "And the way your idiot brother is running around the Continent strewing money it will only cost me more." The little bastard hadn't even returned to London for their wedding. Well, based on what Edward had heard of *Ceddy* that was just as well.

"Now," he said, jerking the door open. "If you wouldn't mind, I've got work to do."

She flounced up from her chair and came toward him with narrowed eyes.

"Oh," he said, placing himself in front of the door so she couldn't leave just yet. "You will curtail your frantic pace for the duration of the Season. I will look through your invitations and decide which functions you might attend."

She was flushed, her substantial breasts heaving, and very, very lovely. "You are *not* the master of me."

He winked down at her, amused when her jaw dropped. "Oh, but sweetheart, I *am* your master—in every sense of the word. The sooner you accept it, the better off you'll be. "

She was fast—amazingly so—and her palm struck his left cheek— bloody hard—before he even saw it coming.

He automatically reached up to feel his cheek, grinning down at her. "My, my, is that a love swat, Kitten? Because it feels like an invitation to play, to me."

He laughed at her expression of horror as she fled, grinning from ear-to-ear once he'd shut the door behind her—she was *pregnant*. He couldn't wait to tell Nora!

❋❋❋

Nora knew when she heard the sound of glass breaking all the way up in her chambers that she would soon have company. She glanced yearningly at her sunroom door, where she'd hoped to take an hour or two to paint. But that had become an impossibility of late. If it wasn't

152

Edward complaining about Catherine, it was Catherine running to her with her most recent complaint about Edward.

Not more than a few moments passed before the door flew open and Catherine—or Cat as Nora now called her, came charging inside.

"He's a *revolting* pig and I don't know how the two of you can be related," she cried, throwing herself into Nora's arms. "Oh, Nora!" she sobbed, her soft, curvy body shaking with the force of her crying. "I hate it, I just hate it."

Nora petted her back and made soothing noises. She wasn't surprised to see her. Indeed, Cat had begun to come to Nora for friendship even before she married Edward. For such a beautiful, spirited, clever girl, she had remarkably few friends. Nora supposed they must all be back in the country, as she'd had little opportunity to meet girls her age—and class—during this rather hectic Season.

So, by default, Nora supposed, she'd become Cat's sister, dearest friend, mother, and confessor.

When Cat learned she was pregnant this morning—from the midwife Edward had hired to hound and harry the poor girl when she'd failed to become pregnant that first month—it had taken Cat less than five seconds to sprint from her chambers at the far end of the hall to Nora's rooms.

She had cried and Nora had cried with her. She'd cried for poor little Cat—who didn't want a baby; she'd cried for herself—who'd never even once had a pregnancy scare in all her years of whoring; and she even cried for Edward, who'd done this to all three of them and couldn't seem to see the disaster that loomed on the horizon.

Nora held Cat at arm's length and gave her a gentle shake. "Come now, you will make yourself ill. And now you have the baby's health to consider."

"Ugh. Don't remind me—the *baby*." Cat scowled and flung herself back against the settee in a dramatic pose and closed her eyes, but at least she'd stopped wailing. "*His* baby," she added in a voice that pulsed with loathing.

Nora was glad the girl couldn't see her right then. She would give up everything—even painting—if she could carry Edward's baby inside her.

"I suppose the good news is that I shan't have to put up with his loathsome pawing for ten months at least."

That *was* good news. Nora knew her thought was selfish—she'd missed having Edward to herself—but the girl had nearly driven herself hysterical whenever Edward went near her and Edward, being Edward, had persisted in exercising his conjugal rights, twice a week. Apparently, that was the frequency the doctor recommended as the most efficacious for pregnancy while not traumatizing a gently bred young lady.

"I hope you are gentle and kind to her," Nora had told him—a rare volunteering of opinion—one night when he'd come to her complaining of his wretched duty.

"Good God, Nora," he'd snapped. "You'd think I was some sort of monster." *That* had made her smile. "I never hurt the chit—unless you consider me putting my cock in her precious cunt hurting her. Lord, I'm as gentle as bloody lamb but she barely allows me to spend in her before she drives me out of her room. I've taken to fisting myself right to the point of coming so that I can get in and out before she stars screeching at me." He turned his scowl on her. "And you. You're supposed to be mine—why are you taking *her side?*"

Nora hadn't known whether to laugh or cry. Sides? "I'm not taking anyone's side, Edward, I just can't conscience cruelty in the bedroom."

That had made his eyes pop open. "But you *love*—"

She'd sighed at his thick-headedness. "Not *that* kind of cruelty."

He'd snorted. "That's just as well—she won't let me put a finger on her, I can't imagine what she'd do if I came after her with a crop."

Nora shuddered even now recalling that.

"Nora?"

"Hmm?" She looked up to find Cat staring at her, intense. "You won't leave me here, will you? I mean … I *know* that Tedward and I row all the time and it's unpleasant."

Nora couldn't help smiling at Cat's derogatory nickname for Edward—a silly, childish name which infuriated him.

"I suppose listening to us must be miserable."

It was, Nora conceded, but also entertaining at times—like watching two children—although it often made her feel a hundred years old.

Cat took her hand and squeezed it. "But it shall be better now that I don't have to let him—" She shivered and then continued, "Although it will mean I shan't be able to enjoy the rest of the Season as he told me that *he* will select what invitations I might accept."

Thank the Lord. Not only would it be better for Nora's sexual needs, but her sanity, as well; she'd hated accompanying Cat to all these vapid, endless affairs but couldn't seem to deny her.

Their late nights had left her exhausted—and sexually frustrated—and she'd been quite surprised Edward hadn't curtailed his wife's behavior before now. But Edward had been allowing Cat a range of freedom he'd never extended to Nora. That, she was sure, was over now that his child was inside her. Nora shuddered to think how Cat would react to Edward's iron control. Unlike Nora—who craved and relished Edward's high-handed, domineering ways—Cat was a remarkably headstrong young woman who appeared just as determined as her husband to get her own way. The two of them never backed away from a fight.

Cat leaned up against her, snuggling under her arm. "You won't go? I'll need you here if I'm to bear having this dreadful baby getting bigger inside me. And I'm terrified of giving birth to it; if his baby is anywhere near as big as his wretched *instrument of torture* it will likely be a fifty-pound monster."

Nora chuckled at that. "Women have babies every day; you shall be fine." Yes, women *died* all the time, too, but what would such information do to help Catherine?

"But you'll stay," Cat persisted.

"Yes, I'll stay." Nora sighed, how had this happened to her?

✳ ✳ ✳

Nora could feel the Thomas's anger as he trotted along behind her. She didn't care—this was the first day in over two bloody months that she'd been Edward- and Cat-free and she needed to talk to Charles.

And the day was beautiful and she'd refused the carriage the pushy footman had tried to thrust on her. Although the servants were all too terrified of Edward to show her any disrespect, Nora wasn't under an illusions about how they felt about her. Only Mary, apparently too naïve to understand the veiled, vulgar comments, continued to believe the laughable fiction that she was Edward's niece.

Nora had hoped the tension in the house would dissipate after the announcement of Cat's pregnancy, but the two were at each other's throats all the time. They didn't just dislike each other, they *hated* one another.

She'd also hoped for some peace and quiet when Edward had been called away to Manchester for ten days but it had just been ten days in which she'd had to rein in Cat rather than paint.

And, oh, but she had wanted to paint! She had a lovely idea for yet another painting of Edward. It would be something that only she would ever see, of course, but that just made her idea more enticing.

But at *this* rate, she'd be lucky to see a paintbrush, not to mention work on an actual painting.

She simply couldn't say no to accompany poor Cat when she asked. The girl—woman, really—seemed younger than her years and was truly lonely. The marquess and marchioness had departed from London even before the Season was over, each of them doubtlessly off to pursue their own pleasure. And Cat's only sibling—Ceddy?

Well, Nora shivered at the coincidence that Edward's new brother-in-law was the vile Viscount Redmond. Luckily the nasty little toad appeared to be killing himself in France or Spain in some brothel—along with some poor whore, she suspected—so Nora would likely be gone from Edward's house before Ceddy ever materialized.

Nora knew she would have to tell Edward eventually—it would be a disaster if Ceddy showed up and opened his poisonous little mouth, but she was afraid what Edward would do. Once, when he'd lighted a half a hundred candles and then fucked her, he'd seen the scars on her inner thighs—he was certainly down there enough—and had demanded repeatedly who'd done that to her.

It had taken all her will to stand against him.

Now that he'd impregnated Cat, Edward behaved as if she didn't even exist—at least not as a person—but only as the vessel carrying his child. He ordered her life, exerting more and more control over what she ate, how much sleep she got, along with a dozen other small, invasive details. As much as Nora loved him, she couldn't help wanting to strangle him.

He'd begun to come to her every night, just like he used to, well-pleased that he was having his cake and eating it, too—that his life was running on the path he'd charted for them all.

But there was a restless to him and she knew he was seeking some kind of distraction from the tension in the house. So, she wasn't surprised when he'd told her several nights ago that he wanted to pierce her nipples. It was inevitable—especially now that his mind had filed away the wife and child problems.

While she would adore being pierced or tattooed or even branded for him (yes, he'd suggested them all at one time or another) she couldn't help being angry with his utter refusal to face reality. Did he not see his young, neglected wife was a volcano waiting to explode? Did he really believe he would just get his two children off her and put her neatly in one of his files? Didn't he understand that someday Cat would learn what went on between them and when she did she would be furious— not because she was jealous—but because they'd made a fool of her?

"We're here, Miss."

Nora stopped and saw that, indeed, she'd marched right past Tosca's.

"Go wait in the kitchen," she told the Thomas, knowing the whores always enjoyed teasing her thick, humorless jailers.

Nora didn't bother sending a maid for Charles but took the back stairs to his room. She tapped lightly on his door and heard a muffled groan before entering his room.

As she'd suspected, he was tangled in bedding, his torso naked and sweaty in the heat of the attic.

"Phew," she said, waving her hand in front of her face and going to his window. "It stinks like sweaty whore in here." She flung open the window and turned to find him propped against his cushion, yawning and not bothering to hide his sleep erection.

"My goodness," she said going closer to look at his cock.

Being the exhibitionist that he was, he grinned up at her and took his surprisingly meaty prick in his hand and shifted it from side to side for her admiration.

"It's an apadravya," he boasted.

"I've seen it before." *Times beyond counting.* But she sat on the bed, curious to actually look at it now that she had her own piercing. She had to admit it was very erotic. Edward's enormous crown would look spectacular with a heavy silver bar through it. Her belly tightened at the thought. It was too bad she could never see him submitting to such a thing.

"I can see you swallowing and know your mouth is watering. I'll let you suck me off if you like." He grinned and stared through slitted eyes as he resumed his stroking. "Anything for a friend, you know."

Nora snorted and looked up from the silver bar that passed through the head of his cock, piercing his meatus. "I'm guessing you've had it sucked plenty already."

"Yes, but I've never had *your* mouth on me and I understand there is none better."

"Finally a word of sense from you," she said mildly.

He laughed wickedly and gave himself a lazy stroke before dropping back on his pillow.

"How long have you had it?" He must have been young, because he'd been sixteen when Nora met him.

He shrugged and yawned, idly caressing himself. "Fourteen."

"What made you do it?"

"Not what, *whom*." He corrected, giving her a lascivious grin. "You've been dying to ask me for ages, haven't you?"

She had enough heart not to tell him that she'd never given it a second's thought, until now. Instead, she said, "Believe it or not, Charles, not all of us go about our days thinking about your cock."

"I don't believe it."

Nora just lifted her eyebrows, knowing he couldn't bear not to share every last detail of his life.

It took five seconds for him to break. "It was the *gentleman* who bought me from my old Ma."

Nora had *definitely* heard about him, some lord or other.

"He fed me up, cleaned me up, and gave me this. He made bloody good use of it, too—especially since he had to wait a good long time to take advantage of it."

"It takes a long time to heal?"

"God yes—months with no in-and-out."

No, Edward definitely wouldn't submit to that. Nora tossed her gloves and reticule on the bed and stood, going to stand by the window where there was some breeze.

"Mr. Smith is quite enamored with it."

Nora turned at that information. "Ah, is he? And how is that moving along?"

"Quite nicely—although the bastard won't be brought to offer for me." He eyed Nora's expensive walking costume with envy. "I want what you've got."

Nora doubted that but didn't argue. "Did you actually ask him?"

"Only a hundred times."

"What does he say?"

"No. Just: no. No explanation, nothing. He's . . . *maddening.*"

Nora grinned. "You've fallen for him."

Charles threw his pillow at her. "Go sod yourself, you silly whore."

She laughed. Ah, it was nice to see somebody else suffer for love for a change.

"He'll only visit me once a week—no matter how hard I try to make him want more."

Nora could only imagine the way Charles was behaving. "Perhaps you might try being less, er, available to him."

He sat up straight. "Is that what you did?"

Was it? Nora didn't think so—she thought she was only being herself, but perhaps she had?—

Down on the street a saffron colored bonnet popped out of a handsome and caught Nora's attention: it looked exactly like the outrageous hat Cat had just purchased the last time she'd dragged Nora shopping. She frowned, wishing her vision were a bit sharper at this distance. It *did* look like her. But why would she be outside Tosca's in a rented carriage?

"Oh," Charles said, while she watched the carriage pause for a moment, start rolling, stop, and finally lurch forward. "I almost forgot—I have a letter for you from Lord Anthony."

Nora's head whipped around. "What? When?"

Charles shrugged as he held the letter toward her. "Perhaps two weeks ago?"

"Charles!"

"What?" he said with his standard innocent wide-eyed stare.

The letter was crumpled and dirty and looked as if he'd kept it on the bottom of his shoe. She examined the back flap suspiciously.

"Don't, worry, I didn't look at the old gimmer's love letter."

Nora cut him a nasty look.

"But you've received no letters about the painting whosey-whatsit," he said airily.

Nora tried to contain her disappointment. The paintings had been on display for some time now and she'd only been able to get away once.

The Thomas who'd accompanied her to the exhibition had behaved as if she'd dragged him to a funeral instead of the most enormous display of art in England.

It had taken ages to find her paintings but she'd been pleasantly surprised to see small clusters around two and a crowd big enough to obstruct the third one: the big painting of Edward.

She'd signed her work Hartwicke, her real name. Although she knew women *did* submit paintings—more every year—she felt better knowing her work was being judged more objectively. She'd paid Charles an indecent amount of money to pretend to be her and deliver the work.

He would have demanded even more if he'd known how much allowance Edward gave her—an obscene amount in addition to paying for everything else in her life. He'd even paid for her books when she'd agreed to stock his woeful library—a compromise she'd made on the subject of housewifery.

And when Edward had learned she spent her own money on her paints and canvases—from one of the Thomas's reports—he'd smiled indulgently, as if amused by her small gesture of independence.

"What are you looking at, Nor?"

"Nothing," she said, pulling her eyes away from the street, where she'd thought she'd seen Cat. It was probably nothing.

She looked up to find Charles beside her, decently robed although he'd not bothered to tie his sash and was idly twiddling with the silver balls that held his bar in place, his cock as stiff and beautiful as ever. He boasted—incessantly—that he could come four times an hour, if need be. Nora had no idea which of his clients would *need* such a service from their whore and she had no interest in finding out. Luckily, she'd been fortunate never to have to work with him or their friendship would likely be over as he wasn't just insufferable, but competitive.

"You're going to wear that thing out, Charles," she said absently, staring down at Lord Anthony's letter. "Now leave me alone for a moment, I need to read this." If she didn't read it now, she'd never get to do so uninterrupted at home.

He yawned and flung himself down on his bed. "Don't let me stop you. Just don't wake me when you leave."

Nora had a bad feeling about its contents, but she broke the seal and opened the envelope.

S.M. LaViolette

Chapter Nineteen

dward admired the marks on Nora's flanks while she posed on all fours on the big sheepskin.

"Wider," he ordered, sipping his drink. She obeyed and he stared at the narrow strip of leather that was cinched tightly between her legs, hiding her cunt and back door from his view.

Edward had always been a backdoor man, but he'd never wanted to keep a woman constantly filled the way he did Nora. If he wasn't able to be inside her himself, he wanted something inside her that would keep her thoughts on him.

Tonight, she wore a new device he'd seen at the select shop where he went to purchase such things. He already knew about chastity devices but he'd always found them aesthetically unpleasing and bulky. This new item was as delicate and graceful as the woman wearing it.

While he doubted the efficacy of such things—after all, he could make Nora come without touching her, so there was no device that could stop her from experiencing an orgasm—he loved the way this on looked her slender body. The belt was hammered silver and it could be secured with a delicate lock to which only Edward had the key. He would like to keep her locked in it all day, but that was not feasible—at least not with this model, although his brain had been coming up with variations.

The portion that went from her front to back was a mix of silver and leather and he'd had it made to hold both a special phallus—modeled on his own cock—and an anal plug that was covered in little nubs.

Right now she had both inside her. It was allegedly punishment for not immediately obeying when he'd ordered her to stop sucking him earlier, but he would have found an excuse to use them on her, no matter whether she'd misbehaved or not. Besides, he knew how aroused she became when suffering for him. And he had no doubt she was suffering right now.

He'd also had the man who made it include a narrow slot in the soft black leather that covered her mons so her piercing would be exposed for his enjoyment. He'd entertained them both earlier by tonguing her until the leather was wet and her clitoris engorged. And then he'd left her that way.

She was a bloody work of art.

He'd always found black leather sexual and nobody wore it as well as Nora. Her milky white skin made the straps he bound her with appear all the more stark and erotic.

Of course, keeping her plugged and locked up this way meant he could only use her hands or mouth, but it was worth the sacrifice to stare at her.

He gently massaged his loose balls and stiff cock as he sipped his drink and stared. Sometimes he kept her this way for hours and she never moved—like a bloody statue. He told himself each time he would wait her out—see if she would twitch, perhaps even tickle her nose or tease her poor swollen nub with a feather. But he always gave in, his arousal outrunning his patience.

And he was particularly low on patience after he learned about the stunt Catherine had been pulling for weeks. Bloody Catherine.

His cock, which had begun to throb just from studying Nora's welted, plugged ass wilted at the thought of his wife.

He took a stiff drink and shoved his free hand through his hair, pinching his temples at the ache that always began when he thought of Catherine. According to the midwife he'd paid to come see her—Nora had insisted midwives were better than any Harley Street doctor— Catherine must have become pregnant sometime that second month, a product of one of their agonizing fifteen second fucks. That had been long after he'd cherished any hope that she'd calm down and come to accept him in her bed, if never actually welcome him.

He snorted, sick of thinking of her and furious about her most recent stunt.

He looked at Nora, as serene and calm as a painting, although he knew she would be throbbing and wanting.

He didn't want to, but he had to ask. "Nora?"

"Yes, Edward."

"Turn around and look at me but remain on your hands and knees."

She did so, her pale eyes almost black in the low light of the room. Sometimes he lit the room like a blazing ballroom just so he could make sure that when her pupils flared, they did so with lust, for him.

"Did you know about Catherine sneaking out?"

"No, Edward, I didn't."

He sighed, relieved. He already felt the two were far too close and often banded together against him. It would have hurt him to know Nora would disobey him by aiding Catherine in such a way. He'd been so furious he'd almost locked Catherine in her room. As it was, he discharged her maid—who'd helped her sneak in and out—and hired a woman with the aspect of a prison guard to act as her body servant. Things were not going well at all. He should have taken one of the homelier, more tractable women for his wife, but he'd been blinded by Catherine's beauty.

"What do you think she got up to when she was out and about?"

"I couldn't say, Edward."

Just what the devil would a girl who had everything need to sneak around for?

"Do you think you could persuade her to go to the country for the rest of her pregnancy?" He loathed the petitioning tone in his voice.

"I don't think so, Edward." She paused, opened her mouth, and then closed it.

He dropped his head in his hand. "God, Nora, I just wish you'd talk to me without me having to drag everything out of you." His plaintive whining made his head hot.

"But that's what you said you wanted, Edward."

His head whipped up. "When did I say such a stupid thing?"

"The first night we met."

"Good God, Nora. That was, well, that was *then*. And this is *now*. Things are . . . I don't bloody know, different."

She gave him a smile he'd never seen before—at least not for him, gentle and teasing. "But, Edward, I'm still your whore. What has changed?"

He flinched to hear her call herself that. But he called her that all the time, didn't he? But he meant it in play, to make her sexually excited. Or did she find it insulting?

Christ. These women were going to turn him into a blithering idiot.

He shrugged away the nauseating self-pity. "So you've been obeying my orders by not talking freely?"

"Yes, Edward."

"Well, my *new* order is to speak without needing me to whip or drag words out of you, do you understand?"

"Yes, Edward."

God, she looked so bloody . . . *untouchable*, even bound and kneeling for him.

He shook the thought away. How could he think that? She was here—she was his, waiting for whatever he wanted.

"What's the matter, Edward?"

He flinched at the question and decided it might take a while to adjust to a freely talking Nora.

"Nothing," he said, not wishing to go into his thoughts: which were largely that he might have made a mistake marrying Catherine, an utterly unthinkable and unbearable thought. He patted his knee. "Come here." She crawled toward him, somehow managing to make the movement sensual, and he took her chin in his hand and held her still for his examination. She returned his look submissively.

He needed . . . *something*. What? Jesus. *What?*

"I'm looking forward to going to Bernina's, Edward." Her words shot straight to his shriveled cock. "You promised you would have me pierced but then you forgot."

His hand tightened on her jaw. "I've not forgotten." He swallowed hard. "You're looking forward to it, eh?"

She smiled—God, twice in one day! "I am. Can we go tomorrow?"

How had she known that was *exactly* what he needed to hear when he hadn't known himself? Bloody hell, she was just a . . . his mind floundered for the right word. *A gift.* That's what she was: a gift.

A trickle of cold terror ran down his spine as he looked at her face, which was now a *part* of him. Their year would be up in less than eight months. Surely the contract didn't matter any longer? Surely she'd stay?

✳✳✳

Nora crawled into bed exhausted, sore, but utterly sated. Edward had been so tender after that brief conversation on the rug—well, he'd been tender in the way she liked, which is to say he'd strapped a collar on her—one that had a ring to clip a halter lead—and held the leather strap tightly enough to almost choke her while he'd fucked her throat.

But he'd not spent in her, instead he'd removed the chastity belt and the two marble phalluses—which had become uncomfortable but only added to her arousal as she loved suffering for his viewing pleasure—and had licked her to orgasm before finally plunging into her and filling her with liquid heat.

He'd slept for perhaps ten minutes before waking and kissing her a sleepy goodnight and reminding her about tomorrow before she'd left their room and he locked it behind her.

She was lazily stroking her sore, overstimulated piercing and thinking about Lord Anthony's letter. He was ill—bed-bound—and he'd asked for her to come see him weeks ago. She would have gone today but hadn't had the time after her visit to Charles. She would go, no matter what, in the morning. Her eyes watered at the thought he might not be there. She'd said goodbye to him the night she'd signed Edward's contract—they'd had their usual lovely session—and afterward, he'd asked her if there was someplace he might write to her. She'd been stunned—and flattered. But also nervous. She'd known even then—before reading Edward's contract—that he'd not want her contacting former clients. So she'd told him to give it to Charles. That he would always know where to find her.

Dammit. She chewed her lip hard enough to make it bleed. She should go to see Charles weekly. She wasn't a prisoner here. It was just—

Nora heard the familiar rattle of wood and sat bolt upright. Could it be the door? Edward needing something? She scrambled out of bed and went to her dressing room. Yes, the door to the room had opened but there was no light inside. Squinting to see in the utter darkness she ran right into a body halfway there—a small, soft *female* body.

Catherine let out a terrified squeak. "Nora?"

Nora almost fainted with relief. And just as quickly gasped with fear. "Catherine, what were you *doing* in there?"

✳✳✳

Before Catherine could answer Nora took her arm and pulled her back to her bedchamber, which was lighter because Nora had only closed the gauzy curtains and light leaked in from the streetlamps that burned below.

Nora went to light a candle and Cat caught her hand. "Please don't. I'll tell you everything, but I'd rather do so in the dark."

Nora hesitated, but finally said, "All right."

Cat saw her move toward the sitting room and asked, "Can we get under the covers in your bed? I'm cold," she lied.

Nora, who rarely said no to anyone—and now Catherine knew *why*—climbed in without speaking and lifted the blankets for her.

"What did you see?" Nora asked.

"You and Edward." Cat couldn't keep the revulsion from her tone.

Nora made an unhappy sound. "Are you terribly angry, Cat?"

Catherine paused in her snuggling, trying to get closer to Nora's body, which remained rigid for a second, but then softened.

"About what?"

She gave a breathless laugh. "That your husband and I are lovers."

"Oh, that. No, of course I'm not mad." Cat pushed a little closer, brave enough to slip an arm around Nora's waist, but worried Nora would be able to hear Cat's heart pounding, would somehow guess—with all her knowledge and wisdom of such things—how the place between her legs was sticky and tight and ridiculously sensitive after watching them tonight. Just as it had been all five nights.

"Cat, I want you to tell me everything."

Nora only used her stern voice on rare occasions. Although she was just six years older than Cat, she might as well have been a hundred

Cat sighed. "I stole the key out of his desk when I was in his office looking for something." Nora didn't need to know that what Cat had been looking for was something of Edward's to break or damage or steal. "I guessed what it was for because I'd seen the door."

She felt Nora stiffen beside her. "You've been in Edward's room?"

Cat grimaced. "Er, yes."

"Uninvited." It wasn't a question.

"What of it, Nora? He came into mine often enough." Cat shivered with disgust at the memory.

"You mustn't do that anymore, Cat. He's—well, he's particular about his privacy."

Cat snorted—he was deranged about it. "I won't," Cat lied.

It was better for everyone if Nora never knew that Cat had prowled Edward's room every night when he'd been out of town in Manchester. She'd done it out of boredom, generally moving his possessions around—he was unexpectedly tidy for such a great slob of a man—and stealing whatever seized her fancy: like a whopping roll of banknotes she'd found under his mattress. She'd never had so much money in her hands in her life. So she'd dropped it into her dressing gown pocket along with a diamond cravat pin, two pairs of gold cufflinks, and his ivory hair brush. Later she'd wondered later why she took the brush and threw it into the rubbish bin in the alley beside the house.

She'd also discovered the door.

Nora sighed. "Go on with your story."

"I didn't get up the nerve to unlock the door before Edward came back."

"When, Cat?"

"I finally got up the nerve one day when he was at work." She twisted toward Nora, even though it was too dark to see her. "I'd never imagined such a place existed, Nora. That *bed* and everything is white and black—so stark. And then I looked in the armoire."

"Oh, Cat," Nora said, stroking her shoulder. Cat snuggled closer.

"I ran out of the room as fast as my feet would carry me but I forgot to lock the door so I had to go back again."

Over the following weeks she'd gone back twice—always during the day when Edward was working and his valet was off on some errand. She was no longer frightened of the things in the wardrobe, although she was still a little disgusted. Mostly, she was intrigued. So intrigued she'd been rubbing the spot between her legs that Edward had tried to touch that first night, amazed at the wonderful things that occurred when she persisted.

"Go on, Cat. How long have you been watching?

"A week ago I hid under his bed after dinner. I went up early claiming a headache and I only had to wait barely an hour before he came in. Nelson undressed him and they'd talked about something or other and then he'd sent the man off. I watched his bare feet—they're disgusting and hairy—move toward the hidden door. Once he'd closed and locked it, I went to see if you'd gone to bed." She paused. "I'm sorry, Nora, but when nobody answered my knock I went in and found the bed untouched. You weren't in your painting room and—" Once again she shrugged. "That was when it dawned on me, that you and Edward were lovers."

Nora was so still it was like she'd left her body behind and gone somewhere.

"Nora?" she asked, ashamed at the frantic note in her voice.

"Yes, Cat?"

"I wasn't mad at you, except I wished that you'd told me. You know I would have been glad. I only wish *you'd* married him and then *you* could carry his wretched baby."

Nora said nothing.

"It's all right, Nora, really. I'd say I forgave you, but I wasn't even angry. About him, at least."

"Oh, Cat," Nora said quietly, and Cat wondered if she was crying. "What we've been doing is not all right, but it is still extremely gracious of you."

Cat preened at the slight praise and continued. "Anyhow, the next night I hid under the bed in *that* room and waited."

There was a long pause and then, "I see. And when was that, Cat?"

"Five nights ago."

"Hmmm. And you've been there every night since?"

Cat could tell by her voice that she wasn't exactly pleased. "I'm sorry, Nora. I know it was terribly gothic of me to sneak around and spy into your privacy."

Nora gave an odd chuckle. "Well, Edward is *your* husband, Cat."

She shivered. "Don't remind me."

"Oh, Cat," Nora said. "What are we going to do with you?"

Cat couldn't help sniffing Nora's hair and neck while they were lying so close together. She smelled wonderful. Faint lavender overlaid by sweat and, she now knew, the tangy scent of sex.

Suddenly a terrifying thought struck her. "Are you going to tell Edward?" Nora didn't answer immediately. "*Please*, Nora. He'll beat me."

That made Nora laugh. "He would *not.*"

She was right. "Only because it would harm the baby," Cat said sulkily.

Nora didn't argue.

"He'll force me to some horrid place in the country."

"Yes, that is likely true."

"Please don't tell him."

"Cat, I won't lie to him if he asks—I never lie to him."

"I know," Cat said spitefully, "I heard *all* about you these five past nights."

Nora stiffened beside her and Cat immediately regretted the ugly insinuation.

"I'm sorry, Nora, really! Please don't—"

"Shhhhh." Nora kissed the top of Cat's head and she felt herself melting at the gesture of affection. Was that odd?

"I can't believe Edward would think to ask such a thing in a hundred years," Nora finally said. "Just put the key back where you found it. *Immediately.*"

"I will," Cat promised, conveniently forgetting to mention she'd already done that after having her own copy made on one of her secret jaunts. Jaunts that were now over, thanks to Tedward.

"And I want you to promise me you won't go in there again."

"*Nora!*"

"I mean it. Promise me or I will go to Edward right now."

Cat knew she meant it—she'd never met a person as loyal and obedient as Nora before—at least the way she was to Edward. "I'll promise, Nora, but—"

"But what?"

"But I want to know *more*. I want t-to *do* some of those things. Not the whippings," she added quickly, shivering. "But some of the other things looked . . . nice." They looked a lot more than that, but Cat kept the business about rubbing herself almost raw to herself. "Nora?" she asked when the other woman said nothing.

"Cat, you know Edward would be very happy to teach you the things you saw tonight. You don't have to do all of them—or even any of them. There are an infinite number of ways to make love. Sex is one of life's greatest joys and Edward is a wonderful lover. He would be gentle and make you very happy."

Cat's stomach pitched at the disgusting thought. She willed herself to say what she wanted but she was too much of a coward. She was more afraid than anything in a long time, not since that very first night when Edward had put his *enormous* breeding organ inside her, making her worry she would break inside or tear in half. Of course five nights of watching Edward and Nora had taught her that Edward had been *exceptionally* restrained with her. She shivered at the memory of how brutally and frequently he had—*fucked*—Nora. Even in her *mouth* and back *there.*

Thinking that word—fuck, which Edward used incessantly, along with other, even more crude terms—made the tingling between her thighs even more difficult to ignore.

"Cat? Would you like me to talk to him for you?"

"No!"

They both jumped at the abrupt word.

"I won't," Nora soothed. "But you really should approach him yourself and—"

"It isn't him I want, Nora," she gritted her teeth and squeezed her eyes shut. "It's *you.*"

Chapter Twenty

Nora was glad it was dark because she could not imagine what her face might have given away: simple shock?

Or would it have been something less flattering—like greedy pleasure that this gorgeous, nubile young woman would never want Edward the way she did?

"Nora?"

Cat didn't sound like her usual, confident self and Nora could imagine how embarrassed she was right now. She was like a virgin experiencing sexual attraction for the first time—at least it sounded that way. Nora chewed her lip. She needed to be careful what she said—she needed to say the right thing. She needed—

"*Nora?*"

"It's all right Cat, I'm sorry—I'm not shocked or disgusted, I was just considering what to say." She realized the girl had pulled away when she made her disclosure and pulled her closer. "Come here," she murmured, kissing her head again. She didn't know why she felt so much older than her. Cat was only six years her junior and she was a pregnant woman— an experience Nora had never had and likely never would.

A tentative hand on her thigh reminded her, suddenly, that she'd gone to bed naked.

She swallowed audibly in the darkness. *Now what do I do?*

Cat's hand slid up her leg, her fingers unspeakably soft and timid, not stopping until they touched her mound and she sucked in a sharp breath.

"Nora?"

"Yes, Cat?"

"You can tell me no if you don't want me to, but I was—" she broke off and her insecurity and misery stabbed at Nora's heart.

"You can touch me wherever you want."

This is a bad, bad, bad, bad, bad idea, a voice in Nora's head shrieked.

"Really?"

Say no.

"Yes, really. Is it my piercing you want to touch?"

She heard a gulping sound and then a hoarse whisper, "All of you. I want to touch all of you."

Nora's heart thudded at the lust in the other woman's voice. It was the same reaction she had whenever she knew somebody wanted her—it was her fatal flaw: she simply could not deny a person she liked—male, female, it made no difference to her—the pleasure of her body. It was, she knew, not normal.

Cat's hand crept further and Nora spread for her, her core already pulsing with anticipation, because—yes—she was an immoral whore.

Cat slid a finger across her shaved mound—which Edward sedulously groomed—and sucked in a breath. "You're so soft." Her finger lightly touched the ring. Edward had sucked her piercing for a good hour tonight and it was sore, but she forced herself to lie still and take Cat's tentative touches.

"Edward likes to tongue it and suck on it," Cat said in a tone that suggested she wanted to know what that was all about.

"Yes, he does."

"Edward seems rather obsessed by your body."

Nora laughed softly. "Yes, he is."

"That must be nice—to have somebody want you so much."

Nora was about to tell her that she would find that one day herself when she remembered that Cat could never, ever, be unfaithful to Edward. It didn't matter if he no longer went to Cat after she'd given him his two children. Edward guarded what was his—those things and people he considered *his* possessions—more jealously than any person Nora had ever met. He would never let Cat go. He would likely kill Nora if he caught them right now.

Naturally the thought of incurring his anger aroused her.

Cat's finger dipped between her swollen lips and swept up and down, from the base of her peak to her opening.

"That feels good, Cat," Nora praised.

Cat's hand shook and Nora heard her gulp.

"Would you like me to touch you—with my mouth?" Nora offered.

You have crossed the point of no return. The voice in her head sounded like what God must sound like—or what her father had always sounded like when speaking God's word.

Yes, of course she'd crossed a point of no return; since when had she ever shied away from anything?

✳✳✳

Cat wanted Nora so bad she couldn't stop shaking.

"Shhh," Nora soothed as she pulled the blankets back. "Can I take this off?" She asked, her hands lifting Cat's hideous nightgown.

"Yes, please." Her voice was a whisper but her body thundered.

Nora's hands were deft and quick and she lifted the gown and Cat ducked out of it. She was naked with another person for the first time in her life. What would Nora think of her body? It looked nothing like her own—sleek, pale, and perfect. Her own breasts were too big and floppy and—

"Beautiful," Nora murmured as she cupped one of Cat's breasts with her cool, soft hand.

Cat's shivering intensified and the place between her legs clenched and clenched and—

"Poor kitten," Nora whispered against her nipple, making Cat cry out. "You need to come so badly."

Her head grew woozy at the crude word, which Nora was speaking to *her.* She hadn't realized she'd spread her legs until Nora said, "What a lovely invitation. May I touch your stomach?"

Cat startled at the question, stunned anyone would want to touch her rapidly thickening body.

"Yes, Nora. Please," Cat added.

Nora positioned herself between Cat's thighs, pushing them wider, making her feel—*wicked, exposed, desirable.*

Cat felt warm breath on her belly and then Nora's hands.

"Mmmm," she hummed, massaging Cat in a way that felt . . . *worshipful.* "May I kiss you—lick you?"

Cat thought her head might spin off. "Please," she croaked, sounding just like a frog.

First Nora's lips touched her navel, kissing softly, teasingly. Then her tongue flicked inside the dimple, again and again.

174

Cat moaned as Nora's mouth and tongue drifted down and down, not stopping at the mass of hair that covered her. Instead, she buried her nose in Cat's swollen crease and inhaled deeply. "Mmm, you smell so sweet."

Cat's face and throat and chest burned with embarrassment at the primitive, *animal* action, but she spread wider and tilted her hips without even realizing it.

Nora chuckled softly. "So eager," she murmured, her hands moving to Cat's lower lips and parting them.

Her mouth, when it finally touched Cat, was like that last drop of water that made the dam break and she shuddered, the now familiar pleasure rippling through her.

Nora tongued her less sensitive flesh, avoiding the source of her pleasure—which was almost painful to the touch, now—while Cat rode out her climax.

It was different with somebody else, she realized groggily as Nora continued to lick and kiss and caress and Cat drifted in a state of boneless pleasure.

Nora's mouth never stopped moving, licking, sucking, and plunging her tongue into *there,* the place where only Edward had ever been.

Cat moaned and pushed against her, wanting her deeper. Nora's finger joined her thrusting tongue and began to pump in and out of her while her mouth moved to Cat's *clitoris*—the word sounding unspeakably dirty even in her mind.

Soon Nora was using two fingers, plunging into her while sucking. It wasn't long before Cat experienced a familiar building in her pelvis; she was going to have another orgasm.

"Yes," Cat murmured, arching and spreading, encouraged by Nora's groans of pleasure to thrust against her, enraptured by the feeling of her hot, soft, sucking mouth that brought her up and up and up and up and—

"Ah, God. Nora," she cried out, muffling the words with a pillow, ripples of pleasure carrying her toward bliss.

This was what it was meant to be like: *this.*

Chapter Twenty-One

For once, Nora managed to slip out of the house without one of the Thomases following her. She simply did not want them reporting to Edward that she'd visited Lord Anthony Howell, a prominent politician and the son of one duke and uncle of another. Edward would know immediately the only way that Nora would have met such a man.

So, she'd put on her old gray cloak, which Mary had stuffed in the far back of a wardrobe and hurried toward the prestigious address on the letter.

She had plenty of money to hail a ride, but she needed to walk after last night. If she was wise, she'd *keep* walking as far as she had to in order to get out of Edward's reach.

Cat had fallen asleep after a shocking number of orgasms and Nora had hated to rouse her, but she needed to at least get dressed. If Cat was found asleep in Nora's bed that could be easily explained—everyone knew them to be friends. If she was found *naked* in Nora's bed …

She'd been adorably shy, her deep flush making her even more beautiful. Nora had enjoyed Cat's body, which was lush and sweet and responsive, but the worshipful look in Cat's eyes had made her question the wisdom of what she'd done more than ever.

"Cat," she'd said just before the girl left. "You must hide this from Edward, you know that—don't you?"

She'd smiled, her lovely face radiant, "It will be our secret, Nora."

Nora had wanted to cry—and start packing; she'd have more luck hiding a volcanic eruption in the house than Cat's euphoria. If ever Nora had seen a well-pleasured woman, it was Cat that morning.

She chewed her lip as she scurried along, dodging early morning delivery wagons, domestics, and a host of other people heading to work.

Nora had decided she'd best be able to hide her excursion the earlier she left. She often painted in the morning, so she'd left a note on the bed for Mary telling her she was painting and did not want to be disturbed. And then she'd frantically searched for the key she'd never used before and locked the sunroom door. Not that she was sure what *that* would achieve in the—albeit unlikely—event that Edward came looking for her. If Edward wanted in and she didn't answer him, he'd break down the door. No part of her, she knew, was off-limits in his mind.

Nora knew before she even walked up the steps to Lord Anthony's town house what had happened: a black wreath was on the door and all the drapes were drawn. It was a house of mourning.

Nora's eyes glazed with tears; she was too late. She squeezed her eyes shut, aware she must look odd standing on the middle of the sidewalk staring up at the house, but unable to move.

"Nora?"

She jolted at the voice, her eyes flying open.

"Oh, I say—sorry to startle you."

She looked up at a vaguely familiar face.

He smiled shyly, his pale cheeks flushing. "You might not recall me. I'm—"

"The Duke of Glenway, Lord Anthony's nephew." As if a whore were likely to forget a duke she'd fucked.

He grinned. "Jolly good to see you."

Nora found his obvious pleasure at being remembered—especially by a prostitute—endearing. "Thank you, Your Grace." She paused, not sure what—if anything—to say.

"I daresay you're here in response to Uncle Tony's letter?"

She blinked, both at his knowledge of the letter and at the thought of such a dignified man being referred to as "Tony".

"I didn't receive his letter until yesterday."

The duke grimaced. "Ah, yes, I see. No, I meant the other letter—from the solicitor?"

"No." She took the crumpled envelope out of her reticule. "This is all I received—a brief message asking me to come see him." She swallowed hard. "I'm terribly disappointed I am too late. I always—" she broke off, remembering she wasn't Nora Hudson, a wealthy businessman's niece, but Nora Hudson the whore.

He nodded, his expression kind and understanding. "Uncle Tony spoke of you more than once."

"He did?"

"Oh yes, he was very fond of you. And impressed by your aspiration to be a painter."

She flushed with a mixture of pleasure and pain. She'd never shown him a painting and hoped he might have seen hers at the exhibit.

"Won't you come inside?" he offered.

"I don't want to put you out."

"No bother, this way I can give you the solicitor's direction so you can get my uncle's letter. Unless you'd like me to send it to you—wherever you are living now." Again the charming blush.

Nora thought of Edward's almost maniacal obsession with everything concerning her and said, "It would be better if I went to fetch it."

"We'll just pop inside and I shall give you their card."

The door opened when they reached the top step and a very old butler greeted them. Crates and trunks were everywhere.

"Pardon the mess," the duke said as he led her out of the very elegant foyer and up the stairs. "I am moving my uncle's things to where I can go over them at my leisure." He opened a door at the top of the stairs and Nora stepped into a lovely two-story library.

"My goodness," she said.

The duke gave her a tolerant smile, no doubt accustomed to far greater grandeur. "Yes, my uncle loved his books. Now," he said to himself, "where would that be?"

While he searched a massive desk, Nora looked at the shelves, which hadn't yet been packed away into boxes. Once again, her eyes clouded over with tears—how was it possible to pack such a grand life as Lord Anthony's into just a few crates and containers? It simply sucked away all one's hope—what was the point of it all?

"Ah-ha!"

She turned to find the duke triumphant. She took the card from him. "Thank you, Your Grace."

He nodded, his cheeks streaked with red. "My pleasure, my pleasure. I'm popping by their offices today and will let them know you'll be coming."

"It might not be for a few days—"

"The bequest is yours, no matter how long you take to claim it."

Nora blinked down at the card. Bequest?

"I say, Nora." She glanced up at his voice, which had dropped several levels and Nora knew what he would say. "I enjoyed Belinda, but I wouldn't mind visiting you sometime—wherever you are working now."

Nora smiled. "I'm honored, Your Grace, but I'm afraid I'm with one man, now."

"Ah," he said, looking disappointed but luckily taking no offense. "Not the sharing type, then." He chuckled.

"No," Nora agreed with a wry smile, "Definitely not the sharing type."

Chapter Twenty-Two

Catherine

Cat was in love and nobody was going to spoil it. Not *Tedward* with his beastliness, not her mother with her letters telling Cat it was her responsibility to leave London and sequester her swelling body somewhere in the country, where nobody could see it. And—most especially—not Ceddy—who'd come back to London with creditors snapping at his heels and some police officer or such, who'd followed him all the way from Paris.

Her brother looked unhealthy—pale, skinny, and always sweating. And his mind seemed to have become addled and he wouldn't stop his nasty insinuations and dirty little digs about Nora.

Even Nora seemed determined to cast shade on what wondrous things they shared with one another in the privacy of her bed—although not as often as Cat wanted.

"Let's run away together, Nora."

It was the dog days of summer and they were sitting in her sunroom, which was sweltering. Nora had stripped down to her chemise and was painting Cat, who wore nothing—not even a fig leaf. She was almost five months along and her belly was rounded and ugly. She personally despised her body but Nora seemed to love it. Indeed, she seemed to view her belly the way Edward viewed Nora's entire body.

When Nora didn't respond to Cat's suggestion—her pale eyes stranger than ever as she painted with an expression of frightening intensity—Cat brought up the subject that ate at her day and night, now. "I don't like all the marks he leaves on you," she said, sounding petulant to her own ears.

"Hmmm?"

"Nora, are you listening?"

Nora seemed to wake from a deep sleep. "I'm sorry, what was that?"

Cat tried to swallow her irritation, but really, the woman could be maddening. She rarely seemed to say *no* directly, yet she always appeared to get her way. Quite frankly, Cat had wished more than once that she could ask Edward how he managed to bring her to heel so easily. Cat grinned at the thought: he'd pop his tightly wedged cork if he had any idea of what went on in this room almost every day. But still not often enough for Cat.

"Nora," she snapped, breaking her pose, which had her lying demurely on her side. "I want you to paint me like this." She opened her knees wide, the bottom of her feet together, looking—she knew—like a wanton harlot. But it finally got Nora's attention, setting that pulse at the base of her throat flickering like the wings of a hummingbird. Cat ran a hand over her already wet slit and then dipped her middle finger into her body. "Do you like me this way?" She moved her finger in and out, her hips pulsing. "Don't you want to come taste me? Feel me?"

Nora's generally expressionless face broke into a smile. "What a little tart you are," she said, but Cat could tell she was pleased with her sluttishness because she put aside her brush—not even bothering to clean it—pulled off her chemise and threw it on the floor before sinking naked to her knees at the foot of the chaise where Cat lounged, her mesmerizing eyes moving from Cat's swollen stomach to her wide-spread sex.

"You are perfect."

The worshipful look on Nora's face and tone in her voice drove Cat far too quickly toward the precipice.

Nora slid a finger—almost casually—up Cat's cunt—that's how she thought of it and referred to it now: her *cunt*. They both groaned.

"So tight," Nora murmured, her pupils huge. "Would you let me paint you this way, Cat?" She sounded and looked as if she were in a fugue state. "Spread wide, wet—perhaps your hand touching you here?" Nora's thumb rubbed the base of Cat's clitoris, which she'd learned was embarrassingly large—at least in comparison to Nora's tiny bud. Nora had assured her that all women were different, but Cat didn't care— she'd have liked to look like Nora. "It wouldn't be a fast painting," Nora mused, wicked fingers stroking. "We'd have to take frequent breaks to keep you swollen, slick, and ready."

Cat's entire body clenched at her suggestion and Nora gave a low laugh as her hand began to pump. "Well, then. I suppose there's my answer."

Cat shivered, spreading like a butterfly for her lover. "Please, Nora, suck me."

She never had to ask her twice.

As Nora buried her skilled, insatiable tongue in her cunt Cat reached down and twisted one of her tiny nipples, which had rings right through them. Edward had taken Nora to Bernina's and had her pierced while he watched. Cat had been furious at not being allowed to go, although she knew it would have been impossible.

It irked her that Edward had—yet again—marked Nora as his, when there was no sign of Cat's possession of her body. So Cat tugged harder, twisting and pulling Nora's small, perfect breasts to cruel points.

"Mmmmm," Nora moaned, her body shuddering with pleasure.

Cat marveled at Nora's bizarre need for pain, wondering more and more if she'd be able to whip Nora to an orgasm the way Edward could. She would be willing to try it as she *loved* handling Nora's spare, svelte body. Her own body was heavy, increasingly uncomfortable to live in, and her breasts seemed to grow larger every day.

"I'm going to look like a cow, soon," she murmured as Nora languidly fucked her with her finger. "Will you still want me? Or will you turn away when I'm distended with a belly so big I shan't be able to see my own feet."

"I'll want you more," Nora said, groaning as if the disgusting picture Cat had just described for her was something that aroused her. And then she bit Cat's erect clitoris almost hard enough to hurt.

Cat shuddered. "My God, Nora!" Perhaps there was something to this pain business after all?

"Will you let me suck on your breasts when they're heavy with milk," Nora murmured against her, her slick hard tongue moving in rhythmic strokes.

Cat's entire body shook at Nora's shocking words and Nora chuckled, adding a second finger to the first, stretching her.

Lord, but the woman could always amaze her with a new, lower, level of filthiness. And how her body *loved* it. Besides, if she was thinking of sucking her breasts when they were filled with milk—and she *would* do it,

Cat knew that—that meant Nora would be staying at least until she'd gotten rid of this lump inside her.

Every day she worried about Edward catching them. Whatever he did with *her*, she knew he'd never let her see Nora again. And if she couldn't have Nora—

Her body began to tighten, the muscles of her sex beginning their exquisite contractions, her mind emptying of thoughts like water down a drain.

"Oh, God Nora," she moaned as her pleasure overcame her and she pressed Nora's head into her convulsing sex. "I love you so—"

"Well, well, well—what have we here?"

✳✳✳

Nora's eyes flew open at the sound of the loathsome voice and Cat jerked upright, covering her breasts with her hands.

Viscount Rowland—Cat's repulsive brother—just chuckled. "Lord, Cat, you look like a bloated whale—please *do* cover up." His nasty blue eyes slid to Nora. "But I like what I see eating your cunt."

Nora pushed to her feet, her mind pulsing with fury at his whale comment. She made no effort to cover herself as she strode toward him.

"Bloody hell," he murmured, his eyes slithering over her like worms. "You've changed a bit since I last saw you."

"What?" Cat demanded behind her.

Nora briefly shut her eyes, opening them again when Ceddy chuckled. "What, didn't Nora tell you that I had her first? Before the Prince of Tin, even." He gave Nora an evil grin. "Quite the arrangement you have here—the master of the house at night, the mistress during the day. What about the brother? When do I get my turn?"

Nora snorted and stooped to pick up her chemise, pulling it over her head before turning back to him. "You've done so many drugs I doubt you can even get hard any longer, *Ceddy*. Let's get to what you really want: money."

His face shifted into an ugly snarl. "Oh, and you have that—do you, along with that magical cunt of yours?"

"I do."

They both turned to Cat, who'd wrapped her silk robe tightly around her body.

Ceddy's eyebrows shot up. "Do tell, sis."

"I have five thousand pounds you can have, if you leave without saying a word to Edward."

He laughed, but his eyes sharpened. Nora could see he would leap on the offer, but first he wanted to toy with them. "Why shouldn't I take the money *and* tell him."

Nora rarely played cards, but she knew an ace when she had one. "Because I will tell him that it was you who beat me badly enough to leave scars on my body. And I think you know what he will do. He'll not only thrash you to within an inch of your life, he'll cut off your supply of money—and likely your prick. He committed to restoring your estates, Ceddy, not your vile habits. I have a fair idea of how much of your debt he paid off when you came running to him for help this last time. What happened in Paris, Ceddy? What will you do the next time if there is nobody to pay off your debts?"

His eyes glittered with poison and she knew she'd made an enemy for life. "I'll take the money and be gone as soon as my man packs my things."

Cat came toward them, her chin lifted, looking bloody majestic. "Leave now—choose your hotel and I will send Pearson with the money."

Ceddy looked like he wanted to argue, but he wanted the money more. His lover—opium—was even more cruel to him than he'd once been to Nora.

Nora shut the door once he'd gone and turned to Cat, sagging against the smooth wood.

"Five thousand pounds, Cat? Wherever will you get that?" Nora's mind raced as she thought of things to sell.

Cat giggled, sounding like the eighteen-year-old she was. "I've already got it."

"Good Lord, what kind of allowance does he give you?"

"It's not my allowance—I stole it from his dresser drawer."

Nora was torn between admiration and terror. "My God, Cat, if he ever finds out—"

"He already did," Cat said, no longer a girl, but a weary wife. "He came to me, of course, and I told him Chrissy took it."

Chrissy had been a pretty parlor maid whom Edward had sacked some time back.

Nora was sick with shock. "Cat! How could you blame your theft on a servant?"

Cat shrugged, arrogant and not comprehending what she'd done. "If it hadn't been her, it would have been me."

Nora wanted to cry at such a callous, cruel reaction.

"What? Why are you looking at me that way, Nora?" Cat demanded peevishly. "You should be glad I took it or we'd never be able to get rid of Ceddy."

She flounced out of the room, which made Nora believe that she *had* realized what she'd done was terrible. Nora would have to find out if any of the servants knew Chrissy. Maybe she could write the girl a letter of recommendation or help her find a position if she hadn't already.

That was a great deal of money to be accused of stealing. What if Edward had thrown the girl in jail?

Nora chewed her lip until she tasted metal. There was only one way to find out what had happened to the poor girl and that was to ask Edward.

Chapter Twenty-Three

Edward collapsed back onto the bed, his body slick with sweat from the miserable summer heat and the vigorous bout of fucking.

Nora knew now was as good a time as any. "Edward?"

"Hmm?"

"You know that parlor maid you discharged?"

Edward opened his eyes and met hers in the mirror over the bed. He snorted. "You mean the one Catherine accused of stealing my money when it was really her?"

She turned to him, rather than his reflection, eyes wide.

He was smiling sardonically. "You must think I'm soft in the head if you believe I'd credit anything that thieving little cat says."

"But—"

His sensual lips curved into a smile. "I like this new look on you—what would you call it? Speechless? Stunned? Worshipful of my mental acuity?"

"How did you know?"

"No great mystery, Nelson saw her sneaking out of my rooms one night."

Nora's heart almost stopped—and he'd not noticed the missing key? She frowned. Had she lied to Nora and really made a copy? Cat knew of Edward's obsessive neatness and orderliness as well as Nora, and frequently mocked him. Cat would know he'd notice a missing key, especially *this* key.

Nora shook her head. Why the little cat, indeed.

"Nora?"

She turned to him, her heart beating faster than it had been ten minutes earlier. "Yes, Edward?"

"Why won't you let us go out of town?"

She almost fainted with relief at the return of this annoying subject, which was far better than thinking about Catherine and her key. Was Cat under the bed right now? Nora grimaced—she wouldn't be bloody surprised.

"Nora," he said in a tone that communicated his displeasure. He liked her talking more, but still demanded obedience.

"I never said *you* couldn't go," she reminded him for the hundredth time. Edward was like a bulldog—once his jaws closed on something, he never let go.

"You said you wouldn't go with us—the same thing."

She sighed and shook her head. Although she talked far more now, she still didn't have the energy to argue as much as he liked to do.

✳✳✳

Edward sensed something was off with Nora tonight, but he couldn't pin it down. He changed the subject. "I'm bloody grateful that leech is gone."

Nora knew who he meant. "Me too."

"Yes," he mused, "I noticed right from the beginning you didn't care for him."

"Is there anyone who does?"

He laughed. One of the things he'd discovered about his Nora when she started talking was that she possessed a wicked tongue.

He reached over and played with one of her nipples, watching his hand in the mirror, watching her body react to his touch like a musical instrument that had been made tuned especially for him. His. His Nora.

"Touch yourself," he ordered when he saw her hips begin to move, tugging harder and harder on her rings. She could work an orgasm out of herself with her fingers far quicker than he could and he wanted to learn how she did it, so he watched her closely.

Her slender fingers flicked and pulled and scratched and prodded faster than he could see. Her skin mottled, not yet over her last orgasm, and she grunted, tensing. God, but she was a lean, muscular woman. Who would have thought he'd find such a spare body so very inviting? Her belly, when it clenched with her climax, was tautly ridged with muscles—reminding him, oddly, of Smith.

She shuddered and Edward stilled his hand and watched her as she tossed her head side to side, her body straining to hang on to her pleasure as long as possible, the cords in her neck like cables.

"That was the fastest one yet," he said.

She shook with tired laughter. "Is everything a contest with you, Edward?"

He considered her question while absently stroking his chest, flexing, and studying his own body in the mirror. Was he becoming flabby? He met her eyes and flushed to find her watching him. What had she asked him? Oh, yes.

"What's wrong with that?" he asked.

She shook her head. "Nothing. I was just asking."

He had to ask; he couldn't stop himself. "When are you going to open that box?"

"Oh, Edward. Please don't."

"What? Aren't you curious?" He'd learned about the bequest the way he learned about everything: through his spies. The only places he didn't employ spies was here and in her chambers. A man had to draw the line somewhere. Still, he wanted to know what was in that box.

"I think it's a priceless jewel," he said musingly.

She laughed and he knew she enjoyed this stupid guessing game they played.

"You are so unimaginative," she chided, her playful tone as arousing to him as binding her body in black leather—*more*, actually.

"Oh?" he said, mockingly offended. "I suppose you've got a more *creative* idea?"

"I think it's the world's smallest donkey."

Edward almost choked on his laughter. Who would have imagined he would enjoy laughing in bed with a woman?

"It's your turn," she said.

"No, I give in." He could never beat her at this game, she always had a more creative, outlandish answer. Which reminded him of something—her paintings. "It occurs to me—rather late, I'll admit, that I've never seen one of your paintings."

She stiffened and turned slowly to him, the closed expression he'd not seen for some time taking over her face.

What was this?

"Nora? Don't you want me to see them?"

For the first time ever, she blushed. "I—well, they're rather private."

"Private," he repeated flatly, his temperature spiking. "You mean from me."

"No, of course not. It's just that some are—well, not ready for public display. I have a few I wouldn't mind showing you—I will bring them out tomorrow."

"You don't need to go to that effort—you paint in the sunroom, don't you? I can come and look at them there."

"I'd, well, I'd rather bring them out. If you don't mind."

He *did* mind. What the hell was all this? He'd never given any thought to her harmless daubing, but if he wanted to enter any room in his house, he would do it—Nora's permission was not necessary.

"Edward?"

His heart was racing as it did when he'd spotted some new angle in one of his businesses. "Hmm?"

"I can see you are going to turn this into an obsession."

He frowned, not caring to hear that word applied to him. "I am *not* obsessive."

She immediately retreated. "I'm sorry, I didn't mean to be offensive."

"Do *you* think I'm obsessive?" He waited. To his knowledge, she had never lied to him.

She hesitated, but then said, very softly, "Yes, Edward, I do."

Rage and some other emotion boiled up inside him—what? Embarrassment?

"About what?" he snapped.

"Well, about many things."

"Name one."

She hesitated again.

"Go on, name one."

"This conversation is a good example. Why do you care if I think you exhibit obsessive behavior? Just because you now know what I think makes no difference. I've thought it all along without you knowing and it never bothered you."

Edward's head spun, as if he'd drunk an entire bottle of spirits. "I can't even begin to understand what that means."

"Edward." She leaned up on her elbow and looked down at him.

He frowned, unwilling to look at her. "What?"

"Don't be angry. I like the way you are—there is nothing to be angry about."

"Except my obsessiveness."

"Well, sometimes that is a very good thing."

He turned to her. "When?"

She wiggled in a way he found adorable—all the more so because she'd never done it before. "Well, your obsession with my bottom, for instance."

Edward felt a stirring of interest in his cock. Oh, he was not stupid, he knew what she was doing—distracting him with her body—but that didn't mean he couldn't enjoy it.

"It's only once tonight—unless you count the other," he pointed out.

She shook her head, her expression serious but her unearthly eyes glinting with humor and arousal. "I don't count my cunt, Edward." He shivered with excitement. He loved it when she used vulgar words. "I only count my back hole."

"It's still early," he said in a deliberately musing way.

She smiled—which he'd still not become used to—and turned onto her stomach before getting on her hands and knees, canting her plugged arse at the very angle most comfortable for him to enter her. His prick—which had already spent twice this evening—was as hard as iron again.

"I want you to suck me, first," he ordered, just to make sure she knew which of them was in control and who made their decisions.

She lifted her chin, her expression demure. "Of course, Edward."

❋❋❋

Nora was exhausted. The last few weeks had been more rigorous than her time in various whorehouses. She lay in her bed even though the sun was already up several hours. She wanted to crawl back under the covers.

Last night was the closest she'd come to lying to Edward—about her paintings. But if he came into her small studio, he'd look and pry and peek and prod. He would find things—no matter how hard she tried to hide them. She would start tucking things away today so perhaps she could sooth his wounded feelings and invite him in tomorrow. And he *was* hurt, she'd seen it. Even when he'd left their bed at dawn this morning—having broken his record and leaving her full of his spend and wearing a very large, heavy plug—she'd known he hadn't forgotten.

There was a light knock on the door.

Oh God. Please don't let it be Cat. My jaw is almost dislocated from sucking Edward to hardness those last two times.

Before she could say to enter the door opened: it was Edward. He hesitated on the threshold until she smiled and sat up—she'd put on a nightgown already—and said, "Please, come in."

She could sense his relief from across the room. His hands were flexing at his sides and he glanced around as if he'd never seen the room before.

"I haven't been here since that first day," he explained, as if she didn't know that.

Nora stood and took her dressing gown from the foot of the bed; it wouldn't do to be seen talking with her *uncle* partially dressed. She secured the tie and gestured to the sitting room. "Do you wish to talk to me? Perhaps sit a while?"

He flushed and she realized, for the first time since she'd known him, that he was embarrassed. "Maybe for a moment."

He took the biggest chair and she sat across from him. "What is it, Edward?" she prodded when his lips remained tightly pressed together.

"I've come to apologize."

Nora goggled.

He laughed—but it too, like his smile—was tinged with embarrassment. "Judging by your expression that is a rare beast, indeed."

"No, no—it's not that. It's just that I wasn't aware you'd insulted me."

"I've been rather selfish."

Edward saying he was "rather" selfish was like saying the ocean was "rather" wet.

"I never asked you about your painting and when I finally did I went bulling in." He frowned down at his hands. "It was wrong of me—in several ways." He glanced up, his dark eyes hopeful. "But I would like to get better about things like that. A man should treat his wi—"

It was like witnessing a rare celestial event—an eclipse or meteor shower, and a hundred—perhaps a thousand—emotions flitted across his face as Edward realized what he'd almost said. And then, it struck him with the force of a mallet to the forehead: what he'd done to her, to him, maybe even what he'd done to Cat.

His blankness only lasted a second before he looked utterly stricken—there was no other word for it. He blinked as if something had—and was still—blinding him, and then lurched to his feet. "I have to go," he muttered, his eyes stark.

Nora watched him walk from the room like a man sleepwalking.

✳✳✳

Edward didn't go to *their* room that night or the next. Instead, he went to the Bellaire, the only place that had no associations of Nora.

There were new girls since his last visit and he engaged two of them, and then a different pair the next day, never leaving his room to go to work or home.

The whores were skilled—very skilled—and they managed to get him off over and over again in spite of the fact he felt like a corpse.

He engaged in every perversion he could think of with the women, hoping he could *feel* something; there was nothing.

But if there was one thing Edward was not, it was a quitter.

So, he stayed for another day and he just kept going forward, like a soldier.

But instead of marching like a soldier, he was listlessly fucking, and had been for what felt like his entire life.

He was currently embedded in one of the whores, from behind, while she tongued and pleasured another woman—an arrangement he had once favored greatly. He blinked his eyes to clear them as he studied the woman being pleasured by her friend. She was tied to the bed—he must have done it—and had done a good job of it, too. He'd securing her ankles and wrists with straps that bit into her skin and pulled her so wide it had to hurt—but he could see she was suffering with a smile on because she knew it meant a great deal of money. It was a sight that would normally interest him—enflame him. But not anymore.

He simply could not go on.

He pulled his already wilting cock out of the woman whose ass bore several of his handprints and a goodly number of whip marks.

"Get out," he said, stumbling as he climbed off the bed. He went to his coat and yanked out his wallet, taking out the fat wad of notes

192

without even looking at them and thrusting them into one of the women's hands. "Get out, *now*."

He waited till they'd gathered their clothes and slipped out the door before dropping into a chair and taking his head in his hands. Edward still could not believe it. How could he have been so stupid? He, who always studied every angle of a transaction as carefully as a game of billiards—looking ahead five, ten moves? How had he not seen where this was going?

How had he not seen it was Nora, all along: Nora.

The last months became dreadfully clear and ugly, just like this gaudy whorehouse looked when exposed to the harsh light of day.

Oh, he *knew* that Nora had enjoyed the courtship phase as much as he did. He'd felt her body quivering and clenching at the exquisite degradation every time Edward fucked her and told her how he would marry and breed another, keeping her as his private whore.

And he'd done exactly that—married Catherine—the spoiled daughter of a marquess who'd hated him from the beginning and—Edward realized like a slow-witted fool—had perfect justification for doing so.

He tried to take some comfort out of the fact that although Edward had made one bad decision after another, at least Nora had received some pleasure out of it. But that was phenomenally unconvincing. He could have given her the same sensations without locking himself into a marriage with another woman—forever cut off from the woman he only now realized he loved. Yes, he was obsessed with her, but he loved her in the only way he knew how.

She's yours—for at least a year, likely longer. What does it matter if she's not your wife? Nora is yours.

But instead of feeling comforted, he lowered his head in his hands and gave free rein to his anguish.

✳✳✳

"*Forget* about Edward," Cat said for the millionth time. "He's probably at some brothel right as I speak." She saw Nora flinch and had a brief pang of remorse. But she shoved it aside. The sooner Nora learned Edward was no good for her, the sooner they could get on with their lives, without him. They could do like those two women who'd moved to Wales together. Although Cat didn't think either of them had been married when they ran off together—and likely not pregnant, either. But those were just details and didn't matter. Besides, now a woman could seek a divorce without fear of public stoning.

Cat realized Nora hadn't responded. They were in the sunroom. But instead of painting and fucking, they were sitting here talking. About *Tedward.*

"Nora, come here, I want you."

For the first time ever, Nora said, "No."

She stood and left the sunroom not bothering to shut the door even though Cat was naked. By the time she'd wrapped her robe around her and went into the bedroom it was to find Nora staring at a small chest.

"What's in that box?"

"A man and woman who love each other and live happily ever after."

Cat couldn't have heard that right. "Nora?"

Nora turned to her and smiled, but it was a strained smile. "Nothing, just a foolish jest. Will you give me half an hour, Cat? Perhaps you might go and put on the gown we chose—the rose one."

Cat squinted, not liking her odd expression. "Of course—if you're sure you'll be all right."

"I'll be fine."

Cat would remember her words later.

❋❋❋

Nora stared at the box, still unwilling to open it although it had been in her possession for over a month.

Something about the mystery it represented soothed her. Or maybe she liked it because it was such an easy mystery to solve—unlike the riddle of what had happened to her life. All she had to do to solve *this* riddle was open the box.

She took the small key from her bedside table and fitted it into the lock. It clicked open easily. Inside there were no jewels or the world's smallest donkey or even a couple who loved one another and lived happily ever after. There was a letter with her name on it and a fat packet of documents—the kind you received after a large transaction. A contract of some sort.

Nora sat on the bed and opened the letter.

Nora:

I can imagine how you must have stared at this box and wondered what I could possibly have to give you. If I know you—and I flatter myself that I do, a little—you didn't open the box immediately."

Nora smiled, her eyes watering.

"I've wondered about you since our last night—questioning whether I did the right thing by not stopping you—by not offering for you, myself. At the time it seemed selfish: you are a young woman and deserve a man your age. But in the weeks that followed, I thought of you daily—not just about all the pleasure you gave me, but about what mark I would leave on the world. I know that is an old man's arrogance, but the thought has been heavy on my mind. Two weeks after you left, I did a bad thing: I pried into your life. I knew from our time together that you were good friends with the young man named Charles."

Nora stopped and shook her head. "Charles, Charles, Charles," she said under her breath. But for once she was glad of his greedy nature.

"He wouldn't take my money—" Nora stopped to offer up a silent apology to her friend and continued. *"But he did allow me to look at the three paintings you were submitting to the Royal Academy. All I can say, dear Nora, is that what I saw humbled me. You are a magnificent artist and will one day be a great one—your name long remembered."*

Her tears fell on the page but she kept reading.

"And this is where the story comes back around to me, my dear, because I'm a selfish old man. I will die soon, very soon. Being with you on your last night at Tosca's was also my last night of pleasure. I was brought to bed shortly after that night, and I will never leave it under my own locomotion. As I've lain here in this bed, week after week, I realize there is a way to snatch a tiny bit of posterity: I can hitch my wagon to a star. You, Nora, are that star. The papers in the box will see to it you are never homeless and hungry. I've given you a cottage—a small manor, really—that has been in my family for generations. I've spoken to His Grace about the disposition of the house and the establishment of a trust for you. He is a wealthy man in his own right and you need not fear any anger or retribution on his part. I hope that you will find shelter at Rose Cottage and that my house, which I loved dearly although I spent so little time there, will feed your spirit. But, most of all, I hope you will paint. And paint. And paint. All I ask of you is that you never doubt yourself and that you keep painting.

I've left enough in trust for you that you will not have to worry. I hope—being the vain man I am—that someday, when you are an old lady comfortable in your incredible genius—you will mention my name, and how you came to live in Rose Cottage and perhaps painted your masterpiece there.

Your friend, lover, and admirer, Anthony.

Nora's heart, which she'd believed was already broken, cracked a little more. And she wept.

Chapter Twenty-Four

Mr. Smith

Normally it was no hardship to go to a brothel, unless you went for reasons other than pleasure.

It was Nora who finally alerted Smith to Fanshawe's condition.

"He's not come home for four days," she'd said, pacing the study at his home, where she'd somehow tracked him down. Smith took a moment to appreciate the artistry of this woman in this particular room. He liked black. He preferred it to any other shade or color. Right now he had this woman—so fascinatingly pale—set against a black background.

Not for the first time in his life did Smith wish he had the artistic skill to capture a moment.

"He's not at Tosca's or Bernina's, I checked. I daresay he's at the Bellaire." She stopped in front of his massive black desk, this ethereal creature in white. "I don't know anyone there—and I'd hate to make a scene asking for him. Will you check, Mr. Smith?"

While he was generally resistant to feminine wiles—or any other wiles, for that matter—he was not impervious. And he had a definite weakness for Nora Hudson. Not the least because she was an awe-inspiring artist. He'd seen the picture of Edward. And then he'd smiled after he'd picked his jaw up off the floor. Of course he recognized him, having seen that magnificent body naked. But nobody but he, Nora, and a goodly number of whores would recognize it.

He'd been disappointed when she'd won some acclaim but not won the grand prize—not that it was very grand, a small purse of money and a partial scholarship to the Royal Academy, which Nora clearly did not need—but the adulation would have been good for launching what was likely to be a spectacular career.

"Mr. Smith?"

"Hmm?"

"I asked if you would check for Edward?"

"Of course. I'll go immediately." He stood.

She blinked those one-of-a-kind eyes in surprise. "Right now?"

He gave her a gentle smile as he came round the desk. "Last time I checked that was the definition of immediately."

She smiled, but her heart was not in it. She feared for her lover—more than Edward deserved, in Smith's opinion, given the way he'd treated her. But love, he knew as well as anyone, was a strange beast.

"Come, Nora. I'll drop you home on my way to fetch Edward."

✳✳✳

Even in the foyer, Nora knew something was dreadfully wrong. She looked at Phelps, the butler, and he gave a minute nod of his head: Edward was home.

She stripped off her gloves as she ran up the stairs, her heart thundering louder than a herd of horses. When she got to her room, the door was open. Inside Cat leaned against the wall, blood leaking from the corner of her mouth.

Nora ran toward her. "Did he—"

"No, he didn't touch me. I fell trying to get to the door before him." She glared at Nora. "You left it wide open."

Nora closed her eyes briefly and then opened them and went to the sunroom.

Edward was inside, seated on the chaise, studying the painting on the easel. Although it was only half-done, it was undoubtedly Cat, naked and spread, her wicked smile so enticing it made Nora want to step into the canvas. *She'd* done that, she suddenly realized. And Anthony was right—she was an artist—perhaps one day she'd be a great one.

But now was not the time to revel in future brilliance.

"Edward?"

He didn't look away from the canvas. "How long?"

Nora knew what he meant. "Several weeks."

"How. Many."

"Eight weeks."

He snorted softly and shook his head, finally turning to her. "So, while I was worried about my *wife* sneaking out to meet her paramours, she was fucking my mistress." He laughed until his eyes teared. "This is too farfetched for the stage."

Nora felt movement beside her and knew it was Cat.

"And you," he looked at his wife as if he'd never seen her. "You never wanted me to touch you because of this—because of your *Sapphic* bent."

She felt Cat shrug and was glad the other woman said nothing to incite him.

He gestured to the canvas and then to the others that were stacked against the walls, rolled up, and some hanging. "How you must have laughed at me—an ignorant philistine—while you could paint like *this*."

"I've never laughed at you."

He surged to his feet and seemed to flow toward her, not stopping until he had her caged between his massive arms, pinned to the wall.

"Edward," Cat said in a shaky voice while Nora and her lover—the love of her life—were locked in each other's gazes. "Please. You don't und—"

"If you say I don't understand I might just throw you on that chaise and show you how very wrong you are." He spoke without turning away from Nora. "Now, if you will kindly *get out,* this is none of your affair."

Even Cat—as fearless as she was in so many ways—did not cross Edward when he spoke in that voice.

Out of the corner of her eye, Nora saw her leave.

"Now, it's just you and me."

He'd looked at her many ways, but never with pure hate.

"I'm sorry."

"Sorry? For what? Fucking my wife? Lying to me about *this?*" he gestured to the room. "I suppose you're the reason old Ceddy left, aren't you. Because it has occurred to me, as I sat here looking at naked picture after naked picture of my wife that Ceddy must have discovered something and you paid him off. That's the only reason a leech like that would ever leave free room and board."

She swallowed. "Yes, he found out."

"How?"

"He saw us."

His jaw worked from side-to-side and she knew the images in his head aroused him. Perhaps if they were—

"Don't," he said. "Don't even think about it, you scheming, manipulative, lying, disloyal, cheating *whore*." He leaned close to her suddenly, making her jump. "Oh, don't worry," he whispered against her ear, his hot breath and cold, cold tone making every hair on her body stand up. "The days of me hurting you for our mutual pleasure are over. They are dead and gone. Just as you are—or soon will be: dead as far as I'm concerned, and *gone*. I'm leaving for one hour. And when I come back, I don't want to find you in my house. I'll leave an envelope with Powell that will contain money and a bank draught for the amount in the contract. You haven't fulfilled the terms, but it is money well-spent to get you out of my sight and out of my life. If you try to contact my wife, you will live to regret crossing me. Now, are we understood?"

Nora looked into the love of her life's eyes and said, "Yes, Edward. I understand."

And then he was gone, and she was where she'd always known she'd be: without him.

Part 3

Chapter Twenty-Five

Edward knew he would have to deal with Catherine eventually. In the month since Nora had left she'd become increasingly unmanageable—*unbearable.*

But he couldn't deal with her tonight.

It had been a long bloody day at one of their manufactories and he was tired, dirty, and sick of life. He'd deal with her tomorrow—when he was fresher and less likely to say something he'd regret. When he—

Something flickered out of the corner of his eye as he mounted the steps and Edward looked up.

"Great, bloody, fucking hell!" He threw his satchel on the ground and ran—faster than he'd ever run in his life, up the interminable steps to Nora's room.

He skidded to a halt at the open door, not wanting to startle her, walking on tip-toes to the threshold of Nora's sunroom-cum-painting studio-cum-bordello.

When he reached the darkened room he vaguely noticed something scattered around the floor. He squinted, paintbrushes, tubes of paint that had been squashed and smeared, canvasses torn and scattered.

But his attention was on Cat, who teetered in the window, seemingly unaware of him. She was naked, swaying like a thin reed with a lump in the middle, her toes hanging over the window ledge.

Part of his brain—that eternally inappropriate part—realized he'd not seen her naked before. Well, aside from the painting he'd found that day and which now was locked—with *new* locks—in *their* room.

Edward shook his head; his own bloody wife and he'd never seen her naked.

She began to sway forward and he sprang towards her, seizing her beneath her breasts, rather than her swollen middle.

She screamed—both startled and angry and, perhaps, thwarted—as he pried her fingers off the window frame and pulled her inside, kicking and screaming, her words unintelligible.

She'd lost an alarming amount of weight in the past weeks and she was *so* small—so horrifyingly slight, the only thing substantial about her was her stomach.

Edward couldn't help staring at her rounded belly as he marched out of the room with her fighting him every step of the way. It should have made him feel manly, successful, triumphant to know he'd put his child inside this beautiful, pedigreed woman. But all it did was make him sad: unbearably, cripplingly sad.

As he carried her squirming body to her bedroom he had to accept that not eating, excessive drinking, and emotional tantrums would not be good for the child inside her. By the time he set her on her bed, which he'd not been to since the second month of their marriage, she was sobbing as if her heart were breaking. Well, likely it was. Nora— Edward knew better than anyone—could do that to a person.

He felt somebody behind him and turned.

It was the maid-cum-jailor he'd hired for Catherine. "I'm so sorry, Mr. Fanshawe, I just stepped away for a moment and—"

He waved the woman away. "Go. I'll stay with her tonight." Likely this was the only way he'd ever be allowed to spend a night in her bedroom, with her unconscious.

He could see his words surprised her and knew the entire household would be aware of the state of things. How the hell could even a dead man have missed it?

You did, for months.

Edward ignored the jeering voice—it was his constant company and he'd gotten as good at ignoring it as he'd once been at not even hearing it.

He laid a hand on her forehead and she flinched away from him— even in her sleep. Or, maybe she was unconscious, he could smell liquor on her breath.

She was hot—unusually so, he thought, although he had no experience in caring for a sick person.

Or anyone at all. Except yourself.

He sighed and pulled a chair over to the bed, looking at her and forcing his tired addled mind to think.

As he studied her, he realized he'd not truly *seen* her in months.

Really, Edward! Have you ever *seen her?*

He sighed. Probably not—and certainly not since he'd successfully impregnated her and then set her aside. And she'd become all but invisible to him after he'd sent Nora away.

He knew he should be angry with her for her infidelity, but even he was not such a hypocrite.

Now Nora's infidelity, on the other hand …

Edward's throat tightened and his heart sped up. Worst of all, his cock—which he rarely noticed these days—stirred with interest.

At first he'd refused to think of her. But that had been a disaster. His mind was like a bucket that was left out in the rain. But instead of filling inexorably with water, it filled with Nora.

So he'd then forced himself to allocate specific parts of the day to think of her—the way he'd consider a problem at a factory.

That didn't work either; he could not think rationally about her. Even now, weeks later, he just saw red.

Or became hard. Or both.

No matter how much he tried to calmly examine his reaction to her that day, he came up with nothing—at least nothing he wanted to face.

He'd told her to leave and she had. He'd told her not to contact him or Catherine, and she'd disappeared like a wisp of smoke.

And, she'd taken nothing of him with her. Nothing.

When he'd looked in her room, he'd found her closet still full and her jewelry casket untouched. Mary told him the only thing gone was the trunk that she'd come with, which had held her old clothing.

She'd even left behind all her equipment and some of her paintings—the ones that must have been too wet to transport. That had included two of Catherine, both of which Edward had immediately confiscated.

There was the painting he'd held that day—a work that was quite frankly, stunning. Even unfinished it was hard to look away from. This was a Catherine he could hardly believe existed. Passionate, flirtatious, lustful, demanding, cajoling—and a dozen other expressions shone from her eyes. Looking at the painting made him feel as if his chest had been stove in by a shovel.

The other painting showed yet another Catherine he did not know. She was nude but demurely posed on her side, only the curve of her bottom, a glimpse of breast, and the rosy swell of her stomach visible.

She looked out at the observer with an expression of pure joy. She looked, he realized, like a woman in love.

These versions of Catherine—and likely many others—must have all been visible to a person who truly looked at her—or maybe just even *glanced* at her. It was true he might never have been allowed a glimpse at the passionate woman that Nora had, but he could have seen some other sides of her if he'd viewed her as something other than a vessel for his ambition and self-glorification.

It was no wonder the poor girl—for that is what she was—had looked for affection somewhere else; anywhere, else.

No, her part in what had happened just left him feeling empty and hopeless—but not angry, and certainly not jealous.

Only Nora left him seething with jealousy more corrosive than acid. She also seemed to reach deep inside of him—even now that she was gone—and force him to look at the very worst parts of himself. Like the fact that he was—even while standing in the utter shambles of his life— obsessed with the knowledge that nowhere in that room had there been any paintings or sketches of him.

Nothing, not even a charcoal drawing like the dozens she'd made of Catherine. Hell, there had even been sketches of the Thomases—or perhaps just one Thomas, it was bloody difficult to tell. She'd even made a sketch of Ceddy, which made him smile even now. It had been most unflattering: Ceddy's head on a shit-fly's body.

Edward's amusement drained away and he shivered. He should probably be grateful she'd never drawn him. How would have he come out on paper? Not well at all, he suspected.

For the first few days after he'd discovered them—when he'd been almost insane with anger and jealousy and a pain that nothing would ease—he'd told himself that Nora had made a fool of him from the first night they'd spent together. She'd hidden this part of herself—this blazing, shattering, stupefying talent—from him. Why?

But then his private tormentor, his own personal inquisitor, had pointed out: *Why didn't you ever ask her?*

Really, it was as simple as that. He'd known she painted if not from their time at Tosca's certainly since she'd begun to live in his house. And yet he'd given almost no thought to what made up her days, assuming she must have shopped or slept or did whatev—

Catherine muttered something he couldn't decipher and groaned, her expression one of agony. He could see that her brow was sheened with sweat. She was becoming worse, not better. This couldn't be normal—had she done something to herself? Consumed something she shouldn't have? Should he summon a doctor—her midwife?

He heard a soggy choking sound and sprang toward her, lifting her and turning her on her side just in time for her to void her stomach all over him.

Well, he thought, rubbing her back as she retched and retched and retched, until only clear bile would come up, it was likely the least he deserved after the way he'd treated her.

Once he was certain she wouldn't choke he laid her back and strode to the bell pull and yanked it hard enough to pull it down. A sleepy footman appeared immediately.

"Send for Mrs. Jackson and Doctor Baker—and tell them both to come quickly, that it is an emergency."

A coughing sound behind him made him turn.

She was trying to sit up, unsuccessfully.

He went to her and slid an arm around her, which she weakly tried to push away.

"Don't want you," she said drunkenly in between coughs. "Want *Nora.*"

Me too, he wanted to say, but didn't

Instead, he held her and tipped a glass of water to her mouth. She sipped a little, but not enough to make up for all she'd lost. Still, she shook her head and pushed away the glass with her limp hand.

"Hate you," she muttered as she slid back onto her pillow.

Me too, Edward thought—hating him and wanting Nora seemed to be the only two things they had in common.

Edward sat back in his chair, crusted in vomit, and watched his wife, who cried even in her sleep.

The midwife and doctor arrived in less than an hour; by then it was too late: Catherine had already lost the baby.

Chapter Twenty-Six

May, 1869
Nine Months Later . . .

*N*ora yawned, stretched, and then climbed over the sleeping body in her bed. Derek slept like the dead and didn't even stir.

It was barely light, but—now that she was her own mistress—she'd learned it was her favorite time to paint. She paused only long enough to brew herself coffee and slip on one of the loose dresses she'd taken to wearing ever since joining the group mockingly referred to by many as, "the artistic crowd."

In truth, she'd never joined any group, they'd somehow managed to accrete around her in the months since she'd moved back to London.

Nora suspected it was more because of the fact that there was always wine and food at her lodgings rather than any great desire to associate with her because of her person or talent.

Some of them, she knew, wanted her sexually. But if there was one thing Edward had taught her, it was to avoid emotional, complex men. So, she'd made it clear she did not share her body with artists. Instead, she enjoyed her models. And why not? For only a few shillings one could have the most physically beautiful men and women in London strip off their clothing and pose any way she wished.

As for what happened after her sessions? Well, she'd not had to pay anyone for *that* yet, either male or female.

The group of men who gathered in her lodgings—uninvited—and consumed her food and drink while arguing art and politics into the night, were the ever-changing members of the Pre-Raphaelite

Brotherhood. As much as these men—her fellow painters—liked to consider themselves the type of artists who innovated and forged paths, they were actually quite shocked by Nora's casual attitude toward nudity and sex.

None of them knew she'd been a whore. She'd not kept the matter a secret out of shame, but because she wanted no connections between Natalie Hartwicke—her real name—and Nora Hudson, the woman she'd left behind and the only name Edward knew her by.

Thus far her identity had remained secret, mostly because the men she mingled with were too self-absorbed to ask questions about her past. Nor was she likely to encounter anyone who'd known her in her past life as they were they the type of men who could hardly afford a loaf of bread, not to mention an expensive whore from a place like Tosca's.

It hurt her to cut off contact with Tosca's—specifically with Charles—but she knew once Edward recovered from his mad fit of jealousy he would not be able to resist finding her, even if wasn't to forgive her, but just to know what she was doing.

When she'd left him that day, she'd gone to an inexpensive, unobtrusive, hotel in a part of town she was unlikely to see him. She'd stayed there until she'd spoken to Lord Anthony's solicitors about the house and attendant trust fund.

What she'd learned had left her breathless; her generous lover had not only left her a sizeable property—and one which paid its expenses from its rents—but enough money to make her a very wealthy woman.

So, she'd packed up her meager possessions—along with fresh supplies, as she'd left everything but her paintings at Edward's house—and went to Rose Cottage.

It was every bit as nourishing to her bruised soul as she could have hoped. But the beautiful light, expansive vistas, and lush landscapes were no longer the views she saw in her mind's eye. She knew, after painting Edward and then Cat, that her preference, at least for now, was for the human form.

So, after six months in the country she'd closed up Rose Cottage, leaving it in the hands of the competent couple who'd once worked for Lord Anthony, and headed for a new start in London, a city she'd somehow grown to care for, like a certain too big, crude, and brutal lover.

Once again, she took a room in a modest hotel and then spent her days roaming the city on foot, the way she'd never been allowed to do before. It hadn't taken her long to recognize those people she now thought of as 'hers': those men—and even some women—who lived on the fringes of wealthy society, both despising and dependent on their rich patrons for their survival and art.

A man named Dante Rossetti, the nominal leader of Pre-Raphaelite Brotherhood—a grand name for a fractious, jealous, and back-biting collection of men with very rigid notions of art—had taken her under his wing. Well, to be honest, he'd wanted to take her under his body—or any way he could get her—but she'd made her position about fucking artists clear.

Rather than be offended, he'd been amused and brought her into his small society, but as an observer to their high-flown ideals rather than a fully-fledged member.

He'd helped her find exactly the type of place a painter needed and connected her to other painters, models, and the lively social circle that thrived on the fringes of fashionable society.

They would gather in somebody's garret or meager apartment—increasingly Nora's—and argue and drink and smoke well until dawn.

At first Nora had found the subjects—the nature of art—interesting. She'd been amused by how fiery they could become over their opinions—like their enduring hatred for Sir Joshua Reynolds—the founder of the Royal Academy, whom they'd dubbed Sir Sloshua.

Eventually, however, she found them rather tedious. All this talking just took time away from *doing*, from painting. And she had much to catch up on, her mind brimming with projects.

They, on the other hand, seemed to become increasingly determined to pull her—or her expensive brandy—into their circle, spending hours haranguing her, all but ordering her to switch from her Goyaesque or Blakeian methods to the Quattrocento style.

Unlike most of them, Nora had no formal training and had, at first, avidly looked up and read about all the paintings and painters they'd mentioned. Even now, almost three months later, there were books covering almost every surface in her sparsely furnished house. After a time, however, she viewed their fixations as a distraction.

She painted how and what she wanted to paint. Unlike most of them, she didn't need to ever sell another painting—a luxury that should have made her feel at least some guilt but didn't. Although she had no reason to put her art for sale, she did it anyway. Her apartment was small and rapidly filling—there was no room for her increasing output. Besides, it made her smile to think of her art hanging on some stranger's walls. She'd instructed the small gallery who handled her paintings to never disclose her location. Now that she was a rich woman, she didn't hesitate to give such orders, not to be cruel or contrary, but to protect her fragile privacy

She began to settle into her new life and, quite astonishingly, found herself in some demand as a model. Mainly she sat for the men she befriended, who, when they discovered she wouldn't bed them, begged to capture her image. Nora never said no to such a request because she knew, from her own experience, that the desire to paint some*thing* or some*one* could be intense—an almost *physical* obsession.

As a result of her willingness to pose, clothed or unclothed or anywhere in between, she was in great demand. Of course, she also did not charge her friends for her time, which she suspected was the true reason behind her popularity.

It didn't matter the reason, it amused her to see paintings of herself in medieval garb bearing a flaming torch, floating naked like a dryad or naiad—she could never recall which—lounging nude (never naked—it was art, after all) in a woodland lake, thundering across a dramatic landscape, wearing flowing garments, on a white steed, and many others.

Her own painting was going very well. Despite the taunts of her associates, she was finding her way, learning to paint only for her pleasure.

She laid down her brush and picked up her forgotten cup of coffee, grimacing at the cold liquid, and putting it aside, her eyes still on her canvas. She must have taken more away from Edward than a broken heart because she appeared to be obsessed with his naked body.

No matter how often she paid for models, she ended up painting from her hoard of sketches and three paintings. The paintings had thankfully been waiting at the Academy that day Edward entered her studio for the first time, or she suspected they might be lying torn at the bottom of the Thames. As it was, they hung in her bedroom—the only art on her walls.

While he was nude in all three, she had no qualms about displaying them because his face was not visible in any of them. The ones she'd painted *after* leaving him, however, that was a different story. Those she stored in her studio, stretched and framed but under protective covers to keep them from prying eyes. Every few days or so she would lock the door to the room—a necessity in an apartment which others felt free to enter at any time of the day or night without permission—and gorge on Edward.

The one she was working on today, was of him sitting on his black leather throne, his powerful arms resting on the arms of the chair, muscular thighs spread enough to display a glimpse of his heavy balls, and his thick, ruddy cock glistening with need. His lips were curved in a slight smile, his eyes glittering with the thought of what he'd just done to her, or what he was about to do.

Looking at it now made her heated and wet.

"Lord, Nat—that's a bit fierce first thing in the morning, innit?"

She startled at the sound of Derek's sleepy voice, the sight of him never failing to bring a smile to her face. He was eighteen, with the body of a god and the stamina of a draft horse, and, she had to admit, the wits of a turnip—and not a particularly wise turnip at that. Still, one couldn't have everything.

She went towards him, pulling off her apron and tossing it to the floor, exposing her naked body to his eyes. She slid her work-roughened hand around his lovely thick cock. "You're one to talk," she murmured up at him when he gasped at her rough stroke. "This is more than a little fierce, itself. Is it for me?"

He pouted in a way she'd captured on canvas, his muscular body as hard and toned as the sculptures of him that were scattered around the city. He heaved a fake yawn, an excellent excuse to flex his torso for her viewing pleasure.

"Perhaps," he said, with a smirk. "But first you'd need to earn it, ducks."

Nora had to swallow the liquid that flooded her mouth before she drown in it, her eyes on his defined torso. She could never get enough of looking at the corrugated 'V' of muscles that separated his smooth, muscular hips. He flexed his abdomen for her, the taut, ridged flesh dropping her to her knees.

She opened her mouth and he slid into her the way she'd taught him to do—the way Edward liked—not stopping until the hard head of his beautiful cock bumped the back of her throat and her lips touched the blond hair surrounding his thick root.

Once he'd filled her, his hands slid into her hair—which she kept even shorter, much to the chagrin of the men who painted her—and he held her there, immobile, groaning as he ground himself into her, bruising her lips, his erection stretching her throat and jaw, rubbing painfully at the back of her throat.

Her sex swelled and evidence of her arousal ran down her thighs as a picture of Edward coalesced. Slowly, almost as slowly as laying paint on a canvas, an image of Edward built in her fertile mind's eye.

And then he began to fuck her mouth, languidly at first, pulling all the way out—until the crown, which he'd let her suck and tongue, tolerating her fascination with the tiny hole she found so very erotic— and then he'd slide all the way into her, filling her in one long glide, harder with each thrust.

And then he began to grunt as he pounded into her with a savagery that never failed to evoke what she craved: Edward—big and hard and cruel.

His dark eyes looked down into her soul, consuming her pain like a delicacy, building on it, taking her further—

"Ooh, that's lovely," Derek cooed.

Nora startled.

"Ah, careful with the teeth, ducks."

His cockney voice obliterated her fantasy lover like a cannon ball blowing a hole through a castle wall.

He rammed himself deep, throating her painfully, fucking her so hard his heels lifted off the ground, his thigh and abdominal muscles taut, hard, and glorious. It was good—painful the way she liked it—but it was Derek.

Edward was gone, and once she lost him, he remained elusive.

Next time, she promised herself, as her orgasm drifted out of reach, her eyes teared, and Derek emptied himself deep in her burning throat—next time she'd instruct him to be silent when he took her.

Chapter Twenty-Seven

"I want a divorce."

Edward looked up from his desk. He'd not even heard her enter he'd been so absorbed in the syndicate's newest project—a machine that could harvest in one hour as much as one hundred men could harvest in a day, all by itself. Why, with such an invention a farmer's reliance on labor would disappear almost overnight. It would mean—

"Edward!"

He realized she looked blurry—he couldn't see her features, only an outline. For a moment he debated about leaving on his glasses, but that would be childish.

When he looked at her without them, he had to blink, suppressing the urge to shade his eyes. She was dressed in the color of the season—Magenta—which some duchess or other had just made popular. He wondered what she'd say if he told her the dye for the cloth had been invented by one of his weavers? No, actually he didn't wonder—he knew she'd tell him to sod himself.

"Did you hear me, Tedward?"

His lips smiled without any order from his brain. He'd begun to enjoy her nickname, never having had one before. He knew it was not meant as a sign of affection, but he liked it all the same. "You want a divorce—was that it"? She sneered. "So glad to know your hearing isn't going the way of so many other things."

She meant his appearance, not doubt, which was gaunt and haggard. And then there was his hair, which had seemed to go white almost overnight.

She flounced forward and threw herself in a chair.

"That color looks well on you," he said, lying. For such a beautiful woman, she didn't appear to have any sense of style or fashion. The color she was wearing was for a dark beauty—not her sunny blond loveliness. He kept that observation to himself, too.

"Save it for somebody who wants it—although I can't imagine who that would be. Perhaps one of your *whores.*"

It was true he'd begun going back to paying women—not that he'd ever really stopped, he supposed. Not to Tosca's or Bernina's or even the Bellaire—where he'd made such an ass of himself all those months ago—but to a new place. A place that was devoted to the sorts of perversions he and Nora had always adored. *Nora.*

He pushed her face away and sat back in his chair, relaxed rather than tense around Catherine as he used to be. Everything had changed the night she lost the baby.

Well, except for her hating him, of course.

She was a lovely, lovely woman and grew more attractive every day. He'd not been the only one to start visiting whores. He knew—not through spies, which he'd never set on her, but from Smith, that she was frequenting Bernina's, that she'd gotten herself pierced, that she employed the whore named Emma, and that she spent enough there to buy a whorehouse all her own.

Smith had seemed surprised when Edward said and did nothing. In fact, it was the only time he'd ever seen his mysterious partner out of temper.

"You need to set your house in order," he'd snapped when Edward said nothing.

"Do I?" he was curious why Smith thought such a thing was necessary.

They'd been in Smith's coal black study at the time and he'd flung his arm at a mirror. "Look at yourself. You look like hell."

Edward couldn't argue; he did. He shrugged. "What of it? Is my contribution to the syndicate suffering? Am I not pulling my weight, doing my share?"

"Goddammit Edward you know you're making more money than ever. It's not that—it's—"

"Yes?" Edward prodded, not really curious to hear the rest but feeling like it was expected.

Smith heaved a *huge* sigh, rolled his eyes, and flung himself into his chair with enough drama to give Catherine competition. "You're my friend, dammit. And a man doesn't let his friend slowly kill himself."

Edward was his friend? That had *surprised him.*

"Edward? *Edward!*"

He looked up from his thoughts to find Catherine standing in front of the desk, her expression furious. "Did you fall *asleep?*" She stamped her foot, not waiting for him to answer. "I want you to tell me right now—will you grant me a divorce, or make things difficult?"

"Contact your father's solicitor," Edward wrote down a name and direction on a piece of paper and handed to her, amused by her opened-mouthed expression. "Tell them to contact mine and arrange something."

Her eyes narrowed with suspicion. "If you try to draw this out like one of your vulgar business negotiations—"

"I won't." He was surprised she'd even noticed his negotiations, vulgar or otherwise, not to mention whether they proceeded quickly or slowly.

"I warn you, I shan't be left a pauper."

"How about half of everything I have? Will that do?" he asked curiously.

She made a squeaky sound in the back of her throat and then swallowed convulsively. "I don't know. I shall have to ask my solicitor."

Edward smiled with genuine amusement. "You do that, Catherine."

She cut him a look of disgust. "You've always been awful and odd, Edward, but since you threw out N-Nora," he was pleased to see some emotion on her face other than hatred. "Well, you've become pathetic." On that note, she stormed from the room.

"How nice to find another thing we agree on, Catherine," he said to the closed door. And then he put on his glasses and turned back to the farm machinery.

Chapter Twenty-Eight

December 1869

ora was reading about Cat's latest escapades in the society pages of the paper. It seemed that people of every class and from every walk of life had talked of nothing but the scandalous divorcee since the news had been made public four months ago.

The gossip columns claimed it was the biggest divorce settlement in recent history—and speculation was rampant as to how much money she'd taken from the reclusive King of Tin, a name Nora suspected Cat had helped the newspapermen come up with.

"Nat?"

She looked up. "Oh, hello Angus—I didn't know anyone else was here." *Why should I? It's only my house.*

He flushed and she realized he must have read some of her sarcasm in her face or voice.

She gave him a genuine smile and gestured to the chair nearest. "Shove all those books onto the floor and have a seat."

"Oh, I can't stay long. I just came to tell you I sold that painting—the one of you with—"

Nora didn't know how he could have painted her in the nude and yet still not be able to articulate the word.

She had mercy on him. "I recall the one. Congratulations, Angus."

His already red face flushed even more. Angus Parker was enrolled at the Academy and Nora thought he had talent. She suspected he would never be a great painter, but he could make a comfortable living if he agreed to do portraits.

"Was that all?" she asked when he continued to bounce on his heels and look nervous.

"Well, not really."

She cocked her head and gave him a patient look.

"I'm sorry, Nat, but the gentleman who bought it asked to meet you."

"Angus, you know how I feel about that."

He nodded, his expression anxious. "I know it's unusual, but he paid a great whopping pile for it."

As if that makes some difference to me. But she smiled to soften her next words. "I'll consider it and get back to you, Angus." *And say, no, but he didn't need to know that.*

Instead of nodding and taking his leave, he kept bouncing.

She sighed. "You've brought him here, haven't you?"

Before he could answer a man emerged from the adjoining room—a dining room she used to hold the overflow from her studio.

"Hello, Natalie."

She had to laugh. "Hello, Mr. Smith. Why am I not surprised that you were the one to find me?"

✳✳✳

Mr. Smith

Once Nora had dispatched the rather bovine-looking Angus with the pocketful of banknotes Smith had given him—after listening to his repeated assurances to Smith that he'd have the painting delivered by the end of the week—they settled in her astoundingly cluttered sitting room. In fact, he'd not been in a house this cramped, crowded, and cluttered in—well, maybe never.

"Would you care for a drink?" she gestured to a decanter and some mismatched chipped glasses which looked none to clean.

"Thank you, but I'm fine."

She grinned at him—the rare flash of amusement that changed her face from intriguing to transcendent. "You're afraid you'll catch some sort of dreadful disease."

To his surprise, his face heated—when had that last happened? Not in this decade. "Ah, go on, then—I'll have a glass of the less brown one."

She laughed and poured them both glasses and handed one to Smith before lowering herself into the opposite chair. She was garbed in a heavy smock-type apron and he was fairly certain she wore nothing beneath it.

He took a sip, pleasantly surprised.

"You see," she said, lifting her glass and eyebrows.

"I'd ask how you're doing but I can see you're blooming."

"Even if I'm doing it on a dung heap."

Smith laughed. She'd always been quick, cutting, and clever. At least with him.

"I know Edward would never send you, but I sense you've come on his behalf."

He blinked at this frontal assault. "You're correct—he didn't send me. He doesn't know I've found you."

"How *did* you find me?" her eyes narrowed. "Oh, wait—*Charles*. What a little rat."

Smith's amusement evaporated. "That little rat just happens to belong to me now, so I caution you to speak carefully."

Rather than cowering at his cold tone, which generally sent grown, armed men running for cover, she laughed.

God, what a woman.

"So," she said, throwing back the remains of her glass. "You still haven't told me why you're here." She was thinner than before—and she'd already been thin—harder and more *concentrated*, somehow. He supposed this was the real Nora, rather than the woman who'd been Fanshawe's kept mistress.

"Two reasons: one, I want to commission you to do a portrait, and two, Edward wants to send you a letter."

She recoiled in surprise—and disbelief. "*Edward* wants. Not you, putting him up to it or, God forbid, actually writing it?"

"No, Edward said he wished he at least had your direction so that he could send you a letter." As lies went, it was fairly pathetic.

"Hmph. And whose portrait?"

"Mine. And Charles's."

That made her eyes open. "You want a portrait together." It wasn't a question.

"Yes."

"I'm not a portrait artist, Smith. There are people I could refer you to who would—"

"Not for *this* type of portrait."

Comprehension dawned quickly in her pale eyes and she smiled a rather wicked smile that made him feel like a boy caught rubbing one off in a closet.

"You want an *erotic* portrait."

"Yes, go ahead, enjoy yourself. I'm not ashamed." Smith took a drink. Not ashamed—but bloody embarrassed. While he was proud of his body, he wasn't sure he was proud enough to have it captured for posterity. Especially not in a portrait that would, if not get both of them killed, then certainly get them run out of the country. But he'd wagered with Charles and the little bastard had won and this was what he wanted. Smith was not a welsher.

She nodded her head, her expression watchful, speculative. But Smith, with his nose for blood and instinct for the kill, knew she would comply with both his requests.

"Give me a week to consider it—both," she amended.

He smiled. He could spend the week deciding in which room of his she would paint their *erotic* portrait.

✳✳✳

"You *saw* her?"

"For the fifth time, Edward, yes: I saw her. As in spoke to her, not passed her on the street in a carriage."

It was a sign of Edward's distraction that he didn't respond to Smith's sarcasm.

"And she said she would welcome a letter from me."

If Smith were a praying man, this would have been a perfect time. Instead, he said. "Yes. Apparently, the last time you two saw each other was . . . well, not a happy leave-taking."

Edward snorted, but there was no humor in the sound. "You could say that." He looked up suddenly, the muscles in his gaunt face taut. "Has she seen Catherine? Are the two—"

He still couldn't say it, even though his former wife's antics were making the scandal sheets millions of pounds.

"No," Smith said, hoping like hell it was true. Just because he'd seen men's clothing—dirty drawers, for God's sake!—scattered around Nora's vile little hovel did not mean she wouldn't be seeing Catherine Fanshawe as well. Nora—or Natalie—even went beyond Smith's sexual tolerance. The thought of Charles touching or being touched by another was enough to make him—

"I'm surprised," Edward said, interrupting Smith in the mental process of beating one of Charles's non-existent lovers to death.

"Oh?" he said, just to keep the man talking. Not an easy task these days.

"I would have thought Catherine would have found her."

"I think Catherine has other interests these days."

Edward blinked and then smiled, wryly. "Yes, I've enjoyed reading about them."

Smith's eyes bulged. "You can't be serious."

Edward shrugged. "Why not?"

Smith did something he rarely did: he sputtered.

Edward did something he did even more rarely—he gave a genuine laugh. "Oh, don't worry about offending me. You are remembering how I controlled her every movement when she lived here. Or the foolish, vain, arrogant, and ignorant way in which I went about marrying her in the first place?"

"Well, yes, actually."

Edward threw his head back and laughed until there were tears in his eyes.

Well, it was a day for surprises—first Nora—and now this.

When he'd composed himself, he sat back in the big black leather chair he favored, his rawboned frame—much lighter these days— relaxing for a change. "I don't care what Catherine does. I just hope she finds some happiness in her life." He cut Smith a quick, almost embarrassed look. "I know it sounds ... *weak* for a man to say this about a woman who divorced him, but I got out of our marriage with far less trouble than I deserved."

That was a bloody lie—Smith knew exactly how much Edward had paid to his wife because he'd had to sell some of his shares to Smith and the other members of their small syndicate to afford to pay it.

"I can see by your expression you're thinking of money," Edward said, surprising Smith with his astuteness. It used to be the man didn't see past the end of his large nose.

"What *do* you mean, if you don't mind me asking?"

Edward shook his head. "You didn't see her that night—the night she lost the child."

Smith knew almost nothing about it and had never dared to ask. He said nothing now.

"She did something to herself to get rid of the baby."

Smith stopped breathing while the other man bled in front of him.

"She never wanted it and she never wanted me. And I swear to you, Smith," he looked up at him with eyes raw with anguish, "As I sat there, believing she would die as well? I couldn't believe that it took so long for me to see what I'd done to her. To me." He gulped so loud Smith could almost feel it. "To Nora. Can you believe I never saw it until that night?"

No, Smith really couldn't. But it was hardly what the man needed to hear right now. "I'm sorry about the child, but she didn't die." Smith scrambled to put his thoughts into words. He truly liked this rather thick-headed man across from him. And he didn't like or care for many people. Indeed, the number barely exceeded one hand. "You can punish yourself until you die, and it will never erase what you did to Lady Catherine or Nora."

Edward snorted. "If this is your idea of how to talk a person out of the—"

"Punishing yourself helps no one."

Edward's intense stare—as if *Smith* held the answer—almost melted his skin from his body.

"Do you want her back?" He didn't have to clarify who he was talking about.

Edward's chest expanded and expanded until he released two explosive words. "God, yes." He dropped his shockingly white head in his hands. "But there is no way—none. The way I treated her—"

"If we're talking about the same Nora I think she loved and encouraged a lot of your bad behavior."

Edward's head swung up. "Tell me what you did that night. Just—tell me."

Again, Smith knew what he meant.

He propped his elbows on his knees and leaned forward, waiting until Edward did the same, his expression filled with such fearful anticipation it was painful to see. "We talked, Edward. That's what we did."

Edward blinked. "You talked."

"Yes, talked." He felt like he was trapped in a loop.

"You never touched her?"

Luckily Smith never hesitated. "Not except to kiss her cheek goodbye." Even that, he could see, made the man's mouth harden. He'd never seen such a jealous man in his life.

Well, except perhaps himself.

Chapter Twenty-Nine

The first letter came the week after she began her portrait of Smith and Charles.

She'd made her decision to paint the men earlier, but the discussion about *how* to paint them dragged on.

"I want you to paint me with Smith's cock buried in my arse," Charles had declared—his declaration surprising neither Nora nor Smith since he must have said it fifty times. "And I want the picture to show the head of my cock—my piercing."

Nora and Smith had exchanged looks and Smith had, yet again, explained why a less graphic image might be preferable. Eventually, there had been a compromise. They'd be painted on a chaise, Smith lying behind Charles, who would have an erect cock—and yes she'd make sure his precious piercing was visible—and the men flushed from an activity that would be obvious to any viewer, not that Smith had any intention of showing the portrait to anyone. Charles, on the other hand, well …

The sessions—or sexions, as Charles humorously dubbed them— were singular in her experience, but not unpleasant. Still, she was less than productive given the show the two men put on so that Charles could have an erection during the sittings. When she tried to explain she didn't need him hard *all* the time, he'd pouted and Smith had given her that look that said: whatever Charles wanted, Charles got. It was accompanied by the sinister stare that she knew was supposed to flay the skin from her bones and leave her a quivering mass of fear. Smith clearly had no idea whom he was dealing with.

So, to keep Charles satisfied—in every way—the sessions were, quite frankly, two-person orgies. If such a thing existed.

They'd offered to include her, but Nora—for all that she was more than a little intrigued to feel a pierced cock inside her—had learned her lesson about being the third leg of a triangle. That meant she usually spent most of the drive home in Smith's fine carriage relieving herself of the build-up of sexual tension that came from watching two fine male specimens fuck each other silly.

While they were both too slender for her taste—she did love a big man: big in all ways—they were fit, toned, and possessed beautiful penises. Charles was proportionate. Smith—she already knew from personal experience—was huge, or at least his cock looked huge on such a slender body.

She'd just finished another session and changed out of her painting smock—she left one at Smith's house for convenience—and was fastening up one of her loose "artist" garments when Smith came in the room.

"Yes?" she said, her hands working at buttons.

He glanced at the open doorway with a furtive look and then said in a low voice. "I need to tell you something."

"So I'd gathered, otherwise you wouldn't be lurking."

"Edward asked me about that night at Tosca's."

She frowned. "Why would he have brought that up after all this time?"

Smith shrugged, as guilty as a fox with a hen in its jaws. "Anyhow, I told him I never touched you except to kiss you on the cheek."

Her hands froze. "*What?*"

Something that looked like embarrassment flickered across his impassive face. "I'm sorry, Nora, but I had to."

"Smith," she said, suddenly furious. "People *have* to get out of the way of a fast-moving carriage or they *have* to stop speaking to so-called-friends who've betrayed them." She paused just to let that sink in. "They don't *have* to lie about matters long past."

"Well, not *that* long—"

"*Why* did you lie to him? I hate lies."

"I know, I know. But I had to."

"I want to know *why?*"

"Because . . ." He shoved a hand through his neat, short brown hair in an unprecedented display of agitation. "Well, because I *like* the man."

Nora raised her eyebrows.

"Oh, not like *that*," Smith snapped. "He's a friend. All right? Are you happy you made me say it?"

Nora snorted. These *men*. Him, Edward, the whole lot of them behaving as if friendship was dangerous to their masculinity.

"I can see you might be a little . . . angry?"

Nora ignored his foolish question. "And what am I supposed to tell him if he were ever to write me—as you've indicated he wishes to do—and asks me about that night?" Nora wouldn't put it past Edward to have the audacity to ask her such a thing, she knew how jealous and obsessive he was.

She could see Smith flushing even with his rather dark olive skin. "Tell him we just talked."

She didn't bother to hold back her laughter. It still made her wet recalling the way Smith had used her that night: he'd been almost as good as Edward with a whip and that big cock of his, which he'd made sure she became very well acquainted with before that night was over. "Oh, is that what you call it where you come from—*talking*?"

"Very droll." He worked his jaw from side to side and then, "Will you keep it our secret?"

"I don't know, Smith." And like a bolt of lightning, it struck her.

"Nora?" he took a step back. "When you smile like that it makes me think I should hide all my knives."

"I'll keep a secret if you tell me one thing. And *no* lying."

"*Nora, please.*"

Nora stared at him, arrested. Who would have thought the stern man could beg so charmingly?

"I want your first name."

All signs of placating and begging dissipated and the look that replaced it really did send a shiver down her spine. "I'm not even going to justify that with an answer."

She felt like a tiny, tiny mouse backed into a corner by a huge cat. But even mice had *some* power.

She shrugged, pushed past his rigid person to pick up her cloak. "Then I can't promise you what I'll say if he asks me."

Nora found herself pinned to the wall that had just been several feet behind her. Smith's powerful hands were on her waist and he held pressed firmly, her feet not touching the floor.

She swallowed, but did not look away from his eyes, which put her in mind of bottomless wells. His face was as tight and haughty as those she'd seen on the Egyptian carvings—gods and kings from long ago. She would, she knew already, have to paint him wearing this expression—not in this portrait, but another with only him.

He leaned close enough to whisper the name in her ear.

Nora's jaw dropped and his eyes narrowed to slits.

"Why, that's a very nice name," she said unable to keep the laughter from her voice.

"You really are a dangerous bitch, aren't you?"

Nora grinned.

As he lowered her gently to the ground, she realized she was more aroused than she'd been in months. She needed somebody like him to manhandle her. Not him but *like* him.

"What are you two whispering about like a pair of thieves?"

They jumped to find Charles leaning against the doorframe. He'd put on a robe but not bothered to tie it: Nora had never met such an exhibitionist and Smith only encouraged his brattish behavior by pandering to his every whim.

Smith was suddenly sweetness and light and said without hesitation, "It's a surprise, darling."

Charles stood up straight, like some kind of pointer hound; his pointer already getting excited. "Ooh, what is it?"

"If he told you it wouldn't be a surprise, would it?" Nora asked him, her sweetness laced with sarcasm as she glared at Smith, wanting him to know she was still very vexed with him, regardless that she now held him in her power.

She fumed all the way home, until she saw Edward's letter laying on the salver in the tiny entryway.

All through her dinner, which she ate by herself after sending Derek off by claiming a headache, which, judging by his reaction—open-mouthed shock followed by uncontrollable laughter—told her that she was a dreadful liar.

She eyed the envelope that lay in front of her, supine and harmless on her cluttered dinner table. But what was inside? Would *that* be harmless?

Should she open it? Or toss it into the grate and let it burn.

After dinner she relaxed in her study with a book about Manet, whose art she found intriguing, but was not sure whether she liked.

Tonight, it failed to capture her attention, as did everything else she looked at except the white rectangle of paper. So, finally, a little after midnight, she snatched a broken paintbrush somebody had left, inexplicably, in a vase of dead flowers, and used it as a letter opener.

She took a deep breath and spread out the letter.

"*Nora,*" she paused, the sight of his powerful handwriting almost like an aphrodisiac. Edward had touched this very paper. She ran a finger over the slight indentations, smiling. He wrote with a heavy hand. Nora snorted, that was no surprise.

She ignored the unsubtle thumping in her sex, and continued reading:

"*I hesitated to write to you even after Smith told me you were hoping I'd write to talk about that last day—*"

"Why you lying, manipulating, interfering, meddling—" Nora realized she was talking to piece of paper and stopped. That bloody, lying Smith. Oh, she'd get her pound of flesh—and more. She'd paint him with a blood wen on his nose, she'd—her eyes were caught by the next line of the letter:

"*Of course, I knew Smith was lying as you would never, in this lifetime or the next, say such a thing. That made me wonder. I knew he must have seen you—but did he tell you about his scheme? Or are you reading this letter right now wishing I'd continued to leave you alone—the way I so angrily demanded of you that last day we saw each other? So, before I go any further, I need some sign from you. If you don't mind if I write, please just send me one sentence. If you don't respond. This will be the last you hear of me. Edward*"

✳✳✳

Nora waited three weeks before she made up her mind. Although most people thought she was shallow and somehow didn't suffer as deeply because she didn't rant and rage, that last day with Edward had changed her and not, she feared, for the better.

She felt as though an ax had sheared off a part of her—something important like a hand or foot, but not outwardly visible. She didn't pitch fits like Cat or Charles or Edward, or coldly threaten to slay people like Smith, but she'd raged inside her own mind for months. After all, she'd brought most of her suffering on herself as she'd always known Edward would eventually send her away. It had been no surprise and she'd always expected it. But that hadn't made it any less painful when it happened.

So why travel a path she already knew was fraught with danger? So she could lose some other part of her?

But the longer she watched Charles and Smith, the more she realized the relations she had with men like Derek—or the young model she was eyeing to replace him—gave her nothing but transient pleasure.

With Edward there would pain—she knew that. Some of the pain would be joyous, some would cut her.

Nora dithered for weeks but finally decided early one morning, before beginning yet another painting of him that she was tired of just existing, she wanted to start living again.

So, she sat down at her small writing desk and wrote: *"You may send me letters until I ask you to stop. I cannot say if I will respond. Nora."*

Chapter Thirty

Nora,

Thank you for agreeing to read my letters, for however long you choose to. I know many women would not want to speak to or hear from a man who'd done what I've done.

I realized as I sat down and looked at a blank sheet of parchment that I've never written a personal letter; thousands of business correspondence, but nothing that required so much thought.

I could fill the next pages with apologies, but I know you aren't the type of woman who values form over function, so I'll say it this once and then move on: I'm sorry for the way I treated you. Not in the bedroom, but in the rest of our lives.

So, what I've decided to do is to tell you how I became the man you knew. I say knew, because I like to think I've changed at least a little over the time since we've last spoken.

I'm not telling you my story because I believe it will excuse my behavior or the man I was when we were together, and, likely, still am in many ways. I'm telling you because I realized I only let you know one part of me and I never bothered to discover any part of you other than what happened in a bedroom.

Maybe you'll read this letter and the others I hope to write, maybe you won't. Maybe you'll read some and become disinterested and throw the rest away unopened. But I have to try.

I just re-read this and realize I sound like a blithering idiot."

Nora laughed out loud.

"But I think you will take my meaning from the tangle of words.

So, where to start? At the beginning is what I would say, but the beginning of what?

I suppose the first twenty years of Edward Fanshawe's life is a tale that takes few enough words to tell. I never knew my parents and grew up in an orphanage. On the surface that sounds grim, and it was, but I can't complain as I believe it gave me the ambition and drive to become the successful businessman I am.

But as to the rest of me? I suppose you could say I became stunted early in many ways. The couple who ran the orphanage was neither kind nor cruel, they were just trying to scratch out sustenance in a meager environment, surviving on lean pickings, and trying to stay alive.

If that meant they sometimes shorted our food rations or kept our dormitory unheated, well, I daresay they did it out of hunger and cold rather than spite or greed.

I was a big boy right from the beginning and took very little abuse. But neither did I see any affection."

Nora dropped her head against the chair back and rolled it back and forth, her eyes tearing for a boy she never even knew. What a grim, grim life. Yet look what he'd made of it? And her? Raised with all the creature comforts and affection—yes, even love—and she'd spurned it all and left it behind the moment she could, and all to become a whore.

The pages beckoned her and she was sad to see there were so few. Yes, she *did* want to know what had made Edward the man he was. Where was the shame in admitting that? Wise, or unwise, he was the only man she'd ever loved, and she loved him still.

"When my twelfth year arrived, I was apprenticed to a farmer, not out of choice, but because my back was already showing signs of being broad, a good characteristic in a beast of burden. I'd never stepped foot in the country and must say, even now, that I am in no hurry to return to it.

I lived at the home of a yeoman farmer in Kent, not so far from London as to be terrifying, but far enough to miss it dearly. I won't go into the dreary life of a farmer except to say it was not the life for me. Once I'd earned back the money the farmer paid for me—one year early, when I was sixteen—I was ready to move on to other, hopefully, greener pastures.

I've left out one thing, a small thing, but it certainly set me on my path in sexual matters and made me the person you met at Tosca's."

Nora swallowed and took a deep breath, debating about continuing reading.

Thinking of the times they'd spent in their room together—well, *his* room—were thoughts she only allowed to invade her mind *one* day a month. On the last Wednesday of every month she took a day to herself. She didn't paint or do any of the thousand small household tasks that always waited. Instead, she packed a small bag and went to a hotel—a nice hotel, now that she could afford it, and it was a treat in her otherwise frugal existence. She dined in her room on whatever foods seized her fancy, bathed in a luxurious tub, and thought only of her times with Edward. She glutted herself on him, like a bear storing up fat for the lean times. She pleasured herself countless times and relived the best nights. And the next morning, she went home, and put him out of her mind for the next month—if she was lucky.

If he wrote about sex, she would likely lose her comfortable schedule—her lifeline to sanity. But wild horses couldn't keep her from turning the page.

"The farmer I lived with often loaned me out to the local squire when he had no need of me. I'd grown to nearly a man at fifteen and would work a full day for the squire, and often go home and work several hours that evening and again the next morning for the farmer. I knew the more I worked, the sooner I could leave—so I jumped at any chance to work for the squire, who paid better than anyone else in the area.

Perhaps the fifth or sixth time I worked for him, the job I was doing kept me late. The squire sent a servant to tell me at dusk that his master had paid for another day, and that I was to find a place to sleep in the barn.

That night, when the rest of the lads were sleeping, the squire's man came for me. His master had summoned me to the house for some urgent reason.

Well, I'm sure you can guess the reason. He was an older man—some forty years older than his young, pretty wife—whom some said he'd lost his head over. She was comely, I'd seen her. She liked to stroll in front of us as we worked and sweated in the fields, often when we were shirtless.

Mrs. Squire, I will call her, had noticed me in particular.

So, I would now have a night job, the squire told me, once he'd brought me to his study, the finest room I'd ever been in. If I kept my mouth shut, I could earn more in a night than I did in a week.

I think you know my feelings about money, Nora. I most certainly could keep my mouth shut to earn so much.

He led me to a room that was not far different than the one I created here, although it isn't boastful to say the Squire's was not nearly as nice.

Mrs. Squire was as naked as the day she was born and that night we began our own theatrical, of sorts. I was to grab Mrs. Squire and force myself upon her. When her husband caught us (he'd been in the room all along, of course, watching as I serviced his wife, an activity he could no long participate in, but still enjoyed as a spectator) he would pretend to be furious and bind her to the posts of a massive bed. I would wear manacles and chains, forced to watch as he whipped her.

His whippings were nothing when compared to the ones I gave you. But then pain was not Mrs. Squire's desire, but exhibitionism.

Once her husband had supposedly left the room (only in the story)—leaving her conveniently tied up, naked, and wet—I would fuck her while the squire watched.

Increasingly the Squire would step out of character. Sometimes he was a procurer wanting to buy a slave for his master and needed to see that she was worthy. He would direct me how to fuck her, where, how hard, and so forth. I'm sure you can imagine my fifteen year-old brain and body were thrilled."

Nora laughed. *As would your forty-year-old brain and body be*, she thought with some amusement.

"I noticed over time that I became aroused by the crop, his small collection of whips, floggers, and other implements. I found leather particularly erotic. What began as once every few months became once a month, and then twice, and then finally every week.

I might very well still be there if the Squire had not keeled over in his sleep one night, thankfully not a night when I was balls-deep in his wife."

Nora laughed.

"It seems Mrs. Squire was not as enamored of my cock up her arse as her husband had been. By the time I bought off my indenture, she'd left the neighborhood, rumored to have a new, younger lover.

I see I've filled several pages with my wittering and reminiscing.

Young Edward, on his way back to the city, is a good place to stop. If you are still reading, please know I appreciate it. Edward."

That night, for the first time since she'd made her Wednesday pact with herself, she broke it, pleasuring herself to the image of young Edward servicing the squire's wife.

Chapter Thirty-One

The night he wrote Nora his first letter he opened the door to their room for the first time since the day she'd left—since the day he'd *thrown* her out. Nothing had been touched since the last night they'd been together. Although he'd never told her, it was Edward who'd been the only servant in their room.

Sometimes it was difficult to get the time to bring fresh linens, to clean, oil, and care for the implements he lovingly used on her body—but it had been, he realized now, his only hobby.

He cleaned the room and prepared it for use, even though he had no thought or hope of every using it again, and then locked it up.

Just being inside the place where they'd had such pleasure—and where he'd been such a fool—left him too out of sorts to go to the Birch Palace, his new haunt. That night, he was weighted with longing and regret and all he wanted was Nora.

It was a struggle to wait a week to begin the next letter, but he didn't want to worry her that he'd become obsessed— never mind that he'd never *stopped* being obsessed—and make her stop reading his pitiful missives.

He'd received nothing from her, but then he'd expected nothing. It took all his will not to look for her and find her—to pry into her life and consume her bit by bit from the outside. He no longer owned her—not that he ever had.

He knew that Smith saw her because he told him.

"She's good friends with Charles," was all Smith replied when Edward asked.

Edward's face had heated. Although Smith had never come out and confessed to being a sod, it had become clear when he'd visited his house and the annoying male whore would come out especially to taunt him.

Well, it wasn't his business, was it? And if Smith and Charles were sods, they would hardly be fucking Nora, would they? So, really, it was the best possible solution. If Edward could manage to behave around Smith—and his little whore—Smith might let things slip about Nora, like scraps from a table to the dog cringing beneath.

Oddly, that notion didn't bother him at all; he'd take whatever bits and pieces of her life he could get and be grateful for it.

✳✳✳

Nora followed the same routine as she had with the first letter and kept it until after she'd fed herself, read a book for a while, done a pathetic amount of tidying in her bedchamber—it appeared she was a slob when left to her own devices—and finally climbed into bed with a glass of whiskey, an indulgence just like his letter. It wasn't that she couldn't afford the finest whiskey money could buy, but she rarely imbibed spirits. Partly because she didn't care for the taste very much, but mostly because it made her control slip. When she'd first begun to socialize with the Brotherhood, she'd drunk a great deal, behaved wildly, and made several very bad decisions when it came to lovers.

Now she held herself to no more than one glass a night.

She looked down at the heavy cream envelope and dragged her thumb over his practical, un-pretentious writing. She'd wanted this letter far too much. He was drawing her into his web, seducing her with words rather than whips, his cock, and his cruelty. She should throw this into the rubbish bin and write to tell him to stop. It would be the wise thing to do.

But since when had she ever been wise when it came to Edward?

Nora,

I hope this letter finds you well. I also hope this has not arrived too quickly on the heels of the last one as to seem intrusive.

I know that Smith occasionally sees you—he told me as much, although he said nothing about your location. He reminded me you are a good friend of his friend, the young man named Charles."

Nora smiled. The second *friend* looked a little shaky, as if he'd not been certain of the word to use.

"In any case, I just thought you should know that, although I suspect Smith will have told you."

No he did *not*. Not after the bollocking she gave him about his lie to her. She'd threatened to leave his portrait unfinished if he didn't immediately promise her that he'd never lie to her again. After much hemming and hawing, he'd agreed. She could have told him that nothing in the world would have stopped her from completing their portrait. It was, she felt, one of her best works yet.

She knew it would never be seen beyond a few people, but rather than making her feel sad, it made her feel like she'd buried a treasure. Perhaps someday, a hundred years from now, sexual standards might be less rigid and somebody would find it in an attic and wonder about the two men it depicted. Two men who were so much in love but didn't seem to know it, letting petty differences and small untruths keep them from loving completely. Well, Nora was nobody to give advice in such matters.

She turned back to her letter:

"I left young Edward on his way to London. Luckily I carried letters from both the farmer and Mrs. Squire. I'm sure you can imagine I encouraged Mrs. Squire to be quite effusive about the loyal, hard-working, intelligent, and honest man she was recommending.

I began work as a carpenter's assistant. The man was only about ten years my senior. He'd inherited the shop from his father, who'd been a fine craftsman. The young man, I'll just call him Employer, was not on the level of his father and the shop was suffering. It seemed that I'd finally found something my overlarge hands were good at besides farm labor. I worked hard, as I do when I've found a skill to be mastered."

"Or a woman," Nora muttered.

"Employer was woefully unskilled, so I learned by visiting other master carpenters, and seeing how their work came together. Watching how they worked with the wood rather than tried to bend it. Would you believe that turned out to be a skill

of mine? Working with something rather than bending it to my will? I'll bet you are smiling."

She was. And he was right; she'd never have suspected this hidden skill of his.

"The shop faltered within three years of Employer taking over. I was making serviceable pieces, but not fine furniture. Employer had taken up with a woman who wanted a gentleman rather than a tradesman. One morning I arrived at work to find the door barred. He'd lost his business, which he'd borrowed money against to keep his expensive wife.

I was fortunate that I'd taken my box of tools home with me—as I did every night—or I would have been in a terrible situation, indeed.

With my skills and tools I went along to those men I'd been studying. I was an arrogant pup to think I was highly skilled. I'm sure you will not find that difficult to believe. The pieces of my work that I showed these men did not impress them.

I'd almost exhausted my meagre savings and was becoming frantic when I came to the man who was last on my list: a fine but cantankerous craftsman whose business had never flourished.

He immediately insulted my work and I stormed out, his criticisms ringing in my ears. It was summer and warm and I was big and strong, so I could sleep on the street. But food was another matter and I was on the verge of needing to sell tools to feed myself. So I swallowed my pride—a hearty meal indeed—and went back to the last man.

After insulting me further, he agreed to hire me to sweep his floor and do small jobs that didn't involve me destroying expensive wood (his words).

This man I will name, because our connection is somewhat well-known: Jonah Spinnaker.

I think Jonah will require a letter all his own, so I will stop my story here.

I'll be gone from London next week, but will write to you from exotic Scotland. It is my first visit that far north, and I've been warned to tread lightly around Scotsmen in their native environment. Edward."

The following week, Nora was expecting his letter. Indeed, she made sure to be home for the post. That evening she sat down to a dinner comprised of a meat pie, fresh bread and fruit, keeping her letter until late in the evening, just to see if she could.

When the clock struck midnight, she tore it open.

Nora,

I write to you from the dreariest hotel I've ever had the misfortune to stay in. It is cold, draughty, and the amenities are non-existent. What I <u>can</u> take heart in is that I might have created a new fashion sensation: all gray clothing outfits. I can't claim the genius for wearing gray linens that were once white and a gray suit that was once black, that honor goes to the hotel launderer.

If there is a surlier creature than a Scot confronted with a Londoner, I have yet to find it and hope I never will.

I'm here to check on three ships we've commissioned. Chatham, I daresay you recall him, believes we are being swindled by the shipping company we employ to transport our finished goods from Britain. When Chatham finally speaks, the rest of us tend to listen and believe him.

Well, now we are being swindled by Scottish shipbuilders. I will be here at least another week to untangle this knot,, a prospect I cannot look upon with pleasure. It is a gray city that seems even dirtier than our filthy London. Or perhaps that is a product of prejudice.

My only enjoyment in this cold, rainy, grimy city has been a rather unusual house of pleasure."

Nora's body, which had been well-serviced by her own hand and could not possibly be wanting, throbbed all the same.

"I hesitate to share such information with you for fear I am overstepping the fragile peace between us. At the same time, it is a subject I know interests you."

Nora laughed. "Oh, Edward, you missed your true calling as a bawd."

"But I've come up with a solution. You will notice I included a piece of paper folded and sealed on its own. If you wish to know anything about such subjects, you merely need to crack the seal. If not, you can toss it in the rubbish bin. I will leave the decision up to you."

Nora turned the small folded and sealed packet in her fingers, her body humming. She set it aside; she would read his letter and decide about reading this extra correspondence afterward.

"In my last letter I was just embarking on my apprenticeship with Jonah. The first year is a blur of work, sleep deprivation, and daily mortification. He told me he would strip me to the core and re-build me with the correct skills, and he did. Was it painful? Yes. Did I ever think of leaving? Yes, every day, usually several times a day.

But I stayed and bore up under his various diabolical abuses (no, nothing physical or damaging—at least not permanently).

At the end of the year he gave me the first minor commission that came in. He watched my progress closer than any hawk has ever watched a field. The small cabinet, I remember it well, was a test to see whether it was worth wasting his time to keep me for another year.

Suffice it to say I passed his test after much brow-beating.

The second year was marginally less miserable. It was during that year I learned my real skill: turning an unprofitable business into a profitable one.

When I wasn't being hectored by Jonah, I studied his disastrous leger. Without going into tedious detail, I'll tell you that he was a master carpenter but a failure at running his business.

First there was his unpleasant, unwelcoming, and uncompromising personality. You are thinking I'm a pot criticizing a kettle, I know."

She laughed. Yes, she certainly was.

"I convinced him to hire...can you guess? Yes, my first employer, the man I've called Employer (I see now that may not have been the best choice of names—he was called Ben). He was out of debtor's prison and wifeless and in need of a way to earn a living. Ben had no carpenter skills but he knew the craft and could engage with customers without insulting them.

Getting Jonah to accept Ben was difficult, so Ben agreed to work for room and board, no wages. At the end of six months, Jonah would decide whether he was worth the expense.

The orders came faster than two men could make them. We needed more hands.

Hiring more carpenters was difficult given Jonah's standards. But Ben and I were growing used to his ways and came up with clever—some would say sneaky— solutions.

By the end of my fifth year there were seven craftsmen. That amount doubled by the end of the sixth. We'd expanded, taking all the properties for lease on our side of the street.

Ben and I persuaded Jonah to buy a building.

Soon I had no time for carpentry as I managed this suddenly exploding empire.

During my twenty-eighth year, Jonah died peacefully in his sleep. I can say with certitude, that it was the only thing he ever did peacefully."

Nora sniffed—here she was, crying for a curmudgeonly old carpenter she'd never known. Edward might have a future writing gothic novels if he ever gave up being a titan of business.

"He had no wife, children, or family that anyone knew of. But he'd had the foresight to make a will. Except for a handsome gift of money to Ben, he left everything to me.

So, it is there I will leave you—an older Edward, on the cusp of great change. Yours, Edward."

The other letter sat beside her like a coiled serpent prepared to strike. There was no doubt in her mind she would read it. The only question was, when?

If she read it now, it would change a schedule that had made her life—her work—and her sanity possible. Once she opened the door to fantasizing about Edward any day she wanted, she would be lost.

Besides, it just so happened that her Wednesday—her Edward Wednesday—was next week.

So, the question was, would opening it now be more of a distraction than waiting one entire week and fantasizing about its contents?

She gave a half amused, half annoyed laugh: already it was cutting up her peace.

Nora stared at the white envelope and swore she could hear Edward's laughter.

Chapter Thirty-Two

Edward stared out the rainy window of the syndicate's private train car, pleased to see the last of Glasgow. The disagreements had been smoothed over and construction on their ships had resumed—for the moment. If matters ground to a halt again it would be Chatham or Smith's turn to come deal with the aggravation.

They no longer used Smith as their weapon of choice in every situation because the man would no longer let them. It was probably just as well as Edward shuddered at the number of unmarked graves Smith must have filled at their behest.

He turned away from the dreary view and winced, still sore a week after his most recent adventure. Apparently, it would be at least two months before he'd feel no twinges, and even longer before he'd want to resume his usual activities at the Birch Palace.

That was just as well. Since he'd begun writing Nora his sexual urges had begun to channel themselves in her direction and he had no interest in anyone else. Besides, the only activity in recent memory that had stimulated him even remotely toward the level of sexual satisfaction he'd always achieved with Nora—although still falling far short—had been his first evening out on the town in Glasgow.

And a big part *that* had come from his decision to write to her about it—a decision he'd made an hour after stepping foot into the establishment.

Edward looked down at the writing desk in front of the plush seat he occupied, his finest pen and a stack of parchment awaiting him.

Today was the day he wrote her: Sunday.

Had there been some twisted quasi-religious notion in mind to select such a day?

He snorted and opened the black leather folder that held his correspondence to Nora. He made a copy of each letter he'd written, to make sure he didn't repeat himself. He flipped through the pages—some failed drafts—to get to the copy he wanted, the one he'd sent about his first experience at Glasgow's only attraction.

The place was called Frau Meisen's. On the outside it resembled every other whorehouse. But inside? Well, if Edward had ever designed and constructed such a business this would be what it looked like.

Like the town it inhabited, the inside of the Meisen's gave one a sense of power derived from iron, coal, and machinery. It lacked the fussy furbelows that filled every whorehouse he'd ever visited. Even the Birch Palace relied on clichéd thick red and gold velvet, gilt furniture, and suffocating draperies and wall-hangings. Meisen's was almost as cold and functional as the ironworking and shipbuilding businesses Edward had explored with Gideon Banks his first days in town.

Naturally, it had been Banks who'd discovered the place.

Banks. Edward snorted and shook his head. The elegantly built, exquisitely garbed, blond-haired, and blue-eyed man resembled an angel as much as ever—but he'd begun to resemble the fallen kind. His eyes were still sky blue, but hard. And his almost too-pretty face was scored by deep grooves from his blade-thin, aristocratic nose to his thin-lipped mouth.

Banks ran through mistresses the way other men ran through stockings—faster, probably. He always kept at least two, sometimes as many as four, setting them up in extravagant love nests which he allowed them to keep after he tired of them. And he *always* tired of them—after only four days on one rather infamous occasion. The amount of money he spent on kept women was staggering. But Edward, who was generally believed—quite rightly—to have given over half of his worth to an ex-wife who'd publicly flaunted her affairs and then divorced him—was in no position to pass judgement.

After spending almost two weeks with the man, Edward believed Banks was teetering on the edge and heading for a fall. If anyone knew what that looked like, it was Edward.

When he returned to London he would speak to Chatham and Smith to see what they thought they might do, if anything.

He put that aside for later and perused the letter he'd last sent her, making sure he began in the correct place.

Once he'd refreshed his memory he glanced at the other letter, the one he'd sealed, which told her about that night at Meisen's. He wondered if she'd read it. And, if she had, had she known what was in his mind when he wrote it?

His cock stirred slightly and he winced at the pain even a small amount of arousal caused. No, he'd better not revisit that letter just now.

Nor would he tell her more—especially not about his last visit to Meisen's. At least not until a cockstand wouldn't bring tears to his eyes.

Nora,

I'm writing you this letter on the train back from Glasgow. I'm hoping that will be the last I'll see of that city.

While the trip took longer than I'd hoped, we should have our small fleet of merchant ships by next summer at the latest.

The last thing I wrote is about Jonah's death and will.

I suppose I should talk a little bit about what I did during that time that was not work-related. I had several lovers after Mrs. Squire—most were other women of my class as I could not yet afford the type of establishment I felt any attraction for. But a pattern began to form. I would enter a liaison with all the hope and vigor of any young man only to find the union flat after a certain point. I'm sure you know what I mean as we are both bent, if not actually broken, the same way.

I believe my 'bent' is why I'm a wealthy man. With no interest in marriage—especially not having watched Ben, who would repeat his disastrous marriage after inheriting money from Jonah—and no lover to make demands on my time I applied myself to growing the carpentry business and finding other investments for the money I now had available.

The carpentry shop would eventually become my first manufactory. I know Jonah is still spinning in his grave to see the cheap works we produce, but they are affordable for a class of people who otherwise would go without.

The next business I acquired was a small textile operation. Again, it was the victim of poor management. The owner had neglected to update machinery as a result of worker disagreements. This was a far more challenging investment, and I learned about the difficulties of operating a business with not two dozen employees, but two hundred.

It took three years to make a return on my investment. By that time, my carpentry manufactory could barely meet demands, it was time to expand. This time, I employed the power of credit to acquire more property, rather than spend my own money.

I also joined forces with another man I'd met in the process of handling labor relations at my textile factory, Mr. Smith.

Over the next decade we purchased a dozen or more failing businesses. We also began to look for areas that were either underserved or neglected. We financed railroad spurs, small canal projects, and several toll roads. Along the way we met and included first Banks, who was a wizard with machinery, engines, and such. He'd been a scholarship boy at Oxford before being tossed out for some sexual infraction, and was selling his services—mental, not physical—to various factory owners.

The last of our number, Chatham, was employed by an accounting firm we used. He came to us with proof of multiple embezzlements by his employers. After Smith recouped our money from the firm—using his special Smith-methods—Chatham joined us.

By the time Chatham joined our number, Smith and I were already wealthy men, with Banks well on his way.

I daresay that is enough dry business for anyone to have to ingest.

Life had been hectic, busy, and rewarding up until that point and I'd filled my few spare hours with willing widows or randy bar wenches. For my thirty-fourth birthday I treated myself to my first whorehouse, the Bellaire. Naturally the name and recommendation came from Banks, who should publish one of those informational guides about such places.

For the first time, I was able to purchase what I could never bring myself to ask for from any of my prior lovers.

But that, I believe, is a story for next time.
Yours, Edward

Edward laid aside the pen and stared sightlessly at the letter. There was a lot he didn't know about Nora: like where she came from, what happened to start her down the path of whoring, when she began painting, or a thousand other things he burned to know. Late at night, when his defenses were at the lowest, he would admit to himself that he would probably never get the chance to ask her any of those questions, and he was the only one to blame.

He folded the letter carefully, his lips pressed grimly at thought. But then, as he sealed the envelope—lighter than the last one by half—his lips curved first into a reluctant smile and then into a full-blown grin. He might not know much about her past, but he *did know* what her reaction would be when she received this envelope with only one letter in it.

Chapter Thirty-Three

ora threw the letter onto the bed. "Next time?" she demanded in a voice that was squeaky with disbelief.

To her profound disgust she picked up the envelope and—like a gin addict with an empty bottle—turned it upside down and shook it to check for anything she might have missed: like a second, sealed letter.

There was nothing.

Nora flopped back against the stack of pillows behind her. What a bastard.

He was, she knew, perfectly aware of what he was doing. Who knew Edward possessed such subtlety? Of course he would have assumed she would have read it already and would be panting like a dog in heat for a second one.

She glanced at her nightstand drawer, which held the letter that had tormented her for *six-and-a-half days*—and which she'd hoped, greedily, might have a second letter to join it when the post came with Edward's letter.

Nora *had* hoped that tomorrow night, which was Edward Wednesday, she'd have *two* such letters to open and enjoy and gorge on.

Perhaps the letter only contains information about some new patent for a sticking plaster that will remove corns? her taunting inner voice piped up.

Ha! Whatever was in that letter was pure Edward, which meant sex.

She'd already made—rather pitiful—plans for her orgy of Edward. Instead of going to a hotel, she'd paid her housekeeper to shop for delicacies and she would lock the door and stay in the comfort of her own bed while she enjoyed the letter. And then, likely, frig herself blind.

Nora picked up the letter she'd just finished, her eyes drifting restlessly across the pages.

The story of his success did not surprise her as she knew first-hand that he worked all the time, even though he was already a wealthy, powerful man. But what it had cost him—years of work and, it sounded to her, a largely joyless existence? That *did* surprise her.

For years he'd eschewed everything for his success: family, children, friends and even, it seemed, sexual satisfaction.

Compared to her life, his seemed impoverished. While whoring had had its costs—some quite high—it had thrown her together with a kindred spirit like Lord Anthony, kind and caring lovers like Felix Lombard. And had also given her friends like Charles, who—admittedly—could be a pest but would still give his last penny to help her.

She smiled at that last thought—he would, but he'd charge bloody high interest.

Nora opened the bedside table and extracted the—she hoped—erotic letter, turning it around and around in her hands.

Nora knew that sexual gratification was not everything in life, but to people like her and Edward—for whom intimacy was inextricably bound up with physical acts—it was terribly important.

Besides, who was to say Edward day had to be a Wednesday. Why not a Tuesday? Why not any day?

Perhaps she should send a message to Clive—the model she'd fucked in a closet during an agonizingly tedious party thrown by one of The Brotherhood last week—and tell him she couldn't see him tonight?

Thinking about Clive, unfortunately, brought to mind Derek and the last time she'd seen him, the day after that party.

Nora grimaced at the ugly recollection. She'd been in a hurry to leave when, as usual, he'd barged in without knocking.

"You *fucked* him!"

Nora had reminded herself to start locking her door.

"You fucked Clive Newcomb," he repeated in a less certain tone when Nora ignored him, instead continuing her search for a pair of gloves that both matched and had no holes in them.

"Did you hear me?" he demanded.

"I fucked Clive Newcomb." Nora shook her head; she really needed to employ a maid. Her glove drawer—along with every other part of her house—was a disaster.

"What do you have to say about it?" he demanded behind her.

"I don't have time for this right now, Derek."

"Oh?" he'd sneered. "Going to see bloody Clive? Or are you already moving on to your new Sapphic lover, that nasty old cunt Simmons?"

News travelled fast in artistic circles.

Nora was indeed headed out to meet with Helen Simmons, a painter she'd met at the same party where she'd enjoyed time in the closet with Clive.

Nora had liked the wry, witty older woman immediately. She'd just been about to ask her to luncheon when Helen beat her to it.

"You'd fuck anything, wouldn't you?" Derek demanded.

Nora held up a brown kid glove that appeared to be brand new and frowned at it; where the devil was the other one? "You're behaving like a child, Derek. You have other lovers and I don't make a fuss. We never agreed to—"

The glove disappeared in a blur as Derek spun her and slammed her against the bureau, the violent action sending bottles, jars, and the inevitable stack of books tumbling to the floor.

"You listen to me, you *bitch*."

Nora reacted instinctively, her knee coming up with all the force she could summon. Luckily, she wore one of the loose, *artistic* gowns she favored and there was no huge crinoline to get in the way.

Derek's strangled yelp filled the room and he staggered back, his head clipping the arm of a chair as he fell.

"Don't ever touch me in anger, Derek," she'd said more coolly than she felt.

He'd rolled back and forth on the floor, his hands cupping his genitals, tears streaming from his eyes. Nora tried to dredge up some sympathy for him and failed.

"I'd hoped we might end our association without me having to bring this up, but you forced the issue. I know you took the emergency money I kept in my study desk drawer—which was at least two hundred pounds. I also know you've taken some of my more expensive pigments and sold them. So, you are mistaken in your belief that Clive supplanted you in my affections, Derek—*you* did that. I cannot conscience a thief. You have less than a minute to evacuate my house or I shall stop off at the constable's office on my way to my appointment."

Nora turned back to her drawer as he grunted and shuffled his way toward the door. "I won't forget this," he said in a squeaky growl.

"Don't forget not to steal from your next lover while you're at it," she'd tossed after him, as he slammed the front door hard enough to knock a picture off the wall.

Nora groaned as she recalled that scene. Was it not possible for her to end things with a lover without such pyrotechnics?

A sharp knock came from the front door and Nora frowned, who could that be? None of her friends would ever knock.

But then she recalled she'd begun locking the door after the Derek incident.

She put Edward's letter in the drawer and locked it before pocketing the gold key and heading toward the door. Nora supposed it was telling that the items in the locked drawer weren't jewels or money, but letters from Edward.

She briefly checked her reflection in the entry hall mirror—adequate—before unlocking the door and opening it.

And then freezing.

"Hallo, Nora."

Nora steadied herself against the doorframe. "Catherine."

Chapter Thirty-Four

Cat's laugh, that same carefree, slightly wicked laugh, made Nora shiver.

"I don't think I've seen you speechless before," Cat confessed, her tone jocular, but her eyes flickering about in a nervous fashion. "Did I call at a bad time?" She laughed again, not the carefree one. "Is *any* time a good time for me to call?"

Nora reached out and took her elegantly gloved hand, squeezing the delicate bones hard.

"I'm happy to see you," she said, wondering if that was really true. "I was just surprised." She opened the door wider. "Please, come in."

Cat entered and looked around, her forehead becoming gradually more furrowed as she took in the narrow, dark entry hall, which was strewn with the detritus of Nora's life: a broken easel, several worn, forgotten, male coats, a hat with no top, and other random items.

Looking at Cat's almost horrified expression created an urge within Nora that she couldn't recall experiencing before: the urge to tidy like a frantic hostess.

"Do you have time to stay for tea, Catherine? Or I have coffee if you'd rather?"

"Well, if you're sure I'm not interrupting."

"Oh no, of course not." Nora cringed at her over-hearty tone.

"I have time. *Loads* of it," Cat laughed again, and this time Nora noticed how brittle it sounded.

She wished, suddenly, that she'd not answered the door, or that she'd told Cat she was on her way out—anything but this. Even when she wasn't looking directly at Cat she could sense the familiar need and desperation that had always simmered just below the surface of her beautiful veneer.

"Please, come into my sitting room."

Nora couldn't help grimacing as she saw it all through Cat's eyes.

What was wrong with her? She never cared about such things!

"Can I take your coat and hat?" she offered, likely oozing a bit of desperation herself.

Once she'd helped Cat out of her elegant coat she realized there was nowhere to put it, so she laid it over her desk and returned for Cat's hat.

"Would you like tea or coffee?" she asked as she deposited the hat along with the coat. "I'm afraid today is one of the days my housekeeper does not work, but it would only take a moment to make it for you." A moment Nora could use to gather her scattered wits.

She could tell by Cat's arched eyebrows—which had been lightened just like her hair, the shade rather close to Nora's own pale blond.

"Actually," Cat said with a wry smile. "I can spare you the effort." She gestured toward the small table of decanters.

It was barely noon; Nora suddenly understood the other woman's gauntness.

"Of course, what would you like? Although, to be honest, I'm not sure exactly what I have. I keep a good selection for several of my friends who are quite demanding." She couldn't seem to quit babbling.

"Anything is fine," Cat said, casually stripping off her elegant gloves, which were a spectacular magenta shade Nora had recently tried to replicate with some pigments. The color was beautiful but it did not, she thought, suit Cat's coloring.

"I've heard about your rather famous—some would say infamous—circle," Cat said, looking around at the cluttered tables for a place to set her gloves before tossing them onto the settee behind her—which, Nora noticed with a grimace—was loaded with sketches she'd been making for her portrait of Smith.

She hastened forward and held out a glass.

"Here you are," she said when Cat didn't immediately look up from the pictures of Smith, whom she certainly must recognize.

Cat took the glass, her expression dazed. "I see you have drawings of Mr. Smith—are these from—before, or are you still acquainted?"

Nora cleared a place to sit while conveniently removing the drawings at the same time, pretending as if she'd not heard the question.

She sat but Cat was still looking with bemusement at the stack of drawings, now on the end table.

"You have?" Nora prodded.

Cat downed fully half the glass of whiskey in one sip. "I'm sorry, what was that, Nora?"

Nora struggled to mask her horror. "Er, I was referring to what you just said—that you'd heard of my friends?"

"Ah, yes, that. Don't worry," she said, reading Nora's expression correctly. "I've not heard the name Nora Hudson, only about the elusive Natalie Hartwicke, whom all the men in the only interesting part of London want to fuck."

Nora flinched at the word, but Cat was too amused by her own thoughts to notice.

"I saw one of your paintings and knew immediately it was you."

That was both flattering and worrisome. "Oh, and which one was that?" She'd not sold many, but she often gave them away. After all, most of them she felt no attachment to when she was done. Only those three.

"Some young Adonis posing as Atlas."

That would be Derek.

"I met him at a party given by a very wealthy and wicked woman I know—Amelia St. John."

Yes, Nora knew who she was: a *very* wealthy woman in her fifties who collected young males along with paintings. Nora had met her a few times and liked the older woman, who could be a bit cattish, but was clever and amusing while doing it.

Cat shrugged. "I knew immediately N. Hartwicke was you. Your style is very distinctive." Her mouth softened a little. "It was a brilliant painting."

Nora's face heated. Even now—after she'd sold pieces for several hundred pounds—she snatched at every morsel of praise.

"He was quite thrilled with the price—Amelia apparently paid a packet for it."

Nora was disappointed, but not surprised, that Derek sold a picture she'd given him as a gift. He was poor and needed to eat and St. John's offer must have been irresistible.

"However, my dear Nora," Cat drawled, her sly smile giving Nora a hint at what was coming. "When I asked him about what it was like to pose for N. Hartwicke he seemed quite . . . well, hostile, I suppose." Cat laughed, a malicious glint in her eyes. "He's terribly miffed that you threw him over but I told him to cheer up, that he was now part of an exclusive club."

No doubt he'd conveniently forgotten that his thieving, and not his person or lack of sexual skills, had been the real reason she'd ended their liaison.

"I shouldn't worry about breaking his heart too badly," Cat said, "Lady St. John appears pleased to add him to her current stable. I daresay he's forgotten you by now."

Nora smiled; Cat's tongue always had been a sharp one, just never aimed at her.

"That one you did of me—the unfinished one—it hangs in your little playroom, you know."

Nora knew which *painting* and which *he* Cat referred to—the one Edward had been holding when Nora found him in her sunroom that day. Why hadn't Edward destroyed the portrait? Didn't it remind him of Nora's betrayal?

"I know he keeps it because it reminds him of *you*—not because it's a painting of *me*." Cat laughed harshly. "The only time he ever got truly angry with me is when he realized I possessed a key to his little . . . *shrine* to you."

Nora opened her mouth to say—what? Cat was correct: she'd been a piece in a game between Nora and Edward.

Cat lifted her glass, which was empty. "May I? Oh, no—you sit," she said when Nora began to get up. "I'll see to my own needs. We are old friends, after all, aren't we? We don't need to stand on formality." Her back was to Nora when she said the words, but they were bitter and it cut her: because she deserved it.

Cat turned, holding a glass that was so full the amber liquid touched the top rim.

"Did you know I kept expecting you to contact me?" Pain and rejection mixed in Cat's eyes.

Yes, Nora knew.

Cat gave a scathing laugh. "He told me he'd forbidden you to do so and said your obedience to him would *always* outstrip any feelings you had for me."

Nora did not contradict her—it would have been a lie.

"He didn't even say it in a taunting way, but with calm certainty. Even so, I didn't—I couldn't—believe it. I *knew* you loved me. Every day I waited for something—*some sign.*" Her voice pulsed with self-loathing and she swirled the liquid in her glass, staring down at it. "You were wise never to come back. The two of us had been bad before, but after you left? Well there was nobody left to act as a buffer between us—to keep us from employing every weapon we could find. But do you know what his greatest weapon was? The one that spread destruction like those terrible guns the Prussians are said to use on defenseless villages?" She paused, her blue eyes leaking tears and hatred in equal measure. "We'd been fighting for days and I'd accused him, again, of separating us—you and me. And that was when he told me what I should have guessed all along. You know what that was, don't you, Nora?" Her laughter held a hint of madness, and she didn't wait for Nora's answer. "It was when he told me that I was just another prop, toy, or implement—no more than a whip or chunk of marble—for the two of you to use to heighten your twisted, perverted pleasures."

Nora knew she should open her mouth and accept the blame, but her jaw was frozen. Besides, what could she say? It was true, and there was nothing she could say to excuse her behavior, nothing she could do to undo it.

Cat stared at the glass in her hand, which shook hard enough to spill amber liquid on the rug. "I know you were in on his plans from the beginning."

Nora startled. Surely Edward would not have been that cruel—?

"No, he didn't tell me." She said as though Nora had spoken out loud, her look sharper than a sabre. "But I know him. And I also know you—*now.* He would have come to you as he planned his *courtship,*" she spat the word, "And he would have told you *everything*. And then he would have whipped you and the two of you would fuck each other into a frenzy of twisted passion."

Nora's soul felt sick and her stomach churned so badly she had to clench her jaws tight to keep back the bile.

But the sad, revolting truth? The images Cat's words evoked made her sex and belly clench for those lost days.

"I'll bet he even came to you on our wedding night."

Nora remained rigid, silent, but Cat laughed.

"Yes, I guessed as much. How you must have laughed together— especially later when I came to you for comfort after those horrid nights with him. I'll bet—" she choked and the rattle in her chest was more than a little alarming.

"Cat—" Nora half-stood but Cat waved her back, shaking her head until the bout cleared.

"Stay away from me," she said in a hoarse voice, blinking hard, as if she could stop the tears that had already fallen. She lowered the glass without looking and it hit the edge of the table and tumbled to the floor.

They both stared at it.

Cat jostled the overloaded coffee table and sent books and sketches tumbling. "I never should have come. You did me a favor by ignoring me—showing me how little I meant to you. You continued to obey his orders even after I'd divorced him, when you knew *exactly* where to find me. I've been a fool; you made your feelings—or *lack* of them—clear." She shook her head, as if trying to dislodge something. "I never should have come," she repeated, snatching up her coat, hat, and gloves and stumbling blindly, bumping into tables and chairs as she left the crowded room, scattering books and other detritus in her wake.

Nora opened her mouth to call after her, to beg her not to go. But Cat's words had been like arrows dipped in poison—the poisonous truth of what Edward and Nora had done to her—and they had hit their mark with deadly accuracy.

They'd both treated Cat abominably—Nora just as much as Edward. He might have been the one to begin their game, but Nora had never hesitated to join him.

She didn't know if she could have stopped him, but she could have tried. She could have told him she loved him any time before he'd offered another woman marriage. She could have threatened to leave him if he married. He might not have heeded her. He might have let her go—or she might have stayed, anyway.

Nora could have put some effort into saving an innocent bystander. But no, just like Edward, she'd sacrificed Cat to her needs, not stopping even after she began to know and like her.

That night when she'd crawled into Nora's bed there had been other options. While none of them were good ones, at least she could have chosen one that didn't put Cat into the middle of their sexual games.

At every fork in the twisty road she'd traveled with Edward, she'd always chosen the path that led to their pleasure at the expense of everything—and everyone—else.

If she went after Cat now, it would be to make herself feel better—not because she believed she could do or say anything that would help her. After all, look at how things had turned out the last time Cat came to her for help?

So, for once in her dealings with Cat, Nora did something for the other woman rather than her guilt-stricken conscience: she let her go.

Chapter Thirty-Five

Catherine

Cat woke up in a bed that was not hers, but there was nothing new about that.

She lifted the blanket to see who was beside her, squinting down at auburn hair and pale, pale skin. It took a moment for her to remember: she didn't recall her name, but it was the new girl at Bernina's.

She stared up at the ceiling, glad there were no mirrors there, as there were in many of Cecile's rooms. Cat didn't look at herself if she could help it. She'd not wanted to sleep another night in this, or any other, whorehouse, but she could not seem to sleep in the huge house she'd purchased after the divorce. A house so big it made *his* pale by comparison.

Cat should feel a sense of triumph that she'd humiliated Edward by *very* publicly flaunting her infidelities during the last months of their marriage and then again by winning a divorce settlement that still made her eyes water, but she didn't.

Besides, it wasn't much of a triumph considering he'd never resisted even one of her demands. She could have had everything of his if that bastard Smith had not come to her.

Smith had *advised*—threatened, really—that she take the half Edward offered her and have done with it. She'd considered ignoring the man, but something about the insignificant looking but somehow menacing businessman—a man who didn't even have a *first* name—decided her against it.

Cat had always known Smith didn't like her. Whenever Edward had insisted on dragging her along to one of his dreary business functions Smith had always been there—along with that creepy Chatham who never spoke but *looked* with those probing eyes, and that disgusting leching Banks, who'd tried to fuck her every time they met.

Mr. Smith had hardly even acknowledged her, making his preference for Nora clear. The two of them had laughed and giggled like schoolgirls whenever they'd been around each other, an activity that had irritated Edward no end. So at least that had been enjoyable to watch.

Yes, Nora laughing with another man had done far more than all Cat's infidelity and public flaunting to torment Edward. The only thing Cat had ever done to hurt him was take away his Nora.

His Nora, she snorted and shook her head, not ready to think about Nora and their last meeting just yet—not until she'd had a few drinks.

Instead of thinking about her stupid decision to dredge up old pain and old memories, Cat did what she always did on mornings after nights with too much alcohol and too much mindless sex: she tried to recall how she ended up where she was, which seemed to grow increasingly difficult.

The evening came back to her gradually. She'd gone to one of the endless string of parties she used to favor—those thrown by rich society women—*her* kind of women—who wanted to rub shoulders, and other things, with London's rougher, wilder element.

After almost a year of attending such functions, the novelty had paled.

There'd been nobody there she'd wanted to talk to or fuck so she'd had her coachman take her to Bernina's and she'd paid a lot of money to forget for a few hours.

Brief snatches of last night drifted through her mind's eye, none of them interesting enough for her to seize and examine.

It was the same, always the same. The redhead still lying beside her had a luscious mouth and tongue and had given Cat just what she'd paid for: a string of intense but empty orgasms.

Cat knew most of the whores disliked her because she used the girls harder even than most men, making them work until their jaws probably felt close to falling off.

Not even Emma wanted to see her any longer, and Emma was the least demanding, least temperamental person she'd ever known. But the last few times Cat had asked Cecile for her, she'd been *unavailable*. So, there was an insult for you—rejected by a whore even though Cat knew she'd always paid Emma at least three times as any other client.

Cat shrugged to herself. Who cared? Other than a passing resemblance to Nora—which faded quickly the moment the woman opened her mouth to speak—she was no better than any of the others.

Certainly no better than her current bed partner, who'd complied quickly and without question to all of Cat's demands.

Instead of being aroused by such submission—as she had with Nora—the girl had only irritated her. Cat kept pushing her, wondering when she'd finally say *no*, making the woman lick and suck her long past the point when it was pleasurable.

Cat reached between her lips and winced. She was raw and sore and knew she should forgo carnal pleasure for at least a few days—better a week. But she wouldn't because there was a party tonight that she actually wished to go to. One of the painters Nora was known to associate with had sold a painting to one of Cat's friends. Well, friend was pushing it. Lady Susan Metford was another woman like Cat—a duke's daughter who'd married an obscenely rich cit who'd conveniently died in the bed of his mistress, leaving Suzie nearly as rich as Cat.

She was almost as notorious for her sexual antics and her parties often devolved—or evolved, depending on how one looked at it—into orgies. Cat never missed them.

What else was there other than parties? She was a divorcee—a notorious, wealthy slut who was no longer welcome in polite company. Or even impolite company.

Suddenly she recalled what had started her drinking so early yesterday, which she tried to avoid but increasingly couldn't control. It hadn't just been that disastrous visit to Nora a few days ago—it had been her mother's telegram from Dover. Ceddy was in a hospital in Naples. He'd been stabbed and was not expected to live much longer.

Her mother and father were rushing off to the Continent and had ordered her to join them.

That had made Cat laugh. And then fire off a one-word telegram of her own: No.

That was the only consolation she'd received from her miserable marriage: her freedom.

Ceddy was a slimy worm who deserved what had happened to him; the person who'd knifed him deserved a medal.

Still, thinking of him dead made her recall when they were little—back before he'd turned into such a poisonous toad. They'd been all each other had while their parents fought loudly enough to wake the neighborhood.

But that was long ago.

Cat still burned with fury when she recalled his attempted blackmail of her and Nora.

It was too bad Edward had kept that painting of her. It really had been beautiful—and not just because it was her, but because Nora had an ability for capturing something other people didn't see.

At the time she'd thought Nora had painted her so clearly because she'd loved Cat. But now, especially after seeing the painting of the big, handsome, and rather thick Derek, she knew that was just part of her skill. The painting of Derek had been riveting not so much because he'd only been wearing a scrap of fabric over his far too masculine body, but because you could see the person behind his façade—his acquisitive, greedy self peeking out.

Well, *others* could see it. Derek had simply preened as he stood beside it at that party, clearly too stupid to realize that Nora had stripped more off him than just his clothing.

While the painting had been good, she'd been more intrigued by the knowledge that Derek must have known Nora, at least a little. He'd been as stupid as he looked, and he'd also demonstrated some other traits she recognized: jealousy, anger, and a desire for revenge.

Not only had he been Nora's model, but her lover. Cat idly wondered if Nora only painted people she fucked. Or only fucked people she'd painted.

She snorted. Anyhow, Derek was another victim of Nora's perplexing siren effect on both men and women.

It was a sign of Cat's own petty character that she hoped Derek would find some way to hurt Nora—which was something Cat couldn't seem to manage.

It would be nice to see Nora suffer at somebody else's hands for a change. Perhaps she and Derek could chat a bit more about his situation. Maybe—

The body next to her shifted and groaned and a smooth warm hand traveled up Cat's naked thigh, knocking the thought of Derek from her mind.

She had to give the whore credit—she was intent on earning her money.

Cat sighed and laid back, her legs already spreading even though she knew it would be more painful than pleasurable.

Instead of thinking of the woman laboring between her thighs, however, she thought of Nora. And Derek.

Chapter Thirty-Six

It took Nora three days before she knew she would not be contacting Cat—either in person or with a letter.

That Wednesday night after Cat's visit had been the first Edward Wednesday on which Nora hadn't thought about him or engaged in her solo orgy of pleasure. The letter she'd so anticipated reading had remained unopened, and she'd wondered if she would ever be able to read something from him again without feeling crushing guilt at what they'd done to Catherine.

But of course she hadn't thrown the letter away.

Instead, she'd put it back in its locked drawer.

And for three days she'd run her encounter with Cat through her head, over and over.

At least a dozen times Nora had been on the verge of calling on her. But then she decided she could explain better, and less emotionally, in a letter. And she'd even begun several letters, but none of them seemed adequate.

Nora *was* sorry about how she'd used her, and ashamed at her ability to treat a person she had liked so horridly.

But the truth, if Nora were honest with herself, was that she would do the same thing over again without hesitation.

That was the result Edward had on her, and visa-versa. They were like chemicals that reacted violently when mixed, and Nora would be a hypocrite to expect Cat's forgiveness.

Nora couldn't heal her, only time and Cat's own efforts could heal herself. If Nora called or wrote, she would only be doing so to assuage her conscience.

That decision had taken three days, which Nora thought of as a vaguely biblical number; not that what she was about to do—finally read his damned letter—had anything holy about it. No, once again she'd had a choice to make, and she'd chosen Edward.

Today had been her last sitting with Smith and Charles, which gave her a pang of sadness although the painting, when she finished it, would be superb. She would still go to Smith's house to complete her work, but sittings were no longer necessary. Indeed, they'd not been necessary for some time, but she'd strung them out longer because they'd been far too entertaining to curtail.

Feeling rather restless, she'd called on Helen rather than going home—an impulsive act that had led to an afternoon of unexpected pleasure. After enjoying an impromptu tea and exploring Helen's shockingly tidy studio, Nora had accompanied her to a show. The painter was a friend of Helen's, another woman whose work Nora had found inspiring.

She'd headed home filled with hope and excitement at making new friends—women painters like herself, rather than more self-centered men.

The afternoon had reinvigorated her and she'd begun her new painting of Smith almost immediately upon returning home, almost setting her studio ablaze with candles before deciding it would be wiser to resume in the morning.

And now, as the hour approached midnight, restlessness began to creep in.

It was usual for her to feel a certain sense of anxiety after she finished one project and moved on to another—as if she were about to embark on a journey—but the truth was her mind had settled, once again, on the letter locked in her drawer.

It wasn't an Edward Wednesday but she'd make it his night after ignoring the last.

She changed into her oldest, softest nightgown, poured herself a glass of whisky and, on impulse, brought the decanter to her nightstand and crawled into bed.

She broke the seal and unfolded the pages.

Nora:

I must confess it arouses me to think of you reading this.

Then again, you are far more likely to use this letter to wrap up a kipper carcass, which is what I deserve.

In the spirit of optimism, not to mention sexual fulfillment, I will choose to believe the former.

My second night in Glasgow I went to a brothel with Banks, who, of course, had already been there on our first night. You know Banks, you could put him down blindfolded in any city in the world and he would locate a whorehouse within the hour.

We were met at the door by the madam, a cruel-looking female of indeterminate years. She had skin as white as yours, but from heavy powder, rather than nature. She was garbed in revealing, sensual clothing intended to draw a man's attention away from eyes that glittered with more sin and acquisitiveness than I've ever encountered.

She knew why we were there, courtesy of Banks, and led us to a room with a minimum of conversation.

The room was stark and spare and unlike any I've seen before in a brothel. It reminded me of <u>our room</u> in its lack of artifice but it was not as elegant or comfortable. There were no plush rugs, mirrors, or even a bed; there were just a dozen heavy chairs scattered about the large space, with men occupying all of them.

Some were alone, some in small groups, a few young, but most around my age.

They shared one characteristic: they all gave frequent, impatient glances toward the other end of the room, which was covered by a black velvet curtain, like the type you would see on a theater stage.

Banks and I were the last of the guests and, after seating us, the madam drew the curtain to expose a heavy iron frame that had the look of the hoists used in the shipyards to lift massive, heavy timbers and such. It had been altered to suit its special purpose, which was immediately apparent from the woman strapped to it.

You will probably not be surprised to hear she was naked and bound. Her arms hung together over her head while her legs were wide-spread in a way that left her exposed. Interestingly, she wore a black velvet bag over her head and face. I have to admit—"

Nora paused a moment, forcing herself to slow down. The letter covered only a few pages—at this rate she'd be done in less than five minutes. She took a few calming sips, savored the rich burn, and continued:

"I have to admit that I found the erasure of her identity arousing.

With no face—no eyes—she was simply an object for our viewing pleasure, a vessel waiting to be filled. She had a lovely body, but nothing about her was out of the ordinary. I realize, now, that she'd been chosen for her very lack of distinction. If a man were willing to use his imagination, she might be whomever he wanted her to be.

I imagined she was you."

Nora picked up the glass with shaking hands. It had been too long since her last orgasm if she could become this stimulated by mere words.

But these were Edward's words—fresh words at that, not the ones she hoarded, those well-used memories that she'd used time and again on her Wednesday every month.

She put down her glass and continued.

"The madam made a summoning gesture and a man entered the room—a great hulking fellow who made me look small. He was garbed in a robe that he dropped upon turning to his small audience.

I must admit the theatricality displeased me and prevented any true sensuality, but, I am happy to say, that changed once the madam left the proceedings.

Like his counterpart, the man was naked. He also wore a mask to conceal his face, although his mask allowed him to see.

He was enormous in every way.

And here is where I need to interject something."

"Good. God. Are you trying to kill me, Edward?" she muttered, throwing back the rest of her drink far quicker than was wise. The alcohol warmed her throat and made a low humming noise in her head.

She refilled her glass. It was unwise, but she was alone and would only make a fool of herself in front of herself.

"After you rejected my first offer at Tosca's I was at a low point. Smith appeared determined to befriend me, cheer me out of my doldrums. You know Smith as well as I do; he has the crookedest mind I've ever encountered.

I realize now that he was attempting to addle me so badly I'd focus on what I really wanted—you—and find a way to make you accept me. I daresay he enjoyed addling me. His first move was to take me to an erotic bath house, where he made sure I was primed, but not pleasured. He also exposed himself—erect—in a seemingly harmless fashion."

Nora's lips pulled up in a smirk at that revelation, knowing what was coming.

"~~I know you won't be surprised that such a sight unnerved me~~.

That is not exactly true. While the sight unnerved me, I found it arousing. I worried I might be a sod. I'm ashamed to say that led to my ill-advised visit to Tosca's with him. After that, he left me to stew on my situation for several weeks before inviting me on another jaunt. I accepted, hoping to prove my masculinity. By that time, I was half-mad and only needed a slight nudge.

This time we went to his club of choice, Bernina's, where he'd lined up Emma. He fucked her in front of me, and, to my mortification, I not only enjoyed watching them, I enjoyed watching <u>him</u>."

Nora snorted, even though she knew it was unkind to mock him. Admitting his physical response to her had doubtless been extremely difficult.

"Smith's plan to set me on the road toward <u>you</u> worked very well.

His actions left a residual fear, but also the realization that I could find eroticism in a man and not be a sod.

Which takes me back to my story.

While the female represented a wide spectrum of physical types, the male in this performance had been chosen to intimidate his male audience. He was slabbed with muscles, his legs corded with massive thews that led to narrow, sleek hips which supported a cock that was, I am forced to admit, even larger than mine."

Nora smiled at how much it must have pained him to write that and took a sip from her glass.

"His entire body had been oiled, including his thick shaft, which jutted above a heavy, pendulous sac. He was truly a goliath. But that was not the surprising part. The surprising part was the silver bar piercing the head of his cock."

Nora had lifted the glass to her lips with her free hand and almost choked. "Good God," she muttered. Could Edward read her mind?

"I've always believed I was a man well-versed in sexual deviance, but I simply hadn't imagined a thing like this was possible.

Yes, I stared. And, I admit, I wondered what such a thing must feel like. Well, after the initial excruciating pain, of course.

His first action was to remove a peg from the frame on which the woman was tied. That simple action allowed him to easily turn it, positioning her any way he wished.

He moved her until she was largely in profile to the audience, and then secured the device. Next he went to a table where several implements had been laid out and selected a light-weight flogger."

Nora shivered and closed her eyes, her inner muscles clenching as the image of Edward with a flogger in his hand filled her mind. She groaned, torn between servicing herself or finishing the letter.

She stroked herself with one hand while the other lifted the letter.

"As you know from experience, a light flogger is the most deceptive of all whips. When wielded properly—as I flatter myself I do—"

"Ha! You *know* it's not flattery," she muttered, taking another sip of whiskey to sooth her strangely parched throat.

"—as I flatter myself I do—the first phase of a well-done whipping will feel more like a caress.

Our Goliath warmed up his massive arm with several light blows—so light his subject barely quivered. It didn't take long for his arm to get into a hypnotic rhythm, the fall of the lash and slight shudder of her body mesmerizing.

Although the big room was silent, the atmosphere of arousal was palpable and added an element to the whipping I'd not experienced before. I found it affecting and was as hard, I suspect, as every man watching.

He was very good at his job and she didn't realize the blows had begun to redden her skin, so slowly did he increase their force. She marked beautifully and began to flinch and whimper as his blows fell harder.

Goliath was as stimulated as his subject, his enormous cock arched hard against his belly, weeping so copiously it slickened his shaft.

Her whimpers turned to grunts as his biceps bulged with the violence of his strokes, both their bodies glistening with exertion. And then she began to shudder, her spread hips clenching and futilely attempting to thrust against their tight bonds as she climaxed.

He tossed aside his flogger and went to stand before her, sliding a huge hand around her slender waist and then another around his monstrous, pierced cock. He was clearly primed but he pumped himself several times to display his length and girth, like a stag displaying its enormous rack before the lesser members of the herd.

He mounted her with one brutal thrust, holding her filled and arched as she writhed.

His thrusts, when they began, echoed his flogging. Subtle movements of his powerful hips, thighs and ass, designed to hold the eye to the point at which they were joined.

It was mesmerizing to watch such a huge organ in motion, and to know the metal impaling him must be heightening her pleasure.

I felt movement beside me and looked away from the riveting display to see that Banks had stood and approached the duo. He'd removed his coat but otherwise wore his trousers, waistcoat, shirt, and even his cravat.

He'd also opened the placket to his trousers before moving toward the stage, and his organ—respectable for a man his size—jutted out through the opening, hard and slickened.

Goliath paused in his thrusting, his huge chest heaving with the effort of restraining his orgasm. He appeared unsurprised by Banks's arrival so I knew the scene must still be following some script.

Trust Banks.

Incidentally, I learned afterward that although Goliath was an employee at the brothel, his female companion was the wife of one of the men in the audience. This performance was the wealthy man's gift to his wife."

"Oh Edward," Nora murmured. "How bloody lovely."

"I sat there aroused and frustrated, imagining that I was this Goliath and the woman was you. I also imagined just watching you with two other men. I imagined all types of scenarios.

I know you'd have reveled in driving me mad with lust and jealousy while you allowed others into those parts of your body that I considered mine.

Why did I never live out such fantasies?

Jealousy and no small amount of fear, I'm ashamed to say. Jealousy is self-explanatory, but the fear? I feared you would enjoy one of the others more than me."

"You foolish, foolish, man."

"As always, you were the stronger one, having never objected no matter how often I brought in other women. And then there was my anxiety about engaging in such an act with other men, worrying . . . well, I'm sure you can guess.

I greatly enjoyed what I'm about to relate, Nora. But I can't help wishing the woman had been you."

Nora groaned, her eyes never leaving the page, her fingers caressing in a way that would draw out her pleasure.

"Banks took his position behind her and, I have to admit, there was something unspeakably erotic about her naked, whipped body pressed against his fully clothed person.

Goliath was still thrusting, but his strokes had become languid and deep.

Banks reached around the woman's body and fondled her breasts while his hips pumped slowly, rubbing his cock against her lower back. He worked her nipples until she began to squirm and moan before exploring the rest of her body and ending at his destination: her whip-reddened, wide-spread ass. He produced a bottle of oil from one pocket, making sure to oil the hand that was on the side of his audience.

I admit Banks surprised me and prepared her like a gentleman, rather than just bulling in. He insinuated a finger, his massaging gradual, heightening her pleasure while whetting the audience's anticipation. And then two fingers, three fingers, her whimpering becoming primitive grunting.

Goliath stilled his thrusting while Banks slicked his cock with more oil, pumping it—a clear act of showmanship.

There was not a sound in the big room as he positioned himself at her entrance— my own body tensed, my cock hard and weeping—and then he breached her. I caught my grunt of pleasure, but several of the audience did not. The air was thick with savagery and sex as he slid in slowly, gently, until he was seated.

Goliath had removed his enormous organ and was casually fisting it, priming it as if waiting for some signal.

It occurred to me the woman was far more fortunate to have Banks at her back entrance than Goliath."

"I would want you there, Edward," Nora whispered, her jaw clenching with the effort of holding her hand in check.

"Banks began fucking her with slow, deep thrusts while Goliath waited until an out stroke, and drove into her, hard.

I confess I've rarely been so close to climaxing in public. I could almost feel the inside of your body, Nora. I could imagine your small pelvis, stuffed with so much cock you felt ready to burst.

Like the men performing before me, we—me and your mystery lover—would fuck you in alternating thrusts. You would straddle the border between pleasure and pain as your orgasm built, your body's contractions taking us with you. And when you reached the precipice we would fuck you in time, filling you with hot spurts of—"

Nora threw down the letter like it was on fire, her hips jerking as the waves of pleasure pounded her. Finally, whimpering with exhaustion and drink, she curled up on her side and began to drift into sleep.

The letter.

The thought woke her with a start and she briefly struggled to sit up. But the combined effects of sexual lassitude and drink overwhelmed her. She closed her eyes and gave herself up to soothing oblivion.

***

"Hallo, Nora," a hot voice whispered in her ear.

Nora gasped as rough hands seized her by the waist and flipped her over.

Her eyes felt weighted, her head heavy and thick as she struggled to place herself.

Strong hands fumbled at her bunched up nightgown and tore it, not in one long rend, but a series of furious tugs.

Nora swam through alcohol and sleep, fighting her way to consciousness like a ponderous turtle. "Edward? Wha—?"

Hot breath coated her ear. "Not Edward you bloody *whore*. And who the hell is he? Your newest cunt-pricker? Already thrown aside poor Clive?" An ugly breathy laugh followed the voice, which she'd never heard so filled with hate and loathing.

"Der-ck?" she mumbled, a hand pressing against her back as his legs straddled her thighs, his hands fumbling and bumping her naked bottom.

"That's right, *Nora*. I've come to take a bit 'o what I deserve." His breath was ragged and something blunt shoved between her cheeks. "You kept me dancing after you were like a right princess, aye?" He thrust against her, his cock breaching her dry, unprepared body.

Nora screamed, or tried to, but Derek pressed her face into the pillow, until she was more worried about breathing than the agonizing tearing and thrusting.

"Treating me like a servant." He thrusted and grunted. "While all the time you were nothing but a fucking whore. Thought kneeing my jewels was funny, didn't you?"

He cuffed her head hard, the blow setting off sparks behind her eyes.

"Thought you'd had the last bloody word *Nora*."

He struck her again. And again.

As she sank into darkness it occurred to her that he'd called her Nora. Derek had somehow found out who she was.

Chapter Thirty-Seven

Mr. Smith

"N ora? *Oh my God! Nora! Are you dead?*" Charles flung himself on the poor woman and was pulling at her shoulder.

Smith strode toward the bed. "Good God, Charles, get off her so she can speak. You're crushing her—look her hand is moving. She's not dead." His voice sounded calm, but inside he was chilled and shaking.

He sat on the mattress beside her. "Nora, can you hear me?"

She groaned.

On the other side of the bed, Charles bounced up and down. "Oh, God! What do we do? We must call a doctor I'm—"

"Charles if you do not sit down in that chair this instant, I will pick you up and lock you out of the room."

Charles's very pretty jaw dropped open and then his eyebrows plunged. He opened his mouth, looked at Nora, and then swallowed whatever he was about to say. The look he cut Smith, however, told him Smith would pay later.

Smith was afraid to look too closely at the blood smeared bedding around Nora's hips. Her torso was naked, the bruises and scratches telling at least part of the tale.

"Nora," he asked, "Are you hurt inside? Do you need a doc—"

"No doctor." The words were muffled, but strong. Her arm moved and at first Smith thought it was to push him away, instead her hand felt blindly until it landed on his. Her slender, work-roughened fingers were cold, and her grip was crushing. And then she began to sob.

✳✳✳

Nora was so mortified by her behavior she didn't want to turn over.

Poor Smith. He'd held her hand and awkwardly patted her shoulders with his free one. Charles had disobeyed him, coming to sit on her other side. The two of them clucking and murmuring so much like broody hens that soon she began to laugh.

Their hands froze. "Is she choking, Smith?"

"I think she's laughing."

The laughter seemed to cut off the torrent of sobs and she finally turned over.

Smith hurried to cover up her naked breasts, which she found endearing.

"What time is it?" she asked, merely to break the awkward silence.

The two men exchanged an uneasy glance that sent a bolt of fear to her heart. "Is it Edward? Did something happen to Edward?" She sat bolt upright, flinging off the covers.

"Shhh, darling," Smith murmured. "Edward's fine. Well, as fine as he ever is given that he's Edward."

Charles grabbed several cushions and put them behind her. "Here," he said, gently pushing her shoulder. "Lie back."

Nora complied, the small hairs all over her body suddenly prickling. "What is going on? Please, tell me."

Charles looked at Smith, who nodded.

"We came about this," he handed Nora a newspaper. It had been folded back to the society section. "Second column about halfway down."

"Is it true? That's what people will be asking all over London this morning. Was N—H—the rising painter and protégée of The Pre-Raphelite Brotherhood— truly a daughter of Mary Magdalene? This newspaper has it from reliable sources that N—H—who has been causing **hart** *ache—"* Nora laughed and then winced at the pain it caused in her head.

Smith nodded, his expression grim. "Yes, very clever isn't he?"

"N—H—who has been causing **hart** *ache in the art world once was employed by a certain M—T— before accepting a more permanent* position*—"*

Nora put the paper aside. "I don't need to read any more of it."

"That is an excellent decision," Smith agreed, his icy tone leaving no doubt in her mind that he was already making plans to get to the bottom of the article.

Nora laid a hand on his, which had clenched into a fist. "I don't want you getting involved, Smith."

"Nora!" Charles snapped, his handsome face suffused with anger. "You need to put your bloody pride aside and let Smith help you. If nothing else, he could teach this newspaper person a lesson that would have them thinking twice before writing anything else about you."

Nora bristled at his bossy stone. "And *you* might want to think twice about your willingness to employ your lover like a club, Charles."

Charles recoiled as if she'd slapped him. "Why you—"

"Not now, children." Smith's tone was one of boredom. He gave the younger man a stern look before turning to Nora. "I won't do anything to anyone without your approval. Fair enough?"

Nora studied him with narrowed eyes, not trusting his acquiescent mildness.

His face hardened. "But I do want to know who did *this*," he made a gesture that encompassed her person. "Unless it was something you wanted or requested," he amended, his tone and expression skeptical.

Nora didn't need him to fight this battle for her, either. "I did ask him for it," she lied.

Both men made sounds of disbelief. "Then why did you weep as if your heart was breaking?" Charles demanded, crossing his arms.

"I'm not myself this morning. I drank a great deal more than I am used to last night—certainly more than I should have. Things got—well, they got rough. But it wasn't anything I didn't ask for." She held Charles's narrow-eyed stare, feeling the heat from Smith's glare burning into the back of her skull.

"Now," she said having to reach deep to find the strength for a brisk, no-nonsense tone. "I have things to attend to today."

Charles stood up, marched to her dressing table and brought back a hand mirror.

Nora gasped, turning her face from side to side. Her cheekbones were badly bruised, even her jaw.

"Now you see why we don't believe you," Charles said. "You can't go out like that and you need somebody to tend to the scratches on your shoulders and back, not to mention your windward passage and likely your—"

"Charles."

Charles looked at his lover, his expression innocent. "What did I say?"

Smith ignored his question, instead addressing Nora. "I'm going to give you some time to think about this—to heal. And we will revisit the subject."

His expression was one she recognized—the one she was hoping to capture in the portrait she'd just begun, the one she hoped to surprise him with.

Nora nodded. "Very well."

"Good," he said as if there were never any doubt in his mind. "And now you will direct Charles and me to pack you a bag."

She frowned. "Why?"

"You are going to stay at my house for a while. Not only do you need care, but I daresay things will be uncomfortable for a while."

She groaned, having already forgotten about the paper. Still—she looked up at Smith and saw the depth of worry behind his hard stare. Why not stay with him? Her eyes began to water at the thought—it had been so long since somebody had tended to her.

And she so needed tending.

Chapter Thirty-Eight

It was Saturday night—or Sunday morning more accurately—and he was alone, lonely, and anxious. And he couldn't bloody sleep.

He leaned over and stared at the bedside table, squinting at the clock. Did that say three o'clock or four o'clock?

"Bloody hell," he muttered, feeling the bed beside him for the spectacles he now needed to read scientific articles. And, apparently, the big face of a clock.

It was a few minutes before three. He grunted. What the hell did it matter what time it was? He thrust back the covers and swung his feet over the side. What was making him restless, he decided, was his desire to write Nora's letter. It had only been through a sheer force of will that he'd waited until Sunday—albeit three o'clock in the morning.

He'd been anxious about this letter because, really, it would bring him to the current date and was the last installment of his life. What could he write about after this? She'd never answered any of his—perhaps she'd never even read them. The pain that squeezed his chest at that thought was too much to be borne.

No, he had to believe she read them—*all* of them.

Today he would re-read the erotic letter. He'd wanted to re-read it several times, just for his own pleasure, but his cock had only recently healed to the point that even slight erections weren't painful. He was ready to test his recovery—gently—by reading what he'd thought was a damned fine letter. Who knows? Perhaps soon he'd be ready to write a second one?

Cheered by that thought he shrugged into his robe and navigated his room by the low glow of the fire. Self-control, he knew, had always been something he'd prided himself on. But Nora had shredded that almost from the beginning.

The gas newel lights glowed dimly as he made his way down to the library.

Edward snorted at the word. Was a library really a library if it didn't have books in it?

Oh, it had some—the books Nora had chosen when he'd finally convinced her to stock it. But she'd been thoughtful with each choice, rather than simply buying books by the foot as he would have just to get the shelves filled. It occurred to him, only now, that a library *should* be assembled the way Nora had done it. Books you would wish to read, even if you might not get time to read them for years.

Once inside the room he went, instead of to his desk, to the six shelves Nora had filled. Six shelves out of hundreds. He'd not really noticed them before, and had certainly not read the spines.

She'd organized them according to a system, alphabetizing by author surnames.

Hmmph. That would be helpful provided a person knew their authors.

Edward skimmed the names: Austen—*five* books—he squinted and his eyebrows shot up: so, a woman writer. Bronte—another woman, no, *three* Brontes. Several by Defoe, Dickens—even Edward had heard of him—Elliot, Fielding, Gaskell—another woman.

He read until the end—Thackery. Out of all those names, he recognized only a few. Was he *that* ignorant, or were her tastes that arcane? Edward suspected it was the former. He couldn't recall the last time he'd read a book for pleasure. Oh, he read plenty, but that was all related to his projects or to develop new ideas. He enjoyed the reading he did, but it wasn't a leisure activity.

He tried to come up with any *title*—fiction, not the article he'd been reading tonight about the advances in electrification—and could not think of a single one.

Well, it was bloody appalling that he couldn't recall *any* book he'd read for pleasure.

Was he *really* that, well, obsessed? Not just with Nora, but with business? With making money, always more money.

Yes, a dry voice in his mind said. *Yes, you are, Edward.*

He snatched one of the Dickens books—people were always going on about him: *A Tale of Two Cities.* Good enough.

He chose the chair nearest the fire and opened the book.

The frontispiece was of a man sitting on a pallet in a jail cell. Edward grimaced. Really, is that what people liked to read about?

He shrugged and turned the page.

"It was the best of times, it was the worst of times, it was the age of wisdom, it was the age of foolishness, it was the epoch of belief—"

"Bloody hell," he muttered, eyeing the desk yearningly. He could always put this aside and go write his letter.

Quitter.

He groaned.

"it was the epoch of incredulity, it was the season of light…"

✳✳✳

Edward was dreaming of Nora. They were in their room and he'd just ridden them both to shattering climaxes. He lay on his back and she'd climbed over him on all fours, naked, moving up his body until her cunt was over his face. He was— impossibly—hard again, even though it had been mere seconds. His cock ached in a way that was excruciating, but he bore it because she crouched low enough for him to open his mouth and stretch out his hard tongue, but he was distracted by the pain, and also the loud clanging and shuffling and—

Edward opened his eyes and shook his head. "Hmmm?" he muttered.

The charwoman's head whipped around and she shrieked and flung her dust bucket in the air. Luckily it was empty and came down on the carpet—rather than the stone hearth—with a rather dull thud.

"Oh, sir," she said clutching her chest. "I'm so sorry, I am. I didn't see you there."

Edward, still disoriented, realized he was holding something in his lap: a book, and it was currently shielding an erection of epic proportions.

282

He swallowed hard and glanced up at the fluttering servant. "Will you please go and tell the kitchen to send up some coffee, Mrs. Er—"

"Carlyle, sir." She dropped a curtsey, wide eyed. "Right away, sir." She snatched up her ash bucket and broom and scuttled away.

Edward relaxed against the back of his chair and forced himself to breathe, relax, and generally wait until his painful erection subsided. He thought about his servants—an annoying subject. Specifically, he thought about why his servants behaved as if they were terrified of him. Edward had no idea why. He rarely fired anyone or even verbally chastised anyone.

When he picked up the book, he saw that he only made it to page seven before falling asleep. He was pathetic. He put the book on the side table, only then realizing his robe gaped open and he wore nothing under it. No wonder the poor woman had been in such a hurry to get out.

Well, it was his bloody house, wasn't it?

He was debating going up to his room and having his coffee sent there when the door opened and one of the Thomases entered with the various newspapers he took.

"Good morning, sir."

Edward grunted and the footman set the papers on his desk and left.

Banks, Edward knew, had his papers *ironed* before he had them brought to him.

"Bloody ponce," he muttered, dropping into his desk chair and picking up the first one his hand landed on. It was his practice to read each paper cover to cover. Not because he enjoyed death notices and wedding announcements, but because a man never knew where he might find his next idea.

He took different periodicals for different days, some focused on politics, some were liberal, some conservative, some social—he read *everything,* his eye constantly looking for something that might spark an idea.

He was half-way through his second cup of coffee when he saw it. At first, he just skimmed it, but the phrase Magdalen's Daughter jumped out at him. He'd never heard it before, but the orphanage where he'd grown up had been fond of the bible and the boys had gravitated to the parts that had even a whiff of scandal. Like whores.

He'd seen the initials of some artist and hadn't paid attention. But then a sentence had jumped out at him:

'N—H—was also, it appears, one of the reasons for the monumental settlement in the K—of T—'s divorce.'

Edward read it again, just to be sure. Yes, it was about him, the King of Tin, the nickname Catherine had so amusingly hung on him. His eyes flickered up and widened as he began to put names with initials.

He was still staring when he heard a commotion in the hall. The door opened and a very flustered Phelps stood on the threshold.

"I'm sorry, sir. I told Mr. Smith you were—"

Smith pushed past him. "He'll see me even if he's in his bloody birthday attire."

"Thank you, Phelps. You may go," Edward said, his eyes on Smith's face, whose eyes were on the paper he held crushed in his hands.

The door shut and Smith said. "I believe I've already discovered the responsible culprits."

Edward felt an ugly smile twist his lips as he stood. "I'll just go throw something on."

Smith's grin seemed to have twice as many teeth as usual. "Excellent idea. My carriage is waiting outside."

Chapter Thirty-Nine

ora knew that a week was more than long enough to recuperate—indeed, her body had recovered after only a few days—but she was hesitant to leave the comfort and security of Smith's opulent, very odd house.

Besides, he'd already told her he was keeping her a month, and that she had no choice in the matter, to consider herself kidnapped.

Charles was euphoric—as if Nora was a new puppy Smith had given him "I'm so glad you're *here*, Nor. Smith works all the time," he confided. "Those sittings with you were the most time I've ever spent with him during the daylight hours."

Nora could have told him she was familiar with that type of behavior. But while she had her painting, she couldn't help wondering what Charles had to occupy him all day, every day.

When she looked at Charles's dressing room, she realized what he spent his time doing.

"Charles," she'd said, not bothering to hide her horror. "Are you mad? Who needs so many clothes?" It made the extravagant selection Edward had bought her pale in comparison.

Charles, at least, had the grace to blush. "I know, I know, but *he* is the one who buys me most of it. He even converted this room, which had originally been a bedchamber, into my dressing room."

"This isn't a dressing room." Armoires, shoes, dressing tables— *two*—plush divans and chaises and, yes—partly hidden by the most enormous folding screen she'd ever seen—was a huge tub in the shape of a seashell.

Nora could hardly stand for laughing. "Oh my God, Charles, it is positively *vulgar.*"

Rather than be offended, Charles nodded. "I know. Want to take a bath in it?"

So, that's where they were two hours later, soapy and pruney.

They lay with their backs at the wide end of the shell. Whoever had built the huge shell had taken liberties with nature for the bather's comfort.

They'd already drained and re-filled the tub three times and were discussing getting out when a voice came from behind them, making them shriek.

"Well, well, well."

They were both silly after sharing a bottle of champagne to celebrate the first time the tub held two people, as Smith refused to share it.

Smith strode into view, crossed his arms over his chest, and leaned against the wall opposite the shell, trying hard not to smile and losing the battle. "This is a nice sight to come home to."

"We like to call it *Whores on the Half-shell,*" Charles said.

"Well, it is certainly a tasty looking dish."

Charles scooted to the far side of the shell, leaving a space between himself and Nora. "There's room to join us."

Smith's dark eyes flared slightly, but he just shook his head. "No, I'll let you two enjoy it. I've got a few matters to attend to in my study, and then I thought we might have a night out?" His eyes were on Nora as he said this; she'd not been out of the house in a week.

Nora experienced a twinge at the thought of leaving Smith's secure luxury, but she had to go out sometime. Didn't she?

Smith was almost to the door when he turned back. "Oh, I almost forgot—I had one of the footmen bring up your post and put it in your chambers, Nora."

A thrill of excitement flashed through her; perhaps there was another letter from Edward?

"I'm getting out," Nora announced, crawling over the side rather than attempting to stand on the slick ribbed tub surface.

Charles hooted. "Thank you for that lovely view—do you expect to get paid for it?" He swirled his almost empty glass and tossed it back. He drank almost as rarely as Nora and his eyes sparkled with champagne. "Ring the bell for me, on your way out, will you, darling? I'm going to soak for a bit more, but I'd better switch to tea or I shall be unable to be my sharp clever self tonight."

Nora snorted as she toweled herself dry and then slipped on one of Charles's numerous dressing gowns.

"I shall have to suggest to Smith that he put a bell closer to the tub," he muttered as he splashed.

Smith, a mind reader even when it came to strangers, knew his lover well and a servant entered as Nora reached for the pull.

"Ah," she said, smiling at the handsome young man, "You're just in time. He's in the halfshell."

The servant grinned. "Thank you miss."

As Nora made her way back to her room it struck her once again how smoothly and comfortably Smith's house ran. He employed only men who shared his sexual bent. That meant he didn't have to worry about loose lips. His servants had quarters on the fourth floor that Charles said were almost opulent.

All in all, Smith's house, with it's odd black on black color scheme in every room except the guest rooms—Nora's was a very pale blue—was one of the most comfortable places she'd ever stayed.

In her chambers she found Nate, the servant Smith had assigned to wait on her personal needs, placing freshly laundered clothing in her dressing room.

"Hello, Miss," he said as he slid a drawer closed and opened another.

"Hello, Nate." She picked up the neat stack of letters. "Are you here to make me look pretty?"

"You don't need any help with that, Miss Nora."

Nora sat on the padded bench in front of her dresser, flipping through the pile of letters until she saw one with Edward's distinctive writing. She smiled and tucked it into her dressing gown pocket. She would read it later, after she came back from her evening out. She put the others aside and looked up as Nate closed the last drawer.

"Mr. Smith says you are going out to dinner and the theater, Miss. As you did not bring any evening clothing with you, he sent me out to bring back a selection of gowns for you." He opened one side of the wardrobe, which had been empty this morning, but was now full of perhaps a dozen dresses. Most of them were white, cream, silver, or some combination thereof, but one was brilliant scarlet velvet. Not the burgundy or reddish colors one normally saw, but the color of fresh blood.

Nora looked at the maid or valet or whatever one called a man who waited on women— "Did you choose these, Nate."

"No, Miss. Mr. Smith did. He is quite particular in his tastes. And, if I may be so bold, he selected some lovely choices for your coloring."

Nora's eyes were drawn to the red gown as though some invisible force worked on her.

"I'll take the red one, Nate."

✳✳✳

Nora realized, as she paused at the head of the stairs, that she'd not felt so apprehensive in clothing since that first night with Edward, when she'd dressed in garments he'd selected for her. That, she knew, had been a sensual reaction. Tonight, her nervousness stemmed from something else—something less desirable: she was afraid to go out in public. People would whisper and stare. She knew why Smith had picked out this gown, and, on one level she heartily approved. But now…well, she would not be able to hide from prying eyes.

She heard something behind her and turned.

Smith stood staring at her. If she'd wondered whether she looked well, his expression put paid to it.

His look of stunned admiration was beyond gratifying. "I have to admit I did wonder whether you would be too pale for it. But when I described you the clerk told me that if you looked good in silver, you would look good in red. You are, according to the clerk, a pale blond, not a golden blond."

Nora's body hummed at the warm approval in his eyes, the memory of another time when he'd looked at her that same way flickering

288

through her mind. "Is that what I am?" she asked archly. "I confess I'd always wondered."

He grinned and offered his arm. "Come, we'll have to wait for at least five hours for the real beauty in our trio.

They'd just reached the second landing when Smith's butler Felson, came up the stairs. Like his entire breed, he was marvelously impassive. But Nora sensed a problem.

"I beg your pardon, sir, but there are visitors here to see Miss Nora."

Smith looked at her. "Are you expecting anyone?"

"Nobody even knows I'm here—unless you told anyone?"

Smith told Felson, "Tell them to come back tomorrow, at a more appropriate hour."

"They say they are Miss Nora's parents, sir."

Chapter Forty

It had, Edward realized, been a very long time since he'd visited this part of London—at least at night and on foot. He'd grown up on the edge of the Dials and had run the streets with as much confidence as the big rats that scurried just at the edge of his vision.

It was an odd coincidence, he thought as he walked through the miasma of sewage and misery that hung as thickly over the area as it had twenty-five years earlier, that the pub where he was going for his meeting was on the same street as the orphanage.

The only warning he got that somebody was behind him was the mere whisper of a scrape.

But Edward's body was ahead of his mind and he ducked and swung around. Two boys, surely no older than he'd been when he left The Dials, stood frozen with cudgels raised.

Edward grinned, pleased that he still had the reflexes needed for the rookeries. They staggered back at whatever they saw on his face.

"You've made a bad choice, lads. If you want to make a good one, turn up at Gateshead Brewery on Monday and I'll have two honest jobs waiting for you."

The boys gaped.

"The choice is yours." Edward pulled his hand from his pocket and they began to retreat. Their expressions of fear turned to comic wonder as he sent two sovereigns flashing through the air toward them. "Use this to buy yourself a bath, a meal, a decent coat, and shoes. Or use it to buy gin. The choice is up to you."

He turned and walked away. The act of charity, he knew, should have made him feel better, but it didn't. Giving away a few sovereigns when he sat on hundreds of thousands of pounds was like pissing on a man dying of thirst. Edward knew many great *philanthropists* gave away thousands of pounds, but—and perhaps this was mere tight-fistedness on his part—he believed gifts of money achieved little.

Old Jonah, whom he'd been thinking about since writing to Nora, had said once, if he'd said a hundred times, "Give a man a fish and you feed him for a day; teach a man to fish and you feed him for a lifetime." To be honest, Edward had wanted to crack the old bastard over the skull with a plank the fiftieth time he'd had to hear that. He'd thought it was horseshit, then. But now he believed Jonah had been right. Although there was an addendum to the quote in his mind: if you taught him to fish, there damned well had better be fish to be *caught*. Meaning: there had to be jobs worth having. The people who worked for the syndicate-owned businesses earned more than those who did the same job at other companies, but that was still little enough.

Edward knew from talking to Smith that he agreed with Edward when it came to worker reforms, although neither of them knew quite what to do about it. Paying too high wages could start a war between the various manufacturers. It was a fucking mare's nest.

Edward hopped over the sewage running down the street in front of the pub, shaking his head. Perhaps these people wouldn't live in such squalor if people like him had a few thousand pounds less.

He shoved the reactionary thought out of his mind; he'd need his wits about him in a pit like this. He pushed open the door and released a gout of noise and smoke into the street. The bar was middling busy.

He glanced toward the right corner and, sure enough, there was the big blond bastard, chatting up a serving wench. Edward's fists clenched as he stared at the man who'd beaten and raped Nora.

You want to hurt him badly, Edward. Not just thrash him.

No, he wanted to kill him, but he'd been sternly warned about that.

"What do you want?" the bartender asked, although—in his accent—it sounded nothing like those words.

"Send two drinks over to the corner," Edward said, slipping into the old speech as easily as slipping into an old coat.

The bartender nodded and turned away, noticing nothing untoward.

Edward knew he had Smith to thank for that. Smith had found clothing that looked as if he'd crawled through mud—or worse—in them.

Derek Brown looked up as Edward neared his table, the line over the bridge of his nose giving his eyes a hard look. He could see why Nora would have chosen him—he was handsome enough and had a big, muscular body—but she'd missed that mean glint in his eyes.

Brown swatted the barmaid's arse and set her on her way.

"Donovan?" he said as Edward dropped into the chair across from him.

"Aye," Edward nodded, struggling to subdue the rage in his gut. This man was easily two times bigger than Nora. What a bloody pig. No, that was an insult to pigs.

"So, my mate says you've got a large amount of something you can't shift." He leered. "If it's what I think it is, I'm in a place to help you. For the right sum of money."

The barmaid returned with their pints and thumped them down on the table. Edward slid a coin across the sticky surface and her eyes widened, her attention suddenly shifting from the golden god to Edward's shaggy gray carcass.

"Leave off, Bren," Derek growled.

Edward waited until she'd flounced off and then pulled a small vial out of his pocket and set it on the table.

Derek snatched it up and squinted, his lips curling back in disgust. "This is it, eh? Mummy Brown?"

"Just a small part of what we have."

Derek looked up. "How do I know this is real ground up Egyptian kings and not some gaffer you dug up yesterday?"

"I've got the box he came in—they call it a sarcophagus."

"Yeah, yeah, I knew that," Derek said, sneering. "So, where is this, then?"

"How do I know you can pay for it?"

Derek glanced around, did something in his coat, and then lifted his hands, palms together, opening them a crack to expose a fat roll of bills.

Edward almost laughed—he might as well glue the bloody bills to his forehead for as guilty as he was acting.

Edward didn't care if the man had any money or not, but it would look strange if he didn't ask. Not that Derek would have noticed, he realized now. Derek was just kicking off his career as a criminal; Edward predicted it would be a short, brutish, and nasty.

Chapter Forty-One

ora sat in Smith's sitting room—a cavernous, cold, startlingly white room she'd never been in before. Her parents resembled a pair of startled turtledoves perched on the corner of a white silk settee, their eyes wide.

Nora felt ridiculous in her red evening gown, but supposed she resembled the whore they knew her to be.

She'd tried to convince Smith and Charles to go on with their evening as planned, but they were waiting for her in Smith's study.

"Natalie?"

She looked up at the sound of her mother's voice. "I'm sorry. I suppose you are here because it is all over Basingstoke. I have a—"

"What do you mean, Natalie?" Uncharacteristically, it was her mother doing the talking.

Her father looked shrunken and old. Nora suspected it was this disclosure that had given him that look.

"I mean the column in the newspaper, Mother."

"Column?" Both her parents blinked with confusion.

Nora frowned. "How did you find out about me?"

Her mother reached into her reticule and pulled out a letter. "We received this."

Nora recognized the almost childish, loopy handwriting, not needing the return direction to know who it was. She glanced up. "May I?"

They nodded, their eyes still wide.

Mr. and Mrs. Hartwicke,

I am writing to inform you that your daughter Natalie is has been living in London under the name of Nora Hudson.

You likely know me as Lady Catherine, the daughter of the Marquess of Blanford. I am also Catherine Fanshawe, former wife of Mr. Edward Fanshawe, and I daresay you've heard both our names this past year.

At the time of my marriage your daughter was living under my husband's roof, posing as his niece, when in reality she was his mistress. It was around the time I learned of her relation to my husband that I also learned of her background.

Before I learned that fact, I grew to care for you daughter a great deal. It grieves me to admit we are no longer friends. That said, I write to you in the hope you might be able to offer her guidance as she is currently living a bohemian lifestyle in one of London's seamier districts. I believe the path she has chosen is one that will end in regret.

Now that I know her real identity, I felt compelled to notify you of her whereabouts and leave you to determine your role in what is—I think we can all agree —a tragedy.

Yours & etc.,

Lady Catherine

Nora stared at the page even after she'd read it twice, her heart thundering in her ears. So, this was Cat's revenge—or perhaps just a part of it.

What else had she done? Had she sent Derek to her? Because Cat had mentioned encountering him at that party and speaking to him about her—about *Natalie*. Had she told Derek her real name? Had she stoked his anger with tales about Nora and who she was—who she'd once been?

"Natalie?"

She looked up at her father's soft voice, so unlike the one that he'd employed in the pulpit.

"Is all Lady Catherine said true?"

Ah, Lady Catherine—and the not so subtle tone of respect in his voice. Well, it was only natural; the Marquess of Blandford was his patron, after all.

"Yes, Father, it is true." *All that and more.*

"Dear God," her mother whispered, clinging to the vicar's arm. "Wh-when did you come back from America?"

"She never went, Dorothy." The vicar's tone surprised her—dry, ironic, and filled with self-disgust, no doubt at his credulity.

"Why?" her mother asked, tears trickling down her cheeks.

Nora stared at these people who had made her and tried to think of a way to describe *what* they'd made without killing them, making them look even older. There was no way that didn't hurt and destroy. It reminded her of her recent struggle with Cat. She felt her lips pull up into a wry smile. Oh, clever Cat had devised a punishment that fit the crime. Nora had to admire her.

Nora couldn't dislike her although she disliked what she'd done. Perhaps now that Cat had carved out her pound of flesh she could direct her cleverness toward something that might actually make her happy—fulfill her.

"I left because I knew I'd only bring you heartache by staying," she said, her voice weary to her own ears.

"Was this because of what happened with Peter Miller?" her father asked.

There was a name she'd not thought of in a long time. He'd been the boy she'd been caught with that night outside the assembly. Her parents had been horrified, as had Peter's, who'd been successful farmers in the area. Peter, she had to admit, had tried to be a gentleman—at least about accepting the blame. It was true he'd kissed her, a chaste kiss that had been more of a peck, but she'd been the one who'd allowed her hands to roam his big, hard, young body, not shying away from his obvious desire for her. It had been Nora who'd opened his trousers and made him come in her hand that first time. The next time he had, rather clumsily, returned the favor. By the time they were caught outside the assembly hall, they'd moved on to their mouths. She couldn't recall Peter's face, but she remembered the feel of his cock in her mouth.

"He would have married you," her mother said, interrupting Nora's journey through her past.

"Yes, mother, I know. That's why I left."

"But—" Mrs. Hartwicke shook her head, unable to finish.

"I didn't want to marry him or anyone else. I wanted to—" she stopped, looking from face to face. "I wanted to live a different life."

"You mean your painting? You could have continued to paint after your marriage. Peter was a kind boy and would have been a kind husband."

Nora smiled. "I don't doubt that. I didn't want a husband. I wanted to explore the world."

"In a *brothel*, Natalie?" her father demanded, his expression one of revulsion.

She moved her jaw from side to side and then sighed. "That was what I found most conducive. And that is why I wrote telling you'd I'd gone to America so my behavior wouldn't eventually shame you. I wanted to spare you. I'm terribly sorry you had to learn about me this way—or any way at all." She paused and then plunged on. "If you suffer from this in any way—if others were to find out and you lost your position. I have a house in a lovely village and enough money to see to your needs."

"Money from what you've done?"

Nora could tell by her father's tone he'd not be accepting any assistance from her even if he was starving on a street corner.

"Yes, father. Money from what I've done."

The vicar opened his mouth and Dorothy Hartwicke squeezed her husband's arm, an action which, surprisingly, made him stop.

"But you don't do that now. You are a successful painter."

Her mother's hopeful, almost pleading words made Nora realize something. "How did you find me here? How did you learn about the painting?"

"We went to see Mr. Fanshawe. It was he who suggested you might be here. He says Mr. Smith is not your—" the vicar could not go on.

The pulse at the base of Nora's throat had begun beating wildly at the mention of Edward's name. "You went to speak to him," she repeated faintly.

"It was the only name we knew," her mother said. "We thought he might know where you were. Mr. Fanshawe said you'd left some time ago and lived on your own. That you were a successful painter."

Nora had to smile at the spark of pride she could hear in her mother's words.

"He said you'd recently been ill and came here—this Mr. Smith is your friend, he said." The deep lines in her father's high forehead grew deeper. "This is an irregular arrangement, Natalie—the man is a bachelor. Surely you—" the vicar stopped as he realized the foolishness of what he was saying.

"Why did you come?" Nora asked.

Her mother's face suffused with red, but it was her father who answered. "You are our *daughter* and no matter what you have done, we love you. You can have no idea the pain you have—"

"We want you to come home, Natalie," her mother said.

Nora could only stare.

"There is a young man—a curate—living in Sarah's room—"

Nora flinched at her sister's name.

"But your room is still empty. Not much different from how you left it."

"Sarah?" Nora said, her heart pounding.

"She married an architect who builds fine houses. They have two children, a boy and a girl."

Nora had a niece, a nephew, and a brother-in-law.

"Does Sarah—"

"We haven't told her. Yet."

They would have to—if her sister hadn't already found out—just in case somebody in her social circle were to put the names and Sarah's family together.

Nora knew they were waiting for her to say . . . something, as if there were some combination of words that would make all this go away.

"I think you know I can't go back," she said.

Nora told herself she was pleased, rather than insulted, when she saw relief behind their regret.

Chapter Forty-Two

Nora had appreciated Smith's luxury and care, but it had been a dream that she'd known she'd have to awaken from, eventually. And her parents' visit had awakened her most rudely. So it was that two days after their visit she was back in her small artist's garret.

It felt good to be back in her own house, even though she'd been home only a few hours. The first few of those she'd spent assuring Smith and Charles.

"I'm fine," she said. "Better than fine." She cut Smith a coy look. "I know I said you weren't supposed to, but I appreciate whatever you did to make that journalist write a new column." She meant the column that had retracted the prior one and admitted it was based on information acquired from a known criminal. The paper itself had printed a public apology for slandering her and Nora suspected they were expecting to be sued at any moment.

Smith shrugged. "I merely contacted their editor and explained the situation." Nora could well imagine. "He was quick to understand—and it is certainly understanding of *you* not to pursue the matter."

Nora didn't remind him that everything was *true*. Wasn't truth a defense to defamatory statements?

"Perhaps the next time he won't accept the word of just anyone— especially not a violent, lying criminal," Charles added.

Ah, yes—that.

Smith cut his lover a quick look of displeasure.

"I'm sorry, Smith," Charles whispered loud enough to be heard a block away, his eyes darting dramatically between Nora and Smith, making it easier—but still not *easy*—for her to smile about such a subject.

"It's quite all right, Charles. I am not so fragile that you can't mention Derek's name in front of me." Although it did make her gut clench, and not in a pleasurable way. "I don't like thinking of him, but I also don't need to be swaddled in cotton wool."

"Of course we won't swaddle you," Smith assured her, his tone soothing.

After she'd ushered them out the door, she began unpacking her valise, putting her clothing away in the drawers rather than strewing them about as she normally would.

Smith, given his obsession with order and control, had sent servants over to tidy and clean her house and it was positively sparkling and inviting.

Other women might have been offended, but Nora was pleased to see everything in its place. It had taken only a glance to assure herself that all her items had not been moved far enough to cause her problems finding them. And, naturally, they'd not entered her studio.

Her housekeeper had also been here, waiting to greet her—yet another example of Smith's attention to detail—and her small larder was stocked with food she could simply take out and put on a plate.

Everything was perfect.

So why, then, did her spine feel as if somebody had inserted a key and wound it tightly, like a clock?

Was it the surprise of learning what happened to Derek? She'd directly confronted Smith about whether he'd done something to land him in jail, and he'd sworn he'd had no part in it. Nora had held his gaze, which had been steady, and suddenly decided she didn't care. She was glad Derek was locked away where he could not hurt her—or anyone else. While she found the knowledge that he'd been involved in smuggling stolen artifacts from the British Museum startling, she couldn't deny that he would know—as well as any painter—that the market for certain pigments, like those made from the ground-up bones of mummies, for example—could be both lucrative and illegal.

Smith believed she was traumatized by the rape—although likely Charles knew better. While Derek's brutality had surely shaken and hurt her, it was no worse than she'd experienced at the hands of several bad clients—like Ceddy, for example.

No, what had really upset her was that she'd not seen beneath his attractive veneer. Was she really so blind? So oblivious? She knew that, in general, she was very lazy. If Derek had not made an ass of himself about Clive that day, she'd likely still be engaging in bed sport with him on a weekly basis, even knowing he was a thief.

Nora startled at the sound of the brass post flap; the mail was here.

Edward's last letter sat unopened in her valise. She'd not forgotten about it, of course, but after her parents' visit she'd been too distracted to enjoy it. Edward's letters—with or without the erotic additions—were a highlight in her weeks.

In the entry hall two letters lay in the post tray. One an invoice from the supply company where she purchased her framing materials and one a letter from Edward; it was a day early.

As ever, the pulse at the base of her throat began to drum. Nora knew it was her giveaway because Lord Anthony had once pointed it out.

"You're so cool, so unreachable and beautiful in your pain, Nora. But your pulse always reveals what's inside you."

Nora knew that was true and had seen evidence often enough during her many times with Edward. He liked to take her in front of mirrors, so he could watch them. Nora had liked it, too.

Her fingers began opening the letter of their own volition and she paused, wondering at her loss of control. She never read his missives without waiting and, often, arranging some ceremony, some celebration.

But perhaps, she thought, as she looked around at her almost unrecognizable apartment, now was as good as any time for a change.

Dear Nora,

I apologize for breaking what has been my routine and sending this letter early. By now you will have guessed the reason.

I knew immediately your parents were who they said they were and not people sent by newspapermen—that might sound absurd, but it happened more than once during my divorce. You resemble your mother closely, but with your father's pale complexion and unusually light hair. Your eyes are entirely your own.

But you would have heard all that before, many times, I'm sure. To me such familial resemblances are eerie mysteries and I cannot comprehend seeing my features in another, or theirs in me. I suspect that is part of the reason I was so desperate to have a child: the urge to replicate myself, maybe to feel a connection. I understand that was only part of my obsession.

I hope I did right by sending them to Smith's. Yes, of course I knew you were there. He told me as much after I read the newspaper column.

Your parents appear to be genuinely affectionate people torn by joy and grief. I don't believe you are cruel, Nora, so I know you must have had your reasons for cutting them off. I wish, more than you will ever know, that I'd asked about your life during our time together.

I can't say that I'm surprised to learn you've become such a respected painter. I know I should be ashamed of the paintings of yours I kept, but I cannot seem to make myself give them back.

If you want them, I will return them.

I'll confess something to you, something that stills shames me. But, I've realized, as I've written these letters, that I feel better after telling you the truth about myself. In my past dealings with everyone—including you—I carefully selected what I wanted others to see, concealing those parts of myself that might expose me as less than what I wanted to appear: a successful man of business. I realize now that vision of myself is limiting. I <u>am</u> a successful businessman, but I hope—and am striving—to be more. Is that a sad admission—a pitiful goal—for a man of almost five-and-forty? Perhaps, but not as pitiful as what I'm about to confess.

My reaction that day in your studio was a complex one. I felt betrayal, pain, anger, fear, insecurity, and a great many other emotions that I continue to think about. The betrayal was painful. But right behind that was the intense pain I felt at having been excluded—no, that's not correct—at having excluded <u>myself</u>—from that entire part of your life. The sketches you left, dozens and dozens—some of Catherine, some even of Ceddy and the servants, but not a single one of me.

Ah, well. There is the sad truth, Nora. Poor Edward, his feelings were hurt.

I started this letter only to explain why I sent your parents to Smith's but, as ever, it has come back around to me.

Respectfully,

Edward.

Nora felt tears sliding down her cheeks.

Poor Edward. She understood the pain he felt, must still feel, at such exclusion. More than anything, she wanted to tell him the truth—to take away his anguish, his feeling of rejection. More than anything she wanted to write him, or even go to him.

But then Catherine would loom up in Nora's mind: a coldly angry Catherine—the way she should have been back then, back when she discovered that her husband and only friend were lovers.

Now, when it should have no longer mattered, it was Catherine who stood between them.

Nora suspected that she always would.

Chapter Forty-Three

October 1870

Edward didn't write her a letter the next week, or the week after that.

Indeed, it was almost seven months now since his final letter—not the one about her parents, but the one before that—in which he told her he'd not write again until she told him there was some chance for them. That it was up to her if she ever wanted to speak to him again.

Edward looked for letters each day, at first, but he'd become better—or at least less pitiful—as the months passed. The days were not as bad as he'd anticipated and he no longer rushed home from wherever he was to check the post. If she wanted to write, she would write. The days when Nora did everything he told her to do were long over.

He was fortunate in that he could still read and hear about her. He'd seen her name associated with several showings. She'd done a portrait of Smith that was generating quite a furor. Smith had come to him before Edward had read about it.

"She did it without my knowledge. She asked my permission to exhibit it this year, and I didn't feel like it was my place to say no."

Edward could tell he was pleased. And why not? Was he jealous? Hell yes he was. He liked to think he'd changed since she'd left, but he doubted he would ever change *that* much.

"Are you angry with me?" Smith asked him one night some months ago, when he'd come to join Edward for dinner—just the two of them. Edward knew Smith was asking because there had been several articles on the painting; it had made quite a stir. Edward read the articles greedily, drinking up the little bits of information about her in a way he suspected was not normal. Again, he was who he was.

"I envy you," Edward said. "But I'm not angry."

And it was the truth, he *did* envy Smith. But he was glad Nora had ended up with Smith as a protector—the man was exactly who Edward would have chosen to protect her, if it couldn't be him.

"How was her showing?" Edward asked Smith the last time they'd dined together, earlier this month, trying to sound casual.

Although they spoke of Nora on occasion, it was usually only when Smith introduced the subject.

"She found it stressful—worrying people won't come, that sort of thing—but her art could not fail to attract crowds and buyers." Smith answered Edward as if his question were normal, giving him hope that the next time he might ask another question, perhaps even two.

Edward had wanted to go to the showing, but of course he hadn't. He'd wanted to send an emissary to buy up every single one of her paintings. But he hadn't done that, either. He'd thought about buying only one, but that had felt wrong, as well—as if he were prying or stealing, even though he'd have paid for it. So he'd merely read about it and tried, unsuccessfully, not to yearn.

Smith had begun to dine with him once a month and Edward found he looked forward to the meals. He still saw the other members of the syndicate often, but Smith, he felt, knew him—or at least as well as any man knew him.

Their growing friendship, if that's what it was, wasn't only about Nora. The two of them had decided to establish a trade-school—the type of place that taught useful skills to boys who'd grown up in bad circumstances. There would be apprenticeships, but with more choice than Edward had received. He still didn't know where Smith came from—or even the man's name—but he knew Smith's experiences must have been similar to his.

He found working on the project fulfilling. Was he lonely? Of course. Did he think of Nora? As much as ever. But there *were* parts of his life he enjoyed. He'd finished his first Dickens and then picked up another book. This one by a woman author, *Jane Eyre* one of the Brontes, whom he now knew were sisters.

He'd enjoyed the story far more than he'd expected. Young Jane's experience was similar to his own, although of course he had no wealthy relatives. And Rochester had been almost as big an ass as Edward—they even shared the same Christian name.

He now read regularly, working his way through what he thought of as Nora's Library.

He'd also taken up wood working again. When they opened their school he was considering offering his carpenter experience if there were any boys interested. He was not a master carpenter, but he knew several and could pass along any promising students.

That was where he'd been tonight—at the new school. It didn't have students, yet, but they'd begun to fill the small dormitory with furniture and the classrooms with chairs, desks, or tools, as the various subjects dictated.

It could only house forty boys, but he and Smith had purchased the building beside it.

Because Edward never had his servants wait up past nine o'clock there were no Thomases in the foyer. He'd found that he liked to be alone when he came home, free to relax in any part of his house without servants hovering.

He went to his study, which resembled a library more and more as he purchased books of his own. There were still many shelves to fill, but he had time. Lots of time.

He picked up the bundle of post from its tray beside the door and took it to his desk. He wore spectacles all the time now, those with a split in them. It was mortifying—a man of barely three-and-forty—but he'd decided to prize utility over vanity. His face had never been much to look at, in any case.

One envelope caught his eyes: it had foreign postmarks and something about the loopy script looked familiar. It took him far longer than it should have to recognize his former wife's handwriting. But then, he'd never really known much about her.

He stood and poured a drink, fearing he might need one, taking it and the letter to his favorite chair beside the fire.

Taking a deep draught, he broke the seal:

Edward,

Here I am doing a thing I never thought I'd do: write you a letter."

Edward snorted and took a sip of brandy. "You and me, both, Kitten."

Smith told me he'd never tell anyone—not you or Nora—about my involvement with Nora's troubles last year. I say troubles, when I should speak the truth: her rape and subsequent public humiliation.

I'll tell you what I told him: I never knew that Derek would do that to her when I told him about her past. I was using him, it was true, to expose her secret—to humiliate her, which, I knew would hurt you. I could say it was really to hurt you, but I wanted you both to feel pain.

While I only expected Derek to take the information I gave him to a newspaperman—which he did—I should have guessed he was the type to take out his revenge in a more physical manner.

I don't know if he told you, and it doesn't really matter, but Smith told me to leave England or he could not be responsible for what he did to me."

Edward hadn't known. He lifted his half-full glass "Well done, Smith."

"I would have left anyhow after hearing what Derek did. I'd like to claim I wasn't in my right mind—that I was addled by drink—but I knew what I was doing by starting down that path.

As the saying goes, 'A man who desires revenge should dig two graves.'

The months that followed my removal to the Continent were, quite honestly, almost the end of me. While I could blame you and Nora for setting me on the path to ruin, I could only blame myself for not getting off it.

I'm not telling you this to make you sorry for me; I'm telling you this because it's important to me that you know I'm well, now.

I wish I could say I was wise enough to have saved myself, but I met a person who saw me at my worst and still loved me. She taught me that I <u>am</u> worthy of being loved.

She convinced me that if I hang on to my hatred for you, I'm harming myself and those who love me.

Having behaved with great cruelty toward Nora—and, by extension, you—I know I'm no better than either of you in that regard.

I accept now that I must forgive you so that you no longer hold sway over me.

I must forgive you in order to forgive myself, Edward.
I will never like you, but I bear you no ill will.
Catherine Fanshawe."

Edward exhaled a shaky breath as he stared sightlessly at the letter.

Smith had *not* told him of Catherine's involvement in Derek Brown's attack on Nora. Edward had to admit that was a wise decision. He wasn't sure he would have been so kind as to offer banishment.

Although he understood Catherine's Biblical impulse of an eye for an eye, he believed she'd maimed the wrong party.

Or perhaps she hadn't. Edward would have much rather have been raped and publicly shamed than Nora, so maybe Catherine's aim had been unerring, after all.

Chapter Forty-Four

Spring 1871

Edward was, he decided, exhausted but happy. At least as happy as he believed himself capable of being. The school was open, the dormitories filled, and the classrooms noisy hives of industry.

Like other schools, they would take an Easter Break. The instructors, most of whom had been selected by the members of the syndicate—Chatham and Banks had, not surprisingly, become involved in the project—were young men selected from their various business enterprises.

Edward and Smith were paying some of the instructors additional wages to stay at the school over the break, during which time they were offering excursions to places most Londoners never seemed to make time to visit. It would be a treat for boys who had, for the most part, grown up without ever having a holiday.

After Smith had shamed him—by leading a group of students on an excursion to the Tower—Edward decided to take a group to visit a part of the British Museum that featured furniture.

He'd grumbled about it to the other men, but the truth was that he'd looked forward to it. With his usual mania for organization and control he'd visited the museum three times by himself to develop a list of questions to ask his students.

When Smith had seen the questions, his comment had been that it was supposed to be *fun*.

Edward was still irked about that. Just what wasn't *fun* about furniture?

Edward was mounting the steps to his house and considering how to one-up Smith's next trip—to Madam Tussaud's, of all places—when the door opened, Phelps on the threshold.

"Good evening, sir."

The reason Edward had chosen Phelps for the position of butler is that he epitomized everything Edward always imagined a butler to be: unflappable sophistication. Today, however, Edward detected as slight tension around the other man's eyes.

"What is, Phelps?" he asked, handing the man his hat and cane.

"You have a visitor, sir."

Edward paused in the act of stripping off his gloves and glanced around stupidly, as if Phelps might have hidden the visitor somewhere in the foyer.

"It's rather late for a visitor," Edward said, pointing out the obvious. "Why didn't you just make whoever it was come back?"

"Because Phelps and I are old friends."

Edward's head whipped up so fast the bones in his neck cracked.

"Nora?" The word left his mouth before he recalled. "I mean—"

"Nora is fine, Edward."

Edward gaped like a child at a circus. "I thought you were in the country," he said, apropos of nothing.

She smiled down at him, which made him realize he was standing in the middle of the foyer shouting up at her. He turned to Phelps and opened his mouth.

"It's already on the way, sir."

Ever the paragon of discretion, Phelps turned and disappeared in the direction of the kitchens.

Edward lifted legs made of lead and made his way toward the stairs. He knew there were only thirty or so, but it felt like a hundred before he reached the top where she stood waiting.

He'd forgotten how very small and slender she was, his Nora. His palms were sweating as his eyes ranged over her like marauding bandits.

"Your hair," she said, with a touch of wonder in her voice. "It's lighter than mine."

Edward foolishly ran a hand through his overlong hair—as if to confirm what she was looking at. "I look like an old man. It happened overnight." He didn't tell her which night, but he could see by her expression she knew. Yes, his Nora.

"And spectacles, too," she added.

He smiled wryly. "I'm only glad you have come on a day when I wasn't using my wheeled chair."

She smiled slowly and his lungs tried to freeze and speed up at the same time.

Once again, he noticed they were speaking in the hallway.

"Would you like to come to the library?"

"That's where Phelps put me, remembering how much I enjoyed books."

Phelps, Edward decided, was getting an immediate increase in pay.

They walked slowly, Edward matching his long stride to hers. "You have many more books than those I chose," she said as Edward opened the door for her.

"Yes, I've taken up reading," he admitted, feeling like a twit for being so proud of such a simple thing. "Well, reading for pleasure," he added.

"There is nothing else like it, is there? A well-written book."

"No, nothing quite like it." He couldn't stop staring at her.

They sat, reflexively, in the chairs they'd occupied the few times they'd sat in the library: he in the big black leather beside the fire, her in a smaller version opposite him.

In addition to gawking, he couldn't stop smiling.

"You look different, Edward."

"Yes, so you mentioned."

"Not just your hair and spectacles, but your smile. You look . . . happy."

His face heated, as though she'd just accused him of some indecency.

"It looks well on you."

If his face became any hotter it would burst into flames.

"How long have you been here?" he asked, wanting to take the subject away from him.

"Only a few minutes before you." She gestured toward her traveling costume. "I just returned to town today."

"Ah. Smith gave me reason to believe you were gone for several more months yet."

Her lips curved in an arch smile that had the predictable effect on his cock—which had already roused at the first sound of her voice. "Yes, well, Smith likes to think he knows everything, doesn't he?"

Edward chuckled. "He is guilty of that from time to time."

The door opened and Phelps himself entered with the tray.

"Thank you," Edward murmured, his eyes riveted to Nora as she turned to prepare their tea.

"I've taken the liberty of putting you in your old room, Miss Nora."

"That will be lovely, thank you, Phelps."

Phelps took in Edward's dropped jaw and dammit if the man didn't crack a smile. Albeit the smallest one visible without a microscope.

The door shut silently behind the butler and Edward closed his jaw.

He wanted to speak, but he was worried this was one of his more frustrating dreams—the ones where he saw Nora on a street and it turned out to be somebody else. Or the ones that—

"Edward?"

She was holding out his tea. "Thank you," he said in a voice not his own. He took a sip of scalding tea and grimaced.

She handed him a plate, on which she'd placed three macaroons. He stared.

"I asked Phelps for them—they were always your favorite." She paused when he still didn't take it. "But perhaps that is no—"

He hastily took the plate. "No, it is still true." He picked one up and took a bite, as if to prove the veracity of his statement.

They sipped tea and ate biscuits, Edward expecting her to disappear like a mirage at any moment.

Nora had always had a shocking capacity for sweets and he was content to watch as she ate thee macaroons and two pink frosted cakes—where the devil had Phelps found those? He was in no hurry to disturb the blissful vision of her inside his house again after ... He struggled to recall the date in his head. When he did, he realized she was watching, her smile knowing.

It was three years to the day since she'd moved into his house.

His heart thudded so loudly he swore it sounded like somebody pounding on the front door, shaking the house, moving the—

"I brought something for you." She picked up a satchel that sat beside her chair and extracted a sheaf of papers.

Edward rose to take them, confused but intrigued. He could see by the structure of the document it was a contract of some sort. He sat and lifted it to read, but her voice interrupted him.

"I'm offering you a carte blanch and that is the contract I've drawn up. It's a—"

Edward stood and marched to his desk, his hand shaking as he flipped to the back without reading anything and signed his name. Hers, he saw was already there.

"Paragraphs two, five, seven, twelve, and fifteen."

Edward's lips curled as he flipped and signed in all the spots where her signature preceded his. His Nora's contract was longer than the one he'd given her. Excitement, hope, and—yes—a smidgen of fear swirled in his belly. He replaced the pen and walked back to her.

She took the contract and cocked her head while looking up at him, her pupils flaring. He laid a hand on the back of her chair to keep from dropping to his knees—even though that was where he wanted to be.

"It doesn't seem wise to sign this without reading it, Edward. I hope you don't come back to me at some later date and try to negotiate."

"I shan't," he said, his lips twitching at her very good Edward imitation.

"Hmmm." She tucked it into her bag. "You may be seated," she said in a dismissive tone.

Jesus. Mary. And Joseph.

Edward walked on wobbly legs back to his chair.

"Where do you think you are going?"

He swung around at her voice. "But you said—"

"*Tsk, tsk*, Edward, you should have read the contract. It's paragraph five—one of the very paragraphs you initialed. It's very clear about your position whenever you're in a room with me." She spread her feet … *wide* and pointed to the floor between her knees. "Kneel."

He knew his haste was unseemly, but he didn't care. His knees made popping sounds as he lowered himself.

"That sounds painful, Edward." She reached behind her and pulled out the narrow back cushion, offering it to him with an arch look that made his already hard cock throb even harder. "We don't want any permanent damage."

Once he was kneeling, she looked down at him with lust darkened eyes. "Take off your coat, slowly."

His hands shook and he made a mental note to purchase only four button coats from now on.

"You may put it on the table behind you. And then remove your tie."

He pulled out the plain gold bar he used and she held out her hand, her smile wicked. "I'll hold on to that for you. Now your waistcoat." And then, "Why Edward, your hands are shaking. Are you nervous?"

You're bloody well right I am. "A little, Nora."

"Hmm, if you're only a *little* nervous I must not be doing this right."

He opened his mouth and she shook her head. "I'll ask the questions and tell you when to speak."

God, he was going to come in his trousers.

"And no orgasms, or things won't go well for you."

Edward knew it would be a terrible mistake to laugh.

"Now, I want you to unbutton your shirt."

Edward's fingers stumbled more than ever. He was leaner—would she notice? Would his body still please her?

First he removed his collar, setting it on the pile.

"Slowly," she ordered as he raced through the buttons.

He complied. And when he reached the bottom, he unbuttoned his cuffs.

But when he reached up to pull it off she said, "No, I'll do that." She leaned forward a little in her chair, her eyes almost level with his; for all that he was on his knees. She insinuated her hands beneath the flaps of his shirt, her eyes never leaving his. When her cool, calloused hands touched his heated skin he sucked in a breath and shivered, his chest rising and falling like a locomotive engine gathering steam.

"You feel leaner," she said, her voice speculative as she explored him with her hands.

He opened his mouth to ask her if she found him *too* lean.

"Ah, ah, ah, Edward, no speaking until you're told to do so."

His mouth snapped shut.

"You *are* leaner. I can feel the individual muscles beneath your skin. I always could, but now you're *harder.*" Her nostrils flared and he swore he'd faint from loss of blood. "Stripped down, more toned—like a racehorse." She smiled, the expression unspeakably wicked. "If I remember correctly, one part of you was already like a racehorse."

Edward clenched his jaws and stiffened—all over as she dragged short nails over his chest, grazing his nipples hard enough to hurt, her fingers continuing down to his stomach.

"Mmm, yes, as hard as I remember. You must have been doing something to keep so fit. Tell, me, Edward, what have you been doing?" She suddenly grabbed his right nipple and pinched it. Hard. "And don't lie, because I'll know it. Have you been . . . *fucking?*"

"Yes."

She frowned and tugged cruelly on his tiny bud. "Yes, *what?*"

"Yes, Nora," he gasped. He grimaced at his mistake. "Or—"

"No, not Natalie—Nora." Her pincher-like grip eased.

"Tell me about your current *fucking* habits."

To be honest, his sexual needs were just as rampant as ever. Would she—

"This hesitation does not bode well for you, Edward," she said in a low, menacing voice.

"I favor a place called the Birch Palace as it caters to, er, well, men with my predilections."

"And what predilections are those?"

She was good at this; he never would have guessed just how good.

"I like to bind my lovers and then whip them. Hurt them." He almost smiled and then caught it. Ah, how he loved that traitorous pulse of hers.

Her hands slid up his belly and stopped on his shoulders. "We shall speak more about that later." She pushed off the shirt, her eyes dropping to his body for the first time. Her lips parted in a way that spelled ruin for his trousers. And then one side of her mouth pulled up into a sinful smile as her eyes rose to his. "Still black here. Are you black down below?"

Oh, Nora. You have no idea what I have down below.

"Edward."

He straightened at her warning tone. "Yes, black everywhere else. Only my head hair turned white."

She nodded thoughtfully and sat back in her chair, her eyes burning holes through him. "Lift my skirt."

He couldn't help it, a groan escaped him.

"You'll be punished for that later," she promised.

She was trying to kill him.

He took the hem of her skirt and began to lift. She dressed in a fashion he knew to be favored by the dress reformers and he had to admit he highly approved—no cage crinoline and only a mid-weight petticoat, which he lifted with the skirts. He paused at her knees and she nodded. So he pushed the skirts up her thighs.

He swallowed and it was a noisy gulp. She wore stockings, but no knickers, no drawers, nothing but Nora. Still pierced he saw, but unshaved, he had to swallow repeatedly.

"That will be one of your tasks," she said, her voice not as brisk as it was. "Keeping me properly groomed."

"Yes, Nora."

She gave him a regal nod. "You may proceed."

Edward didn't need to be told twice. He took her beneath the knees and jerked her toward him, his rough action earning a gratifying squeal.

✽✽✽

Good God she'd missed his mouth.

He yanked her legs over his broad shoulders—he was even more defined and hard than ever—and positioned her the way he wanted.

There was no finesse, no gentleness. He sucked her into his mouth and ravaged her, the thick middle finger of his hand slamming into her hard, his thrusts deep and remorseless.

Nora plunged her fingers into his thick white hair, holding him firm while she ground herself against him, spreading wider and fucking his tongue, his lips, even his rough chin, which scratched skin that was almost virginal it had been so long since it had last had contact with anything but her hand.

Not like Edward, who'd been fucking and whipping women other than her all along. The familiar swirl of lust and jealousy filled her belly and overflowed into her womb, her body pounding with a primitive throbbing for him.

Her inner muscles contracted and her first orgasm in months—with another person—seized her by the scruff and shook her until she threw back her head and grunted his name.

As ever, he read her body like a book, knowing which parts were too sensitive and shifting his attention to her puffy lips, sensitive thighs, and even the thin skin behind her knees. By the time she pulsed for more he'd already worked his way back up, the soft, hot suction of his mouth shoving her toward yet another climax.

Her hips jolted and shuddered, her hands still buried in his hair, which she'd pulled hard enough to hurt. Or so she hoped. She shoved him away roughly when his greedy mouth moved toward her entrance.

"Enough," she panted. "Down. Put me down and go back to your chair."

He gently lowered her rubbery legs to the floor; Nora had to admit she thrilled at ordering this big, powerful man around.

He slid his hands around her corseted waist—her only concession to modern fashions—and lifted her with ease, setting her against the chair back before returning to his own seat.

Nora didn't bother covering herself up—she *loved* having his eyes on her. In fact, she hitched one knee over the arm of the chair, an action which caused the vein in his temple to stand out, its tempo matching the throbbing in her sex. She dropped a hand to her swollen lips and idly stroked herself, thrilling at the straining cords in his neck.

His cock, she saw, had soaked the front of his trousers.

"Did you orgasm, Edward?" she asked the question in a lazy voice as she languidly stroked. "Look at me when I speak to you," she ordered sharply.

His eyes flew up with gratifying speed. "No, Nora. I didn't spend."

"You've been a very good boy so far."

His jaw clenched and Nora had to bite back a smile. Ah, her Edward was not born to take orders.

Nora gave an exaggerated yawn. "My, my. I don't know why I'm so exhausted." She lowered her leg and carelessly pushed down her skirts, enjoying the thunderous expression on his face as he watched her nudity disappear before his eyes.

She stood and he stood with her, wincing with discomfort.

"I'm for bed," she said airily. "You will not touch yourself tonight," she reminded him as she strode toward the door, tossing over her shoulder. "Fetch my satchel and bring it up to my room before you retire for the evening. Just leave it inside the door and don't disturb me. Good night, Edward."

She opened the door and spun around before she delivered her final words, gratified by the sight of his unhinged jaw and flaring nostrils. "Oh, and I'll want you in my room at six o'clock sharp tomorrow morning." She frowned. "I dislike tardiness."

And then she left him there, furious and as hard as a pike.

Chapter Forty-Five

Edward thought he might have to actually tie himself to his own bloody bed to keep from tearing the door off the hinges and storming down the hallway.

A quick glance at the heavy brass clock on his nightstand told him he'd been tossing and turning for almost two hours.

Nora was here in his house.

She was *here.*

But was she? Perhaps he'd merely hallucinated the entire episode in his library?

It was a testament to how crazed he was that he almost yanked on the bell pull beside his bed and summoned Phelps to reassure him that yes, Nora-Natalie-Hudson-Hartwicke really *was* in his house.

His body was hard—every damned part of it—and it felt as though somebody had delivered a bolt of electricity that raced around and around under his skin. As he laid there, his cock throbbing and leaking, he cursed all the nights he'd not pleasured himself—all those lost opportunities.

"You bloody fool," he muttered. "Why don't you just get your arse out of bed and go check for yourself?"

"Yes, you fool, why don't you?"

Edward screamed like a bloody schoolroom miss and leapt out of bed.

"Goodness, Edward—you appear rather . . . on edge."

Edward had clutched at his throat with one hand like a trembling virgin in a gothic novel—which, he was embarrassed to admit, he'd read more than a few of these past few months. He hastily lowered both hands to his sides.

It wasn't until his clenched fists brushed the skin of his outer thighs that he realized he was naked—and erect—in front of her.

A gasp came from the pale figure in the darkness. *"Edward."*

Did he grin at the wonder in her voice? Perhaps just a bit.

Nora had no time for his face, her eyes riveted to his cock as she closed the distance between them.

"Yes, Nora?" he said, wondering if she heard the hint of smugness.

She dropped to her knees in front of him. "Light your bedside candle," she ordered, her voice pulsing with . . . well, something that made his condition even worse.

He complied and was pleased when she gasped again.

"It's—it's *magnificent.*"

He preened. And then yelped when a touch lighter than a feather brushed over the sensitive, impaled head.

"Does it hurt?" she asked quickly, still not looking up at him—at least not his face. He now knew what she must have felt like when he couldn't take his eyes off her pierced hood.

"No. It's long healed."

"Hmmm." Her breath was hot on the swollen head and his other head reeled.

And then her hot, wet mouth lowered over him.

✳✳✳

Nora's carefully planned evening of seduction and torment flew out the window the moment she saw the glint of silver on the crown of his oh-so-very-lovely cock.

Her lips and tongue began making all her decisions and she took him into her mouth, groaning at the familiar taste and feel of him—even with this very unfamiliar, and wildly exciting, addition.

Above her, he moaned in a way that told her he was quickly slipping past the point of any control. She was glad—it was time to end this farce; she *hated* having to scheme and plan and plot to drive him mad. She was not, she'd always known, a woman who enjoyed having the whip hand. It was exhausting having to think two steps ahead. She just wanted . . . well, she wanted this: she opened her throat to him and lowered her head.

"God, Nora. If you do this—I can't, it won't—oh *God.*" He shook as she swallowed around him, again, and again. His sounds were those of a man pushed too far past his limits to endure her torments for much longer. And when his big, powerful hands landed on her head, she shivered with pleasure. "Yes," he hissed in a gravelly, guttural growl, his hips moving with minute pulses that rubbed the hard silver against the back of her throat, the sensation something new to acclimate herself to—the friction almost painful.

Nora swallowed yet again and he gave the low, wicked chuckle that gutted her. "Mmm, my Nora. Nobody has a throat like you." He flexed into her sharply enough to startle a muffled cry out of her, held the hard silver ball against the tender flesh of her throat, and whispered. "And believe me I've fucked numerous throats in search of a superior one."

Her body clenched, heated, and thrilled with furious jealousy at the thought of him rubbing this glorious new part of his gorgeous body against another.

"Shhh, I can feel you shaking," he said, his voice heavy with dark amusement as he released his hold on her, and then just as quickly thrust back in. "Such a jealous thing to deny me any pleasure when I *know* what you've been up to." He pumped, slowly getting into a rhythm. "You know how many nights I lay here alone, fisting myself to you—don't you, my Nora? My exquisite lover, my perfectly trained whore, my temptress and torment." He pulled out until only his thick head remained, leaning low at the waist. "My heart and my only love."

Nora's mind could not contain the almost painful joy of his words: his love. She was his only love.

"My poor Nora," he whispered, his hips resuming their pumping, his hand briefly grazing her wet cheek. "You've missed this just as much as I have." *This*, being a thrust so brutal it almost choked her. He chuckled at the sound. "I can see you're out of practice and in need of my firm hand and hard cock." He held her head in an unbreakable grip while he drove into her with increasingly savagery, plunging cruelly, with no care but for his own pleasure, pushing her dangerously close to the edge.

"No," he ordered harshly.

His selfish command was more powerful than the most exotic aphrodisiac and almost sent her over the edge. But her body, if not her mind, responded without question to his mastery.

"My Nora." He rammed himself deeply, his thick cock spasming and filling her with the violence of his orgasm.

✳✳✳

Edward blinked up at the dark wood ceiling above his bed, intensely aware of the small, sweaty body alongside his.

"I've never been in your bedchamber before," Nora said.

Her beautiful face was clear in the bright light of the candle. Her delicate lips were swollen and pink and slick and her chest—still covered beneath her nightgown, he realized with a frown—rose and fell with harsh breaths.

She turned her eyes to his and Edward's own breathing stuttered. Those eyes; he would never ever get over those eyes.

"Thank you," he said.

Her lips twisted. "I thought to make you suffer all night, but decided I was suffering more."

Edward snorted. "I doubt that very much. But when I said thank you, I meant—"

"Shh," she said, her cheeks flushing. "I know what you meant. And I came to you as much—no, *more*, for myself than for you. So don't believe me to be selfless."

"Oh, I don't."

She laughed, and if there was a more beautiful sound in the world than her laughter, Edward could not recall it.

"I wanted to write you," she said this in a softer, more serious voice.

"I wanted you to."

"I did write you several times, but each time it didn't feel right to open the door again on what we had. I first needed to make some, well, some repairs to my life. You might know I spent a month with my mother and father?"

"Yes, Smith told me."

"I told him to, Edward. Just because I wasn't in contact didn't mean I wanted you to worry about me—and I knew you'd worry if I disappeared from London."

Edward knew he should have been ashamed that she knew how dependent he was, but he simply didn't care.

Edward didn't want to talk about himself; he had her near him and he didn't know for how long. He *had* to ask her things. "Tell me about your family, Nora. If you don't mind."

"I don't mind." She inhaled deeply and then let out a long sigh. "I had a wonderful childhood. Until I was fourteen or so, I loved my life. And then Brandon came along."

His gut clenched. "Good God, Nora—did he—"

"What?" she frowned at him, her mind obviously on something else. As her eyes slowly focused on him she smiled. "No, Edward. He didn't hurt me. That, you see, was the problem."

He forced himself to wait while she gathered her thoughts.

"He came to visit his uncle, the local squire. He was a strapping youth." She cut him a sly look. "Although not as big as you. And he was perhaps only a year or two older than me. We came across each other one day while I was out riding. My father kept horses for Sarah and I even though it was a cost he could ill-afford. But he'd inherited a small competency from his own father and wasn't entirely dependent on his living. He used the extra money to purchase the horses, a few extra gowns and furbelows, things of that nature." She shrugged. "So I was out riding by myself—I had permission to roam the squire's lands, but not to leave them. Brandon's horse had thrown a shoe and he was leading him when I came upon them. Well, one thing led to the next and then the next. I gave my maidenhead to him by the river some weeks later. It was—" she gave a sad smile, "less than memorable. Poor Brandon! How could I expect him to know what I wanted when even I did not? He breached me, came inside me, and was finished in the time that is—I now know—usual for very young men. He avoided me afterward. It is a sign of my naturally wanton nature that I did not avoid him. I *wanted* to do that again. Indeed, I thought of little else. While my elder sister dreamed of wedding gowns and children, I fantasized about the different ways to join with a man." She'd turned to the ceiling, but now turned back. "You see that I've been unnatural from the start."

Edward leaned forward and kissed her, a quick, hard kiss. "I was just thinking you sounded remarkably like me as a young man." His lips twitched. "And even as an older man."

She laughed. "But you are a *man* and I? Well, I was supposed to be a gently bred lady and yet my mind was rife with very *un*ladylike thoughts of breeding. Brandon left after the summer and I found another playmate. My next experiment went better but was also worse because we were caught."

Edward winced.

"It happened at an assembly and our parents both agreed the best thing for all was for the two of us to marry." She chewed her lip, her expression pensive. "It was a horrific thought. Not that I disliked the man—or boy, really—but the last thing I wanted was the end of life's excitement at the age of fifteen. I rarely spent my pin money and my father was more than generous, so I had a sum saved up that would get me to London and perhaps keep me for a month—or so I believed then."

Edward was horrified at the thought of this young vicar's daughter venturing to London alone. "Good God, Nora. What were you planning on doing?"

She gave him a long look from eyes dark with sin. "I knew I couldn't marry a respectable man without confessing my transgressions, and I didn't want to do either. So, I left the vicarage very late one night. I walked some miles to a village too small to have a station. When I arrived at the post house there I went directly to their stables. I knew post boys often loitered and I found one whose eyes told me what he wanted from me and that, my dear Edward, was my first experience with whoring." She chuckled. "I believe I received the better of that deal as the postboy managed to steal me onto the next stage headed to a town with a train station. He, on the other hand, endured what was surely an extremely rough and toothsome mouth-fuck."

Edward couldn't laugh with her. "Weren't you frightened?"

"Of servicing my first customer? No. Of leaving everything I knew and heading into the great unknown, oh, undeniably. But if there is one thing it is easy for a young woman to find in London, it was employment in that oldest of professions. I was smart enough and possessed enough coin not to have to leap at the first opportunity. As a result, I went to work for a decent enough house. I was young enough looking that the madam sold me over and over for almost a year as a virgin."

Edward rolled onto his side, laying his hand on her flat stomach. "You never became pregnant all this time?"

She shook her head, her jaw tight. "No." Her tight whisper told him how she felt about that. "I—I know you want children, Edward. And I don't expect you not to have them—"

He slid his hand around her hip and pulled her toward him. "That's enough," he said sharply, forcing her chin up, until she had to meet his gaze. "Don't you think I learned my lesson where that is concerned?"

She chewed her lip, her huge eyes becoming glassy. "But I *want* you to have a child. I want to hold a baby of yours."

Her words tore at him. "The only woman I want to put a child inside of, is you, Nora." He hesitated. "Could you not love any child? You know I came from an orphanage—there is no shortage of children filling them. When I was little, it was a dream to go to a family."

Her eyes opened wider and wider.

"Careful," he said, his face heating at her expression. "Your eyes are in danger of popping out."

"Oh, Edward, you mean you wouldn't mind taking in some homeless child—even one not of your blood? But I thought—"

"I know what you thought—that I had to have a copy of myself. I was a fool." He gave her another hard kiss, this one to mask the shaky feeling inside him. "I'd give you anything," he whispered. "Haven't you realized that yet, my Nora?"

She became pliable under his hand. "Anything, Edward?" She nipped at his chin and he groaned.

"Yes, I'll give you that—as hard and as often as you deserve. But first I want you to finish."

She gave an exaggerated sigh. "I did not heal the breach between myself and my family during the month I spent with them, but my visit opened a door. It is now their decision whether they wish to take it any further. Anyhow, I'd just returned to Rose Cottage when I received the letter from Cat."

Edward frowned. "When was this?"

"Perhaps three weeks ago—didn't you get one? She said she was writing both of us."

"Yes, but mine came months ago."

Her eyes widened. "Ah! I'd wondered. This letter had been terribly water damaged and it seemed a miracle it had even found me. Cat, as you know, is careless in such matters so I wasn't surprised by a lack of a date. But I could not read the frank. So," she gave him a look of sudden comprehension. "No wonder you looked so surprised to see me. If you received your letter months ago you must have—"

"I thought you might write and when you didn't?" he shrugged.

"Oh, my poor, poor Edward." She slid an arm around him and snuggled closer. "You must have wondered at my continued absence." The words were hot muffled breaths against his chest, and his cock was very interested in this sudden development.

"I did," he admitted rather wryly—able to sound calm now while he'd bled inside for weeks and months waiting for her. "What took you three bloody weeks?" he demanded.

She laughed, the sound wicked. "Oh, I had to deal with Charles— didn't you know about he and Smith?"

"I *know* about them. But what do you mean?"

"No, I won't say anything yet. There is still room for misunderstanding with those two ninnies." She burrowed against him, her hand dropping to his cock, her fingers curling around his shaft, her thumb rubbing his head. "Oh, God, Edward. This is such a wonderful development."

"You little witch," he chided, but his body was arching against her, his prick already taking charge of matters. "I've wanted to fuck you with it for so very, very, very long."

She wriggled in his arms, purring while her clever fingers stroked.

"Did you like that letter I wrote you?" His voice was a growl as he thrust his hips, pushing his diamond hard erection into her skilled fist. "Have you thought about it? Touched yourself?"

She ground her hips against him. "*Please.*"

"Shhh," he chided into her hair. "You've been terribly bad, I'm not sure you deserve such pleasure." His hands moved to her hips, which were no longer beneath the blankets with all her wiggling and shifting. "Who has been shaving my cunt in my absence?"

"Just me, Edward. Nobody but me."

"Hmm, well that will stop immediately." He positioned his middle finger at her opening and entered her with a smooth thrust. Her small body arched and curved to accept him and he sucked in a noisy breath at the feel of her tight, silky sheath. "How I've missed this," he murmured, slowly exploring inside her while his thumb circled her already hard peak.

She shuddered in his arms. "Oh please, Edward. Let me come."

He pushed her onto her back and knelt over her, pumping her hard. "Do you want me inside you? Do you want to feel that cool silver grazing this tight heat?"

Her knees opened wide and Edward stared as his finger—big, masculine, and blunt—slid in and out of her. He pushed her thighs wider with his free hand and bent low, sucking her tiny silver ring into his mouth hard enough to make her squeal. He pulled away without releasing his suction, stretching her until she squirmed and begged.

Her pale skin was splotchy and red with passion, her knees spread in a position of wanton submission. Edward came close enough to position his aching cock at the entrance to her body, breaching her again and again and again with only his crown.

"That feels—it feels—"

"What does it feel like, my greedy little whore?" he grinned down at her, his eyes flickering between the sight of his prick stretching her and her slack, expectant, mouth.

"I need it, Edward. I need to feel you inside m—"

He slammed into her hard enough to drive her up the bed almost a foot. He took her roughly by each thigh as he spread his own knees for better stability and fucked her with pent up need borne of their long separation.

They came, clumsily and quickly, but together.

"Nora!" he gasped as he filled her with everything he had.

"I love you Edward. I love you. I love you. I love you."

Chapter Forty-Six

Edward waved away Nelson's hand. "I'll do it," he said. "I don't need you anymore," he added rather rudely.

Well, that was just too bad. He was feeling rude. He'd woken after his explosive session with Nora to find a brief note on his nightstand:

Edward,

Remember, you are due in my chambers at six o'clock sharp. And do not expect my generous behavior in your bed tonight to erase the fact you signed my contract.

Do not be late.

Nora

He'd paced the next three hours—not easy with an erection that could pierce the hull of a ship. Why had she left him? Hadn't they formed some understanding? Was he doomed to constantly be confused with this woman? He was . . . irritable. And hard as he imagined going into Nora's room in—he glanced at the clock: only nine minutes now.

He finished tying the most disastrous four-in-hand he could recall, considered summoning, Nelson, decided against it, and looked at the clock again. Still nine minutes.

He shoved a hand through his hair, wincing as he encountered his tender scalp. And then throbbing as he recalled the way it had *become* sore down in the library.

God. He wanted her *so* much. He would have done anything to keep her here, as was evinced by his actions last night. Never in his life had he signed any document without reading it at least *five* times. Until last night. Christ. He must have been mad.

But he'd do it again in a heartbeat.

While he'd rather be ordered around by Nora than fucked by any other woman, he had to admit his nature was not submissive. He envisioned spending the year ahead tied to a post being whipped, or whatever other diabolical punishment her devious mind could concoct and shivered. Likely she would not always come to him as she'd done last night. Likely she would become even crueler as she eased into her dominant role.

Hell!

Edward shrugged into his coat and adjusted his tortured cock—it didn't help—before buttoning his coat shut.

The truth was he'd take her any way he could get her and be bloody grateful.

He would have crawled across London naked to have her back.

Yes, he could take a year of beatings and torturous arousals with a smile and—

Edward froze as a terrifying thought struck him—what if she controlled his orgasms the way she'd done yesterday—or at least for part of the evening? What if she kept him hard for an *entire* year only dolling out pleasure when she felt like it?

No, he shook his head at his reflection, as if to convince himself. No, she wouldn't—couldn't be so cruel.

Oh yes, she would.

❋❋❋

Edward knocked on her door at *exactly* one minute to six.

Nora considered making him wait the extra minute but decided she'd probably tortured the poor man enough by leaving him with that note this morning.

Her heart did an odd lurching dance in her chest at the sight of him. She wanted to gorge and gorge and gorge on his harsh beauty. Because he *was* beautiful to her.

"Good morning, Nora."

She gave him a smug smile, enjoying the lines of tension around his eyes and the slightly petulant twist of his lips. Oh, Edward didn't like anyone to control the orgasms in his house except Edward. No doubt, after a night to think about it, he was wondering just what he'd signed.

330

Nora *never* would have wagered he'd sign anything without reading at least three times. It was, she thought, the clearest declaration of love she'd likely get out of him. It was enough and more for her—but that didn't mean she wouldn't enjoy teasing him until the very end.

He'd worn a double-breasted frock coat today and she knew what he was trying to hide. Her mouth watered at the memory of his delicious cock—made even more tasty with that lovely silver impaling it.

Take yourself in hand, Nora. You're not done yet . . .

"I've decided to paint your picture," she announced, tickled by the widening of his dark eyes and the parting of those thick, sensual lips she loved so much. A slight darkening at the top of his cheekbones—more prominent now that he was so lean—told her he was pleased, but also embarrassed.

"You don't need to paint me because of what I wrote to you, Nora. I know an artist paints according to their . . . well, muse. I—"

"Excuse me. Did I ask for your opinion?" She arched her eyebrows and attempted to look down at him, a difficult task as she had to look up a good nine or ten inches to do so. "Don't mistake my laxity in your bed last night—allowing you to take your pleasure without my express permission—to fool you, Edward. I will punish you instantly and severely if you do not obey me in every way." She spun on her heel, torn between enjoying his shocked expression and being too eager for what was waiting to draw out his torment. "Come along, now," she ordered.

The door to the sunroom was closed, but she'd already prepared it the way she wanted it.

She opened it and stepped back. "Gentlemen before ladies, this morning."

He hesitated, his brow furrowing, but then entered. "Good God!"

Nora grinned, stepped inside, shut the door, and then locked it for good measure.

❊ ❊ ❊

Edward couldn't stop gawking and consuming. It was him: just him—everywhere. Him clothed, him naked, him from the back, him from the front, him aroused—bloody hell he looked *good* with an erection!—him in dozens of other ways. There were paintings—at least a dozen—and

331

what looked to be hundreds of sketches. It was . . . well, it was—bloody hell, he had no words for what it was.

He turned around. She was smiling, her arms crossed as she leaned against the doorframe. Looking very, very pleased with herself.

He had to ask, "These are things you've drawn and painted . . . lately?"

She laughed. "No, Edward. These are things I started drawing right after I met you." She strode across the room and pointed to a charcoal drawing of a stern, terrifying image of himself.

"Did I really appear that way to you?" he asked in wonder, turning from the powerful black and white drawing back to her.

She nodded, a solemn expression on her face. "You also looked like this." She pointed to a different sketch and he caught his breath.

The perspective was as if the artist had been looking up—as if she'd been on her knees. He wore his shirt, but it had been unbuttoned and exposed a broad column of stomach and chest. He appeared *massive* and his eyes as they looked down were cruel and satanic, his grin the feral smile of a man about to orgasm. It was powerful, sexual, and painfully arousing—and he'd *already* been painfully aroused.

"This one," she said, pulling his attention away from the mesmerizing image and directing him toward the biggest canvas: a painting of his naked body on its side, facing away. There was nothing overtly erotic about the image, but something about the posture—*his* posture—spoke of sated passion. The room in the portrait, he realized suddenly, was *their* room.

"It's beautiful," he said, and then winced. "Am I allowed to say that about a picture of me?"

Nora laughed, a joyous, gurgling sound he'd heard so very rarely. He turned to her and grabbed her by the waist lifting her up to kiss her— the kiss he'd dreamt about for months—*years*. Her arms wrapped around his neck so tight it was difficult to breathe.

"I missed you so much, Edward." She squeaked when he held her even tighter.

His eyelashes were wet. Once upon a time that would have terrified him. "Nora?" he said her name against her neck, not wanting to stop kissing her.

"Yes, Edward?"

"Was there anything in that contract of yours about, er, marriage?"

She stiffened so utterly his throat shrank to the size of a pea and he could hardly suck in air. Had he ruined things before they could get started? "I'm sorry, Nora, I didn't—"

"You'd have to tell me, Edward."

He held her out so he could see her. "I'd have to tell you what?"

She smiled. "Whether there is anything about marriage in the contract. After all, you're the one who wrote it."

"What?" he demanded even though he'd heard her. "You gave me my *own* contract to sign?"

She nodded, biting her lower lip.

"Why you little wretch." And then something occurred to him.

"Oh, no—" she said, "I recognize that look."

Edward gave her an evil grin as he swung her into his arms and stalked toward the door of the sunroom. "Open it," he ordered.

"But, Edward? Where—"

"*Nora.*"

"All right, all right," she grumbled, but he could hear the pleasure beneath her words.

He strode to toward the room he'd cleaned every month, but never really hoped to use again.

"Edward? *Edward!* Just where do you think you're going?"

"I think you know the answer to that, you little witch."

"But it's six in the morning."

"I don't care what time it is. You need to reach in my pocket and get out my keys, I've rather got my hands full, darling."

She stopped squirming and her beautiful opal eyes widened. "Am I, Edward? Your darling?"

"You're so much more than that, Nora, you're *everything* to me." He had to clear his throat and blink rapidly before looking down at her again. "And when I decide to let you out of this room—perhaps a few months from now—I'll make you my wife."

The look she gave him was dewy—there was no other word for it. "Oh . . . Edward. I love you."

"I know you do." Edward said, proud of the fact there was no quaver in his voice. "But right now we're going into our room and I'm going to punish you properly for playing such a vile trick and getting me to sign my own damned contract without reading it. If word of that ever got out, I'd be ruined."

"That was bad of me." She blinked those huge, beautiful, pale eyes up at him. "I'm terribly sorry, Edward."

"*Hmmph.* You will be. Now, open the bloody door."

Edward didn't need to ask twice.

About the Author

SM LaViolette has been a criminal prosecutor, college history teacher, B&B operator, dock worker, ice cream manufacturer, reader for the blind, motel maid, and bounty hunter.
Okay, so the part about being a bounty hunter is a lie.
SM does, however, know how to hypnotize a Dungeness crab, sew her own Regency Era clothing, knit a frog hat, juggle, rebuild a 1959 American Rambler, and gain control of Asia (and hold on to it) in the game of RISK.

S.M. also writes under the name Minerva Spencer

Read more about SM at: www.MinervaSpencer.com